A WICKED AND BEAUTIFUL GARDEN

WITCHES OF THE ISLAND

KATIE MCGARRY

KATIE MCGARRY LLC

PROLOGUE

*C*assie was five when she learned she would one day play chess with the devil.

It was a normal spring Saturday: the sky blue, the clouds puffy, and the sweet scent of the first rose blooms hovered in the air. The dishes had been washed, wet clothes had been pinned onto the outside line to dry, and Cassie swept the floor while her grandmother kneaded the bread they would eat with dinner.

Once the bread was set out to rise, the two of them sorted through the large plastic containers stored in the wooden shed adjacent to their remote cabin. In most of the bins were mason jars they used for fall canning, but the bottom containers were Cassie's favorites. In those were her great-grandmother's "recipe" journals, diaries akin to the meticulous ones her grandmother kept.

At the bottom of the stack was an ancient chest made of gray oak, and inside that was a box stained a dark reddish brown—the color of rust, the color of dried blood. Her grandmother handled the box with the same reverence as she did with the newborns she had delivered in their community. At a skip, Cassie followed her grandmother out of the shed, crossed the yard that was fresh with new green grass, danced in the fragrant wildflowers and eventually joined her grandmother at the table on the porch.

Cassie loved that she shared so much with her grandmother, including the same shiny hair the color of sun-ripened acorns, the same rosy cheeks, and the same sun-kissed freckles along the bridge of their noses. Her grandmother's skin, which had been fair from the winter months, was now tanned from the hours she fussed over her garden during the heat of the day. A few wrinkles outlined her mouth, a product of her ever-present kind smile.

Her grandmother unpacked a chess board and intricately carved mini-statues. "Your game pieces are granite." The rock figures were gray and cool to the touch. "It's a stone of protection. My pieces are hematite." A crystal as black as a moonless night. "Hematite is helpful in healing. Watch me and place your pieces to mirror mine."

Cassie edged to her knees on the chair to study each figure her grandmother held in her hand and listened intently as she gave each one a name. Cassie then mimicked her grandmother by finding the appropriate piece and placing it on the correct square.

"Every game has a story," her grandmother continued. "A beginning, middle, and end. The game of life isn't an exception. A long time ago, God created the heavens and the earth, the humans, the angels, and the animals who roam the land. There was a great angel named Lucifer. He loved God, and the Creator loved him very much in return. God gifted Lucifer beauty, wisdom, strength, and, like all of his children, the Creator gave Lucifer free will.

"Eventually, Lucifer fell in love with himself, worshipped himself, and became envious of God when all of creation

grandmother to stand in front of her when her mother's boyfriend had tried to hit Cassie with a broken beer bottle.

"Can you do that?" her grandmother asked. "Can you protect a queen so she can, in turn, protect her king?"

Cassie hoped she could be as strong and brave as her grandmother. Maybe she could be…someday.

CHAPTER 1

*I*nsomnia was a mean bastard. When I was experiencing exhaustion only the dead understood, the idea of sleep invited me into a warm bed with a fluffy comforter and a soft pillow. Eyes closed, drift away and then *bam*—insomnia smacked me awake two hours later feeling as if I'd been punched by a linebacker for the New England Patriots. Every night the same weird yet realistic dream would disrupt my slumber and leave me with an unsettled pit in my stomach. No matter how I tried, there'd be no more sleep. Yep, that was me—every night.

Fortunately, the Bambi Bar and Grill, a truck stop near my apartment, was open twenty-four/seven. Even though the kitchen portion of the bar was closed from midnight to four AM, the co-owner, Killian, liked me enough to make an exception when I showed between those hours. He'd cook me a grilled cheese sandwich or a hot ham sub. He'd also pile onto the plate healthy doses of whatever leftovers from the dinner rush he could find in the fridge. Most weeknights at two AM, it was me, Killian, a few townspeople wasting their money on cheap alcohol, and whatever lonely truck drivers were taking refuge from the road in the rustic room.

Bambi's would scare the hell out of the sophisticated and snobbish. The walls were 1970's dark panels. The wooden floor was nicked, worn and on the verge of crumbling into sawdust. The tables, booths and the bar were so sticky they probably hadn't been washed in twenty years. The entire place smelled like spilt beer and grease left warming for too long. There were the typical neon beer signs on the walls, deer antlers over every door, and lonely men and women who nursed whiskey, bottles of beer and their sorrows.

Tonight, Killian outdid himself with two types of cheese on the sandwich, potato salad so good it had to be illegal, and the pièce de résistance: homemade cherry pie that made me want to marry whoever cooked it. I worked thirty hours a day, eight days a week, so I ate dessert. I damn well deserved it.

According to science, there were only twenty-four hours in a day and seven days in a week, but that didn't stop babies from being born and people from being sick. Somehow, as a health professional, time didn't run on the same speed for me as it did for the rest of the world.

With my back against the wall and jean-clad legs resting on the bench of the booth, I sipped my lemonade. I would have preferred a beer, but, unfortunately, like six other days of the week, I was on call. Drum roll please...with the nearest MD over fifty minutes away at the hospital, I was the lone midwife and nurse practitioner in our area. Crashing of symbols and me jazz handing. For my small town, I was the sole medical option, which was sad for everyone.

In the past thirty-six hours, I had single-handedly delivered two babies. Needless to say, I should have been deep in dreamland, but as previously mentioned, insomnia and I were tight. Especially since my dreams over the last several weeks had been vivid. Each night a baby reached out to me as if she were in mortal danger. I felt to the depth of my bones that this child was begging me to save her. I would wake up shaking, swamped by the sensation that the baby must be found, and that if I didn't find her, she'd die a terrible and painful death.

No doubt it was a stress dream. Too much work, not enough sleep, too many patients who weighed on my mind, and now that I had turned twenty-eight, I kept thinking of my grandmother and the stories she used to tell me about the remaining pieces of the supernatural chess game she believed would pop up into existence this year. Just like all the other stories she told me when I was younger, there was no doubt the tales were fables. Still, since my birthday, I kept waiting for something magical to happen. But there was no magic. Just me, alone, in this small town that liked me just enough to pay my salary. A job, a roof over my head, food, and stress dreams about babies in danger—what more could I ask for?

The lone TV near the bar showed one of those twenty-four-hour news channels, and two news anchors, who thought their opinion mattered, discussed why everyone in the United States should be forced to participate in genetic testing. Without the testing, Fae blended so well into human society that humans had no way of distinguishing between who was human and who was Fae.

I considered it a silly argument, but the country was gripped by groups whose desire was to identify Fae. Some wanted to take more extreme steps, such as physically marking the Fae, incarcerating them or outright executing them. Some were convinced the Fae were going to round up the humans and imprison them in camps so they could feed upon our souls. A hundred years after people had learned of the Fae, that had yet to happen, so I felt relatively safe from human soul-reaping camps.

Truth was, Fae had no interest in human affairs and kept to themselves. Sure, there were a few Fae who acted as representatives with the world's governments when humans treated them unfairly. Sort of like the union rep for the local 120. There were some Fae who confessed who they were to humans, but those were as rare as me taking vacation days from work.

Tomorrow would be the one hundredth anniversary of the day when Fae had broken out beyond folklore and myth. According to my grandmother, people woke up "knowing" Fae were part of the world, knowing it as easily as the sound of their own name being called on the first day of school. It was as if that piece of information had been downloaded into everyone's brains at the exact same time, as if the drapes over the world had been lifted. No one, including the Fae, understood why such a thing happened, but it caused an inferno of upheaval, and the embers of that fire still burned today.

When humans learned of Fae, it was a terrible time. People were terrified, demanding trials like those held in Salem for witches. Problem was, there was no way to pinpoint who was truly Fae—at least not until the 1980s, when the scientific explosion of DNA research provided a way to identify Fae by their genetic makeup. And even that was of little use; it wasn't like Fae were lining up to hand over their blood for analysis.

"Damn fairies," muttered Hayes, one of the men sitting at the bar. He had a beer gut the size of Texas, and his normally pasty skin was peeling from a recent bright red sunburn that made him the color of a tomato. "They better keep to themselves and not come around here. They're an abomination."

"They know better than to come here." Jim said as he stroked his long, gray, garden-gnome beard. He was a weathered man due to the years of brutal outdoor work, and his copious alcohol consumption created streaks of broken capillaries along his pale skin.

"If they come to our town," Hayes said, "we'd rip them to shreds."

Idiots. Fairies were everywhere. Killian was Fae, and they considered him one of their best friends. There were even a few Fae who owned farms in the county. In fact, I had recently delivered a baby to a sweet Fae couple who owned a successful apple orchard. Did they know I was aware they were Fae? Nope. How I knew they were Fae was a secret I kept strictly to myself.

My thoughts on Fae? Due to my poor judgement and even poorer track record with the fair folk when I was a teen, when it came to the affairs of the heart, I avoided them.

"I bet them Fae are killing our women to drink their blood," Jim said.

"You're right," Hayes agreed. "Fae shouldn't be allowed to live."

I had heard the Fae-consuming-human-blood rumor but had no idea if it was true. Fae neither confirmed nor denied the rumor, and there was no actual evidence to verify the claims. I had a habit of tilting to scientific evidence instead of ramblings of old men at bars. To my knowledge, no Fae had ever outright physically harmed a human.

"What do you think, witch?" Hayes threw a glance at me over his shoulder. "Do you agree with us and believe Fae are evil?" Jim turned on his barstool to witness my reaction, and Killian's head popped up from whatever he had been reading on his laptop.

"This witch says you have an appointment for your six-month checkup on Monday morning, and I'll be pissed if you're late. By the way, I asked you to cut back on the salt and beer, and I've watched you eat and drink both." Yes, I was aware, HIPPA violation, but that was how Hayes and I rolled.

If I didn't hound him, he'd die of a heart attack. The man annoyed me, but I cared about him and everyone else in this town. They were my responsibility, and I took that very seriously.

Killian chuckled, Hayes huffed, and Jim tipped his beer toward me then returned to watching the TV. Was I a witch? I didn't think so, as last I had heard witches weren't real. But it would explain much if I were.

My cell rang, and I pulled it and cash out of my back pocket. Four in the morning, so this call must be a laboring mom. Maybe this time it would be the baby who was haunting my dreams, and I could finally sleep again. I shook off the constant unease the dream created and answered my phone. "This is Cassie."

I walked across the room, threw the money on the counter near the cash register and gave Killian a wave as he raised his chin at me in goodbye.

CHAPTER 2

*B*eing an empath, I was socked in the stomach with three emotions when Dee opened the door to the cramped apartment: nervous excitement from the expectant mother, joy radiating from the baby in her belly...and then there was my own complete shock at seeing my once lover, Orion MacAleese.

Shock was an understatement. I had watched Orion die. I remembered nothing from the accident nine years ago other than the sight of his bloodied body on the pavement. He'd been driving me home from an evening at the beach and then...my memory failed.

My hands shook. Maybe the apartment was shaking. Maybe the core of the earth had collapsed upon itself and the world was crumbling beneath my feet. Orion MacAleese was alive, and he was on the couch in the living room of Dee's home. Maybe it wasn't him. Maybe it was his doppelgänger. But as I inhaled, I caught the scent of dark spices with a hint of the ocean. He mirrored my disbelief before voiding his face of emotion.

I stood in the doorway stunned. For years, every happy

moment had been tinged with the overwhelming sadness that consumed me over his death. He was alive, and I had the urge to run across the room and hug him, but he wasn't moving. He wasn't speaking my name. In fact, he glanced away from me to focus instead on the hand he was holding— the hand of another woman.

I had loved him. I had grieved for him. For me. For us.

He raised his eyebrows at me in a plea not to blow this for him and to keep my mouth shut. Stupefied, I squeezed the pack in my hand to stop the trembling in my fingers. Orion was alive, and he remembered me, which meant he had abandoned me. With a shake of my head, I forced the emotions away. I wasn't nineteen anymore. I was twenty-eight and in control of my own destiny.

"Come in, come in." Dee waved me in and then coughed her smoker's hack. She'd recently traded her thirty-year addiction to cigarettes for vaping, as she believed the latter was healthier. I gave her a side-eye, as I approved of neither habit.

Dee had shown me enough pictures of her daughter Brittney for me to know she was the one on the couch, but Dee had neglected to mention that Brittney was dating Orion.

He was holding her hand. Holding. Her. Hand. We had spent an entire year together. Inseparable. I thought he had died, and he was here...holding *her* hand.

I caught the emotions of almost every person I came across, but reading Orion was like attempting to tune an old analog radio with its knobs missing. Which was a shame because I needed to know why he was here, in upstate New York, and why he was holding the hand of a woman whose protruding and dropped belly suggested she was easily nine months pregnant. More importantly, how did he survive?

The last clear memory I had of Orion, we were on the beach in South Carolina, and he hugged me so tightly, I was whole. It was a glorious feeling: warmth and joy and being bathed in sunshine. I had a head full of dreams of him becoming my knight in shining armor, carrying me from the nightmare that was my life. We were incredibly close, or at least I thought we were. We were a flirtation, lovers, then there was love, and then he died….

Apparently, he *didn't* die, and he'd been too busy to stay in touch with me. He also apparently had been *very* busy nine months ago. Refusing to concede he could still burrow under my skin, I pushed forward with my job.

I set my backpack full of medical supplies on the scratched coffee table. The apartment was the space above Mateo's auto shop. The walls were yellow but were faded in patches from where the sun had bleached the paint, and there were water stains on the ceiling from the leaking roof. The apartment smelled like a combination of lemon-scented Pledge and car exhaust, but the room was clean, neat, and decorated with the care of someone who clearly loved her home: from the checkered tablecloth on the kitchen table to the daisies in the vase on the living room end table, and framed pictures of Brittney from kindergarten to her senior year adorning the wall.

"I'm sorry for calling so early," Dee said. "But Brittney just arrived, and she's been having contractions."

"They aren't bad." Brittney protectively placed her hand over her stomach. "I can't believe she called you in the middle of the night. You're overreacting, Mom."

"It's okay," I said. "Dee knows I'm a night owl, and even if I wasn't, this is what they pay me the big bucks for." I winked then squirted sanitizer on my hands and rubbed them together. "Let's start at the beginning. Hi. I'm Cassie, the town's midwife and nurse practitioner. Your mom mentioned that you've been living out of state?"

"Yes, John and I drove from South Carolina." The girl had

a natural perkiness to her. She was maybe twenty-one, and that was if I were being generous. Brittney was summer. Blond hair, big blue eyes, pixie nose, and pure exhilaration of life. "I moved to South Carolina with friends, but I didn't like it there, so Mom told me to come home."

"Welcome back." I met Orion's stare head on, a challenge, and he didn't bat an eyelash. "John, is it?"

Orion merely lifted his chin in response. He studied me, the same serious way he had when we were together. During those days, while I waitressed, he would sit at the corner table soaking in my every movement as I bustled from table to table. His gaze had held the promise of how he was going to kiss me the moment my shift ended. I possessed too many memories of us at the beach on those late, warm, sensual nights.

"Do you mind giving me space?" I asked John/Orion. Translation: stay out of my way. He rose to his feet, but Brittney grabbed his hand.

"Stay," she pleaded. He did.

"South Carolina..." My smile stretched wide because faking happy in this moment was the equivalent of yanking out my fingernails. "I lived there once." Sure did, and obviously Orion had stayed there after I left. I wasn't sure how I felt about his silence. Grateful, angry, a bit like slapping him for letting me believe he died.

As always, Orion was beautiful. Dark eyes that pulled me into them whenever I stared for too long, and a handsome face that left me insecure at nineteen that a guy like him desired to be anywhere near me. As he had been years ago, he was taller than me, but Orion was now easily six feet in height. The last time I saw him, he was also much leaner. But the years had been good to him—or maybe he was shooting up steroids in the morning while eating an entire carton of eggs for breakfast. In addition to his extra inches, he had gained massive muscles. His golden-brown hair, which had subtle hints of red, was a tousled mess and hung sloppily over his forehead, and on his face was several days' worth of reddish-blond stubble.

Beautiful. Like all Fae, damningly beautiful, and I hated him for it. From the time I was knee high to a grasshopper, my grandmother begged me to avoid the Fae. I'd thought she was old and biased. At nineteen, lying in a hospital bed for months with no one by my side, I wished I had listened. I used to believe the negative Fae stereotypes were unfounded and wrong, but maybe everyone was accurate. Fae were irrevocably selfish, self-absorbed, and cruel.

Yet out of old habits, I scanned Orion for any of the visible scratches, cuts, bruises, breaks, sprains or bullet holes that were often associated with his job. I didn't spot any, but some could be hidden beneath his T-shirt and jeans. Orion was dangerous in every way imaginable. His family, as he called them even though some weren't blood related, profited from dabbling in the illegal. His lips lifted as if he'd noticed the glance, as if he were the one who could read thoughts through emotions. That was Orion, though—catching the gestures no one else did.

I tried to touch his emotions but found only the strange buzz that belonged to Fae. Orion tilted his head as if he felt me probing. He wasn't aware of my strange quirk. That was a gift I had acquired after our time together. Detaching mentally from Orion, I refocused on the task at hand—Brittney. "Can I examine you and your baby?"

"Yes, please," Brittney said. "I should warn you, I don't have insurance."

"We'll figure it out." Part of the reason I'd accepted this job was because the town council was searching for someone who was interested in healthcare community outreach.

"I'll try to give you something," Brittney said. "But I don't have much. If it wasn't for John's generosity, I wouldn't have been able to afford the trip."

His generosity? When had it become generous to care for the mother of your baby? A sliver of anger dripped into my veins, and Orion shifted as if uncomfortable. "Can you lie back and lift your shirt? I need to examine your baby."

Brittney lay back and drew up her shirt, which was already so small on her that her belly was hanging out of it. I rubbed my hands together, placed them an inch from her stomach and taste-tested her emotions before making physical contact. Skin-to-skin contact could overstimulate me if her emotions were too strong, and the overload would cause me to vomit. Not exactly proper bedside manner to puke on a patient.

A quick read told me Brittney was excited about the baby, nervous about the delivery, and scared. Scared at what labor was going to be like, scared about whether she would be a good mother, and terrified that she wouldn't be able to financially or emotionally care for her child. She was also frightened of someone she'd left behind in South Carolina. I frowned with the intense fear. Whoever this person was must have hurt her terribly.

Brittney also carried guilt. Innocent guilt though— remorse that she hadn't kept regular prenatal visits. I gently settled my fingertips on her belly. "Do you drink? Do drugs?"

"No, ma'am. Can't afford alcohol or drugs, but even if I could, I wouldn't." The mother-to-be's sadness kicked me in the gut, and I snatched my hands back.

Pain roiled through my gut, and I wavered, dizzy. Orion flinched as if he wanted to move toward me, and I extended a hand out as a stop sign. Last thing I needed was for him to touch me. His eyes snapped to the silver scar on my neck, and a chill ran along my spine with the horrendous confirmation—Orion knew about the injuries I had sustained in the car accident and chose to leave me alone during the awful weeks in the ICU and then the months of recovery. He knew and he didn't care.

"Are you okay?" Brittney sat up, but I fluttered my hands to keep her lying down.

"I'm okay. A bit of lightheadedness. I had two deliveries in the past thirty-six hours and not a lot of sleep. But the good news is the mothers and babies are fine."

"Oh, great to hear. Not about you being lightheaded, but about the moms and babies."

Readying for round two, I took a deep breath, rubbed my hands together and tested her emotions. The sadness was still there, but not as strong, just a trickle. Someone she loved had an addiction and she hated drinking and drugs. It was clear, Brittney was determined to never become like them.

"You're going to be a good mom." I gave Brittney a sincere soft smile.

"How do you know?"

"I have a good instinct about these things."

Peace flooded through her, and I placed my hands on her swollen belly. As with any skin-to-skin contact, a rush of energy raced through me, and because Brittney had momentary peace, it was a fantastic sensation. Brittney was happy, the baby was full of joy, and touching someone who was blossoming with such life was an intense and fantastic high. Like floating on a cloud.

"My mom said you're a bit strange with how you do things, but to trust you. She said you have a magic touch," Brittney said. "What are you doing?"

"Feeling for your baby's position." It was true, but I was also searching the baby for signs of distress. Besides a low-level thrum that felt like a headache, everything was normal. Head down and the feet pointed toward the rib cage. The sweet baby was cramped, but content. The child was so agreeable that the thrum headache didn't worry me. Strange headaches when running into dead ex-boyfriends were to be expected. So was the growing heartache in my chest.

The baby turned toward my touches, as if delighted I was here, and had sparks of happiness each time Brittney spoke— a clear indication the baby had fallen in love with their mother. There was no panic, no pain. Just a baby ecstatic to meet me and who was safe and protected by the mother.

And this brought us back to witches. To my knowledge, witches with actual magic weren't real, but who was I to judge? People used to believe Fae weren't real, but they were.

Witch, Fae, or whatever nonhuman creatures existed, it didn't change that I was an empath. At least that was what my internet searches concluded. An empath was a person who could sense others' emotions and could gain an idea of what they were thinking from reading those emotions.

Was being an empath normal? Nope. I wasn't born with the trait. It developed slowly as I recovered from the accident —an accident in which I had suffered severe trauma. In fact, I didn't think there was another person in the world who could do what I did. Well, maybe one of those midway carnie psychics could, but otherwise, I was one of a kind—and not in a good way.

Odds were, it was the brain damage. Or there was something wrong with my genetics. Or I was a witch. There was the possibility I was insane. Any were acceptable answers.

The muscles in Brittney's stomach contracted, and I felt the wave gather strength and then build into a crescendo. Fighting the natural instinct of her body to work with the contraction, Brittney tensed and held her breath. The baby didn't like her reaction, nor was it a fan of being squished.

I focused and murmured telepathically to the baby, *This is normal. Each squeeze means you're closer to meeting your momma.* A headache rumbled through my skull, and I grimaced with the brutal anguish of using telepathy. But I didn't regret it, as the baby's fear lessened. "Brittney, you need to breathe through the contraction. Do it with me. Breath in and out."

Brittney breathed, the baby relaxed, and then relaxed further with the release of the contraction. I sat back on my heels and rested my hands on my knees as I waited for the dizziness and pain to lessen. The good news was, beyond the normal emotions of labor, the baby wasn't in terror. Meaning there was no cord wrapped around the neck, and no positioning that created a risk to the baby's life. Everything at the moment was exactly how it should be.

"Do you want John and your mom here as I finish the rest of the exam?" I asked as my strength returned, and I pulled on gloves. "I'll need to check how much you're dilated."

Orion went to move, but she held onto his hand and yanked him to stay by her side. "I want you to stay. You and my mom."

All righty. I kept my voice cheerful and welcoming as I explained what I was doing and what to expect during labor. She white-knuckled Orion's hand as she soaked in the information.

"How long have you been having contractions?" I repositioned her skirt, properly disposed of my gloves, and reapplied sanitizer.

"She's had them on and off for the past two days," Orion said. "It's been twenty-five minutes from the last one."

His voice was an intimate caress along my skin, and it created a warm, pleasing sensation in my blood I hadn't enjoyed in years. It brought on memories of his hands in my hair, his lips on my skin, his body on mine. My mouth dried out, and my heart beat so hard my frame vibrated. I couldn't look at him even though he was staring at me. "Are the contractions regular?"

KATIE MCGARRY

"No." Just that one word in his deep voice caused a rever-beration in my soul.

I met Brittney's questioning gaze. "You're not in full-blown labor yet, but you will be soon. Keep track of the contractions. I'll give you a cell number, and when the contractions are regularly fifteen minutes apart, call it." I dug out the list I had ready for appointments like this. "Let's go over this together." Places where she could find food, government resources, and the on-call cell I shared with the doctor at the hospital. She paid close attention, nodding along. "And no strenuous activity, not until a few weeks after the baby is born."

Crestfallen, her lower lip trembled. "But I don't have anything, and I know my mom will help me, but she doesn't have much either. I need to work."

"I have money," Orion finally said. "I'll make sure you're okay."

Yes, if Orion was still doing what he was when I was nineteen and he was twenty-one, I was sure he had plenty of money. Maybe that was the issue—his family didn't approve of Brittney, like how they hated me, and he was dumping his latest girlfriend on her family then was returning to the comforts of home. I leveled a smirk and a pissed off glare at him. "How *generous* of you." Then attempted to paint on a sweet smile for Brittney. "See, it will work out. Even if you didn't have this extra money, the resource list can help you and your baby." I shouldered my backpack. "It was nice to meet you, Brittney."

Brittney and Dee thanked me for coming, and I ignored that Orion said, "Wait, I'll walk you out." I then blocked how Brittney grabbed for him again.

I jogged down the steps, and friendly familiarity skipped through me as I noticed the light on in Mateo's office in the auto shop below. He always woke early to work on paperwork before the garage opened. This was one of the reasons I had accepted this job—the community and the routine comfort of small-town life. But as I walked toward my car, the peace faded, and I paused.

It was late, a million stars danced above me, and dawn would be breaking soon. I was exhausted and heartbroken. Orion was alive, he had abandoned me, he didn't care for me nearly as much as I had cared for him, and he was holding onto the hand of another woman—a pregnant woman. He had moved on and it wasn't with me.

CHAPTER 3

"Cassie!" Orion called out at the top of the stairs, but I started again, this time walking faster. "Cassie, you know I'll catch you."

I stopped because it was true. Under the glow of the light from the utility pole, I kept my back to him and tried to steady my rapidly beating heart. Hundreds of memories flipped through my brain, of us talking, laughing, touching... kissing. Breathe. Breathe through the pain.

Many evenings on the crowded boardwalk, people would part for Orion like the Red Sea had done for Moses. Orion was beautiful and he was deadly. The sixth sense people possessed to keep them alive told them to run from danger, and Orion was the definition of a threat. But even as people gave him a wide berth, passersby would be pulled in by the subconscious attraction that left them thinking of him for days after a chance meeting. It was like Orion was a virus and none of us were immune.

Orion glided in front of me and had the audacity to glower as if he were exasperated to see me. "What are you doing here?"

My eyebrows shot up. "What?"

"*What* are *you* doing here?" he repeated as if I hadn't heard him. Oh, I heard him. I just couldn't believe that was the question he had for me. "You're supposed to be in California."

Rage charged through me. "Why would you think I was in California?"

He shoved his hands in his front pockets and struck that lazy, self-possessed pose of his while drinking me in: head-first, down to my toes and back up. "I heard you had received a full ride from USC. I figured you would have stayed out there."

Because I had once shared with him my dream of putting my toes in the Pacific Ocean. "You mean the 'full ride,'" using my fingers to create bunny ears, "from your family's foundation? You mean the full ride I magically received after the accident that almost killed me? A car accident where my last memory, besides your broken body on the pavement, was hugging you at the beach? The accident where when I woke at the hospital, I was told you were dead!"

Orion palmed the back of his neck. "I didn't die."

"I grieved you! I cried for you! I spent an entire year feeling as if my soul had been ripped out of my chest and that's all you have? *I didn't die?*"

"Cassie…." His sympathetic tone grated against my skin, and I started walking again…right into a pothole. I tripped, Orion's strong hand steadied me, and the moment we came in contact, an electrical charge rattled through him and into me. I stumbled back and expected my skin to be singed, to see the hair on my arms smoking, but there was nothing. I wildly glanced at Orion for his reaction, but he watched me with an infuriating, unreadable expression.

I shook out my hands and attempted to ignore the after-shocks of energy rumbling through my body. "Let me get this straight. You heard about the scholarship—the money your mother said was in exchange for my silence that you're Fae—but you didn't hear I was in the hospital? You didn't hear I nearly died? You were oblivious to my months of rehab?"

"I can explain." Orion averted his gaze as if my words caused him pain.

I wanted to shove him, but instead kept my hands at my sides and balled my fists. "I'll do it for you. I became broken, and I wasn't fun, so you moved on with your life. You didn't have the courage to break up with me, so you had your mom do it for you by having her tell me you were dead and that she had spread your ashes at the beach. Perfect solution, right? It doesn't matter—I'm not that stupid nineteen-year-old kid anymore."

I stalked off, but Orion followed. "Cassie," he called, but I ignored him. "Cassie, please." His fingers wrapped around my wrist and the emotional surge from the unexpected contact caused me to convulse from the inside out. He snatched his hand back and stared at me, wide-eyed, as if he had also felt the sensation. "What was that?"

"I don't like being touched." It was true, even before the accident, but that reaction wasn't normal, even for me.

"I'm sorry," he said, his deep voice sincere. He slipped toward me again, in that elegant, swift way of his. Concern liquefied his dark gaze, and tears pricked my eyes with how much I missed that whispered intimacy between us, with how much I had missed him. I had grieved for him. I had grieved for me. "I forgot."

Yes, he had. He had forgotten how unexpected contact could frighten me, and he had forgotten there were times when even a kind and welcomed touch could cause me to tremble with horror. But what was worse, he had forgotten me.

"Leave me alone."

Orion didn't backpedal as I'd hoped. His beautiful eyes searched my face, and he seemed everywhere at once. Not just his body, but his dark masculine scent, and I was drowning in the memories. The sweet pressure of our last kiss was upon my lips and the salty sea was on the tip of my tongue. I turned my head to breathe in anything but him. "I told you to leave me alone."

"When have I done anything anyone asked of me?" he questioned with a hint of the devious smile I remembered. I hated him for that look and hated myself more that the nineteen-year-old in me melted.

The answer was never, and that was what had drawn me to him. Even belonging to an unorthodox family, Orion lived by his own set of rules. Everyone else be damned. Me included. Orion was late nights on his motorcycle at breakneck speeds. He was freedom when much of my life had been spent locked in rooms by my mom and her boyfriend. He was that sweet taste of rebellion. He made me feel like I belonged when the truth was, I was an outcast.

"Cass," he said in a hushed voice, the same way he had under the pier when we were alone. Him caging me in with both of his hands against one of the massive poles, peering down at me as if he wanted to press his body to mine and kiss me until we both died. How many nights had he and I strolled along the beach, the tide lapping and tickling my feet, and I would lose my breath at the way he'd be looking at me?

"I didn't think I'd see you here," he murmured. "I didn't think I'd see you again."

Neither did I.

"¿Estás bien, Cassie?" Mateo's voice caused me to jump, and that helped create space between me and Orion. Mateo could speak English perfectly, but knowing him, he was using Spanish to confirm I was okay.

"Estoy bien," I replied.

Mateo called from the safe distance of his garage, "No te ves bien." *You don't look okay.*

"I'm leaving, and he's heading back upstairs," I said to Mateo while staring Orion down.

"Who is he? And why is he laying claim to you?" Something dangerous flared over Orion's face as his eyes flickered to Mateo.

My shoulders rolled back. Like Orion had any right to ask such a question or use the word "claim" in reference to me. Recalling how Orion loved a good fight, I eased between them as adrenaline pulsed through my veins. "Not that it's your business, but he's a friend, and I helped deliver his baby." The cord had wrapped precariously around the baby's neck, but I had sensed what was happening before the cord had cut off circulation. I was able to rush his wife and baby to the hospital in time for a C-section. "Tell me, is Brittney aware of what you are?"

His eyes narrowed. "What exactly is it I should tell her?"

"That your family makes money doing things they shouldn't, and you make sure people do what they're told. I found a way to make that romantic at nineteen, but you hurting people isn't romantic or adventurous. The mother of your baby should know you're a killer."

A muscle in Orion's jaw twitched as if my words bothered him, but why should they? He was the one who chose to become an enforcer for his family's business, doing whatever illegal things they did to make them obnoxiously rich. Seeing his reaction made me bolder, and I leaned into him as I whispered his secret, "Is she aware you're Fae?"

"That's none of her concern." His fierce gaze snapped to mine, and my mouth dried out with instinctual fear. I had attracted the attention of a powerful predator and I was his prey.

"Even for you, that's not fair. She's human and deserves to know she'll give birth to a...." I dropped off as the realization violently bounced along my insides. The baby was human. I'd been so absorbed in the agitation of Orion's presence that it didn't register that the baby didn't have the high-pitched buzz of a Fae. Blood drained from my face. Something was wrong here, terribly wrong. *Danger.* Danger from what, I couldn't fathom, but this was bad.

"How do you know she's human?" Whispering furiously, Orion loomed over me. "How do you know Brittney's not Fae?"

"I didn't..." I lied. "I assumed...." I was sputtering. "I have to go." I readjusted my backpack on my shoulder as Orion rooted me to the spot with his glare. Taking in a deep breath, I found my resolve and raised my chin. "I need to go. Now."

In that deceitfully lazy way he had, Orion slid to the side, waving me forward to pass. It took every ounce of energy I had to keep my eyes forward—to not look back to see if Orion was still watching me. He would be. That was the way Orion was. Each lift of my foot was heavier than the step before; the pack on my shoulders weighing a thousand pounds.

I fumbled my car keys, dropping them twice, and then finally made it into the safety of the driver's seat. I started the engine, backed up without checking the road behind me and tore the hell out of Dodge. Shaking so hard it was difficult to grip the wheel, I pulled over into St. Mary's Church parking lot. My feet hurt, my head hurt, my soul hurt. I yearned for a hot bath, to drink a beer and to sleep for the next ten days. But the water heater in my apartment was out, I couldn't drink with Brittney close to labor, and it didn't help that insomnia was my best friend.

My head hit the back of the seat. Hot against my skin was my grandmother's small gold cross. I had stopped praying a long time ago, but desperation often caused me to do things I normally didn't. I closed my eyes and I prayed. Prayed this pain in my chest would leave, prayed my soul would heal, and desperately prayed Orion MacAleese would leave and never return.

But my silent pleas were in vain. God had stopped answering my prayers. That was wrong—he had never answered my prayers. It would be hard to answer when God never listened.

CHAPTER 4

*A*rnica is a flower. Yellow. Beautiful. Aromatic. The women my grandmother gathered with called it wolf's bane. She had spent the morning boiling the flower and then making an oil. As her calloused fingers gently rubbed the ointment onto my skin, she told me it would help with the bruising. I had expected her to mention that the potion could alleviate the pain, but she didn't. Many recipes in her cookbook could soothe my body. The heart and the soul were harder to heal.

My grandmother was in her favorite rocking chair on the front porch of the cabin. I was eight and still small enough to cuddle on her lap. The summer air was cooler than normal, and the nocturnal animals of the forest were coming to life. Crickets and owls created a symphony grander than Beethoven could have imagined.

The bruise my mother had left on my cheek was sore, and I wondered if my grandmother was mad at me. I should have known better than to make noise. Mom and her boyfriend liked to sleep in, and they usually had headaches if woken too early. Even though my mom had yelled at Grandma that she and her boyfriend should have been allowed to sleep in one of the two bedrooms in the cabin, Grandma refused and tucked me into my twin bed before tucking herself into hers. Mom and the man had to sleep in the living room on the floor.

That morning, I hadn't meant for the pots to fall from the cabinet. I thought everyone would have been proud of me for doing housework without having been asked, but Mom was furious and so was her boyfriend. They screamed at me, and after Mom had smacked me, my grandmother became angry and threw them out. If I hadn't been there, my mother would have stayed. I was the reason they were apart.

My grandmother's arms around me tightened and she kissed my head. "No, baby. Your mother's choices have nothing to do with you or me. They have everything to do with her. I love you, and I'm happy you're here, on my lap, enjoying this night with me."

I snuggled closer to her. "How do you do it? How do you know what's in my head?"

"When people are connected like me and you, it's an easy read."

I didn't know what that meant and I didn't care. I felt safe in her arms, I felt loved.

In the woods, the fireflies sprang to life, and when I lifted my head in awe, my grandmother patted my back in encouragement. "Go, play. Feed your soul, child."

Play I did, frolicking in the yard as I chased after the glowing bugs, catching them and watching in amusement as they crawled along my skin. Twilight was my favorite time of day—pure magic. As if I were standing between the cusp of the real world and a realm of mysticism where there was peace. In this realm, there weren't mothers who left. No boyfriends who hit. No hate, no cruelty or insecurity.

The forest would come to life during this time. The

insects singing songs to one another, frogs croaking, the call of an owl, the chirp of the bats. Sometimes, if I stared long enough into the woods, I could catch the phantom shimmering eyes of the coyotes. If I was lucky, a wolf.

As I danced with the fireflies, curtsying to my chosen partners on the night of this grand ball, a sparkling light on the edge of the woods caught my attention. Brighter than the fireflies and inviting. Curious, I edged toward it and when I peered into the forest, I saw a baby. Tiny, even smaller than the premature baby my grandmother had delivered to Ms. Sarah on the other side of the mountain last month.

The baby watched me like I watched her. "Who is this?" I called out to my grandmother.

"Your future," she said. "Someday, this baby is going to need your help and you're going to have to decide if you will help her."

That made no sense. "Why wouldn't I help her?"

"Because doing so will mean great pain for you. Life isn't tidy, Cassiel. Neither are people. Choices are never all good or all bad, and neither is the fallout of our decisions."

I observed in wonder as the baby reached out toward me, and as I stretched my finger in her direction, we touched. An electrical shock stopped my heart, and I woke gasping in my bed in my apartment in upstate New York.

With a heavy sigh, I glanced at the clock. Midnight. I rolled over, hoping to sleep, but not sure if I should or if I could. Why was sleep impossible and why was the past—both Orion and my grandmother—haunting me again?

∽

MY LIFE WAS ON REPEAT. It had been for years since coming to this town, and normally I loved the reassurance of routine. Same people, same conversations, same smiles, frowns and waves. I kept my business hours at the clinic, made house calls, and attended births at the hospital, my clinic, and at homes. I then spent the rest of my time at Bambi's eating awesome food and listening to the other patrons who discussed world events as if they had doctorates in every field known to humans. But after seeing Orion yesterday, I was restless, edgy, and my contentment had faded.

Damn Orion for stealing that from me, too.

It was two in the morning and I was once again in my favorite booth at Bambi's. After the initial dream involving my grandmother, I had tried to sleep, even drifting off once, but I dreamt of the infant again. She was in distress, kicking furiously, her emotions begging for me to help, and that left a weight on my soul.

Was there a baby who was in trouble? One who needed to be saved? Or had the stress of my job and my jumbled emotions scrambled my dream neurons?

Killian placed a large slice of chocolate pie in front of me with a healthy helping of whipped cream on top. "You look like you could use this."

This was my one night off, as the doctor from the hospital the county over was taking my calls so I could relax. I gave Killian a halfhearted grin. He was Fae, and like the rest of them, was gorgeous. Red hair, sharp green eyes, late twenties like me, and he had the fast Fae buzz I could recognize, but other humans couldn't. Killian, part of the town council, was one of the people I had interviewed with and he had no idea that I knew he was Fae.

"Rough day?" Killian asked.

"Do I look that bad?"

He flashed me the sexy smile that packed this place every evening. "You always look good, Cassie."

I winked. "Flattery will get you everywhere. That and free pie."

"I'll be heading out of town tomorrow for a few days. Going home. I'll make sure the fill-in knows to give you dinner at night." He paused. "You didn't answer about the bad day."

I carefully weighed my reply. From the moment we had met, he was attracted to me. Over the past year, his emotions regarding me were growing, but I wasn't interested in dating another Fae. "It wasn't the best."

Killian scanned me, and I glanced away, toward the bar, when I captured a single thought—*ask her out*. Nope. Didn't want that, and I didn't want my friendship with Killian ruined if he asked and I gave a rejection.

"Damn fairies." Hayes was, once again, in the middle of another Fae rant. His voice passionate, his face flushed. "The moment we learned Fae were real, people should have wiped them off the planet."

Hayes had never been a Fae fan, but ever since his niece a few towns over was murdered, he had become worse. Police thought it was her boyfriend but couldn't prove it. Hayes, on the other hand, was searching for any scapegoat for his grief. Still, I couldn't stand this anymore, especially not with Killian listening. "Fae aren't any more evil than humans," I called out. Truth was, other than Orion breaking my heart in the most detestable way possible, I had never heard of a Fae hurting a human. On the other hand, I had real life experience on how humans horribly abused others.

He glared at me. "Are you sticking up for them because you're a witch?"

I raised a condemning eyebrow as he refused to pull his hate-filled gaze from me. "Witches aren't real."

"Fae weren't supposed to be real either, yet they are. That alone should prove witches are real, too."

This was ridiculous. I had saved his life last year when he

had a heart attack. "What are you going to do if I am a witch, Hayes? Burn me at the stake?"

"That's exactly what we would do!" Hayes darted off his stool, saliva flew from his mouth and his finger shook in fury as he pointed at me. "Don't you dare defend the Fae! They're evil! They're the devil's work!" He spit onto the floor as if that were a catch-all for expelling these evil forces.

Killian jumped in between me and Hayes. "Enough! You know she's not a witch."

"Are you Fae, Cassie?" Hayes leaned around Killian so he could see me. "Is that why you are how you are?"

"How am I?" I challenged Hayes.

"You know things. Things you shouldn't be able to know about people's health. She knew I was lying about smoking again."

"We all know," Killian said. "You smell like a tobacco field that was set on fire."

"You know what I'm talking about, Killian," Hayes shouted in his face. "She's not like us. She's not normal."

"She's a trained nurse practitioner and midwife." Killian's voice was steady, but the growing bite was clear. "She's going to know more things than we do. It's what she went to school for. The town council spent one year trying to find anyone to fill this position and no one applied. She did, and she came with great references, and I'm happy she's here. Otherwise, we'd have to drive an hour one way to see a doc. We're lucky to have her, and you know it."

Jim came alongside Hayes and nudged him with his elbow. "There's no Fae in these parts. We'd know it if there were. She's weird, but she's no Fae."

Hayes slowly turned his head toward Jim. "What if she's a witch?"

"She's no witch either. On Halloween, she delivered the Robinson baby in Spring Cove, and then ate dinner here with us, which means she wasn't in the woods worshipping Satan. If she were a witch, that's what she'd be required to do. Besides, she's worn the cross around her neck since the day she arrived, and no witch would do that."

Good for Jim for sticking up for me in a seriously weird way, but this entire conversation was asinine. As I opened my mouth to inform them of their stupidity, Killian shot me a look over his shoulder begging me to relinquish the fight. I shrugged an "okay…whatever." He nodded his appreciation and gave a roll of his eyes that he agreed—they were small-minded.

Jim and Hayes watched me as I slid the small gold cross along the chain. I once lived in a loving home. I once belonged. My grandmother swaddled me every morning in a hug, she had warm cookies waiting for me the moment I hopped off the school bus, and she tucked me into bed each night with a song. She believed in God. Loved him as much as she loved me and wore this cross as part of her devotion to a faith I couldn't understand. If God was as good and loving as she said, why did he take her from me and abandon me to the wolverines?

Deciding that Hayes and Jim had ruined the mood, Killian retreated to the kitchen. The door to the outside opened, and every cell in my body awoke when dark eyes fell on me. There was a sizzle in the air, the feeling of a caress along my back, and as much as I desired the touch, I was equally annoyed. If I were the witch everyone thought I was, sharp knives would be soaring across the room, wind would be shattering glass, and lightning would be doing some serious smiting.

"Regardless, if fairies come anywhere near this town," Hayes started up again, but in a lower voice to make sure I knew I wasn't invited to take part in his conversation with Jim, "we'll take care it." Neither Jim nor Hayes had any realization the dangerous Fae that concerned them was literally at arm's length.

Orion didn't even give them a side-eye. Instead, he kept his pace toward me, his gaze drinking me in the entire time. There was a tingling in my blood with that long look. The type of tingling that made me feel as if Orion were thirsty, and I was the last drop of water in the middle of the desert. The type of long look that reminded me how marvelous it was to be that drink and how I had never felt that way with another man in my life.

I, on the other hand, took a long drink from my beer and tried to ignore how magnificent he was in his jeans that hung lazily on his hips and in his white T-shirt that was stretched tight against his muscled shoulders. I hadn't planned on drinking more than one beer, but I considered ordering more. Maybe not. Orion was smart, and I needed to stay sober.

He stopped in front of my booth, and I wasn't having it. "If Brittney's in labor, you need to call the number I left. I'm off duty."

"Brittney delivered the baby at the hospital. Both are doing well."

"Good to hear. Shouldn't you be with them?"

"That information isn't why I'm here." He completely ignored my question.

"Bar's that way. If you tell Killian you had a baby, he might give you a free beer."

"I'm here to see you, Cassie."

I pursed my lips. "Not true."

"Why would you say that?"

An over shrug of my shoulders. "Because it's not possible for you to know where I was going to be at this moment, especially when I didn't know I was going to be here."

Without asking for permission, Orion slid into the booth. "I took a chance."

No part of me believed that. When we were together, Orion had a weird foresight. He would refuse to answer how he happened to "know things," and I swept away my concerns because I had loved him like I was a sad puppy dog. Well, he could have his secrets, because I had mine.

Orion leaned back in the seat and kicked his long legs out under the table as he examined the bar. "You still like the underdog places."

"Not much open at two in the morning."

"If it were two in the afternoon, I'm sure this is where you'd still choose to be."

It was, and I was already tired of our conversation. "What do you want, Orion?"

"Brittney's very human baby was born to her very human mother."

Yeah, I decided silence was the best approach on that one.

"Earlier, you said Brittney was human and was about to say she was going to give birth to a half Fae, but stopped. How did you know Brittney and the baby were human?"

"Normal assumption." I smirked at him with all the bitterness of the sludge coating my insides. "You were, after all, holding her hand."

"How did you know they were both human?" he pushed, ignoring my jab.

"Statistics. There're more humans than Fae in the world." I had absolutely no idea if that were true. "My turn to ask a question: Who is Brittney to you?"

"A means to an end." Couldn't get much more of an Orion answer than that. "If I lay my cards on the table as to why I'm here, will you lay yours as to what you're hiding?"

"I'm not hiding anything."

"You're lying. The stench is pouring off you, Cass."

Stupid Fae power of his. "Don't call me Cass," I snapped. He lost that privilege.

"Doesn't change my question," he lazily continued.

Not a chance I was telling him about my gift. I hadn't told anyone, and I sure as hell wasn't starting with him. "You want to lay stuff out, let's do it. There are four titanium pins holding my spine together. The doctors weren't sure I'd walk again. My neck was slashed open from when I went through the glass of the windshield, and they said it was a miracle I didn't bleed to death. Let's not even get started on the brain trauma."

His face had become blank, unreadable, and his voice void of emotion. "You healed."

I had healed, at a rapid pace, but I still had pain. I still had to relearn how to walk, and I had to learn how to control the chaos in my brain. It took me a year to recover. A miracle, the doctors had said, but it was a year I lost. "I saw your broken body. You were dead."

"There is no way you saw that," he said simply. "Not with the injuries you sustained."

"You knew how bad I was and abandoned me? I know we were…" Lovers. "I thought at the very least we were friends."

He mashed his lips together. A sign he wasn't going to answer. The doctors had said there was no way I had seen Orion after the accident, but I had. The image had been burned in my brain and it plagued my nightmares. "Why did your mother tell me you were dead?"

He stared at the table between us.

"Did you tell her to lie to me?"

More silence.

"Why didn't you come find me?"

Making the strands a rugged mess, Orion shoved a frustrated hand through his hair. "What do you want me to say?"

I slapped my palm against the table. "I want the truth!" I

whisper-shouted. "I want this black hole in my brain to be gone. I want to know what happened to us!" I stopped and berated myself for blabbering. I hadn't meant for the hurt to pour out but it had, and now I was ashamed. "Forget it. Do me a favor and stay away. I moved on, you moved on, and we're both better for it." I went to slide out of the booth.

"I'm searching for someone," he said in that easygoing manner that tunneled into my nerve endings. "Fae in this area. Can you help me with that?"

"Nope." I stood. "Have a good life and stay out of mine."

"Cass," he said as if I were the one being unreasonable.

And I was officially done. I turned from him, and Orion moved swiftly out of the booth. So fast, my hand brushed his arm, and the skin-to-skin contact caused a rush of his emotions and memories into me. I saw us laughing, hugging, holding, touching and making love. Felt his love, his devotion, and his sadness…as if he were the one who was devastated at the loss of our relationship. The touch was warmth, a caress, a reminder of when I was wanted.

I swung back around and exploded in anger. "Leave me alone!" I hissed as not to draw the attention of anyone else. It was bad enough that Mateo had watched the scene between me and Orion. I didn't need anyone else asking me about Orion, reminding me of memories I needed to forget. "I'm not helping you, and I'm not staying around to be played."

Orion stared at me, and any easiness that had been there was gone. Pain seeped through his wall of static and punched me hard in the gut. Fighting to stay upright from the emotional wave, I clutched a hand to my stomach. As fast as the emotion hit me, it quickly retracted.

"I have reason to believe there are Fae in danger," he said quietly, as if the words themselves were a solemn secret. "I think you can distinguish who is Fae and who isn't, and because of what you do for a living, you have contact with nearly everyone in the area. I need your help."

"Can't you tell who is Fae and who isn't?" I asked.

"Yes, but I don't know who is Fae in this area. I believe you do." His dark eyes bored into mine.

I was transfixed, wanting to tear my eyes away from him, but couldn't—not as I thought of Killian and the other Fae who were my friends. "Who are you looking for?"

Orion kept his gaze locked on mine. "A mother and a baby."

A baby. The baby from my dreams? I flinched and his ever-searching eyes caught the movement. "You know a Fae mother and baby in this area?" he asked.

A million questions screamed in my mind, and if I yelled each one, he wouldn't answer. He would be cold and stoic, acting as if I didn't exist. The Fae played by their own set of rules. They had their own wars, problems, and vendettas.

Even though I was exhausted and it would bring on the mother of all migraines, I touched his mind. My forehead scrunched, as reading him without contact was like listening for faint voices through static, with an occasional ear-piercing shriek. I couldn't read his thoughts, but I could decipher that he believed what he was saying was true, and I also detected his undercurrent of concern for this mother and baby. Then in an instant, the static became aware. Aware I was there and not liking it. The static curled in on itself then shot out toward me in the form of a spike. Pain crashed through my skull and I recoiled.

"What's going on with you?" he said so softly I barely heard it.

I resisted the urge to drop my head into my hands and to rub my throbbing temples. "How do I know you aren't the danger? I remember plenty of nights you came to me scraped, bruised and recovering from wounds with no explanation of what happened."

Orion leaned forward. "Call the mother. Tell her Orion MacAleese wants to meet with her. She will welcome me."

"You think a lot of yourself, don't you?"

"Yes."

Besides Killian, there were three Fae families in our county. Clara's baby was a week old. "I'll think about it. Meet me here tomorrow around noon and I'll give you my answer."

Orion shook his head. "Now, Cass."

Exasperated, I threw out my arms. "It's the middle of the night."

"And they could be in danger. Call them. Now."

I didn't trust him, but who was I to stand in the way of Fae issues? And how could I live with myself if Orion was right, I did nothing, and something happened to Clara and her sweet baby? My eyes darted around Orion's face searching for answers I would never receive. With a roll of my neck, I pulled out my cell from my back pocket. "Give me a moment."

Orion gave me a nod and kept his eyes glued to me as I walked to the back of Bambi's to where a small hallway led to the bathrooms. Feeling stupid for calling so late, I rested my head on the wall as I held the phone to my ear. One ring. Two. A third.

"Cassie?" Clara said in a groggy and panicked voice. "Are you okay?"

"I am. Sorry. I know it's late, but I have someone who is adamant to meet you." I glanced up and found Orion's heavy stare pinned on me. "Now."

"Now? What? I don't understand?" A pause. "Who?"

"Orion MacAleese."

Silence on Clara's end. The deep type I could throw a

stone down and never hear it hit bottom. "Send him to us. Send him straight away."

I met Orion's eyes again and barely registered that Clara had hung up. This was real. Orion was here, and Clara was possibly in danger. I registered the sound of my shoes tapping against the old wooden floor as I approached Orion. I thought of my grandmother, her warning to me, and the baby in my dreams. Twenty-eight. I was twenty-eight. Maybe this was it—the beginning my grandmother had promised.

Maybe. Or maybe I was losing my mind.

At the table, I took a paper napkin and a pen left by Killian and wrote down the address. "Clara and her husband don't know I'm aware they're Fae, and I'd appreciate it if you kept that to yourself. I don't want my Fae patients who are trying to pass as humans to shy away from me."

After reading it, he pocketed the address and gave me a look that said it was time to leave and I wasn't invited. Sadness settled in my stomach when I reached out just enough to taste his resignation of letting me go. It had been that simple to him. I was in his life and then I wasn't. I had reappeared again, and he was ready to leave—as easy as releasing air from his lungs. Once upon a time, I had fallen in love with him, and to him, I was nothing more than a momentary distraction.

"Don't let anyone else know you can distinguish between Fae and human," Orion said. "That could make you dangerous enemies."

"I never said I could do anything. You're the one making wild assumptions."

"All the same, stay silent about this." Orion studied me so closely I became uncomfortable. He could smell lies, but could he sniff out specifically which words were the truth and which ones were false? "Are you happy, Cassie? In this town? Are you happy?"

Pure guilt rolled off him, and I wasn't searching to read him. At least he felt something. Was I happy? Not as much as when I was in his arms, but that wasn't real. It had been delusion and fantasy, and I had learned the hard way happiness was an illusion. I was content now and that was all I could ask for. Orion had a life to save in a war I didn't understand. I was outraged at him for lying to me about his death, but I could respect him for rescuing a mother and her baby. With a pounding headache and head heavy with exhaustion, I forced a small lift of my lips. "I have a good life. Please, go. I couldn't bear it if something happened to Clara and her baby."

Without another word, Orion left the bar. Not even a glance over his shoulder.

Killian returned from the kitchen and headed to the two old fools at the end of the bar. He gave them a bowl of pretzels and then met my eyes. I inclined my head to let him know I was leaving, and he gave me a chin tilt as a goodbye as he watched me place cash on the bar for my bill. I walked out into the night and scanned the sleepy town's two-story, 1800-era buildings stacked beside each other. There were no glowing red taillights of a car either way down the long straight road, nor any sign of Orion. He was gone.

It was a five-minute walk from the bar to my apartment, and it was one I enjoyed. But somehow the shadows appeared darker tonight, the clouds in the sky rolling and ominous. A gust of cold air caused my skin to prickle. I edged toward the bar, then shook off my childhood fear of the dark. All was fine, one foot in front of the other, and soon I would be safe.

CHAPTER 5

The moment I entered my second-floor apartment, I flicked on the lights and sagged against the shut door. I developed a distaste for the dark after my mother's boyfriend locked me in a closet for two days because he said I was disobeying.

That was one of the things I loved about Orion. With him, my fears vanished. It was with him I stayed up all night, watched my first sunrise since my grandmother's death, and celebrated as the darkest part of the night was dispelled by the rays of the glorious sun. On the beach, Orion had settled me between his legs, wrapped his arms tight around me, and rested his chin on my shoulder. He would alternate between placing pleasing kisses on my neck and explaining to me Fae lore, rules and wisdom.

"We're called to the sun," he whispered in my ear. "It gives us our power and strength. It offers peace even in the midst of battle. Don't be scared of the dark, Cassie. Without the dark, we can't fully appreciate the sun. Without darkness, we would never appreciate the light."

Nine years. It didn't seem that long ago. Instead, it felt like the blink of an eye.

I threw my keys on a desk littered with unopened mail I had saved to go through on my day off, then tossed my jacket onto the living room chair. I had a studio apartment—probably not much more square footage than Dee's, but it had windows. I loved windows, light, and not feeling closed in.

My place was homey. The walls were painted lavender, my furniture was beige, and the comforter on my bed a relaxing soft pink. A copious assortment of green plants were on tables and hanging from baskets, while larger vegetation rose from huge containers on the floor. Greenery was my attempt to heal the huge hole within me. Each plant was like having a piece of my grandmother: chamomile for anxiety, echinacea for wound-mending and colds, garlic for overall health, ginger for stomach issues. The list went on and on.

I waited for the comfort of being home, but that didn't happen. It couldn't. Not with Orion on my mind. I rummaged through the closet and found the box I had promised myself I would never explore. I should have burned it years ago, but the strength to do so evaded me. I brought the box to the couch, sat, took another deep inhalation, and dove in.

On top of the stack of photos was one of me and my grandmother. An ache rippled through me at the sight of her, but I forced myself to not turn from the memories. My grandmother wasn't the old silver fox type. She had given birth to my mom in her early twenties, and then my mom conceived me when she was sixteen. I could have easily been my grandmother's daughter instead of her granddaughter. From her, I had received my dark chestnut hair, my dark eyes and my fondness of fireflies, teacup roses and the smell of honeysuckle on the vine.

KATIE MCGARRY

My grandmother was my light. Even when Mom would leave, my grandmother was there. Even when Mom would reappear schlepping whatever awful boyfriend with her, my grandmother stood in front of me and put my needs first. She loved me, I loved her, and the familiar fury that she was stolen from me at such a young age raged through my heart.

The case had remained unsolved. My grandmother and I had been cooking dinner. Two pots were boiling on the stove. The long handled aluminum pot contained spaghetti. The other, a black iron pot, was full of rose petals to make rose oil to help lower my grandmother's blood pressure. The summer breeze coming through the open window was forgiving, and as my grandmother asked me to wash the lettuce we had gathered from her garden for a salad, her head popped up at what sounded like the echo of a woman singing. I hadn't liked how her face had paled, how she drew me closer to her, and then how she told me to stay in the house with the door locked and not to let anyone in until she returned.

That was the issue. She didn't come home, and I was left alone.

Unable to handle the following memories, I flipped to the next picture. It was of me and Orion, and there was a fresh wave of bloody pain. When I met him, I believed he was an angel my grandmother had sent to fill the hole left in my life after she died. I thought he was my answer to the cold and loneliness. I looked like a baby in the photo. My smile was so bright, so hopeful, it was hard to fathom that had been me. Orion had his arms around me and was kissing my cheek. How could that have been a lie? We appeared in love...I thought we were in love...

Curling my legs beneath me, I sifted through the rest of the photos to find Orion, Mercutio and Shaw posing shirtless on the beach. They were Orion's best friends, brothers they called themselves, even though they didn't share blood. Shaw with his sly smirk, naturally sun-kissed tan, and surfer boy good looks. Acting the clown, Mercutio flexed his biceps, his skin a beautiful dark umber, and, as always, he wore a contagious grin. And then there was Orion with his lazy, mischievous smile. Mercutio and Shaw had been my friends, but I guess, in the end, they weren't. After the accident, they, too, had disappeared.

The next picture was of me and Wren. My heart twisted in pain. My roommate. My friend, which was an honor because I had learned quickly that she didn't easily do friendships—if at all. Wren was my first friend in South Carolina.

I rested my head against the couch and allowed myself to drift to sleep as I contemplated Wren, with her dry wit and her glossy black hair. She grew up in foster care, and after years of being sick and tired of wondering about her heritage, she had swiped her file to discover her birth mother was originally from Japan before coming to America.

Wren had a distinctive style I admired. Badass meets chic. Tight-fitting jeans with rips, off-the-shoulder shirts, an arm full of bracelets, multiple necklaces, and a short black leather jacket she wore even when it wasn't cold. The bracelets and necklaces were full of stones my grandmother had taught me helped with protection.

After Wren had answered my "roommate wanted" ad, we shared a one-bedroom apartment over a Thai restaurant near the beach, and if we leaned far enough out the window, we could see the ocean. Our apartment was tiny, but cheery, and it was the first place that had come close to echoing the tranquility of the cabin.

One day, Wren sat cross-legged on the floor at her favorite spot. The place where the afternoon sunlight streamed through the windows and the ocean breeze could catch the ends of her hair. "I have a gift for you."

That caught me off guard. We couldn't afford a couch—we could barely afford the bread for the toaster we scored at the Goodwill—but Wren found money for a gift for me? "What?"

She pulled a necklace out of a bag. A stone hung by a silver chain. "It's black onyx." She slipped it around my neck, overlapped it with my grandmother's cross, and I marveled at the smoothness of the stone to hide the rush of emotions I didn't know how to handle. The shock and joy at the gift, the confusion as to why she cared for me, the lump in my throat that was tough to work through to say thank you.

"Black onyx wards off harmful spirits and captures bad energy," I said.

"Correct," Wren beamed, probably believing she was the one who taught me that. It was easy for her to assume as I avoided discussing my grandmother with her or anyone—even Orion.

My mouth flattened. "Is this another perils-of-dating-Orion lecture?"

"You need to be careful with him."

"You and Orion are friends." In fact, we were a group of friends: me, Wren, Mercutio, Shaw and Orion. We ate take-out in our small apartment, played on the pier in the evening, and walked the surf at night. After my grandmother, that group was the closest I had to a family.

"I don't do friends," Wren said as if there were something bitter in her mouth.

"If you don't do friends, what am I to you?"

"Different."

"But you were friends with them before I was."

"The boys and I have shared interests. I scratch their backs, they massage mine. Our world is more complicated than what you believe."

"You mean Orion's world is complicated." He and his friends were Fae, and we weren't.

Wren tilted her head as if she comprehended what I didn't. "No, the world is complicated for you and me."

I frowned, as this wasn't how the conversations went. I surveyed the room, and while the contents were familiar, something was off. "Because we both had crap upbringings?"

"No, because of what we were born to be."

In actuality, Wren had informed me she had heard from an old friend who needed help and that she was taking the next bus to Massachusetts. She had promised to return in two weeks. Five days later, I was broken in the car accident and she became one more ghost in my past.

The hair on my arms stood on end as a chill entered my blood. There were shadows in the corner, as if the room couldn't complete itself correctly. This was a dream. I had fallen asleep and this was a dream, but it felt real—too real. "I'm dreaming."

"Yes, you are, and someone is waking us," Wren said.

"I'm not ready to wake." The shadows on the fringe became darker. Maybe I was ready.

"There won't be many who will like being awakened. Have they found you yet?" As if being hunted, Wren frantically glanced over her shoulder, right and then left. Her eyes were wide and wild, and she breathed heavily as if she had been sprinting.

"No," I automatically responded as if my soul understood the question, but my head had not. "I don't know. What do you mean?"

"You need to wake up. As in physically open your eyes, snap out of this dream, and avoid any place people would search for you. Find somewhere safe to lay low and I'll find you through dreams. We're not safe. The world's gone mad and it's angry at us."

The shadows in the room rolled inward, like a wall cloud before a storm. Anxiety pushed through me, and my instincts were screaming for me to run. "What's happening?"

"Cassie, wake up!" Wren roared, and a loud bang caused my eyes to shoot open. I had been asleep and now I was awake. Lying on the couch, confused and disoriented, I sat up. At the sight in front of me, I swayed. On my coffee table was a large, old and worn book. *Grimoire.* The word rang through me like a sigh and I had no idea why.

An icepick pierced my skull, and I bent with the pain. Emotions. Too many emotions were pummeling me, and each was strong, fierce and terrifying. Fear. Anger. Vengeance. A swirling hurricane advancing in my direction. A pounding of a fist on my door, and I flinched with each hit.

"Cassie!" Mateo yelled. "Cassie, open the door!"

A flash of warning inside me. Something was wrong and I hesitated.

"Cassie, there's a problem!" Mateo shouted as he continued to bang on the door.

His family. They must need help. I raced across the room, and the grimoire opened. Pages flipped of their own accord. Fear made my blood turn cold. My thoughts galloped, yet moved too slow. What was happening? Pounding on the door again. "Cassie, please," Mateo begged. "Before it's too late."

I rushed to the door and opened it. Mateo bust through, then swiftly closed the door behind him. "We need to go."

"Go?" Confusion was a thick fog I couldn't swim out of. "Go where?"

"Anywhere not here." Mateo raced across the room and grabbed my purse. "The town's coming after you, and they're hungry for blood."

I shook my head, to wake myself up, to force this to make sense. "What are you talking about?"

Mateo stalked over to me. "Everyone woke up two hours ago. The whole town. Probably the whole nation. The world. We just woke up *knowing* witches are real. The whole town knows, Cassie. They know about you, and they're coming for you. I can't let that happen. Not after what you've done for my family."

I was still shaking my head. Still not understanding. "I didn't wake up." Was I awake? I was dreaming of Wren, but somehow, she was real…and now? The world was inside out. "I don't know what you're talking about. What do you mean witches?"

"Cassie." As if trying to get me to snap out of this disoriented stupor, Mateo wrapped a hand around my bicep and slightly shook me. "We know you're a witch."

Leaving me dizzy, the blood rushed from my head. "I'm not a witch."

"Hayes called the town council together. Everyone but Killian was there, and word got out about the emergency meeting. Tons of people showed, and Hayes convinced them to kill you. They're on their way, and we need to go." Mateo dropped his fingers from my bicep to my wrist and pulled me toward the door.

"I don't understand." As I dug in my heels to protest, Mateo opened the door. The air rushed out of my lungs at the sight of the mob on the landing outside my door and flowing down the stairs. Jim was front and center, and his eyes turned completely red. The outline of his body shivered as if it were smoke, his tongue darted out and it was that of a serpent's—forked, thin and long. I yelped and jerked back. "Did you see that?"

Mateo gave me a glance like I was insane, but placed himself between the mob and me. "Everyone go home. We'll talk when everyone's had a chance to calm down."

Jim tilted his head in an unnatural way then winked. The

smoke disappeared, his eyes returned to normal, and the forked tongue retreated back into his mouth.

Four men I had helped throughout the years pushed in, two of them shoving Mateo out of the way. "Leave Mateo alone!" But my cries were cut off as the two other men grabbed me. Their fingers dug into my flesh, but the pain was hidden by my shock. "What are you doing?"

"Cassie Strega," Hayes said with pride and joy, "most of the town council has met, and you have been found guilty of witchcraft and will be burned at the stake."

A dream. A nightmare. I was still asleep. "What?"

"You're a witch." Hayes spat at my feet. "Shame on you for doing the devil's work. Delivering our children and speaking Satan's words over them to make them your followers."

"What are you talking about? None of this makes sense!" Soft rustling of pages flipping. I slowly turned my head toward the sound, and my heart stuttered at the golden glow radiating from the book.

"Her spell book is alive!" Hayes jovially exclaimed to the mob. "She's a witch!"

Yells and jeers thickened the air, and I trembled with fear. Jim tilted his head to the side again as if it were broke and smiled at me in a way that made me want to dry heave. He stepped forward, and I fought to get back, but grasping hands held me still. Jim leaned forward and his breath was sour as he whispered in my ear, "He's free now, witch, and he sees you. He said to save yourself you must use your power."

Then I was thrust forward. My arms bound behind me. My hair was pulled, my face slapped. My teeth chattered, tears cascaded from my eyes, and my breath caught in my chest, as though trapped between sob and scream. I was heaved down the stairs from one person to the next. Unable to catch myself, I fell, my face smacking against the steps. Someone picked me up, ground their nails into my skin and threw me into the crowd full of people I had helped heal, people I had cared for over the years.

Propelled out the door of my apartment building, I lost my footing and slammed onto the pavement. My side ached, my skin burned, and as I was dragged onward by my wrists, my arms were scratched and sandblasted by rocks. I cried out as someone jerked me up by my hair.

"A witch worships the devil!" Hayes announced to the crowd.

I convulsed at the sight of a stake in the ground surrounded by a heap of wood. Cries arose from the mob for me to die. A column of flame whooshed upward as Hayes pulled a lighter from a homemade torch that smelled like it had been doused in gasoline. The town had descended into madness, and they were going to kill me. I was yanked forward again, and I refused to comply. Tugging, digging my feet into the ground, I fought my captors, but I was wrenched forward so violently I shrieked with the twist and snap of my wrist. My pulse hammered as I was lifted to the stake. I kicked, thrashed, and as I was bound to the pole, a surge of adrenaline coursed through me and I screamed, "Enough!"

My voice echoed in the night, and like a boomerang, it circled back, but louder, and everyone froze. A fire ignited within me. A fire I didn't understand. The crowd cowered. "Let. Me. Go." *Go* boomed like a grenade. Many covered their ears, and the leaves of the trees shook as a burst of wind blew past me and into the mob.

Hayes wound back his arm to throw the torch to the wood, and my hands became scorching, but my skin didn't burn. My binding loosened, and my free arm stretched out toward him. He was tossed to his back by the wind that whipped around me in a frenzy, yet I was the calm in the storm. I surveyed the crowd and the trees bowed with my fury.

Limbs plummeted from above, and lawn chairs from patios soared across the grass. My once friends scattered, hunkered to the ground, and shielded themselves from me. As the wind continued to blow, the clouds above swirled, and there was a shakiness, a dizziness, a heat flushing my face and a cold sweat along my neck. I jumped off the wood, rain broke from the clouds, and the battering drops stung my skin. I fled into an alley, my feet stomping into puddles. The shakiness started to win as my eyes darted about to figure out which way was safe.

I sprinted into the forest that bordered the town. Ignoring the pain in my body, I ran through the dense thicket. My wrist hung unnaturally, and I cradled it to my chest. Blood oozed down my skin, soaked my clothes. One of my once friends shouted to find me, to finish me. This time, if they found me, I'd die at their hands. I stumbled and fell to the ground. I crawled to a large, towering sugar maple and crumbled against it. My head dipped with exhaustion, but I tugged my chin up and ignored the deluge of pain.

Through the sheets of rain, I glanced at the dark sky about to give way to the dawn. Several feet ahead of me, a dark mist slithered out of a tree. The obscurity grew into a looming cloud. I blinked through the rain, and the mist solidified into a physical form. A hallucination. The blood loss, the exhaustion, my mind shattering into a million pieces. The smoke formed into the shape of a human, then back into a shadow, the head twisting and turning as it curiously looked me over.

"You are the one," the black shadow hissed. I scrambled back, but hit the tree. The shadow of smoke slinked into my personal space. "You freed him. Move not! He is on his way to collect you."

Terror and anger caused another surge of power. Thunder rattled through the forest. Streaks of electricity illuminated the clouds. A bolt of lightning struck the ground in front of a massive man who appeared out of nowhere. The lightning hitting both the man and the shadow.

They disappeared, only for a gunshot to ring out. Wood from the tree trunk splintered next to my chin, piercing my skin. More blood trickled down my cheek.

"There she is!" Hayes yelled as he stumbled toward me. I lifted my head, watched as Hayes raised his rifle, aimed it at me, and there was a spark of lightning in my soul. One last drive to control it and smite my enemy to the ground...but I couldn't. He was the father of three beautiful girls, the husband of a wife he adored. Who was I if I took his life? I closed my eyes, waited… and *bang*!

Shots fired, hot flames through my body, a pull on my hand and then pain. Agony. The air in my lungs squeezed completely out. I was no longer in the forest. I was everywhere. I was nowhere. I neither was nor wasn't. Sharp knives sliced along my arms, my legs, creeping up my stomach and carving into my soul. A scream tore through me and scratched at my throat, but the sound was muffled by the sensation of hot asphalt being poured down my windpipe. Something had my arm and was dragging me through a series of metal doors slamming shut. Some of them I passed through, some of them the sharp metal grazed me as I slipped past, and then others I was squeezed into near nothingness and passed like light through a windowpane. Finally, I was thrust through the other side.

Landing on a floor, I gasped for air, smelled the salt of the ocean, and heard waves crashing on a beach. How apropos that as I writhed in pain, bleeding out from two billion cuts along my skin, I was experiencing my favorite memories before my death.

CHAPTER 6

*T*here were whispers in the darkness. A buzz of a million hushed voices that rose and fell with my suffering. I alternated between no awareness and excruciating anguish. A baby cried—one belonging to a newborn. The infant from my dreams. She needed me, and I ached in my soul. Her agony was worse than my cuts and broken bones. I couldn't reach the baby, and yet she called to me. Days, weeks, never ending...or maybe just hours, minutes or seconds.

A pressure on my forehead, the warmth of a calloused hand, and the whispering halted. I opened my eyes and saw a smooth white ceiling above me and pillows surrounding me. The bed below me was soft as a cloud. The sound of waves crashing onto the beach was a comfort, the scent of the salty ocean a welcomed smell. The seagulls calling out to one another a lullaby. There was no pain now, not even a twinge of a muscle.

The large semi-circle room with beige walls had open French doors leading to the ocean. Each floor-to-ceiling window was dressed with sheer curtains that danced in the gentle breeze. The floor was the color of sand, and there wasn't another piece of furniture in the room.

I sensed Orion's presence before I saw him. Expecting an onslaught of pain, I hesitantly sat up on my elbows. I marveled at my wrist, how the bones were healed, how my skin was untarnished from cuts and bruises. Not real. None of this was real.

Orion stood at the French doors. His shoulder rested against the doorframe, his back toward me as he surveyed the ocean. "From the moment I saw you, my world changed. It's not a euphemism. It's as true as the sun that rises in the morning and the stars that shine at night. I saw you before you realized there was anything like me. The ground beneath me gave way and I fell hard...I fell fast. I knew in that moment that God had made me for you, and it was my job to love you, care for you, protect you, putting your needs before my own—even if your happiness meant my suffering."

I held my breath, wondering, wishing, but none of it was true. This was a dream....

"Having the gift of foresight, my mother saw your arrival. She warned me that you and I, as a couple, were cursed. She told me you would bewitch me and what we would experience would be an intense fling. She said if I allowed it, I would desire you, need you emotionally and physically in ways close to unnatural, but keeping you...loving you...lying with you," his voice deepened with those words, and I shivered with the sweet memories of his body touching mine, "would bring pain, madness, and death."

My mouth dried out as I wasn't sure I wanted this conversation. "For me or for you?"

"Both of us. My decisions damned us both. The two of us, as a couple, are cursed."

Unable to argue, I remained silent.

"I believed I was invincible, that I could change the future my mother foresaw, and my arrogance almost killed you," Orion continued. "After the accident, my mother looked into your future and told me you'd be better without me, so I chose the path that held the greater odds for your happiness. I chose to leave you alone."

He relaxed his back against the doorframe and swung his beautiful dark eyes to me. "All Fae women have the gift of prophecy, but some are stronger in the gift than others. Their premonitions show us the future in the hopes we can change the outcome. That's why Fae exist—we are to save humans from their own destruction."

Orion gave a sly smile that used to mean very wicked and wonderful things. "We're bad enough to do the dirty work God won't allow his angels to do, but we're just good enough we believe humanity deserves another try." His grin dropped as a dangerous glint hit his eyes. "I have to admit, after what I saw in those woods, I'm not sure they're worth saving."

"Am I dreaming?" I asked.

"Yes."

Explained so much. I inched up to be supported by the headboard and leaned against the pillows behind me. "Is this real?"

"What is real, Cass? Fae and witches once weren't real. Was the pain you suffered because of me real? The year in the hospital? The months of therapy? Was that real? The people who just tried to kill you, were their friendships once real?"

"Even though that answer was vague," I said, "you're being unusually forthcoming."

He didn't say a word, only moved his gaze back to the sea. There was the Orion I knew.

"How did you find me?" I asked.

"We are…connected," he answered slowly.

I waited a few beats, making it clear I was waiting for a

better explanation, but he permitted the silence to grow. "Connected how?"

"If you live, I will answer that."

That was a definite twist in the conversation. "How bad am I?"

"Bad." The weight of his simple answer caused me to flinch. "There's a bullet lodged close to your heart, but that's not the only reason you're dying. If I didn't shift you out of there, move the way Fae do through time and space, you would have died in the forest. Shifting with a human is precarious at best. It requires exact manipulation of energy, but you were dying, I had to rush, and it harmed you further. I'm sorry. Truly I am."

Going through the wall, the choking, the flattening, the millions of cuts—"shifting," he had named it. Even when we were together, I was unaware of this ability. Nor was I cognizant of the premonitions, that the Fae have a purpose, or that he was aware that pursuing a relationship with me would lead to my fall. My stomach sank. When Orion told me he was a Fae, I felt so special, so included in his life. When he lifted the veil of his being Fae, I assumed it meant our relationship was real, but he knew being with him would hurt me. How could he keep that from me? We weren't real. He and I…we were a facade.

I pushed the hurt feelings away. "Am I going to live?"

"Your condition is fatal enough that a human doctor cannot save you, but I can. The Fae Council has instructed me to do so, but I won't do it again—not against your will."

"What do you mean *again?*" I paused. "Why do the Fae want me to live?"

"Because, according to Fae visions, you play a critical role in saving the world."

I snorted as my mouth tilted up. I doubted I was critical to anything. What I liked was the short-lived smirk he flashed, as if he could read my mind. But as my half smile faded, so did his, and the seriousness of the situation left me nauseous.

"If, after we talk, you want to live, I'll make sure you do. If not," Orion placed a hand over his heart as if making a solemn vow, "I promise you'll experience no pain as you pass from this life into the light. I give you my word, you'll be swaddled in peace."

I slipped off the bed and walked toward the French doors. Outside was a brick patio, and beyond was the beach. The water sparkled in the sun and the sand was golden. The light breeze played with the palm trees, and I inhaled the sweet scent of Carolina Jasmine. This was South Carolina, on an island off the mainland. A place I had once dared to love as home.

Gunshot wounds, crazed mobs, witches, and shifting. Would I wake in an asylum? I leaned against the opposing side of the doorframe from Orion. "Explain."

Orion was silent for several long beats, rubbed his hand along his jaw, and then pushed forward. "You called me a killer."

My narrowed eyes challenged him to tell me I was wrong.

He gave me an amused side-eye. "I am. I'm a warrior for the Fae. You'd understand me better if I described myself as a soldier. My job is to keep Fae and humanity safe."

"Safe from who?"

His brain working overtime, he held my gaze. "The demons of hell."

The smoke shadow. Jim's red eyes. Dizziness overwhelmed me, the feeling of all the blood rushing out of my face, down my body and out of my toes. A blink and I was on the bed, Orion standing over me.

"What's happening?" I asked.

"We're running out of time. One of our prophetesses had

a premonition there is a baby who will decide the fate of our world. That premonition sent me to Brittney. I thought they were the baby and mother I was searching for, but they weren't. I then assumed Brittney was a steppingstone to where the baby was, as that's how premonitions often work —like a riddle. But then the mother and the baby you sent me to weren't the ones I was searching for either."

"How do you know?"

"I just do. I have to find this mother. I have to protect this baby. The demons are searching for her, too, and they will kill her. They want this world to burn, and they will murder and destroy whoever and whatever stands in their way."

I shook my head, not understanding, but the movement caused my gut to spasm and I winced. Orion gently took my shoulders and looked straight into my eyes. "There's something going on with you. I felt it the moment you entered the apartment, this push and pull in my brain and when we touched…."

It was becoming harder to think as a low-grade throbbing swept through my body. "Evidently, I'm a witch." Was that why I was an empath?

"Yes, but beyond that. You know things—like being able to tell the difference between Fae and human. I saw how you touched Brittney, watched the energy surrounding you as you focused on her baby. There's something different about you than there was before, and I need to know—whatever this difference is, does it have anything to do with the baby I'm searching for?"

The pain intensified, causing me to cry out and double over. "What's happening to me?"

Orion cupped my face with his hands, the familiar pressure a comfort in the midst of hell. "You're dying, and it's causing me to lose the connection with you. Your pain is too intense for you to stay with me in this dream. I won't keep you alive again, not against your will. Honestly, you should be dead, but you keep calling out to find the baby. Are you searching for the same baby we are, Cass? Is that why you're holding on?"

A wave of anxiety and panic smashed into me, and as I tried to solve the riddle, my eyes darted over his face. The baby from my dreams. Was she real?

"We're struggling to find the baby and her mother, but the council believes you can help us. They now believe the premonitions involving Brittney and upstate New York weren't about finding the baby, but about finding you. In their new premonitions, they see you holding our queen. They think you can help me track this mother and her baby, and they want me to save you, but I will not force you to live, not again."

Trepidation was etched on his face. Desperate to understand, I touched his arm, but I couldn't read his emotions. "What aren't you telling me?"

"My mother says you'll be cursed if you stay. You will experience unbearable pain. I stole the peace of the portal from you years ago, and I won't steal it from you now. You have lived a valiant life, Cass. In my world, your name would be written on our walls. Your urn placed upon crystal and glass. Your name spoken on the lips of many on the Day of Souls. You protected the vulnerable, the sick, the mothers, helped bring new life into the world and helped souls move into death. There is no greater honor than this. You've lived a full life and there's no shame in choosing the light."

Caring for the sick in my community, loving my neighbors, holding my mothers' hands during childbirth, whispering my babies through labor and into the world for their first breath…no greater honor…it was a life I was proud of, but it was as if something was missing.

Warmth to my right. The most magnificent sensation.

Like the rays of the sun gently kissing my skin. A blazing light appeared, more luminous than I had ever encountered, but I could look upon its brilliance without having to squint. It shined brighter than any inferno, than any stadium lights, even more radiant than a supernova. There was a gravitational pull, one that was uncomfortable to resist. I desired to run toward it, arms open, and fall into the waiting love.

"You see it, don't you?" Orion said in awe. "The portal?"

"It's beautiful." Tears sprung to my eyes as my heart soared with the feeling of home.

"That's what our legends say. My grandmother said whatever I could imagine heaven to be, I still couldn't comprehend the portal's beauty."

I stretched my hand toward the light, and the serene glow warmed my fingertips the same way my grandmother's hot chocolate used to on cold, harsh nights. "Do you see it?"

"No, but I pray I will when it's my time to pass."

Here was the man I remembered. The tenderness in his eyes, the possessiveness in his face. Like he had hundreds of times when we were together, he lovingly tucked my hair behind my ear. "Go on, Cass. The road has risen to meet you. The wind is at your back. The sun is warm on your face. The rain has fallen softly on your fields, and God is waiting to hold you in the palm of his hand. You have fulfilled your purpose, and it's time to go home."

Yes, yes it was. Orion placed his fingers under my chin, and his eyes smoldered as he sought permission. I nodded, and my pulse beat hard as he leaned down and brushed his lips to mine. I missed him, I loved him, and we were saying goodbye.

He pulled back and gazed at me as if he were memorizing the moment. His fingers reverently caressed my cheek. Something within me changed, and my eyes widened at the miracle. Orion kept his promise. There was no pain, no sorrow. No nagging, worry or fear. I laid a hand on my chest as I had never felt this way before—untainted by life.

Orion tilted his head toward the portal. I stepped for the light, toward peace, and released a final exhale...and then heard the cry of a newborn. The baby from my dreams. My head whipped toward the sound, toward a hallway that wasn't there before. It was shrouded in darkness, dripping with a black, oily substance that stank of decay and contained the cold of death.

I reached out with my mind and I recoiled when I connected with the baby. Through time, through space, I shared her deep pit of hunger, cringed with the frostbite burning her skin, and became hollow with her horrible despair of abandonment. She was alone. A monster had left the baby alone. Terror coursed through me. The baby—she was being tortured.

"What's wrong, Cass?" Orion moved to block me from the hallway.

"Don't you hear it? See that?"

He shook his head. "I only see the room I created for the dream."

"The hallway,"

"There's no hallway."

"The baby is there. She's in pain, and she's alone." I inched toward the hallway, and Orion threw his arm out, stopping me. The compulsion to find her became consuming, and I fought to sprint past. "She needs me."

"Shaw, someone's in the dream, which means they're nearby." Orion unsheathed a golden dagger from the small of his back and pointed the sharp tip toward the dark hallway, toward the cries of the baby. "Find them." He tried edging me back with his arm, but I stood my ground. "Go on, Cass. You need to enter the portal. Your job here is done. I'll find the baby and keep her safe."

The infant wailed. The sound ripped at my brain. "You need my help to find her."

Orion captured my chin, forcing my gaze from the hallway, and the intensity of his eyes shocked me. "Not if the light is calling to you. Staying here will mean pain. The portal opened. You made your choice—the right choice. Now go."

The baby shrieked, and I bolted toward the sound, pushing against his arm, but he kept me locked next to him. "No. The enemy is baiting you. They want you to stay, which means you're safer if you move into the light. I want you safe, I want you happy. Go!"

"What difference does it make if I die now or later?"

"Because if you reject the portal, it might not open for you again," he shouted. "Do you hear me? You will be cursed. Your life will have pain. I will not allow you to become lost. I don't want you living a cursed life. Not for me, not for the council and not for the world. Go!"

"I'm not going. Not until she's safe. I'm staying! I'm choosing to stay!"

Pounding and irrational pain shot through me, my knees gave, and I opened my mouth in a silent scream. Orion let loose a string of curses and the world went black.

CHAPTER 7

*M*y eyes opened, and I was in a small, dimly lit room with dirty walls. A single bulb hung from the ceiling. My lungs burned as I gasped for air. I was choking—on what, I didn't know. My fingers flew to my neck to discover what was preventing me from breathing, but there was nothing. Fluid, there was fluid in my throat drowning me.

"She's crashing!" Mercutio shouted as he pressed his hands near my heart. "She's bleeding from everywhere. I can't stop it. She's dying."

"I'm aware," Orion retorted as he raised a dagger to his own wrist.

"I sensed the portal," Mercutio said. "Her heartbeat stopped then she shot back. What happened?"

"I don't know," pure menace dripped from Orion's tone, "but if Shaw doesn't slit the throat of whoever entered the dream, I will, and I will end their life slowly and painfully."

I tried to scream as Orion sliced his wrist and blood flowed freely from the wound.

"Orion." There was warning in Mercutio's voice. "Are you

sure you're the one who should do this? What this exchange will do to you…to her."

"No other Fae's blood will dwell in her veins. I will deal with the repercussions."

"It's not your repercussions that concern me," muttered Mercutio.

Orion pressed his bleeding skin to my lips. Repulsed, I blanched, but Orion put his hand behind my head and guided my mouth to his wrist. "I know, Cass," he soothingly said. "But this will heal you. You've done this before, but this time you will be able to take all you need. Give it a second and it'll become natural."

As I struggled to breathe, a metallic and salty taste entered my mouth. I gagged, but as his blood dripped into my throat, the obstruction in my airway was repelled by the warmth coating my windpipe. I sucked in a clean draw of air through my nose and I calmed as it hit my lungs.

"That's right," Orion said in a steady voice, "focus on your breaths. In and then out."

The warm liquid coated my stomach, and an explosion of heat dashed through the rest of my body. As if I were being bathed in sunshine from the inside out. The pounding pains, the agony, the aches, and the soreness were being chased away. Suddenly, I was thirsty, parched, and Orion's blood became sweet nectar. It was as if I was death and the fountain of life was cascading from him into me.

"Cassie," Mercutio said from somewhere in the room… Mercutio, my once friend, a member of my once family. "The idiot giving you his wrist is a whiner and a big baby. Seeing a couple of drops of his own blood is going to cause the imbecile to drop. I know he doesn't deserve it, but do you mind letting him onto that bed with you? Because otherwise, I'm going to have to haul his sorry ass to the Fae doc when he faints and busts open his head."

"Don't worry," Orion said. "I'm strong."

"Strong enough to put a hole in the drywall when you faint."

"If you don't keep your mouth shut, I'll throw you through the wall. She deserves better than me beside her in any bed."

"Like you can throw me anywhere."

"Haven't seen you kick my ass once," Orion said.

Even with the familiar banter, I couldn't help but focus on the fact I was swallowing his blood, that he was beside me, and that there was an intimacy being created between me and Orion. His spicy masculine scent was all I could smell. Even without him in the bed, it was as if his arms were around me, drawing me close, as if his lips were on my neck, on the sensitive spot behind my ear, and there was this growing pulse throughout my body that begged for contact with him. For me to press myself as tight as I could to Orion and start a slow delicious rhythm.

Mercutio continued, "He needs to lie down because you're going to require a lot of his blood. He won't join you unless you invite him."

Require a lot of his blood. My eyes opened. Orion was on his knees beside the bed with his head drooped. I attempted to close my mouth, to reject this gift, but Orion wouldn't yield.

"Not saying this for you to quit," Mercutio said. "He'll be okay and it's his gift to give, but he'll be better lying beside you."

Orion lifted his ashen face and scowled at the man he called brother. "I can't."

In that heartbeat, his heartbeat—my heartbeat—the single one that made us completely in sync—Orion's eyes snapped to mine. I became swamped with his confusing emotions. The most acute being his guilt, his sadness, and this aching loneliness of not being able to lie next to me. I trembled with my own growing desire and an irrational craving for his touch.

I made myself smaller on the already tiny bed, and Orion shook his head. But I wasn't allowing his rejection. Not this time. How could he not understand? *Our hearts are beating as one*, I spoke into his head. *How can you not lie with me in this bed?*

Orion's eyes widened then he blinked several times as he searched my face.

It's me, I said into his mind.

"How?" he whispered.

Doesn't matter. Do as I say. I feel your desire. The same desire I have to touch you.

The fingers of the wrist I drew life from caressed my cheek. "Once you're healed, you'll regret having allowed me near. You will remember I betrayed you."

He did betray me, and there was no doubt that truth would kick me in the stomach with a vengeance, but with the craving for him raging within me, I was unable to stay still. *I will deal with that then, but I need you now.*

"There're intense energy threads coming from Cassie," Mercutio said. "Want to fill me in on what's going on?"

"Are you sure, Cass?" Orion asked as if he were imploring me to change my mind. "I climb into this bed and the instincts of this act may overtake us both. My blood is mixing with yours, calling me to you. I'm like a sailor being called to a siren."

I pulled Orion toward me then threw out my hand in the direction of the door. It banged against the wall as it opened and cold air blasted in.

"Damn, that was impressive," Mercutio said. "She's going to be one hell of a witch."

As I went to whisper into Mercutio's mind for him to

leave, Orion gave a sharp glare in warning. As if he wanted me to keep my gifts to myself. Orion climbed into the bed with me. "Leave us, Mercutio."

"Cassie?" Mercutio asked. "You sure?"

My heart swelled with Orion's decision, and a gust of wind swept through the room and out the door. "I'll take that as confirmation," Mercutio muttered. "I won't be far."

The door shut, Orion gathered me to him, and I quaked as his massive body came in contact with mine. "Take what you need from me, Cass." His hot breath tickled my ear. "Take everything and all you need. I'm yours."

Feeling his warmth, his mind, our hearts beating as one, I was overcome with this frenzy of passion. One that was a pulse, a driving need. I released Orion's wrist and he pulled me close as I took his mouth. The kiss was ecstasy, it was sensual, and it was like entering a fevered dream. Our lips moved in time as our tongues danced. Orion gripped my hips and lifted me atop of him, shifting me to an oh-so-beautiful position, and trailed pleasing kisses down my neck.

Liquid warmth traveled through me, causing me to become edgy in an…exciting way. He turned his neck, and I was drawn to the drops of blood coming from a small cut in his skin. A smile slid across my face as I licked the life-giving force, sending me higher. Orion released a satisfying moan, hugged me, then his fingers caressed my back. We glided together in a rhythm, one that wound me tighter and begged for release. I wanted Orion. I needed Orion. I longed to feel every part of him on every part of me.

But there was a prickle in my brain, an uncomfortable feeling I wanted to ignore. It grew more insistent by the second, like a tornado of emotion. Within that cloud was anger, fury and the intent of death. The hair on my arms stood on end, and I disengaged from Orion in alarm.

"Cass?" Orion angled my chin to look into my eyes. "What is it?"

I opened my mouth, but no words came forth. I didn't know how to explain it, but being connected to Orion, I felt this strange surge from within him. He was searching, throwing out his energy as if he possessed the ability to see past walls, time and space. Coldness washed over his face as his energy pinpointed the swirling and mobile emotions, and a single word circled in his head: *enemy*. "Mercutio, Shaw—to the south. Cass, I promise, we will protect you."

A blink and Orion was gone. The terrible emotions became stronger, coming in faster than any human could maneuver, and the anger and rage was so powerful it became a shriek in my mind. The door to the room exploded open, and a grey cloud of soot and smoke barreled in. The acrid stench burned my nostrils. Pure terror caused me to scramble off the bed.

A flash of light, and Orion appeared behind the cloud. He raised his dagger, and as he swiped at the vaporous mass, it formed into a person. At least the shell of a person. Tanned skin, blond hair, the clothes casual…he could have been any man who had walked into Bambi's, but his eyes were completely filled with the color of blood. The man howled as Orion's dagger sliced into his side. Orion achieved another blow to the chest and the figure disappeared.

Animosity and bitterness still surrounded us, but on the periphery. I sucked in a breath to scream when another being appeared at my side. I placed a hand over my hammering heart as I saw it was Shaw and then Mercutio.

"Get her out of here," Orion spit out. "Get her safe."

"Is she healed?" Shaw asked.

"Enough, but she'll need rest." Orion approached me, and when he touched my forehead, he murmured, "Sleep."

CHAPTER 8

A baby cried and I woke with a start. The wails ceased, and the silent void was filled with waves crashing against a beach. As if I had too much alcohol the night before, my head swam with heavy disorientation. My muscles were lethargic and my mental state unstable. Was this awakening real or the latest in a litany of dreams?

"Good, you've been boring asleep." Wren sat in an overly stuffed chair, where she closed a worn, frayed book and unceremoniously dropped it onto the antique, marble-top table at her side. The book made a loud plop in the otherwise quiet room, and the hanging crystals accenting the scalloped top of a 1920s-style hurricane lamp shook with the impact.

Wren stared at me and I stared at her. At one time, I would have described her as a friend, but friends didn't abandon each other. Though she did contact me in a dream to warn me…after years of silence. Did one action outweigh the other?

"Hey," she said tipping her chin at me. I mirrored the motion, but annoyed that she had ghosted me for years, I chose to stay silent.

Wren was pure renegade. Her raven hair was shorter, and it spilled out in multiple directions from a ponytail at the top of her head. Her bangs were cut into a razored edge, and her dark eyes were full of curiosity as she surveyed me. She wore black stilettoed boots with chains, ripped black jeans, a white top, and the leather jacket I remembered from when we were nineteen.

She was a stark contrast to our surroundings.

The floor and the intricate woodworked trim in the room were dark hardwood, and the walls were papered in the style of Louis XVI. Sunlight struggled through the thick, roping green velvet curtains of the four-post bed, and the same type of curtains covered the three windows. There was a massive, ornate fireplace in the room and intricately carved into the stone mantel was a lion's head caught in a roar. This antique room gave me the overwhelming sense I had traveled in time to the past.

"How are you feeling?" Wren asked.

"Hungover."

"I've heard Fae blood is a hell of a high. It makes sense for there to be a fall."

Fae blood. Good god, was any of it real? Did I want any of it to be real? No, I didn't. I raked a hand through my tangled hair and shoved away the grief at losing my old life. My job, my home…my friends. "Am I dreaming again? Because I'm having 'what's-real' whiplash."

A "phsh" escaped her lips. "This isn't what I'd choose for a dream world. If you and I were going to hang together, I would have snapped us to New Orleans. That place is gold. While I'm pleased you're very much alive and awake, I'm less than thrilled to announce you're in the guest room of the great MacAleese family: the rulers of the Western Hemisphere Fae and home of the lead prophetess and the lead warriors."

Fantastic. I was in a waking nightmare. The MacAleese owned nearly everything on the island, including the bar I waitressed in and the apartment I lived in when I was nineteen, and they had a disdain for me that was palpable. Not only did they own businesses and property on the island, but they also held diverse interests around the world. They also had a specific sneer reserved solely for me, but they always had a conflict with someone, somewhere. Orion was the one who performed their dirty work for them. Until recently, I thought he killed for money. Now, I had no idea who or what he had been fighting this entire time.

Rulers? Lead prophetess and warriors? My skin crawled with the implied complications. "That sounded formal and fancy."

"It's a damn lot of politics, red tape and intrigue," Wren said.

"Why am I here?" Orion's family hadn't liked me when we were together, and I couldn't imagine much had changed. "The boys couldn't have dropped me off at a Red Roof Inn?"

"Mommy can control you and the situation better if you're under her roof."

"Super." Mommy would mean Orion's mother, Nessa. Picture the most beautiful supermodel: long, thick blond hair, a serious face with high cheekbones, and cold blue eyes that cut straight through me whenever she gave me a dismissive glance—which was often.

"At the moment, Nessa thinks you're useful," Wren said. "Plus, it would be in bad taste to kick you to the streets since three quarters of the blood flowing through your veins is Orion's. If Nessa is anything, she's a traditionalist in reinstating the old customs. Some good, some bad."

Orion. My legs rubbed together at the memory of his body under mine, and of the rhythm we had created. "Is Orion okay?"

Wren snorted. "Don't worry about him. After he took a power nap, he was swamped in Fae business. Which means he's killing something somewhere."

So much to learn, and I preferred ignorance. My head swam and I rolled my neck. Orion was in my life again, his blood ran through my veins, and we'd went at it with each other as if we were animals in heat. Wasn't sure what it meant that he wasn't here. The clearest and easiest answer: he saved me because we shared the same goal to protect the baby. The rest of our relationship belonged in the past. At least Orion's absence gave me space to clear my head—which was appreciated, as there was a vibration under my skin that yearned for him…more specifically, for his body.

As much as I didn't want to roll in bed with Orion, I couldn't promise my body would comply with my mind if he walked through the door. In fact, I'd more than likely leap up, wrap my arms and legs around him, and…. "Am I safe here?" I switched the train of thought fast.

"No."

That was blunt. "Care to expand?"

"We're witches surrounded by Fae. At the end of the day, no matter how Fae spread their propaganda that their destiny on earth is to protect the human race, they will protect their own interests first. So no, we're not safe."

"Should we leave?" I was actually asking whether I should leave, and her mouth quirked as if she read my mind. Which for all I knew, she had.

"Outside this mansion, humans are holding their newest witch trials, which, so far, make the ones that took place in Salem look like child's play. Congress is gathering in a special session to vote on mandatory genetic testing. If that resolution passes, we'll never be safe. Oh, and they are compiling a list of witches. Your name and picture are already there. I checked."

Awesome. "I'm assuming Fae won't be safe anymore either."

"Possibly, but the Fae are better organized, have money and influence. Nothing could have benefited the Fae more than our outing. Humans may hate Fae, but they hate us more."

I thought of Mateo. "Not all humans hate us."

"No, they don't, but the ones who hated the Fae have turned their sights on us. These people are loud, they're angry, and they have a lot of attention and support. People not only awoke to the knowledge of witches, but most woke with the names of witches on their lips. Maybe things will settle, but today, I'm not tempting fate."

So many unanswered questions. The storm that developed from my voice the night of the mob, the wind from my fingertips, and the lightning from a scream in my heart. My stomach sloshed with sea sickness. Dee, Killian, Mateo, Brittney, her baby…all of my friends…did I hurt them? "Are we dangerous? Should humans be concerned?"

"Depends if they piss us off. Can I give you a word of advice on how to go forward? Don't trust anyone. Orion included. Everyone here has an endgame, and none of their original plans included you."

I studied Wren, head to toe. "If you're a witch, why are you here? In fact, what have you been doing with Orion and the Fae all along?"

"As I said, we all have our endgame." She was as stoic as stone.

Which meant I couldn't trust her either. Once again, I was alone. Story of my life. Not only was I alone, but I was also covered in my blood and Fae blood—and both were flowing through my veins. Dried blood was crusted on my shirt, jeans, and hair. Even my skin was stained. Thank God the sight of blood didn't freak me out; otherwise, what was left of my fragile mind would have shattered. I should have gone into the light. "Is there a shower around here?"

Wren inclined her head toward the other side of the room. "There's a bathroom through that heavy-ass door. Towels, a change of clothes, everything you need to wash and feel alive again is in there. Before you ask, yes most of the blood on you is yours. I know Orion is sorry for the scars. He thinks you should have gone into the light. Me? I'm happy you're still around. Nessa likes meticulous order, and you've always been interesting chaos. It's a pastime of mine to watch Nessa squirm, and no one has ever made her squirm as much as you."

Scars. I lifted my arm, saw nothing, but as my skin caught the dim light, I saw them. Hundreds of glowing tiny silver cuts. But when I moved my arm again, the cuts disappeared.

"They're magical scars," Wren explained. "Humans can't see them, but magical folk will be able to spot them in the right light."

Just super times infinity. Disappointment and grief welled up in me, but I couldn't deal with that now, if ever. I slipped off the bed, my bare feet cold against the hardwood, and I walked into a modern bathroom as large as the bedroom. The walls and floor were made of thick marble and lava stones. Like anything the MacAleese family owned, the bathroom was opulent—an extended soak tub, a device to warm towels, and a lounge chair. At the sight of myself in the mirror, I sighed. I looked like the victim in a horror movie. Guess I was…or not. In theory, I was a witch. Maybe I was the monster.

I reverently took off my grandmother's cross, placed it carefully on the marble countertop and stared at the necklace longer than needed. What would my grandmother think of me? As a woman who entered the house of God every Sunday as if her life depended upon it, my grandmother's mortification of who I had become was easy to imagine.

I finally peeled off the blood-caked clothes, kicked them into the corner, and stepped into the shower. There were multiple showerheads on the three enclosed walls and one on the ceiling. Warm water flowed from all of them, caressing me like a gentle, tropical waterfall. I took my time washing off, scrubbing the clumps of dirt and blood out of my hair, and trying to ease the tension out of my muscles.

After an easy twenty minutes, the water was still magically hot, yet I turned it off and dried myself with an amazingly thick and fluffy towel. Precisely folded on a table were lace undergarments in my size, designer jeans tailored to my curves, and a white button-down shirt made from pima cotton with a cut that nicely showed my cleavage. I opened the cabinets and found every personal product, hair to skin, I used when I was nineteen. I equally loved and hated the thought put into all of it.

I combed and dried my hair, applied the rose-scented lotion I used to lather myself in before I met Orion for a date, then marveled at wearing clothes that cost more than my annual gross income. Taking a good look at myself in the mirror I focused on my eyes and into my soul.

I had died. I touched the portal of light but had dragged myself back, and Orion gave me life. I refused heaven for the baby. Find her, make sure she was safe and then I would settle into another small town in the middle of nowhere, someplace where no one knew who I was, and I'd start over caring for the sick, my mothers-to-be, and their babies. I would reclaim my life. I would find some sort of happy again. My life would be complicated if genetic testing did pass, but I would figure it out. Essentially, I had been on my own since I was young. I was a survivor.

I lovingly put my grandmother's necklace on and touched

the cross as if I were hugging her. Being a witch...my God. Other than that I somehow had the ability to create storms when I was emotional, I had no idea what being a witch meant. The storms, the wind, the lightning, was this something I could conjure at will? Then there was the book, the grimoire.

My hands dropped to the counter, and I gripped the marble as I closed my eyes. I had no idea what the book was or why it was in my apartment, but it must have been important; why else would it have been there? Why else would I enjoy such intimacy, closeness, and fondness for it? I concentrated on the book, on how I knew its name, as if it held secrets only I could discover. As if it truly belonged to *me*.

"Whatcha doing?" Wren appeared in the doorway.

Startled, I placed a hand over my rapidly beating heart. "I didn't hear you come in."

She narrowed her eyes. "That's because you were deep in concentration casting a spell."

"No, I wasn't."

"Yes, you were."

Agitation weaved through me. "If you know what I was doing, why did you ask?"

She merely lifted an eyebrow. "I was curious if you knew you were casting a spell."

No, I didn't. "Where's Orion? He and I have unfinished business."

"I'm sure you do. I've heard rumors about the bonus pleasure of ingesting Fae blood, and how the heat will endure after the encounter."

I crossed my arms. Not a conversation I was having with anyone.

"Fine. Keep the details to yourself. I've been instructed to keep you distracted and to make sure you stay in this room. Everyone assumed it would be easy to do. One, they thought you'd be asleep for longer than eight hours. Understandable, since you did technically die."

Wow. Eight hours. I couldn't remember the last time I had slept that long.

"Two," she continued. "I'm a witch, you're a new witch, and we were once…friends." She let the last part linger as if trying to assess the situation. I stayed quiet because I didn't have answers for what we were either. "They thought you'd ask me a million witch questions, I'd show you the handshake and spill the secrets of the witch way and then we'd eat ice cream. Eventually, after they figured out how to handle you, they were going to send for you and tell you whatever you're allowed to know of the grand plan they concocted."

Slow on the uptake, I tilted my head. I wasn't automatically feeling Wren's emotions. There was a bit of panic that maybe I had lost my ability, but with a simple push, I found I could read Wren crystal clear. She was curious, hesitant, amused, but focused. There was also the important thread of honesty weaving through her, and it was red hot, like burning embers. Maybe it was just Wren, but it would be nice if I could choose to feel people's emotions instead of being bombarded by them. As I pushed further to read her actual thoughts regarding me, about our "friendship," I flinched—hit by a sharp pain as a wall slammed shut on my connection with her.

Did you enjoy reading my emotions? Wren telepathically asked. *At least the ones I allowed you to discern?* My gaze snapped to hers. She waggled her eyebrows. *I also have secrets.*

Are all witches empaths and telepaths? I was amazed how easy it was to use telepathy with her and was giddy with the absent migraine.

Wren frowned. *A witch's magic is individualistic, but yes, some of us are telepaths, though not all. Empaths? No. You're the first empath I've come across or heard exists.*

How did you know I was reading you?

A tickle in my brain. You need to be careful who you share this with and who you try to read—specifically another witch. Being different, even amongst witches and Fae, is dangerous.

How many are there of us? I asked.

Witches? Her eyes widened with the question. I nodded. *Before yesterday morning? Maybe less than a hundred throughout the world. After people woke up, there were a ton of us. Now? We have lost more than we should have.* Grief gushed off of her and her pain twisted my gut. She mourned for people she once knew, mourned for those she didn't, and was unaware that she was loudly broadcasting and that I was reading her.

I weighed her warning and honesty. "I didn't decline heaven so I could sit around and wait for someone else to decide my fate." Or the baby's fate. This baby had chosen me, and I wasn't going to be a passive player. She needed me, and she was my priority. "How do I find Orion?"

Wren gave me a slow and devious smile. "Why are you asking me? You're the one who has his blood flowing in your veins."

"And?"

"Besides the benefits of experiencing exquisite lust, you should be able to find your boy by closing your eyes and concentrating."

Much there to unpack—my curiosity piqued on the lust part—but I was too caught up in the power of Wren's statement. "I can track Orion?"

"I sure as hell hope so, because if you can, I can't wait to see Mommy's face when she discovers this new gift from her little boy's witch. Seriously, Cassie, I don't know how we managed to live without you. You're what makes this strange life entertaining."

CHAPTER 9

On the hunt for Orion, I closed my eyes and concentrated, but when I focused on him, weird things happened that I didn't want to overthink. My heart switched to a different rhythm, my inhales and exhales became longer, and there was a pleasurable vibration in my veins that made my skin sensitive, even to the slightest movement of the air. I had to keep rubbing my hands along my arms to take off the edge. It was easy to become lost in contemplating Orion. His hands on my body, his lips skimming my neck, the way we moved with each other, but also when I fixated on Orion, he felt…distant. He wasn't here, in this opulent mansion. He was gone.

The baby…my attention needed to be on the baby. I pushed thoughts of Orion away and came across a different pull, and literally one foot in front of the other, I followed. The draw was gravitational—not even a choice. With Wren trailing me, I jogged down a grand staircase, crossed a white marble floor, and stopped before a massive, floor-to-ceiling door painted with gold vining and leaves. I stretched to place my fingers on its shiny knob.

Wren shot across the foyer and smacked my hand. "I'm into mischief, but I don't recommend going in there. My letting you leave the bedroom is going to anger Nessa just enough for me to have fun, but this is Nessa's private study. No one goes into that room without her permission. She has killed people for doing less, and do I need to remind you that you're her least favorite being in this world?"

A pulse of warning pushed out of me—a gust of air that blew about strands of her hair. "My book is in there." My brain had no idea what I was saying, why I was saying it, but my soul understood and that was what mattered.

Wren narrowed her eyes at me as if I was crazed. "What did you say?"

The pull was too powerful for me to ignore. My fingers gripped the door handle, I turned the knob, and there was a whoosh in my ears. I blinked and found myself inside a study that made my Louis XVI room look like the servants' quarters. Three of the impossibly high walls of the study were lined with shelves that contained books, many thousands of them, and on the floor were multiple glass cases that held relics, antiques and priceless works of art. This was an extravagant private museum.

My forehead furrowed. No doors to exit, no Wren, and then my hands covered my ears as a chorus of ear-piercing hisses and screams drowned out even my own thoughts.

"What are you doing here, witch?" screeched a voice. "You don't belong here."

A gust of wind not caused by me, and I was face to face with Orion. The world zoned out, and there was just he and I. My inhale became his, and our heartbeats became in sync. Every cell in my body sizzled with need, crying out to be touched, but there was a stronger song being sung to me, the only one that promised me real peace, the only one that could rival the serenity of home...my *grimoire*.

"Leave this room and don't return." His voice was pitched low, a threat of fury.

After the intimacy we shared, his anger was a slap in the face. At least it was clear we were on two separate sides of a battle. "Give what belongs to me, and I'll happily leave." And find the baby on my own.

The clicking of heels caused the hair on the back of my neck to stand at attention.

"Orion." Nessa's lyrical voice was still like sandpaper against my skin. "Leave! I will not have you die on the battle-field, especially not because of her." She punched through Orion, like he was mist instead of man, and he disappeared as if he were a ghost. I gasped, staggered backwards and was stopped from tumbling to the floor by an armchair.

"Please try to take care," chastised Nessa. "Queen Eliza-beth I sat in that very chair. It's bad enough you've rudely entered this room, and it will only hurt your cause if you break more things of mine you cannot repair."

The world moved in slow motion as I regarded the woman who was glowering at me as if I were her hired help. Nessa was perfection, so beautiful it almost ached to gaze upon her. Cascading blond hair, blue eyes as cold as a clear winter New York sky the morning after a blizzard, and a striking face no one could forget. Her nails were long, painted blood red, and she wore a dark pink form-fitting business suit with a pencil skirt. Diamonds dripped from around her neck, wrists and fingers.

When I was nineteen, I had yearned for her approval. As her son's girlfriend, I'd craved for her to accept me. She showered Orion and her chosen family—blood and nonblood—with love and affection. I pined for someone to maternally love me, and I had desperately desired it to be her. But that never happened. I was eventually thrown out like trash. A feat that must have brought her joy. "Where's Orion?"

"Fighting for his life because of you. Sending a piece of himself to tussle with you will leave an energy path for his enemies to follow. You are not worth the trouble you have brought to my family. I'm of half a mind to slit your throat and let you bleed out before Orion arrives home."

My hands tingled as if they were sparking with electricity, but there was no lightning springing from my fingertips. Though a slight breeze did dance throughout the room.

Nessa cocked a perfectly plucked eyebrow. "It's true. You are a witch."

I cocked my head as the wind grew. With the mob, I had no idea how I summoned lightning. With Nessa in front of me, the lightning was speaking to my soul as if we were lovers.

"Nice parlor trick, child. I suggest you stop while you're ahead."

"And if I don't?"

My arms were flung to my back. The storm that had been brewing inside me dissipated. Nessa's heels clicked against the wooden floor as she paced. "You're a day-old witch. An infant who should be suckling at her mother's breast. I promise you this is a fight I would easily win. Are we clear on the rules of this game?"

"What rules are those?" I struggled out as something unseen wrapped around my lungs and constricted them.

Nessa inclined her face a centimeter from mine. "I like things simple, and I like them easy. You do what I say when I say it, and you stay away from my son." She snapped her fingers, and the invisible bonds squeezing my chest disappeared. My hands were forced to the armrests, but I was still unable to stand, and the magic that flowed through my veins when I was angry had vanished. It was unnerving, and I should have been terrified, but it had been a weird forty-eight hours and I was plain pissed.

Nessa placed space between us, leaned against the edge of a Victorian-style writing desk, and gave me that familiar once-over of disdain. "I trust the accommodations I've allowed you to occupy are beyond the standards you're used to. From what I remember of you, and from what I've heard you've done for yourself, I'm sure you prefer things a bit more rustic. You are the first human to have slept here so I'm dying to know your thoughts on my home."

A cruel twist of my lips. How easy it was to forget Nessa did shower me with things...she had rained millions of back-handed statements. At nineteen, I would have deflected my gaze, worried my hands together, and stammered through the conversation in need of her approval. Oh, how I loved not being nineteen and thoroughly enjoyed twenty-eight. "Your home is lovely, but I'm afraid I'm unimpressed with the hospitality."

"You broke into a room you have no business being in." She sniffed dismissively. "I need you to tell me what witchcraft you or Wren used to do it. Any security breach is unacceptable."

"We didn't break into anything. I simply opened a door, blinked, and ended up in here."

Nessa studied me in that cold ways of hers, and I tested her emotions. Of course, she was like Orion, fuzzy like an out-of-tune radio station. I did taste fear though, and that gave me a great sense of satisfaction. "Let's say I believe you," Nessa said, "which I don't. What were you thinking of when you tried the doorknob?"

My book...my *grimoire*. It still tugged at me from a book-shelf on high. But I also felt its hesitancy, a whisper in my brain to keep her a secret—at least from Nessa. *She'll try to use me, she's using you. She will dispose of us both when you've fulfilled your purpose.*

I'm aware, I responded to the book. I was losing my ever-loving mind—talking to and listening to a book.

I'm not just any book. I am the grimoire.

With a heavy sigh, I answered, "I was searching for Orion."

"You were searching for Orion," she repeated slowly and nodded as if this was the missing puzzle piece. "And you share his blood."

Yes, as everyone kept reminding me. "I had no idea entering would create havoc."

"Havoc? This is our most sacred ground, and by waltzing in here with your disregard, you are disrespecting our ancestors and every Fae alive. You, who have no friends, should tread lightly, especially in my home. This room is reverence. This room is respect. To enter there are ceremonies to be done, cleansings, and you show nothing short of impiety and blasphemy."

My breath caught in my throat. Urns appeared. So many urns with names engraved upon them. The room stretched longer, grew wider, and nothing in reality was what it seemed. A mausoleum. This room…no…this wasn't just a room…this realm…was a Fae mausoleum and shrine.

I hated Nessa, she hated me, but one thing I was not was purposely disrespectful. "My deepest apologies for having entered. I had no idea. I opened the door, and I was drawn in. It's a mistake I will not repeat." The not returning part was a lie. One that came easily. I had no intentions of dishonoring their dead, but I would retrieve my book.

Yes, you will. You must. She cannot learn I exist. But come soon, for you will need me in order to fight.

Who are we fighting? I asked.

Our enemies.

Mind narrowing the list for me? I laid the sarcasm on thick. *Multiple people and beings have tried to kill me over the past couple of days.*

Such is the life of a witch, the grimoire answered.

Nessa rolled her shoulders and I regained movement in my arms, but was still unable to stand. "This room and most of my home is off limits to you. My family has sworn to protect the contents of this study. I do not allow outsiders within my home, and I will not allow anyone who is a threat inside this room. Anyone who has ever tried has met with death. No exception will be made for you again, are we clear?"

"As I said, I was searching for Orion."

"And he will find you when he is ready, but otherwise you stay in your room. I have been more than generous in providing for you. Try showing some class and gratitude."

Translation: please try to act like a good little girl. "If you dislike me, why am I allowed in your house?"

Her lips flattened to the point they became white. "Because you are my son's witch slut who has his blood running through your veins. Once again, he has chosen you as his mistress—he servicing your needs, and I'm assuming you are servicing his."

I flinched, wanting to argue, but not sure if I was anything more—to her *or* Orion.

"I do not share the council's enthusiasm that you have joined our fight, nor do I find your choice to shun death admirable. We can find our queen without you, but I am merely one member of the council and had little sway in the time I was given. It is my goal to persuade the council to abandon their faith in you, and to leave finding the infant instead in the capable hands of my son."

"Once again, if you hate me so much, why am I here?"

By Fae law she cannot deny shelter to anyone who shares her family's blood, my book whispered.

You know about Fae? I asked.

I know all.

"You and my son are cursed," Nessa said. "I have personally foreseen that you are my son's destruction and that he is yours. All possible futures that involve the two of you together lead to death. Contemplate that and how it would be wise for you to abandon this journey."

She snapped her fingers, and I was, once again, in the foyer outside the doors. My hand was on the knob, and I snatched my fingers back to keep from re-entering the Fae graveyard.

"Did you think they were going to leave the door unlocked?" Wren asked beside me. "They're serious about no one going into that room. I've never even had a peek."

Had I actually entered? Maybe this was a hallucination. A dream within a dream. *Are you real?* I reached out to the grimoire. *Are you in there?*

The reply was rapid, but so faint I had to strain to hear it. *Yes. I will tell you when to return. I'll be waiting.*

"Wren?" Nessa said from behind us.

Wren and I glanced over our shoulders.

"If Cassie leaves her room again, my goodwill towards you will end, and I will truss you like a turkey on Thanksgiving, brand the label of a witch upon your forehead, bind your powers, dump you off at the most closed-minded town I can find, and roast marshmallows off the flames that will burn you to hell." With a flicker of light, she was gone.

"I would have never guessed it," said Wren.

I would have never guessed any of the past few days. "What?"

Wren offered me a sly grin. "That Nessa eats marshmallows. And the joke's on her." Wren wiggled her fingers and each one had a small lit flame as if they were candles. "I can't burn at the stake.

CHAPTER 10

On the dining-table-for-two that magically appeared in my quarters was roasted chicken, green beans, and rolls. The combined scents made my mouth water and my stomach grumble. The last time I'd eaten had been at Bambi's the night Killian defended me against Hayes— when he accused me of being a witch. How prophetic.

From the window, I watched the waves rolling up the beach. "Would Nessa poison the food?"

"Yes," Wren answered. "But she would wait until you weren't expecting it. Nessa doesn't like to be predictable."

"Comforting," I murmured to myself. "What is a grimoire?"

Wren opened the last of the thick curtains, and warm sunlight filled the dark room. She dropped into the chair at the table and tossed her plate of chicken into a garbage can. "Easiest explanation—it's your spell book. In layman's terms, a grimoire is a witch's diary, where we keep our spells, charms, and recipes for potions, but it is also a record of successes and failures.

"I journal in mine—my thoughts and feelings. As you'll

learn, your magic—or sometimes the lack thereof—is a reflection of your experiences and moods. Magic is very personal. Lots of trial and error, and there is no cookbook for you to follow. What I can do as a witch is not the same as what another witch can do with their magic. We can mentor each other, but it's not the same as teaching someone their times tables in order to do Calculus down the road. If the book allows it, a parent may pass it on to their son or daughter, but each witch has their own grimoire. It belongs solely to them and can be read only by them. Aside from a family book, I've never heard of anyone being able to read a grimoire that doesn't belong to them."

"What do you mean if a book allows it?"

"Grimoires are…" she searched for the proper words. "…alive. They don't breathe or eat, but they do have a personality. They are furiously loyal to their witches. I find it impressive yours has followed you here." Wren eyed me curiously. "Because that's what you said when you tried to go into the room—that you felt your book was in there?"

Uncomfortable, I fought the urge to fidget. "Do they follow their owners?"

"Is that what you think has happened?"

I wasn't going to answer first. "Do books follow their owners?"

"My grimoire was a twenty-five-cent spiral notebook I swiped at Walmart when I was five. It consisted of crayon drawings of me lighting sticks on fire. Of course, it's grown and evolved since then. Sometimes it looks like a two-thousand-year-old book with teeth that will literally bite your arm off if you touch it, and sometimes, it still looks like the cheap-ass, ratty notebook I pinched off the discount store shelf. A witch creates her grimoire when she is ready. That is one of the main points of being a witch—it's your personal journey and choosing to pursue magic is never thrusted upon you. You choose when to start your grimoire, your grimoire does not find you. You find and you create."

I attempted to find solace in the peace of the ocean beyond. "You're saying if my book did follow me here, that would be unusual?"

"Hundreds of people learning they're witches is unusual. Maybe the universe took pity upon you and gave the new witches a starter pack to soften the blow. What makes you think your grimoire is in that room?"

Answering with, "*It spoke to me*," sounded insane. "I felt drawn toward the room."

"You bled out," Wren said. "You were dead. Most of the blood in your veins is Orion's. Maybe your pull to that room is actually his blood being called and not yours. When a witch is ready to start her grimoire, it is a gravitational pull. Maybe your need to start your book, to discover your magic, is getting confused with the Fae things that attract Orion."

I doubted it, yet said, "Probably." The subject needed to change. "When you contacted me in the dream, you were running. Who were you running from?"

"Nessa," Wren said matter-of-factly. "She wants me to spy on you like I did when we were younger."

My feathers were ruffled, and a breeze blew through the room. "Is that what our friendship was? You spying on me?"

"It was part of it."

"Did you agree to do it again?"

Wren shrugged. "As the Rolling Stones said, you can't always get what you want."

"Did you know about the accident?"

"Yes."

A dangerous coiling within me. "When you left a few days before my accident, you said you would be returning. Did you have intentions of coming back?"

"No. You should stop asking because I'm done answering."

"I'll stop when I want to stop." A whirlwind swept into the room, creating a baby tornado of dust in the center of the wooden floor. "Are your loyalties with me or Nessa?"

"With myself." A calculated warning, the chicken on the table burst into flames. "My loyalties are with myself."

I'm not scared of you, I pushed into her brain.

The fire extinguished and steam rose from the chicken. *Maybe you should be. I'm more powerful than you.*

No doubt she was.

"We were close once," Wren returned to talking aloud. "Even though I was watching you for Nessa. At least, I'm here now to help you navigate being a witch. Most aren't that lucky. And this time around, you know where I stand."

"I don't have any idea where you stand."

"As I said, at least now you're aware." Wren paused. "We'll need to be careful with Nessa. She's smart and conniving, and she hates you."

My list of allies was zero. I didn't trust Wren and she didn't trust me. Until I gained a better grasp of the new world beyond these walls and of how to be a witch, she might be my single source of help. My little whirlwind died, and the specks of dust descended lazily to the ground. "Nessa doesn't care for you either."

"That is possibly the world's biggest understatement."

Wishing all of this were a nightmare I could wake from, I returned to staring out the window. I wanted to go home. Back to my tiny apartment and back to saving lives and delivering babies. Off in the distance, at sea, were dark gray clouds. A storm cell was brewing out in the open water, even though sun shone on land. Electricity skipped along in my veins, and I wiggled my fingers like a spider weaving a web to control this…itch. "You can manipulate fire."

The candles in the room danced to life. "And I heard there was one hell of a squall that magically appeared in upstate New York," Wren said. "I'm assuming that was you?"

"I don't know how I did it."

"At first, our powers only manifest with strong emotion. Eventually, you'll learn how to control it. The misinformed say witchcraft is the result of deals made with the devil, but our power is planted in nature. We connect physically and emotionally with nature and can unleash abilities according to our natural-born talents—mine with fire, yours with storms." I envied the peace that crossed her face. "There's nothing like being in tune with the magic inside you, to be one with the earth. Being a witch isn't a curse, it's an incredible blessing."

Hopefully she was right. "If our power comes from nature, what is the source of the Fae's power?"

I felt Orion before he knocked. I slowly breathed in and then out. It didn't help that the inhale was full of his dark scent, didn't help that with his presence I could feel his fingertips brushing along my skin, feel the heat of his gaze undressing me. And it certainly didn't help that there was a bed in the room. A bed I longed to crawl into as I shed my clothes and begged for Orion to tangle himself with me. A million fantasies flashed through my mind of how he could touch me, of how I desired to be touched, and how hot the pleasure would be. Problem was, I didn't know if those were my fantasies, his fantasies or the wild dream-child of both.

"That sounds like a question for me," Orion said. Even though I wanted to resist, my gaze swept in his direction, and I became hypnotized by his dark eyes.

He leaned his shoulder against the doorframe and was as handsome as ever. Damp wet hair as if he had just walked out of a shower, a red-blond scruff along his jaw that screamed wicked nights, and a T-shirt that stretched tight against his muscles. Orion looked like a lazy panther about to pounce on his dinner and I was to be his prey.

"Was there something wrong with the food?" His deep melodic voice caused liquid heat to pour into my veins. Craving to be touched, feeling desperate without it, I rubbed my hands along my arms, but it made the desire worse.

"We didn't want to eat," I said.

Orion's forehead furrowed. "You're hungry. You've been hungry since you woke. That's why I requested dinner for you from the kitchen."

"How do you know what I am?" I snapped.

"My blood runs through your veins," he said casually, as if people drank daily from his wrist, and the thought of another woman drinking his blood caused an irrational rush of anger. "It connects me to you."

My eyebrow rose, and before I could allow a single word to come out of my mouth, Wren said, "We're concerned your mother poisoned the food."

Orion pulled his attention from me and playfully glanced at Wren. "Are you afraid my mother's claws are sharper than yours?"

"Your mommy didn't like us playing with you when we were younger. I can't imagine the depth of hate she has for us now. And while my claws are sharp, I'm smart enough to be careful in an angry bear's den."

"She threatened to bind Wren's magic and have her burned at the stake," I said, trying to make him understand the gravity of our situation.

Orion's lips twitched. "Wren can't burn at a stake."

"See," Wren threw out her hands, "that's what I said. I'm a bit concerned for your mother. She's losing her touch."

She forced me into a chair and froze me there, I said to Orion. *She also threatened to kill me. She doesn't want me here, and I'm inclined to agree I should leave.*

His humor disappeared, and the wave of fury that burst out of him stole my breath, but he quickly masked his expression. "Shaw and Mercutio bought waffles and bacon from the Breakfast Nook for you, Wren. If you want to eat, they're hanging out in our rooms."

"You mean your wing of the house?" Wren didn't get up like I expected. "Do you think waffles are going to put you and your pack of hyenas in my good graces?"

"No, but it's a start." He let a beat of silence pass. "I need to speak to Cassie."

"Speak," Wren retorted. "I'm not stopping you."

"Alone." Good God, the word *alone* caused the cells in my body to vibrate.

"Do you want to be alone with him?" Wren asked.

Yes, and absolutely not. My heart beat faster at the idea of us being unaccompanied, but we needed to talk in private. "Do you want to see Shaw and Mercutio?"

"No, but I will eat their waffles." Wren stood. "Call me if you need me." Meaning telepathy. She crossed the room, rammed her shoulder into Orion's and didn't close the door behind her as she left. That gave me hope, but that hope vanished as Orion closed the door and turned to look at me. He slowly moved in my direction, his eyes undressing me, and I thanked whatever God was above when he stopped six feet away.

"I'm sorry for this," he said softly.

I had to swallow in order to speak. "For what?"

"For the side effects of the blood exchange. For the lust, for the need…the desire." His deep voice was like a physical touch—a ghost of a caress along my cheek. I shivered.

Even though it went against the instinct pleading to run toward him, to wrap myself around him, to kiss every inch of his body, to worship him, I angled toward the open window and welcomed the breeze free of his scent. "Is it just me?"

"I don't understand your question."

I hugged myself in a pathetic substitute of his embrace. "Do you feel like this, too?"

"That every breath is a tease of what it was like to have your body against mine, being lovers like we were all those years ago? Then yes. Walking is damn uncomfortable."

Lust rolled off of him, magnifying my need. I didn't know if Orion also suffering made me feel better or worse. "How long will it last?" I asked.

"As long as it takes for your body to replace my blood with your own."

My medical knowledge informed me that it took forty-eight hours for the body to replace volume and eight weeks to replace lost red blood cells. I groaned and rested my head against the cool windowpane. My resolve was already weakening, and it had only been a few hours.

"The need will lessen though…day by day."

I flipped with my back flat against the wall. "If you touch me will it be worse or better?"

"Better. So much better," he replied with a wicked grin. "But to be fair, I'm biased and having a hard time finding reasons as to why it would be a bad idea to give in."

I snorted then let out a small manic laugh. "Of course, you are."

"We were good together, Cass."

Yes, we were very good together. Orion, if anything, left me extremely…satisfied. Without thinking, I pushed off the wall, and we were chest to chest. With our breaths in sync, my breasts skimmed across his chest with our exhale and my heart fluttered. I only needed to raise my head, lift onto my toes, and we could kiss. His lips would be soft, then rough against mine. His hands would touch me reverently, then grip me with possession. There would be a push and pull between his hands through my hair, my hands along his shoulders, his fingers curling into my hips to drag me closer. … "But what if touching makes this worse?" I asked.

"What if it helps ease the need?" he countered.

"What if we start and we're unable to stop?"

"Then I will die happy."

I raised my head, and the entire world paused. Orion hadn't touched me yet, wasn't lowering his head to mine, but his longing for me amplified my own need. This close, he was easy to read. He coveted me, needed me, and as much as he yearned to take me, as much as he craved to slip this shirt off my body, place his hands upon my breasts, feel my body against his and taste my skin on his tongue, he wasn't going to make one move. This was a play I controlled, and one where I decided the rules. As much as I respected him for it, damn him to hell.

I was so deep in Orion's emotions, I could tell I was the utmost in his desires, rooted in his marrow. I was the single flame within him that burned. He would end time to worship me…and I wasn't even *touching* him. With an effort that caused me to shake, I snapped out of his brain, and the rushed movement created a whiplash. Orion was thrown back and I crumbled to the floor. His eyes widened in concern and he moved toward me, but I placed a hand in the air. "If you touch me, we will end up in that bed, and that is not what I want."

Actually, it was. I desired him naked on that bed for me to do whatever I wished. Hell, I would be happy permitting him to do whatever he craved, because experience had proved he was so good at making my body sing. "You let me into your head." And he returned to a fuzzy radio station. While the urge to touch him was still there, it wasn't as heightened.

Orion scrubbed his face, then assessed me, looking as frustrated and exhausted as me. "The fact I have to work to keep you out of my head is new. Are you ready to admit what's going on with you, or are you going to keep lying?"

I didn't trust him. "We need to find the baby." Then I needed a million miles between us. I tested my legs, and I wobbled like a newborn fawn.

"Then tell me what you know about the baby and about these abilities you've acquired." Orion's eyes smoldered as he focused on my lips, and God help me, I wanted him to kiss me.

"Maybe we should talk with you on the other side of that thick door," I suggested.

"We were gasoline and fire before the blood exchange. You think this attraction is going to disappear if I place a wall between us?"

Nope. "But it'll keep us from touching."

"You give me the green light, and there isn't a wall thick enough to keep me from you."

The images that statement conjured caused me to go weak in the knees again. Orion dug his hands into his pockets and produced a set of keys. "Let's get out of here. Get some air."

"Your mother banished me to my room, and Wren said the world is burning witches."

He cocked his head toward the bed. "Being confined isn't helping, but I'm more than happy to stay. As I said before, just give the green light."

I set off for the door. "If I remember correctly, the beach is lovely this time of year."

"Yeah," he said behind me. "It is."

CHAPTER 11

I followed Orion to the six-car garage and paused when he selected a helmet then headed over to the parked Harley. The bike was beautiful—a sleek, black and chrome Fat Boy. A special edition. I had hundreds of memories of riding with Orion on his motorcycle: my body pressed to his, the wind in my hair, and the complete wild feeling of freedom.

"I don't think this is a good idea," I said from the safety of the doorway.

Orion swung his gaze over his shoulder to me. "I kept you safe on the bike before."

"Not what I'm referring to."

He continued to stare.

"Riding a bike requires me to touch you." To hold onto him. "I thought we had established we needed space and air."

"That's why we're taking the bike. Nothing but air."

I pointed at the five other outrageous cars. "The Ranger Rover, the Lamborghini, the Ferrari, the Aston Martin, or the Jaguar—do none of those work?"

"No," he answered simply.

"I'm not riding on the back of a motorcycle with you."

"Cassie." He said my name slowly, seductively. "If you and I end up in one of those cars, I will drive us to someplace private, drop the walls in my mind I've built to keep you out, allow you a brief taste of what I'm feeling and make love to you for the next fifty years."

"What's the difference between the bike and the cars?"

"Tinted windows." A shadow of something dangerous crossed his face.

My mouth popped open, and the sole sound that escaped was that of a squeak. Unable to come up with a proper response, I shuffled in his direction and awkwardly stood in front of him.

"This," he extended the helmet, "is for you."

"You never asked me to wear one of these before."

"That's because I never believed any harm could come to you while you were in my care. I was arrogant, and that is a mistake I won't repeat."

Orion moved so he could place the helmet on my head, but I stopped him by wrapping my fingers around his wrist. Wow. He really had found a way to shield me from his emotions. "Were you injured the night of the accident?"

Even with the wall, his grief and guilt sliced through my brain like a serrated knife. "Yes." His eyes flashed to the scar on my neck and then to the hundreds of tiny ones on my skin. He dropped his arm and I let go of his wrist. "A lot of time has passed between us, but one thing that hasn't changed is that my mind will not be moved. You will wear this helmet."

"I'm not that naïve girl anymore who thinks you're a god to follow."

"I know," he said as if he truly heard what I was saying to him. "But we're going to have to figure out how to work together and the best way to do that is to define our boundaries. One of mine: I'm not wired to allow people I care for to take risks. I've hurt you before, and I will do everything in my power to not do it again."

I swept my hair back into a ponytail, then accepted the helmet from him. His eyes softened in gratitude.

"I'm not doing it for you." I settled the helmet on my head. "Helmets reduce the risk of death by thirty-seven percent and head injury by sixty-nine percent."

The right side of his mouth cocked up. "Learn that with your fancy degree?"

"That and a whole lot of other things. Like don't fall in love with a Fae."

Orion straddled the bike and watched as I climbed on behind him. "In which college class did you learn that?"

"Nessa MacAleese 101."

The powerful engine roared to life under me. The garage door opened and Orion rocketed out, going from zero to ninety in a heartbeat. Having forgotten how fast he loved to ride, I threw my arms around Orion's waist then jumped with the electrical shock that struck when my hands touched his stomach. My front slid to his back, and his chest vibrated with laughter. Unhappy with his amusement, I smacked his thigh. He laughed harder, captured my hand and held it over his heart as we rode into the sunset.

～

ORION HAD PARKED on the beach, across from the Shell Comber, a lonely food shack Orion and I used to frequent on my rare days off. There was a comfort in the familiar as he ordered two double cheeseburgers, two large fries and a large chocolate milkshake. I chose the Italian sub with oil and vinegar dressing.

We went up and over the dunes and onto the beach. The

sky was a gorgeous combination of marmalade and honey, and far out on the horizon, I spotted the lights of the freighters passing by in the shipping lane. The air held the perfect combination of sweet blooming honeysuckle, jasmine, and the saltiness of the sea. Above us, the last of the seagulls squawked before flying to their roosting place for the night, and the sound of the waves crashing on the beach brought on the same repose as when my grandmother would hug me when I returned home from school.

This wasn't a part of the beach the tourists flocked to. The vacation rentals were farther away. This was a small slice of heaven that belonged to no one. Not the Fae of the MacAleese family, not the holiday beach goers, just the natural world. Except for a few crabs, the crowds across the street enjoying their dinners and a few lovers walking the surf, we were alone.

We ate as if he wasn't a Fae and I wasn't a witch. As if I hadn't died and come back to life. As if he hadn't abandoned me when I was terrified and injured. As if we hadn't been tasked with finding his queen. Orion delved into his feast, and I savored each bite of my sub.

"Am I to understand that your family isn't part of the mafia and you don't kill people who piss your family off?" I asked to break the silence.

"Is that what you thought? We were Fae mafia? Mercutio is going to love that." Orion smirked then shoved a handful of fries into his mouth.

"How was I to know what you were? Your family is filthy rich, and after you would disappear for a few days, you would show up with cuts and bruises. You always tried to act like the scars had been there before, but I knew they were new. And you knew I knew."

The idiot grinned like a madman fondly reminiscing. "I have some great battle stories."

I pursed my lips as I'm sure he did. "It was infuriating not knowing."

"What was I supposed to say? 'Hey, Cassie, how was your evening?' I fought in a raging battle last night against demons, but it's okay though, because I healed this morning?'"

"You could have tried explaining it to me. You had told me you were Fae."

The good-natured humor faded and a part of me was sad to see it go. "I broke rules by telling you I was Fae, and doing so had repercussions with the Fae Council. They threatened you, but then agreed to leave you alone as long as I accepted my punishment and I didn't tell you anything else."

Repercussions. Threatened me. Storm clouds were building in his eyes, and I thought of how Orion had been gone for over a week after he had told me he was a Fae. I also thought of how he had come home to me exhausted, dirty, bloody, and his body weak. I remembered how I had loved him that night, cared for him, cherished him because I had sensed he had walked through hell. Had he?

Nonverbally asking me to let it go, Orion shook his head and glanced away. If he had gone through hell, I would drop this conversation...for now. "You said you're a soldier. Who do you fight?"

"Demons," he said matter-of-factly. "Fae are fallen angels. Our ancestors followed Satan out the backdoor, but once they fell, they had a change of heart. Satan didn't fall from heaven straight to hell, he fell to earth, along with anyone else who followed. A great battle was waged with Gabriel the Archangel leading the charge. The war was bloody, it was savage, and it was won when my ancestors turned their backs on Satan and joined Gabriel. Together we cast Satan and his loyal followers to hell."

I felt like I was five again and was cuddled tight to my

grandmother as she read me fairytales before bed. "What happened then?"

"God forgave the angels who had initially renounced Him and then proved their loyalty in the end, but he would not return their immortality. Instead, we became Fae. We live longer lives than humans, are harder to kill, have power, and eventually die. As long as we live a valiant life, when we die, we then go into the peace of the portal of heaven. Some Fae, like me, are warriors. Others have different tasks to complete, like caring for the natural world. Regardless of our given task, every new generation of Fae picks up where the last generation left off—fighting the greatest and unseen threat to humans—we battle demons."

"What are demons?" I asked carefully, not sure I wanted the answer.

"The bad boys are the fallen angels who stayed loyal to Satan. The less powerful foot soldiers were humans when they were alive."

Humans. That caused a physical ache. "What are the two of you fighting over?"

"Earth," he said. "They want to rule over it which means the destruction of the human race. My job is to keep that from happening and to annihilate as many demons as I can. Regardless of what the Council ordered, I wanted you to go into the portal. As long as you walk on earth, you have free will, which means there's still the chance you could lose your soul. If that happens and you die, it would be a different portal that would open for you upon your death, and there would be no beauty in it. No rest. No peace. You deserve peace. You should have been allowed to die."

Uncomfortable with the conversation, I switched up my position on the shifting sand. "What, if anything, do witches have to do with any of this?"

"Some help us," he said. "Some help the demons, but most

stay neutral." After several beats of silence, he glanced over at me. "What made you want to be a nurse practitioner and a midwife?"

The question was solid. Comfortable. "After the accident, I was in the hospital for two months, and then I was in a rehab hospital for even longer. My nurses were wonderful. They inspired me to be more, to become more…."

"Than the girl who was with me?" Orion finished for me.

"You said it." But I did think it. When I was with Orion, I didn't have goals other than to be by his side. Part of me wished I could slap the girl I was, shake sense into her, force her see that there was more to life than a boy she worshipped. I had limited myself, had tunnel vision, and was more than happy to wait in his bed for the table scraps he threw in my direction.

"What about the midwife part?"

"In nursing school, I loved my rotation in OB and labor and delivery. Rural areas suffer from a lack of medical care, especially care for pregnant women, so that's why I became a midwife and a nurse practitioner." My grandmother and I had lived near an extremely small town. Our home was a cabin built of logs. We lived on well water, had a septic tank, and had electricity when the weather was good. We heated our home with the wood-burning stove, and the shade of the ancient trees was our air conditioning.

The women in our community called for her when they were in labor, and I would tag along and play outside the house until the sweet new baby cried. My grandmother and I didn't have much, but we had everything we needed.

"I remember the first time I delivered a baby on my own. It was absolutely terrifying, and it was also the most exhilarating experience. Thankfully the birth was textbook perfect. It was a baby boy. He came out screaming, but quieted when I put him in his mother's arms. He had this head full of dark hair, and he was absolutely beautiful." As I delivered the baby, I had felt a connection to my grandmother, as if she were there with me.

"So, you were happy in your life?"

I thought of my apartment, my friends, my patients, my mothers and their babies. "I had a good life." I watched the waves roll in and the cloud-to-cloud lightning dancing across the sky in the storm cell off the coast. The air had that rich, earthy smell of rain, and the wind whirling off the ocean was warm. My body was vibrating again, not because of Orion's closeness, but because the more I concentrated on the storm, the more I was becoming one with it. I became the core, the wind, the electrical charge, and the drops of rain being held together in the cloud that was ready to burst.

"When I asked you the other night if you were happy," Orion said, "this is the expression I was hoping you'd give."

I touched my face, and I was truly shocked I had been smiling. Other than when I held the babies I delivered, I didn't smile anymore. Not my real one, not this absolute feeling of joy.

"It was the sub, right?" He gave me a ghost of his devious grin.

"Yeah, it was definitely the sub." I gestured to the storm cell. "It's beautiful, isn't it?"

"Yes, it is." Orion wasn't looking at the storm, but at me. He tipped the milkshake in my direction. "Want some?" We used to do intimate things like that—share drinks.

I went to take it, and then froze. What was wrong with me? A few minutes alone with Orion and I had slipped into old patterns. He had betrayed me, he had *lied* to me…. "We aren't together anymore, and we aren't going to be. You didn't just break my heart, you shattered it. There are some hurts that can't be forgiven." A gust of wind blew down the beach, and the swirling sand stung my skin. Similar to how being with Orion again stung my soul. "We need to find the baby, but your mother plainly stated she wants to kill me. That doesn't exactly bode well for a good working relationship."

Orion rolled his shoulders back. "I have dealt with my mother, and she will apologize. You have no need to worry about her. She knows her place and will keep it."

Nessa would apologize to me when tutu-wearing hippos jazz-handed out of the sky. Instead of hippos, rain erupted from the towering thunderhead hovering over the open water. "Your mother needs to do more than apologize. She needs therapy."

"My mother was acting in the best interest of everyone."

"Did you miss where she threatened to kill me?"

"In her defense," Orion said, "by entering that room, you desecrated the memories of our ancestors."

"Maybe if the room was such a big deal, it should have been locked."

His eyes burned with fury. "It was guarded with enchantments only the highest of our order can unlock. You should never have been able to enter, and you're damn lucky to be alive. I don't know why it let you in, but you must promise me to not enter there again. That room is not what it seems. It will protect itself at all costs." Orion swore under his breath. "You have no understanding how close to death you were the moment you entered."

"From your mother, I know. I was there."

"She saved your life," he retorted. "If the room labels you as a threat, it will torture you, and I wouldn't be able to stop it. You don't understand. I can't stand seeing you in pain, and that's all I would have been able to do—see you wither in agony. There are rules, and there are expectations, and as long as you accept our protection, as long as you are by my side as we search for our queen, I need to know you will respect our rules and abide by what I say."

His anger fueled mine. "What are the rules, Orion? Stay in my room until you escort me out for food? Do whatever you say because you said so? Because that's how you were at twenty-one and I thought that was romantic then? The alpha male protecting me isn't cute anymore. You have a centuries-old family to protect you. I have myself, and no one to trust. So, tell me the rules. Spell them out for me. If I do exactly what you say, how you say it, after I find this child, what happens to me? You throw me away again? I go out in public and risk being named a witch with barely any way to protect myself from a hateful mob?"

"I didn't throw you away," he said. "I made the decision that was in your best interest."

"You tossed me out like I was wadded-up trash," I continued. "I gave you my heart, my soul, and you showed up close to a decade later after I thought you had died. I didn't like this game the first time around. So please, Fae warrior, kindly explain to this witch, who was only good for warming your bed, the proper rules so maybe I can survive!"

Orion flinched as if I had slapped him. The wind whipped around us, the storm in the ocean began to rotate, and I felt as if I were being pulled apart. My muscles and tendons being stretched to the point of snapping.

"Try to relax." Orion searched my face like he was concerned for me. "Find calm."

"I am calm!" I wasn't. My entire body was buzzing, and not in a good way. In a way that made me want to peel my skin off. Whatever wall that had been created when I woke as a witch, protecting me from emotions, crumbled.

I crouched into a ball, trying to make myself smaller from the onslaught, and rubbed my temples as they throbbed. Down the beach, a younger couple began to argue, their anguish and guilt suffocating me. She longed for him to love her, she wanted him to stay. The diamond ring on her finger was supposed to mean a white dress, happiness, babies and forever and he…he threw it all away.

He never meant for that night to happen. He had too much to drink, hadn't meant for the flirtation with the woman to turn into more. He felt trapped by the wedding plans, trapped by a full-time job that he hated, and he loathed the idea of more bills and a mortgage. She wanted to start a family after the wedding, and the more she talked, the more he felt smothered. Then there was the other woman. She smelled of cigarettes and tasted like cheap whiskey and freedom. He liked how she wanted him, liked how she wanted him to do things in public while people in the bar watched. He liked the wildness of it all. He hadn't gone there searching for this woman, hadn't meant for it to happen, and he had hurt his fiancée who he now realized he loved….

Their suffering turned into an icepick headache, and I fought the need to sob. Whose pain was I feeling? Theirs, mine or both?

"Cassie?" Orion was by my side. "What's going on? What's happening?"

He lifted my hair covering my face, and with his touch, lightning struck the sea. This harrowing connection between me, Orion and the storm caused me to feel like a lifeboat caught in a hurricane. My stomach rising and falling with the mountainous waves. "Pain," I whispered.

"Tell me what's causing you pain?"

"Too many emotions." Then I was lost.

CHAPTER 12

*M*ultiple voices screamed as I was inundated by the two billion confusing emotions of people on the beach, from the people in their cars, in their homes and my mind stretched further and consumed the emotions of people in high rises and hotels.

I shrank as I was overrun. Too many people, too much to process. My ability magnified in a way it had never done before. I clutched my stomach as I dry heaved—my mind moving too fast to absorb the assault. My head pounded, a terrible migraine threatening to split open my brain. Something wet trickled down my nose and I tasted blood in my mouth.

"I have you, Cassie. It's going to be okay."

I was lifted, and too overcome with the onslaught, I couldn't fight the horrible sensation of skin-to-skin contact. Of connecting with Orion's too strong emotions—his fear, his anxiety. His guilt was so overpowering that it wrapped around my lungs, squeezing like a python.

A splash of water, the cold causing me to shiver, and then I was completely submerged. With water filling my ears, the sound of the world muffled, the thousands of screeching voices and emotions abruptly stopped. I opened my eyes and stared into the blackness of the dark sea. I rose with the waves, dropped to the bottom as they lowered, and I closed my eyes again as I held my breath so I could stay under longer. I wasn't calm on land, not even close, but in the water, there was no noise, no emotions, no chaos. Just a floating peace.

I saw a light, not as bright as the portal, but brilliant all the same. There was a hand, a tiny one that reached out to me. I stretched my fingers, and when we touched, the cold of the surrounding water was chased away by the baby's warmth. Peace at her contentment, serenity of her rocking and floating in utero. The baby was thriving and happy.

Where are you? I whispered into her mind.

She tilted her head in acknowledgement and exuded security.

Do you need me to find you?

A flash of joy. That would be a yes.

Why must I find you?

The baby kicked, and there was another sensation… alarm, cutting fear, sharp like a blade. But it was a removed emotion from the baby. Not quite hers, but surrounding her like a shroud. The fear belonged to her mother. But the baby herself was the epitome of calm and peace.

My lungs burned, and I ached for air, but I needed to know more. There was a yank on my wrist, and I was pulled to the surface. I gasped and wildly searched for Orion, but he was nowhere to be seen. I was adrift in the water, past the breakers, and alone.

"I'm here," he said from a distance behind me. I circled, and in the moonlight, watched as he treaded water six feet away. "Whatever is happening with you seems worse when we touch." A pause. "From my limited knowledge, witches are connected to the elements, and I thought the water might help you relax."

He let the statement hang open, giving me room to speak, to explain, but I couldn't clarify anything. "It worked." A pause. "Thank you."

"You're welcome. Look, Cassie, you and I—"

"I saw the baby," I cut him off because he and I weren't important. "When I went under the water, she appeared in my mind. She hasn't been born yet." A smile spread upon my lips. "She's beautiful and happy. The baby indicated she was safe, but her mother feels fear."

Orion swam closer, but kept a healthy distance. "How did you do it? How do you communicate with her?"

"Telepathy, I think." I frowned. "Before this, I dreamed of her. Before waking as a witch, I had only been able to use telepathy when I was touching someone, but maybe now that I'm a witch the ability has broadened?"

He nodded as if to a conversation in his head. "You were speaking to Brittney's baby in upstate New York."

"Yes," I confirmed. It wasn't like I hadn't already used telepathy with him.

"Babies speak with you? That's amazing."

That wasn't exactly how it worked. My frown deepened.

"What is it?" he asked.

"It's more than that."

"Tell me," he coaxed.

"I don't trust you." And it saddened me that I didn't. At one time, I trusted him more than anyone, had more faith in him than any religion, loved him more than I loved myself.

"I know, and I'm working on gaining that back."

My trust was something he couldn't have again. There were physical scars on my body that weren't as deep as the one he created on my soul.

At my silence he said, "Cassie, I swear on my life, I made

the decisions I did years ago to protect you. Not to hurt you. Staying with me," he shook his head as if he were struggling, "a fast death would have been a mercy, but that wasn't what was in store for you. That wasn't a car accident that hurt you, but a demon attack. Being with me was putting you in danger. I couldn't allow that."

His mother said we were cursed as a couple. "You should have talked to me—let me decide if the risks were too much."

"But you would have stayed," he talked over me.

"It should have been my choice!"

"I couldn't watch you in pain!" he shouted, stunning me. "And that's what your future held if you stayed with me. Endless torture and pain. I made a mistake, my enemies learned of you, and that put you in danger."

"Am I still in danger?"

"Yes. They can track you when we're a couple. I had to make sure I kept my distance." His eyes pleaded for me to let this go, but there was much that was unanswered.

There was a way to affirm if he was sincere, but I was terrified to do so after what happened on the beach. Needing to know, I swam forward and touched his wrist. I trembled with the rush of emotions, but bobbing in the water, I could control the flow.

My hands on his skin, I closed my eyes and forced my way into his head. It was a complicated maze. Colored threads moving in different directions. Sadness, resentment, anger, grief, loss…but the anger was the most resolute. I concentrated and saw a memory…of me riding shotgun in his car, of him looking at me and there was laughter and love in my eyes. With one hand on the steering wheel, he took my fingers with his free hand, kissed my knuckles and then my entire body lurched forward with an impact, glass shatter-ing….me lying on the pavement, shadows advancing toward me as he withdrew his dagger…the static in his brain recoiled from me, struck out and I jerked to another memory….of his mother standing over Orion, wrath in her eyes, Orion on his knees, covered in blood, and his grief caused hot tears to swell in my eyes.

Please, he begged. *Help me save her and keep her safe, and I'll do anything you want.*

A whirlwind, the memory caught in a tornado. A door in his mind slammed shut, and I flinched with the impact. He wrenched his wrist from my grasp, and he studied me as if he had grown new eyes. "What's happening with you? Don't lie. I let you in then forced you out."

I stayed silent as we treaded water.

"You don't trust me, and I don't blame you. But this isn't about you and it isn't about me. We can't let this baby down."

No, we couldn't. "As I recovered from the accident," I said slowly and deliberately, "I started to feel people's emotions. I gained the telepathy later, but rarely use it because it takes too much energy. When taking care of my patients and my babies, I read their emotions."

"You're an empath," he said with awe. His brain was working fast, and I wished it would slow down, because maybe I had made a mistake by sharing. "Can you read anyone's emotions?"

"As long as they're in proximity. I read some people better than others. There are some I need to touch to read. But since waking as a witch, everything is stronger. Sometimes the emotions are easier to control and other times…"

"We just learned controlling emotions can be harder."

I had migraines before, but I had never felt as awful as I did on the beach. "Yes."

"But there's a difference between feeling an emotion and knowing a thought."

I didn't want to validate his correct assumption. My teeth chattered as the cold water nipped at my skin, and my muscles were exhausted from treading. "I need to head to shore."

Orion snagged an arm around my waist and pulled me to him. My breath came out in a rush with the impact, and I was amazed he could hold my weight as he swam for both of us. "Can you feel me now?"

Our wet bodies pressed tight? The friction building between us? The heat of his gaze? Yes, but that wasn't what he was asking. "No." I read no emotion from him. I didn't sense his lust either, or mine. "Why is that?" His face was void of emotion, and frustration leaked into my veins. "I trusted you with my secret, and if you can't—"

"There are demons who can read our signature—our auras. Given what I do as a warrior, I need to be undetected. The same tactics I use to shield myself from them keeps you from feeling the effects of our blood exchange and it keeps you out of my head."

"Is it hard to do?"

His eyes said yes. "It takes concentration. A lot more when I'm close to you."

"Can all Fae do this?"

"No. Sidhe warriors,"–he pronounced it as shee–"are the only ones, and there are some who can't master it. It's like building a wall of concrete in my mind, having to lift each heavy stone, and then having to focus on keeping it up while the world is trying to demolish it. Be honest, can you read minds?"

Orion treaded water easily for us as we crested with a wave and then bobbed down. This was it—the moment to be honest. Doing this made me extremely vulnerable as my past told me he couldn't be trusted. "Sometimes, if the emotions are clear enough."

His expression darkened. "It's bad enough you can distinguish between Fae and humans. Fae won't like that you can read emotions, and they'll hate that you might be able to read their thoughts. We're protective of our privacy. Does anyone else know what you can do?"

"Wren," I said. "She could tell when I was testing her emotions for thoughts."

His arm tightened around me as if my response bothered him. "It's going to be complicated to keep you safe in my world, especially if you can't control your abilities. You and Wren will need to start working on your witchcraft immediately."

"I'm more interested in how we find the baby and her mother. How can we find them when all I can do is wait for her to connect with me so I can sense her emotions?"

"We'll figure it out." Orion turned his head toward land. "I'm being called."

On the beach, now dark with the night, was the outline of a delicate form. The low-level buzz coming off the water told me this was a Fae. "Friend or foe?"

"Depends if she was sent by my mother or not."

Oh, goody.

CHAPTER 13

I felt and looked like a bedraggled rat stumbling out of the water. The Fae who had been on the beach had disappeared, and when I glanced behind me, Orion was gone. My heart stopped, my eyes frantically searched the ocean, and I jumped in surprise when Orion magically appeared in front of me. He was in dry clothes and held in his hands a pair of sweatpants that were way too big for me, one of his T-shirts, and his black leather jacket. The one he used to wear when we would go for long motorcycle rides during cool fall evenings. Butterflies took flight in my chest, and no matter how I tried, I couldn't wrangle them up and tie them down.

"I thought there was another Fae," I said.

"She's still here, just shifting back and forth until we're ready. I assumed you wouldn't want to meet anyone looking like this." His gaze traveled my body, and I became aware I was wearing white, that my clothes were clinging to my skin, and were now see-through.

A sharp image in his mind came barreling through: We were coming in from the beach wet and covered in sand.

Orion led me to the shower before I even had a chance to take off my shirt. I stood there before him, under the current of warm water, as he slowly undressed and devoured me with his hungry eyes.

Orion took off his shirt and jeans, and my mouth went dry as I watched the water drip down his chest of solid muscles. Instead of stripping me quickly, wrapping my legs around his waist, and taking me exactly how I wanted, he pulled toward him and kissed me tenderly as his hands whispered caresses, promises of what was to come, along the inside of my thighs. He lazily slipped my shirt up and over my head then spent too much time torturously peeling down one bra strap, then another, before undoing the clasp. It fell to the floor of the shower, and the two of us became lost in one another.

I shook my head to force myself away from the memory.

On the beach, Orion's smoldering gaze met mine, and a streak of white-hot lightning zapped through my blood. My thighs rubbed together and there was a heavy ache, an emptiness within me begging to be filled. It was Orion who I needed. His body on mine, his lips on my skin, his hands on my….

The way Orion was drinking me in, it was clear I wasn't the only one feeling this incredible longing. I swallowed and forced distance between us, but each step felt like agony. "I thought you could stop the lust?"

"I can." Orion raked his hands through his hair, and the intensity of the heightened need between us began to lessen. Now I was left with normal desire—which between me and Orion—was the same chemical make-up as nitroglycerin. "But then I remembered…." Yes, I was aware of what he remembered. "And my concentration slipped. Are you okay?"

Nothing we couldn't solve in a bed or here on the beach or just about anywhere, but that wasn't going to help the already complicated situation between us. "I'm fantastic." Hardly. "Is it difficult to keep us from feeling the desire of the blood exchange?"

"It takes a lot of concentration, but I can contain it," he said. "For you."

"You can't stop it for yourself?"

"That's not how my wall works. It keeps energy in, instead of allowing it to roam freely."

My eyes widened as I let that sink in. As he protected me from the razor's edge of that ferocious lust, he felt it the entire time. Dear God, how was he standing it? "I'm sorry you have to feel this way."

"I'm not. To have you in my life again is a gift I never thought I'd receive. Of course, if you would like to help ease my need, I'll be more than happy to comply." That wicked seductive grin almost made me relent.

The wind blew. I shivered and crossed my arms to warm myself, but then noticed how that made my breasts rise up and squeeze together. His eyes fell to my shirt again, and I didn't think either of us were going to survive a round two. "Turn around." After the "freak" storm, the beach was empty. "Let me change."

With a mischievous glint in his eye, Orion unhurriedly gave me his back. I peeled the shirt off my body but left my bra on. Taking it off was asking for trouble. "Shirt, please."

He tossed it over his shoulder. I caught it and pulled it over my head. Being that he was a giant, the ends of his T-shirt hit my knees. It was more arduous to wrestle off wet jeans, and Orion circled back as he offered me his sweatpants.

"I could have been naked," I said, and then we would have christened this beach with our reunion, regardless if the beach was empty or not.

"My T-shirts are like dresses on you. Besides, I've seen you naked before."

Every inch of me became hot, and that was without the help of the blood bond. Good God, how many mornings had I walked barefoot around his condo in one of his shirts while he cooked us breakfast? We'd eat at the table, and then fall back into bed again. "You haven't seen me naked in years, and we're not starting tonight." I attempted to banish the memories of us laughing, the whispered conversations as we were tangled up with each other, but I was devastatingly unsuccessful. I shoved a foot into one of his massively long pant legs. "This isn't going to work."

Orion held out his hand, and I stared at it warily. "Is that a good idea?" I asked.

"The wall in my mind is firm," he answered. Yeah, well, the wall in my mind wasn't. Still, I accepted his offer, taking his hand to steady myself as I tripped over the left leg.

"I retrieved these from my penthouse on the beach," Orion said. "Do you want me to collect the clothes in your room? It'll only take a minute or two. Wren warded the mansion, so it takes a bit more maneuvering for me to shift in and out of there."

"No." I drew the drawstrings tight, and the pants still fit loose. "I'll manage."

He offered his motorcycle jacket, and as I accepted, there was a feeling of nostalgia. I slipped my arms through it, nuzzled my nose into the collar, and breathed in his dark scent. I used to love this jacket and what I thought it represented: belonging, friendship, family, and love.

I sighed at how wrong I had been. In the moonlight, I didn't need to be an empath to read the regret and anguish on Orion's face. "If you can build this wall in your head to keep me out and hide yourself from you enemies, why can they still find me?"

"We're blood bonded, and that type of connection creates a signature." He paused as if choosing his words carefully. "While the wall I create can protect me, the blood bond makes you fully visible to other Fae and to demons. It's a specific aura that wraps around you—marking you as mine. The stronger the bond becomes, the brighter the signature, which makes you easier for my enemies to see."

A pinprick of panic entered my bloodstream, and I reeled as the world became more complicated and dangerous. "How bright is it now?"

"We recently reconnected, so it's dim. It's highly unlikely they can see it and find you…yet. But the longer we are together, the brighter the bond will become."

A million thoughts—and they were colliding. "When you talked to me in the dream, you said you didn't want to save me again. Did you give me your blood the night we were attacked?"

"I couldn't give you enough to fully heal you because I was in a weakened state. You'll never understand how sorry I am for that, and for the fact I didn't protect you properly."

Uneasiness dried out my mouth. "But the attack was the reason you gave me your blood, which means we shouldn't have been blood bonded. At the same time, you seem to be saying they found us because we were blood bonded. Before the accident or demon attack or whatever you want to call it, I never took blood from you."

Orion shoved his hands into his pockets. His gaze fell to the scar on my neck. On impulse, I covered it. "We're blood bonded because I drank your blood," he said. "Your drinking from me only strengthened the bond."

I positioned my hands in a stopping gesture. There was no way I had correctly processed those words. "You drank my blood?"

"Yes."

"And I let you?" My voice entered a higher octave, and Orion offered me a sympathetic nod. I was frozen solid yet screaming internally. Shock. I was entering shock. I rubbed my hands along my arms as if I were cold, but at the same time a searing heat was causing me to sweat. "I don't remember any of this."

"I begged my mother to snap the link and wipe as much as she could of that night from your memory. It's rare for a Fae to be able to cut a link, but she is one of the few who can. It cost her physically to do it, but she did it for me. For you."

"Lucky us," I said with no emotion. As if that was a hardship for Nessa. She probably had been dancing with joy. "But we shouldn't be blood bonded anymore, yet we are." My words were coming out too slow, too overpronounced. Weird, considering I should have cracked hours ago, but hadn't, and this was the information that was going to do me in.

Orion lowered his head, and after a few heartbeats, he met my eyes. "The bond can be temporarily cut, but it can never be broken. The moment you touched me outside of Brittney's, the cord that tethers you and me was reconnected. The desire we're experiencing—that's because I shared my blood with the person I am bonded with…which would be you."

It was hard to not turn and bolt. "Did I agree to the bond?"

"Yes. The only thing I have done without your permission was give you my blood the first time, saving you from death. It was selfish of me, but I couldn't…" he struggled to talk, "I couldn't lose you."

"Yet you did." And he had forced me to believe I had lost him.

My spine straightened with the sixth sense that we weren't alone. I was engulfed with the impressions of fall—

the cool, crisp air on my skin, the smell of matured pump-
kins on the vine, the rush of wind on a blustery day. My eyes
snapped to the right, as did Orion's gaze, and a woman shimmered to reality before us. Her bouncy, shoulder length curls
were the colors of autumn—blazing red, striking gold, brilliant orange. She had a face of an angel, vivid violet, intelli-
gent eyes, and couldn't be an inch over five foot nor much
older than eighteen. She wore tight jeans, a blue blouse and a
knee length, red cardigan.

Orion placed a hand over his heart. "Relle. Your visit is an
honor."

"The honor is mine, bellator." Along with a short and
swift curtsey, she bowed her head to him, and I raised an
eyebrow at the exchange.

"This is Cassie, my amans." He nodded toward me, and I
made a mental note to ask him what amans meant. "Cassie,
this is Relle. She's the youngest to ever be named to the
Conclave of Honored Prophetesses, and it is Relle who had
the first vision of you holding our queen."

A confident smile perched upon her perfect lips. "Don't
forget to add I'm one of only a handful of Sprites in our
history who has the gift of prophecy."

Orion gave her a side smirk. "And that."

Her eyes danced as she turned to me. "Not that the Sidhe
were happy that a Sprite has the ability of foresight, and they
were particularly not thrilled that my visions are clearer than
any of theirs. It about killed them to put me, a Sprite, on the
Conclave of Honored Prophetesses."

I stole a glance at Orion for reassurance of what was
happening, but he merely watched me with humor. Relle
inclined her head in respect toward me. "It is an honor to
meet you. Beyond an honor. Prophetesses rarely gain the
opportunity to experience the reality of our visions, as it is
our warriors who play out such tasks. It's an archaic rule,

but the Fae, if anything, move painstaking slow with change."

"The Council will not be happy you've left the safety of the Prophetess Gardens." Orion turned serious, and he possessed the same protectiveness older brothers do for their beloved little sisters. "You made a promise to the Council to abide by their rules."

"Everyone believes I've taken to being sequestered to our garden on earth for meditation. They will not look for me soon, but I cannot be gone long. So, we must hurry. I've a new vision and the Council moves slowly. Time is not on our side. They refuse to share with you until the next meeting, that is if they share at all. Nessa stands in the way of anything involving Cassie and the baby. I agree, there isn't much to my vision to go off of, but I don't believe that's the Council's call to make. It's yours Orion. Yours and Cassie's."

The muscles in my neck tensed and I rolled it to help. Nessa was literally going to be the death of me. A muscle in Orion's jaw ticked and he crossed his arms. "Go on."

"Two evenings from now, the mother will be at a castle and she will be in danger. Shadows surround her. She believes she is safe, but she is not."

"Have you seen the mother?" Orion asked. "Her face? Caught a name? Seen if she's Fae? Can you give me more details of where this happens?"

Relle immediately started shaking her head in dismay. "All my visions are from her point of view and are like flipping through snapshot pictures. I caught the date and the time from a cell phone. As for where, the castle was near water."

Orion extended his open palm toward her. "May I?"

"Of course." Relle disappeared and then reappeared in front of Orion. She placed her hand over his, and they stood there for about a minute, unblinking, staring at each other.

With a sigh, Orion disengaged and Relle reappeared back to where she had been.

"Thank you for your help," Orion said. "I will stay quiet about this meeting, and Cassie and I will take care of this."

"You're welcome." She rolled her shoulders back as if readying for battle. "May I fight?"

Orion crossed his arms over his chest, the muscles flexed with agitation. "No."

"I have studied the texts of the bellators, and being a Sprite, I am versed in combat."

"While I have the upmost respect for the courage of the Sprites, Sprites do not fight demons of the levels the warriors encounter. You have more to learn. Plus, when you were named an Honored Prophetess, you made a pledge to stay in Fairy or the protected garden on earth."

"Orion—" she started.

"Enough, Relle. I fought hard for you with the Council for your position, and you promised me you would not take this honor lightly."

Relle lowered her head in resignation then sent me a quelling glance. "Orion, there is talk that the Council wants to meet with you both."

"I've heard the same," Orion said. "There is no need to worry, as I will handle it. Thank you again, Relle. I have much respect for you and the risks you have taken to come to me. As always, I am in your debt."

With one last nod, Relle disappeared. Orion stared at the sand as if it had all the answers to our problems. I listened to one cycle of the waves rolling in and then out. "A little harsh with her, don't you think?"

"Relle is young, and while she does have battle training, she doesn't have the experience needed to make it out of battle alive. I can't watch after both you and her and guarantee safety and success. Maybe someday she can join the fight, but the time is not now. Not when she is the only prophetess with clear visions about the mother and the baby."

"What do we do now?" I asked.

"We do what Fae have been tasked to do since the dawn of time—we stop the vision from happening and we save lives."

CHAPTER 14

*O*rion guided me into a wing of the house opposite of the one that contained my room. This area was more modern than the Louis XVI décor that had made me feel like I was one wrong move from having my neck stretched out at the base of a guillotine. The hallways of Orion's wing were beige, the lighting warm and recessed, the paintings on the wall abstract, and the flooring a light grayish tile that resembled the worn wood of the stairs at the beach.

"What magical Fae thing do you do to decipher the vision?" I asked Orion.

"I use a laptop and start searching."

We entered a huge living room. The light brown suede sectional, overly long and large, dominated the middle of the room and faced a grand fireplace. Over the fireplace was a massive television with a picture so sharp it was hard to tell real life from the projected image. Speakers were built into the walls and ceilings, and there were multiple gaming systems and electronic equipment with lots of flashing lights in a freestanding cabinet. In front of the couch was an oversized coffee table, and off to the sides were three cushy, over-stuffed leather recliners. The artwork hanging on the light gray walls depicted the beauty and terror of storms at sea, but what drew me to the room were the floor-to-ceiling windows overlooking the ocean.

I headed to the French doors, opened them, walked onto the brick patio, and felt immediately energized with the breeze coming off the water. In the distance were the lights of a passing freighter, and stars twinkled in the sky. "Wow."

"I have to say I like it, too."

Joy and grief at the familiar voice. A friendship from long ago. I spun on my heels and Mercutio gave me his patented contagious grin. With outstretched arms, he asked, "May I?"

A shifting inside me…he remembered I didn't care for an unwelcomed touch. I nodded, and he erased the distance between us in two steps and lifted me at my waist, so my feet dangled. "Long time no see!" Mercutio hugged me like a beloved doll. "I missed you."

I wholeheartedly hugged him back. "You can let me down now."

"Not until I get my fill." With one last squeeze, he gently placed my feet on the ground, and I became lighter with him beaming at me with such warmth and enthusiasm. "Nine years was a long time without seeing my girl." And like he used to, he yanked a strand of my hair, as if I were younger than he, as if I were a little sister.

I snorted. His girl. It was what he used to playfully call me to piss Orion off. Mercutio and I were the same age, and he used to tease Orion that our shared age meant he and I had more in common. I never understood why Orion allowed it to get under his skin, but I did understand the massive amount of amusement Mercutio received from ruffling Orion's feathers. Like I did at nineteen, I glanced at Orion for his reaction. He was leaning against the doorframe, watching me with his expression masked.

Like Orion, Mercutio was taller than he was in our youth, his muscles more filled out, his hair a fade on the sides with curly twists on the top, and somehow his grin more contagious, which I wasn't convinced was possible. His smile was like soothing aloe on a festering burn.

"You could have visited me," I said.

His smile fell a fraction. "I wanted to, but couldn't, and we're not going to dwell on the past. You're here now and that's what matters."

Message clear: let it go.

"That was one beauty of a squall that formed out at sea," he continued. "Never seen anything get nasty that fast."

"It was unique," I replied. "Where's Wren?"

"She had business to attend to. Unique. Nice description. I have a question for you."

Not sure I wanted to answer it. "What?"

"How does a witch tell time?"

My mouth flattened. Oh, how I didn't miss this. "How?"

"She looks at her witch watch." He chuckled. "This one's better. What do you call two witches who live together?"

I crossed my arms and cocked out a hip to show my annoyance, yet he continued, "Broom-mates." He laughed deeply at his own joke. "Wait, wait, this one will crack you up. What do you learn at witch school?"

"Are you done yet?"

"Spelling, and I'm just getting started."

"I get it. I'm a witch."

"A witch!" Mercutio exclaimed as proudly as if I were walking across a graduation stage to accept a diploma for my doctorate. "Our baby girl is growing up so quickly."

"Take a swim, kid?" Shaw strolled out from the darkness of the patio. He, too, was taller and broader, his features that of a chiseled man. Just as I remembered him, he was clean cut and cleanly shaven. His designer cargo pants and collared shirt fit him perfectly—not a wrinkle in sight. His blond hair was precisely styled, and there was a hint of his aftershave lingering in the air. Shaw was meticulous, beautiful, and dangerous. There was a glint of death in his eyes that made my soul shiver. "Or did you get caught up in the storm? I can see how it would be easy to have gotten lost in it. That was a magnificent outburst."

"A beaut," Mercutio agreed. "We raised her right."

"If we raised her right, she would have fried Orion with lightning the moment she saw him."

"True." Mercutio stroked his chin as he assessed me. "Orion should at least be nursing minor burns. How does the lightning work? Do you snap your fingers? Let's do a walk through. Practice makes perfect and all that. Hey, Orion, do you mind heading out onto the patio? I don't want the house to be scorched when she uses you for target practice."

I wasn't going to hit anyone with lightning. "What's with everyone's preoccupation with the storm?"

"Even I was impressed." Shaw gave me a devilish wink.

"Very impressive," Mercutio echoed. "Works of art should be appreciated. In fact, if I could, I'd hang that storm up on the fridge for everyone to see."

"Enough about the storm." I questioned Shaw, already knowing the answer: "No hug?"

"Later. When there's less sand on you. I don't do dirt, kid. Not when I just took a shower and have the Nikes on."

I felt the grit clinging to my face and caked in my hair. "Do you like it? It's the new trend."

"I'll pay you twenty dollars if you walk through Shaw's room and shake out your shoes in his closet," Mercutio said. "Specifically, his loafers. His loafers piss me off."

"I'll pay you fifty if you cause it to rain in Mercutio's Land Rover," Shaw countered.

I smiled in spite of myself, forgetting how they could be with one another, and amazed that they picked up like they had seen me the night before instead of nine years ago.

"One hundred if you lie in Shaw's bed, roll over his expensive sheets, and grind as much sand as you can into the silk," Mercutio continued.

"She's not rolling on anyone's bed." Orion's voice was deep with warning, and that caused Shaw and Mercutio to grin like wolves sensing prey.

"Do you see that, Shaw?" Mercutio gave a low whistle as he tossed a glance at him.

"It's damn bright."

"Damn bright," Mercutio repeated. "You see what we're seeing, Orion?"

Orion surveyed them as if he were lazily contemplating the different ways to tear the limbs from their bodies. He had mentioned other Fae could see our bond, and I didn't like the idea of anyone else seeing something so intimate and private. "I thought you said it was dim."

"It is," Orion said. "They're idiots. We have a guest bedroom if you'd like to take a shower and rest."

I studied each of them again, none of them appearing as though they were going to let me in on their secret conversation. "Lead the way."

"Knock, knock," Mercutio called.

Didn't want to play, but he would be relentless if I didn't. "Who's there?"

"Broken pencil."

"Broken pencil who?"

"Never mind, it's a pointless joke."

I hated it, but that one made me snicker.

Mercutio beamed. "I'm glad you're here, Cassie. We missed having you around."

"Get some rest, kid," Shaw said. "And don't worry. We have your back."

Wasn't sure how true that was, but regardless, I nodded my thanks.

On the way to the guest room, Orion showed me a fully loaded kitchen that contained state-of-the-art everything and told me to raid the fridge if I was hungry. We passed a half bath, and then we entered a long hallway where Orion pointed out where Wren was staying, Mercutio's suite, Shaw's suite, the suite of someone named Tierney, who Orion said I would meet later, and at the end were two more rooms. He tipped his head to the one on the right. "That's the guest suite."

"Whose room is that?" I gestured toward the one directly across.

Orion tried for innocent, but instead he offered me a seductive tilt of his lips. "Mine."

My blood tingled with the possibilities. I entered the guest suite, and my soul sang at the wall of glass doors showing the ocean. The room was painted a light blue and was furnished with an off-white living room set that included a sofa and two high-back end chairs facing a fireplace. Over that was a mounted television, and on the other walls were either fantastic replicas of Claude Monet's Water Lily paintings or the real deal. Up on a two-step platform was a California king four-post bed that had sheer white curtains hanging from the poles. The bedding was white, as were the dozens of perfectly placed pillows.

"Wow," I said, and wow was an understatement.

"You say that a lot," Orion said behind me.

"I grew up in a cabin in the middle of nowhere until social services yanked me out after they discovered I'd been living on my own. After that, I lived in whatever squalid place my mother chose. Since then, I've lived in studio and one-bedroom apartments. This is a guest bedroom, in a wing, of many wings, in a massive mansion, so yeah…wow."

Orion's discomfort bristled along my skin. "I didn't know that."

"You knew I grew up broke." Because his mother had a background check done on me.

"I didn't know about the cabin or that you had lived alone so young."

No, I didn't discuss any of that with him. "You were a rich Fae and I was me. You already had enough reasons to not be in our relationship. I didn't need to supply you or your mother with more ammunition." Irony was, he left anyhow. "Shower in there, I presume?" I walked toward the bathroom to move the conversation away from my childhood home.

"Yes."

The bathroom was more opulent than the one I had used earlier. There was a walk-in shower with a bench seat, and next to that was a long soaking tub built into the floor that faced a window that overlooked the ocean. I could spend hours lying in there staring at the sea.

"No one can see in," Orion said. "The glass is tinted. Also, the cabinets are stocked."

I opened one of them and found the same lotions, soaps and shampoos that were in my previous room and that I'd loved when I was younger. On a hook was a fluffy, white robe. Similar to the one I sometimes wore at his penthouse after we made love. The attentive touches were there, including teacup pink roses. It was clear Orion remembered me, and even clearer, he wanted me comfortable. Part of me felt the butterflies of nineteen. The other part of me didn't know what to do with any of this. I wasn't nineteen anymore. I was twenty-eight, and this lavishness, no matter how much I had once loved it, wasn't me. "When did you have time to do this?"

"I can move fast." As if proving his point, he disappeared, reappeared on the other side of the room, and then reappeared again in front of me within the lapse of a single blink. "If there are other brands you'd prefer, I'll have them brought in for you."

"No, I'm fine. Thank you. But I would like a laptop so I can start searching for this castle near water." I was sure there were only a couple thousand castles on the earth.

"I'll get you one, and I'll start searching, as well."

Silence stretched between us, and in the mirror, I saw how he hooked his thumbs into his front pockets as if he were unsure what to do and what to say, which was a strange turn of events. When we were together, I used to be the awkward one, the one who fretted whether my next uttered word would be good enough. But as I reached out to touch his emotions, I read the heaviness of concern and worry. The dark brown strands twisting and choking him.

"What's wrong?" I asked.

"The Fae Council has summoned me. Mercutio, Shaw, and I will meet with them later this evening, but I will be back before sunrise. Wren placed wards on the mansion, so you are protected. Still, I don't like leaving you here alone."

I wasn't sure how I felt about it either. Hopefully, whatever wards were, they were good. "How did you know Clara's baby wasn't your queen?" I asked.

"Relle had a vision where I hear the baby's heartbeat by no magical means necessary, just by being near her, and I know, without a shadow of a doubt, she is our queen. Also, when I hold her, she glows with the light of heaven. That didn't happen with Clara's baby or with Brittney's."

"I guess that's a way to rule out who is and who isn't."

"I'll jump into the other bedroom," Orion said, "grab

clothes for you and leave them on the bed. Goodnight, Cassie."

"Night." As he turned to leave, I rolled the bottle of shampoo in my hands. "Orion?" He glanced at me from over his shoulder. "Thank you, truly. None of this is easy. Being here, seeing you, finding out I'm a witch, dying, living…" I shrugged. "I miss my old life, and it's nice to see familiar things." Even if they're items I was familiar with years ago.

Orion offered me a nod that felt like a solemn promise. "Anything. Anytime." He left, closing the bathroom door behind him.

~

WITH MY HAIR in a towel and the white, fluffy robe wrapped around my body, I walked into the bedroom to find the lights dimmed, flames dancing in the fireplace, and on the bed, a laptop and a neatly folded pile of clothes. My chest constricted. No, it couldn't be. My fingers shook as I touched my favorite pair of stay-at-home jeans and my most cherished Imagine Dragons T-shirt, which I had purchased last year at a concert I had gone to with Nancy, a nurse from the neighboring county hospital. We stood on our seats, screamed our appreciation for the band the entire time, and then sang along to their music the rest of the way home.

I wondered if Nancy thought of me. I wondered if she hated me now or if she still considered me a friend. In the midst of so much that wasn't me, this T-shirt was. So were those jeans, those PJs, and that brush—all items left behind in my apartment in New York. My heart stopped. My grandmother's brush. Her silver brush. The one she said her mom had passed down to her. The one she said had been in her family for several generations. The one I watched my grandmother brush her hair with every night. The one she brushed my hair with as I sat at her feet. I loved the sensation of the bristles running through my hair, the slight scrape against my scalp, and the caring way my grandmother would pat my shoulder when she was done.

Orion used to watch me brush my hair with it, but I had never told Orion why I cherished that brush. I never spoke much to him about my grandmother. Those memories were too raw for me then. They still were. I reverently folded the T-shirt then cradled the brush in my hands. My grandmother. Orion brought me my grandmother. My throat tightened and my eyes burned. There was no greater gift anyone could have given me...ever.

Thank you, Orion, I whispered to him telepathically. *Thank you.*

CHAPTER 15

After spending hours searching the internet for castles and bookmarking the ones that could be possibilities, I fell asleep and my dreams were weird. I dreamed of Orion changing out of his clothes and into a pair of black silk pants. Multiple scars marked his muscled body. I dreamed of Wren speaking in a hushed voice to a group of women huddled in a circle. Of Nessa, unmoving, on a balcony staring out onto the ocean, her hair whipping in the wind. Then there were whispers, lots of them, like steel voices scratching at my mind.

I was in a long, dark hallway, walking slowly through puddles, trying to ignore the cold and the smell of death. I didn't know how I ended up in the tunnel and had no idea if I was going deeper, if I was heading out, or if there even was a way to escape. A baby cried behind me, and my lungs seized. I spun and sprinted toward her. She wailed louder, the sound echoing along the walls, and I skidded to a halt at a fork in the tunnel. Her sobs were coming from multiple paths. My heart thrashed. I had to find her, but how?

"Cassie," called a voice in the cave. A sweet voice, a luring voice…*enchanted.* "Cassie, she's waiting for you, and she will not survive without you."

The world twirled, the baby's cries ceased, and I was in the Fae mausoleum. The room was dark, moonlight drifting in from windows near the ceiling. The ticking of a grandfather clock thundering. Two fifty-nine in the morning. The growling pit in my stomach calmed—my grimoire was near. *Cassie, awake. The Fae are gone.*

I opened my eyes and sat up. My mouth was as dry as a desert. I swallowed hard and glanced at the clock on the bedside table. It was three a.m., and my head tilted at the sight of a white lace sundress hanging on the bathroom door. A dress that hadn't been there before.

Feeling groggy from my dream, from my lack of sleep, I slipped out of bed and padded on bare feet to the dress. Pinned on it was a note in Nessa's elegant handwriting: *Orion will not be able to keep you from the Council forever. When you are called to Fairy, you will be respectful. Wear this. No shoes. You will be collected if you are needed.*

Screw you and your little dog, too, Nessa.

The TV over the fireplace flashed on, and what I saw sent fear into my soul. The station the old men used to watch at the Bambi Bar was on, and there was a video of a mob pulling a woman through the streets with the words Witch Hunts as the headline. The mob was spitting on her, hitting her, one man grabbing her hair and nailing her in the face with his knee. When she collapsed, they continued to drag her on the street and onto a pile of wood surrounding a stake. Heat sickened me, my palms became clammy and a dry heave raced up my throat. As they tied her to the stake, as she cried out for help and then sobbed when help was denied, the TV turned off, causing me to jump.

My room was possessed. Not caring to linger, I went out the door and nearly squealed when the door shut behind me.

The hallway was dark, the boys' wing of the house silent, as if there wasn't another soul around. A gust of air pushed at me from behind, encouraging me forward, and I couldn't hear past the pulse pounding in my ears.

The breeze continued to blow, and I had a choice: return to psycho room or follow the wind. Both held a slasher movie's promise of tragedy. At the moment, I was okay with the idea of leaving this house and taking my chances with the mobs. The wind pushed at me again. In theory, I had already died multiple times and had survived, so what did I have to lose to pursue the breeze down the hallway? I walked past the kitchen and the living area, entered another hallway, and descended the winding grand stairs. The breeze died at the entrance of the Fae graveyard.

Fantastic. The door of the damned. The room where Orion said I would be tortured for a millennium. But the same gravitational link I felt with Orion, that string to be pulled, I also felt for something within this room. *Are you there?* I sent out telepathically.

Yes, my grimoire responded.

Are you the one who woke me? Sent for me?

Yes. You have much to learn and not much time. You need to understand your power so you can fulfill your purpose.

I sighed heavily. *Orion said the room is cursed.*

It is, but I am stronger. I will protect you.

I wasn't exactly reassured. *Why not appear for me like you did in my apartment?*

I cannot be left unattended in this house. In this room, I am protected.

I nibbled on my bottom lip. *How did you know I was here?*

I am, I exist, and I will be, my grimoire said, as if that were an acceptable answer. *Do you trust me?*

No. The answer was simple and the truth.

I trust you.

Nice to hear, but it didn't change anything. *If I enter, if I follow directions, won't Orion find out? Won't Nessa kill me? They said the room hurts those who enter.*

I will keep them from detecting you and I will protect you from the dangers in this room. It is no longer time for questions. It is time for faith. You called for me. I came. Either enter and learn or follow your lack of faith and leave.

Faith. What an ugly word. The small gold cross around my neck said I had faith, but God ignored me. When I was a child, my knees met the ground as I fell in complete submission, begging God to save my grandmother. Instead, he instilled in me this pain of abandonment that I could never allow another living soul to experience—not as long as I could prevent it. But where God failed, I would succeed. I was going to find this baby.

I turned the knob and found myself in the Fae graveyard. This time, I was on the second floor, and I was looking over a golden railing. Below me were the urns, the glass cases of artifacts, and even the chair Queen Elisabeth I had sat in. Last time I was in here, I didn't remember there being a second floor, but this room was more than it appeared.

I waited for Orion to show, for Nessa to appear and slit my throat, but there was nothing more than the ticking of the grandfather clock somewhere below. Then the ticking stopped.

Red smoke streamed from the urns, combining together, and the room filled with the sound of steel fingernails against a chalkboard. A caustic stench burned my throat and caused me to cough, to gag, to choke. The red smoke rotated as a tornado, and my heart beat out of my chest as eyes appeared within the twister and glared at me. The tornado lashed out and threw itself toward me. I stumbled back, flung my arms in front of my face, preparing for the impact, and gasped when the red smoke slammed into an invisible shield.

The stench faded, and the smoke raced around the balcony, but was unable to discover a way in. The two eyes multiplied into hundreds, if not thousands, and they blinked in unison. I shivered as the coldness of death entered my bones.

Cassie, the eyes called, the sound of millions of angry bees buzzing. *You will die.*

Cassie, the book whispered. *You will live, but you have to choose to believe I am real.*

I turned toward the voice and was astounded. The literal breath stolen from my body. My book was on a round wooden table, twelve thick candles creating a circle around it, giving the old, tattered manuscript a soft glow. There was nothing about its physical appearance that left me in awe, but the feeling of raw power that pulsated from its pages nearly knocked me off my feet. My skin prickled as I slowly walked toward it.

Familiar scents drifted from the book: grass clippings, the smell of the forest after a rain, basil from the garden, and finally the subtle hint of hot chocolate chip cookies. There were flashes of images: fireflies glowing in the dark July night, lightning striking out of a towering cumulonimbus cloud, a full moon in a star-filled sky, and the sun rising over the horizon of the ocean. Sounds overwhelmed my ears: the pitter patter of the rain from a summer storm against a tin roof, waves crashing against the ocean, the song of a warbler, my grandmother whispering she loved me.

Sight, smells, sounds, tastes, and there was one missing: touch. I reached between two flames, placed my hand on the cover and an electrical current streaked through me, causing the hair on my arms and on my neck to stand on end. A bright exploding light and a wind pushed me back. A cloud of white rose from the book, the table, and the burning candles. Adrenaline shot through me as the cloud formed into the shape of a human, and, within a breath, I was staring into glowing tawny eyes.

I searched myself for fear, but found none. Searched myself for alarm, dread, panic, but instead I discovered understanding, a knowing, and this weird sensation of grace.

"I know you," I said.

She was a woman with flawless skin the color of golden-brown topaz. She had long black hair in tight curls that hung to the middle of her back, and she wore a form-fitting blue dress that touched the tops of her bare feet. She regarded me as I regarded her. "Of course you know me."

"How? We've never met."

"I've been watching over you since you were God-breathed into a new soul. As I explained to you, I am."

"Are you my grimoire?" I asked.

"I am *the* grimoire. I belong to everyone and no one."

I circled her and she matched me step by step. "Are you a person or a book?"

"I am."

"Do you always answer in riddles?"

"My answers are not riddles. I am bigger than a question or an answer."

"If you are not my grimoire, why did you find me? Why did you follow me?"

"I am everyone's grimoire. I belong to you as much as I belong to everyone else, and that is why I am also not yours. As for why I am here, you called for me. I will help you refine your powers so you can protect the babe."

I came to a halt. "Shouldn't we find the baby before we worry about me protecting her?"

"She did not choose you because you have the power to find her, though that is helpful. She chose you because you contain within you the power to protect her."

"The Fae will protect her." It was clear Orion, Mercutio,

and Shaw would give their lives for the baby. "I'm here so I can help them find her."

"She has chosen you, and when you refused the portal, you chose her, as well. There will be no more questions and I will give no more answers." It wasn't like any of her answers made sense. "First, you will need to learn how to mask the connection between you and your Fae. He can track you through it."

I contemplated that. "He said the room is dangerous, and it appears it is. He came for me the last time I entered." I glanced at the tornado eyes still glowering.

"The items and beings in here are dangerous, especially in the presence of the untrained."

I wanted to ask if she were dangerous, but instead smashed my lips together. The grimoire gave me an approving smile. "You have always been a fast learner. Come, open the book. Let your instincts guide you and you will find the exact enchantment you need to mask yourself when I call on you to visit me next."

"You mean snap the connection Orion told me exists between me and him?"

"Snapping the thread will alert him something wrong has occurred, and it will cause him great pain. He will be compelled to leave wherever he is to search for you. That is not what we need. Instead, we will create a false connection that will exist long enough for him to believe you are safe. I do not like lingering among the Fae. The next time we meet, it will be away from here and I cannot allow your Fae to follow you to me."

Sounded like she understood Fae much better than I did, so I was all in. "Let's get started." A surge of warm light raced through me as I flipped through the pages and permitted my heart to guide me to what I needed to learn.

CHAPTER 16

*W*hen I woke the next morning, Orion knew. The moment I walked into the kitchen where he, Mercutio, and Shaw were camped out searching for castles near water, which narrowed it down to the thousands, Orion's head popped up. The smile on his face faded, not as if he were upset, but as if he were curious. His eyes narrowed slightly as his gaze studied not really me as much as the air surrounding me. He didn't say anything, not immediately. Orion stood, asked me if I wanted eggs, and I accepted. I then said good morning to Shaw and Mercutio, they said a good morning back, and when I went to the corner of the kitchen to grab a cup of coffee, Orion came up behind me, placed a hand on my back and whispered seductively into my ear, "You've been using magic. Complicated magic."

It was hard to not meet his eyes, even more difficult to pour coffee into the mug without my hands shaking. "I haven't."

Orion smirked, edged in closer, and his hot breath tickled my skin. Pleasing goosebumps formed on my body, and whatever walls he had in his mind disappeared. I was swept away with a tidal wave of desire and leaned into him as his fingers glided along the curve of my waist. Orion skimmed his nose along my neck, and as he turned his head so that our lips were a breath's distant apart, he whispered, "Liar." And immediately the walls went back up. I blinked as the haze of lust moved from irresistible to slightly controllably.

He winked at me as he moved away, and I felt suddenly cold after being completely enthralled in his warmth.

Liar.

I sighed heavily at myself. I was a liar and had forgotten his stupid Fae power to smell out such falsehoods. I was also probably radiating some stupid magical force field Orion could spot. Sort of like this invisible bond between us anyone else in the room, but me, could see. I also sighed because, right now, I wanted Orion. More than I wanted this cup of coffee and I really loved coffee. More than I wanted air or food or to sleep again. Part of me hoped Orion would drop his guard again just so I would have a justifiable excuse to end up in his bed.

Liar.

But this time that was an admonishment to myself. *All* of me wanted to be in his bed, not just part. Question was— could I live with myself after? Especially when he would leave me again. Especially when I couldn't trust him. Especially when he had hurt me so.

From then on, we searched for the castle and for the baby. Day turned into night, night back into day, and we were running out of time. We'd find castles online that possibly matched the vision. Orion, who had seen the vision through Relle, shared it with Shaw and Mercutio, and then the boys would disappear to visit and later reappear shaking their heads.

As I had been countless times over the last two days, I was

currently in the ocean, deep within, holding my breath for as long as I could and hoping for a connection with the baby. My lungs and throat burned and, unable to keep the air in any longer, against my will, little bubbles of air left my mouth. What was frightening was the draw in of water. I hadn't meant for that to happen. I choked, panicked as water continued to flow into my body, and was yanked up to the surface by a strong hand.

Orion treaded water as I coughed uncontrollably. His eyes were almost black with concern, anger, and pure fury. "You can't keep doing this to yourself, and you sure as hell aren't going to do this alone again. You could have drowned."

I had been alone and was shocked to see Orion with me, happy, but shocked. I wanted to ask how he knew where I was when he was supposed to be halfway around the world in Ireland checking out a castle, how he knew this attempt was going wrong, but couldn't as I continued to cough. Odds were, it was the connection between us. Finally, I could breathe without hacking up a lung and attempted to tread water on my own. But exhausted, I went under again. Orion grabbed me and held me close as he swam for both of us.

"This is maddening," I said. "How do you do this all the time and still stay sane?"

"Usually visions have more details," Orion answered. "There's a reason why the Council didn't pass this vision on to us. It's an unsolvable maze."

Close to two days without substantial sleep, my muscles were heavy, my vision doubling. I rubbed my eyes, then raked my hands through my wet hair. Behind Orion, the sun was setting. We were running out of time. In a few hours, the demons would find the mother and the baby. "Give me a second to catch my breath, and I'll go under again."

Orion smashed his lips together. "You go under again, you'll drown. You're exhausted."

"You'll keep me from drowning."

"This is ridiculous."

I slapped my hands against the water. "Ridiculous? Any more ridiculous than the three of you jumping from castle to castle, going through hundreds of them when there are thousands in the hopes you find the right one?"

"We'll find her," Orion said calmly. "I believe in this. I need you to believe in this, too."

Did I believe? Would doing so mean I needed to believe in him? In us? Without waiting for a response from me, he swam us to shore. Weak from being in the ocean for thirty minutes straight, weak from doing this more than I could count over the last two days, just pure exhaustion from being completely enthralled in this search, my legs were jelly when we hit the sand. When I faltered, Orion swept me up into his arms and carried me. He sat me on the towel laid out on the sand, and I had to fight the burning tears threatening to fall. I couldn't fail this baby, and I was on the verge of doing just that. "What do we do?"

Orion wrapped a dry towel around my shoulders and crouched next to me. "We'll continue to hunt for castles to see if they match Relle's vision. She'll let us know if she sees anything else."

I rolled my neck as I sighed heavily. "Put me to sleep again and wake me as soon as I finish REM." Not that sleeping had connected me with the baby either.

"You need to sleep longer," Orion said.

"I can go into the ocean again."

Orion placed his hand over my eyes and murmured, "Sleep."

～

IT WAS A LOT LIKE WAKING, yet not. More of a dawning of

consciousness. The world was dark, not a hint of light, but there was movement. A swaying from side to side that was like being rocked to sleep by my grandmother. There were faint voices. A woman. A man. A contentment at the sound of their familiar voices chatting along to one another. There was an undercurrent of recognizable anxiety I had felt before…The breath caught in my lungs with the realization. The baby. I was connected with the baby. *Are you okay?*

Delighted with hearing my voice, she perked up. The baby was safe.

Where are you?

She went still, and that made my heart stall with fear. She was unusually quiet and calm. As I was about to ask another question, I heard it. The muffled voices. Specifically, a higher pitched voice, a female voice. I mentally nodded as I understood. The baby wanted me to listen. I couldn't catch all the conversation, just a few snatches of distorted words.

"…dinner." Her mother was eating or had eaten dinner. "…loved…walk…water."

Water.

Something about "too bad" it was "so late." "ferry… castle…heart…."

An electrical zap raced through me. I needed to wake up. I needed to wake up now!

My eyes flashed open, I woke with a gasp and sat up immediately. I was back in the boys' living room, and Shaw, Mercutio and Orion turned and looked at me from where I'd been asleep on the couch. "I found her. Relle's original vision had it correct. The baby is in New York."

CHAPTER 17

inished tying my sneakers, I stood with the air of someone about to go into battle. From the kitchen, Orion's jaw ticked as he surveyed me then he went back to discussing a plan with Shaw and Mercutio. It didn't take a rocket scientist to see he was angry, and I wanted to know why. I reached out and tried to mentally wade through the fuzziness to test his emotions, but he shoved me out before I even got near the periphery.

I'd been asleep for an hour and a half, and we were running out of time. Doubt sloshed around inside me. What if I was wrong about this? What if Boldt Castle wasn't where the mother and the baby were located? What if she were someplace else? What if I made the wrong call and that meant they were going to die?

At the table, the boys studied a map of the small town of Alexandria Bay that sat across from Boldt Castle on Heart Island. "Shaw," Orion said, "scan the castle and the grounds just in case. Cassie's right, it's closed for the night, but I want to make sure the mother didn't somehow manage to go there. Mercutio, I want you to do a perimeter check around the town."

"What do we do if we find them?" Mercutio asked.

"If they're Fae, I approach. The mother will go with us then. If she's human, I'll need a fast car and we need to do a grab and go. We drive until we can get to a secure location to bring her to Fairy."

"A grab and go?" I called from the living room. "That will scare her to death. And there was a man with her. What if he's the father? We just kidnap his wife and child in front of him?"

"We have demons breathing down our necks. I can't risk them snatching the mother first. If that is the father, we will make plans for him...later."

"Let me talk to the mother first," I said from the kitchen entrance. "The baby will recognize me. Maybe the mother will, too."

Orion exchanged a short glance with Shaw and Mercutio. "You aren't going. Once we have the mother safely in Fairy, I'll bring you to her."

I crossed the room and stood tall in front of Orion. "I did not turn from heaven so I could sit on the sidelines."

He straightened to his full height and towered over me. "And I didn't give you my blood to watch you die again. I've done it twice now, and I don't have it in me to do it a third time. You'll stay here, I'll save the mother and the baby, and I'll bring you to them."

"Brilliant plan. So, what happens when you magically appear in Alex Bay and grab the first pregnant mother you see? What if you bring me to her and I tell you that you took the wrong woman? Because there are more pregnant woman in the world than just the mother we're searching for. Last I heard, you can only tell if the baby is your queen if she's been born."

Orion's jaw ticked with anger, but he remained silent. Mercutio, on the other hand said, "She has a good point."

"If it turns messy, Mercutio and I will take care of Cassie," Shaw said to Orion. "We have your back." Mercutio nodded as if in agreement.

Orion scrubbed his hands over his face and tilted his head in some sort of nonverbal agreement. In a blink, Shaw and Mercutio vanished. Orion, the mighty warrior, leaned forward and rested his elbows on the back of a chair. "We'll have to shift again." With just a mere mention of the word, the hundreds of tiny cuts on my arms glowed to life and then faded back into my skin. "I'll keep you safe, but if things go bad, I won't be able to get you out quickly. I'll need you to do what I say, as I say it. My instinct and urge will be to protect you, but…." Orion's face contorted as if he were struggling to finish the sentence.

"You're to save the mother and the baby," I said for him. "They're the priority. That's why I need to go. I can help you locate them. I'm not important. They are. Don't worry about me. I'll be fine."

His dark eyes softened as he looked at me. "You are the most important being in my world, Cass. I'll move heaven and hell for you in a heartbeat, and it's hard for me to put you in a position of danger knowing you can't be my first priority."

Emotion exploded out of him and into me, like the energy of a sun flare barreling toward the earth. He was torn, angry, concerned, grieving and apprehensive. But just as fast as it happened, he drew the emotion back, so quickly that it created a whiplash effect and I had to reach out to the table to stay upright.

Orion offered me his hand. "You ready?"

As I placed my fingers in his, my heart skipped a beat. At the missed intimacy of his strong touch, with the fear of "shifting" again with the memory of the pain of last time still fresh.

"It's okay," Orion said as if he could sense my fear. "This time, I will be able to keep you safe." He kept his eyes locked on mine, and his hypnotizing gaze warmed me from the inside out. "Keep looking at me. Nowhere else. Just on me."

As he laced our fingers together, he drew me into him. My breasts pressed flush to his chest, my legs tangling with his, and my eyes closed as a delicious tension weaved between us, making me feel as if we were once again one flesh, one body, just one. Moving in unison to our own personalized rhythm that created universes, where stars would be born and die upon our will.

Orion leaned down and his breath tickled the sensitive spot behind my ear as he whispered, "Eyes on me."

I opened them, met his gaze, and the warmth surrounding me expanded into a glowing bubble of light with us as the center. His fingers began a slow caress along my spine, a brush of his fingertips that I felt to the tip of my toes. Slowly his fingers climbed along my back, between my shoulder blades, onto my neck and there he traced the crescent scar, sending pleasurable shivers along my skin. My breathing hitched when Orion tucked a wayward strand of my hair behind my ear and then skimmed his fingers along my cheek.

My heart rate increased, as did this need to touch Orion. I raised both of my hands to his chest, and Orion responded by pressing me tighter to him. He cupped my face with his hand, his thumb stroking my skin, and the pull was magnetic. I licked my lips, and his eyes narrowed in and tracked the movement. Desire smoldering in his gaze.

His mind opened, and I sucked in a breath. The rush of his hunger for me created a liquid heat that spread swiftly through my veins, and in a passionate fervor, his memories touched my mind. A snapshot of us laughing, of the first time he took my hand in his, of my shy smile as I proudly walked next to him on the boardwalk with our joined hands connecting us. Of the way my body felt against his the first time we hugged, of the way I lifted my head, and he captured the moment to kiss me. His lips crushing down on mine, and I opened myself up to him.

I was drowning in the growing intensity, of his love, his devotion, his need, his lust, his desire. As the glow surrounding us brightened, I needed him. Wanted him, and I was tired of fighting the attraction. I pushed off my toes, wrapped my arms around his neck, and Orion leaned down. Our lips met, and it was magic. My cells sparked to life, and I was lost in the explosion. Our mouths parted, our tongues danced, and I couldn't get enough. Orion was everywhere, kissing me, touching me, his memories causing me to relive the first time he had slipped off my shirt, the first time I had kissed along his chest, the first time he….

Orion broke off the kiss, and the cooler night air was a like a slap in the face as the warm bubble surrounding us faded. He gazed down upon me as if I were the brightest star in the universe, and I searched his face, unable to understand the two million conflicting emotions waging war within me. I kissed him. He kissed me. What did that mean? If anything? With one tight squeeze of me to him, Orion released me and took a step back. "We're here."

Here. I wildly glanced around and breathed out to calm my pounding heart. Here. Alexandria Bay. Alex Bay. The St. Lawrence River. A place not too far from home, and a place I had visited with Killian to watch an outdoor concert. A place that represented my old life. My normal life. A life that was once safe and routine.

The spring evening was cooler than South Carolina, but unusually warm for being so far north. Alex Bay was small, even by small standards, but still not as small as my town. The main street was made up of late nineteenth-century stone and brick buildings stacked next to the other with a business on the first floor and the second for apartments. The neon signs of the nineteen fifties still hung outside of the restaurants and bars, and most of them still worked. Thankfully, it was off season, a weeknight, and the streets were relatively empty.

Mercutio and Shaw appeared next to us and reported to Orion that both the castle, Heart Island, and the periphery of the village were clear. I knew I should be listening, but I couldn't. As they talked about how to split up, their voices died out as did the music flowing from a nearby bar. There was a tug, a feeling that made me a puppet, putting one foot in front of the other regardless of conscious thought. It was the sensation of being dragged by the soul, and I didn't fight the inclination. I followed.

"Cassie," Orion called, but his voice was too distant to reach me. "Cassie," he said again, but this time he was in front of me. His hands landing on my shoulders to stop my forward motion. His concerned eyes flickered about my face. "What are you doing?"

I shook my head, as I didn't know—but at the same time, I somehow did. "The baby," I said slowly, and then my eyes widened with the words. The baby. The baby had to be the pull. As if coming to the same conclusion, Orion stepped out of the way. Super focused, I kept going, and Orion twice had to place a hand on my arm to keep me from walking off the curb and in front of a car.

Are you there? I reached out to the baby telepathically. *Are you near?*

A stirring in the back of my mind, and I stopped dead in my tracks. It was her, and it was…recognition. "She's near enough I can contact her with telepathy."

"Good." Orion had a glint of encouragement in his eyes. "Keep going. Find her for us."

As the enticing draw grew stronger, my eyes narrowed, as if I could see beyond the trees across the street. But that stirring in the back of my mind flashed with a warning. My head swam, and I winced as the warning became pain. I doubled over with a dry heave. Orion drew nearer. "What's wrong?"

"There's anger," I gasped out as I grabbed my stomach.

"From where?" Orion demanded.

When my vision cleared, I found myself staring into a pair of eyes from a person across the street. It was just a woman in a pink spring sweater and a pair of pressed dress pants. Blond hair, petite frame, red eyes. The entire whites eaten away by the bloody void. The woman bizarrely tilted her head. All the way to the side as if the neck were broke. I stumbled back, and Orion caught me before I rammed into the window of a closed shop.

"What is that?" I whispered at the same exact time Orion shoved me behind him.

"Shaw, Mercutio," Orion's voice dripped with venom, "we have scouts."

Shaw appeared behind the woman, a golden dagger in his hand, and in a swift motion, he grabbed her and the two of them disappeared in a swirl of smoke. My heart lurched, I stepped forward to find them, but Orion yelled, "Move," as he pushed me away.

Another person with red eyes. He leapt for Orion, both hands outstretched as if going for his throat. The air shimmered, Mercutio emerged and produced a dagger of his own. When he grabbed hold of the man, the two of them disappeared. A scream crawled up my throat, but before I could release it, Orion took me by the shoulders. "Cassie, we have to find the mother."

A freezing cold wind blew down the street, causing the

trees to sway, and there was a screaming in my ears that ended with the explosion of a bright, blasting light. In the silence, a towering man appeared. He was beautiful, with brilliant blond hair and a sharp angular face. His muscles bulged beyond his black T-shirt, and his mere presence radiated violence.

With a flick of a wrist, Orion produced a long, golden sword and placed himself between me and this danger.

"Slow your roll, Orion." Appearing annoyed, the man crossed his arms over chest. "I'm here to share a message."

Orion twirled the sword in his hand but kept it in front of him, as if readying for the attack. "What is it, Moloch?"

The right side of Moloch's mouth twitched up in amusement. "Can you believe they were going to send someone else to visit you? But I insisted that I be the one. I knew you'd be happy to see me."

Orion appeared lazy, but I could sense a furious tiger crouching in wait. "Did you have a good trip?" Orion asked with a taunt.

Something dark flashed over Moloch that caused me to take a step back. His diamond cutter blue eyes snapped to me, and the moment our gazes connected, it was as if someone had struck a tuning fork within my soul. Chills went down my spine, and I had to work to stay still. He nodded his chin in greeting. "Witch."

"Don't talk to her," Orion said. "Keep it between us."

"That's just it," Moloch said. "It's not between us. The message is for her."

He's here for me? I whispered into Orion's mind. *Not the baby? Does this mean the baby is safe?*

Orion raised his sword. "Leave now, Moloch. You have no message she needs to hear."

Moloch shrugged a shoulder. "Fine with me. I was told to

keep it short and civil, but I have no problem killing you first and then giving her the message."

"No." I stepped forward, but Orion threw back his hand and a gravitational force prevented my forward progress. "Just tell me and leave."

"See, Orion?" Moloch waggled his eyebrows at him. "She wants to hear." Then not waiting for Orion's response, Moloch continued, "I've been instructed to tell you that you belong with us. Not the Fae. I'm assuming they fed you the 'we're the good guys and they're the bad guys' bull. Nothing is all good and nothing is all bad. Only the Fae deal in absolutes. We deal in reality. Whatever Orion or the other Fae have said to you for you to follow them is a lie. Think of human fairy tales. Fae are the great liars. Their greedy bastards like that."

Unfortunately, I couldn't argue.

"I didn't realize you were the poster child for truth," Orion countered.

"Truth depends on the point of view, and I believe the witch will like our truth more than she'll like yours."

"You don't know me to make that judgement," I said.

"Guess I don't, but when you awoke as a witch, I broke what I was told were unbreakable chains. Your power freed me." He gave me a wink then a smug smirk to Orion. "I heard you reached her mere minutes after she used her power for the first time. Mere minutes. What did it feel like to have completed the ultimate failure, Orion? To have, in theory, sentenced me to an eternity chained to the lake of fire only for this witch to release me upon her birth of power?"

Bile sloshed around in my stomach. "I didn't awaken anyone."

"No matter what the Fae tell you, you aren't safe with them," Moloch said to me. "Even as we speak, they plot your death."

"Leave before I end you for good," Orion said calmly, as if he hadn't threatened death.

"Witch, you can either come with me of your free will and learn the real truth," Moloch said, "or I'll take you against your will once I kill Orion. Your choice."

The static in Orion's brain lifted. His heartbeat reverberated through my soul, my heartbeat responded in kind, and then they synchronized into one. Orion turned his head just enough to look at me. Our combined hearts squeezed together, like a hug. It was as if he was pouring all his devotion into me, and I blinked as Orion became an open book, the easiest read. He was resolute, and the words in his head were clear, *Find the baby.*

Moloch waved his hand and a silver sword was in his grip, accompanied by the sound of thunder booming overhead. He swung the blade toward Orion's head. As I stepped to shove Orion out of the way, Orion pushed me back again with the force that came from his hand and lightning crashed to the earth as metal hit metal. In a blur of speed, the swords of Orion and Moloch struck one another again, a sound wave bursting from the impact. I closed my eyes against the fallout, and when I opened them, the breath caught in my throat. They were gone. Both of them gone.

I wildly turned in a circle and I was alone. Completely and utterly alone.

The baby. I needed to find the baby.

Adrenaline raged through me as I reached out to her. *Where are you?* Even if the demons came here for me, I didn't want her anywhere near them. *I need you to get somewhere safe.*

A wave of concern washed over me, and I felt the baby being jostled. The baby was silent, but as I concentrated hard to listen through the muffled sound, I could pick out her mother's voice: "Need...to...go."

The screaming returned, growing louder, a terrible noise,

scratching and clawing against metal. The screeching pierced my eardrum, and I slapped my hands over my ears. My skin prickled as fear was injected into me, and the shadows of the night became darker. Misty forms appeared in the growing gloom, and they reached out toward me with long-fingered, bony hands. I stumbled backwards and ran into something hard, something cold. Sour breath assaulted the back of neck and a dry heave raced up my throat. The stench of tobacco and decay was all too horrifyingly familiar, along with the deep, slow chuckle that in my past had meant pain, too much mental and physical pain. He'd found me. My mother's boyfriend had found me again.

From behind me, a hand wrapped around my throat, but I wasn't doing this again. I wasn't going to let him win. I wasn't a child. I wasn't a weak teenage girl. I was strong, and I would rather have us both die then to have him touch me again.

I placed my hands over his and screamed toward the sky. Another gust of wind, but this one warm, and the building next to us rattled with the hurricane-force gale. Then there was the roaring of thunder. The air on my arms rose with the static electricity gathering in the air, and the arm that seconds before was trying to choke me was now trying to break free from my grasp. The more he pulled away, the more I held on, until I felt the frenzy of the electricity build to a climax. I let go, screamed again, and lightning struck right behind me. The current of the energy burned my back, propelled me into the air, and as I hit the pavement, the last thought I had was a desperate cry to the baby, *Run.*

CHAPTER 18

My head pounded. An internal banging on the inside of my skull. My hands went to my temples, my fingers rubbing my scalp, but none of that helped. I need Tylenol and a CT scan. Odds were, I had a concussion and I should be mentally evaluated. What was I doing? Why couldn't I have just gone into the portal of heaven? Why was I so obsessed with this baby?

"Because she's a part of you."

My body jolted with the familiar female voice. I sat straight up as my eyes snapped open and the air left my body. I wasn't in Alex Bay. I wasn't at Orion's mansion in South Carolina. I was nowhere. Everywhere. The middle of a green, lush forest. A prairie to the north. The ocean far off to the east. The mountains to the west. The desert to the south.

The grimoire the book was next to me, and next to the book was the grimoire the woman. In a long, blue summer dress made of sheer fabric, she looked as if she were relaxing at a picnic with her knees folded to the side. I was anything but relaxed and shook from the adrenaline coursing through my body. "My mother's boyfriend—"

"Was never there," the grimoire cut me off. "That was a phobos. A demon who paralyzes you by using your fear."

A million questions sprang to my mind, but there was only one who mattered, "Is the baby okay?"

"Thanks to your warning to her, yes, she is safe."

Through the massive migraine of a headache, I perked up. "The Fae found her?"

"No and neither did the demons. She convinced her mother to flee and they escaped."

I rubbed my head again. I was experiencing delusions. It was the only sane explanation. "How can a baby in the womb make her mother do anything?" Even though I was the one who sent the warning.

The grimoire gave an impish grin. "The baby is strong, tenacious, convincing, and not like other babies."

She could say that again. "If the baby can do all that, can I give her directions as to where we can meet up? She can choose. A Target? Panera? Maybe a local park?"

The grimoire gave a small laugh. "That's not how it works."

No, not much worked in my favor. "So, we failed."

"Tonight was not a failure. The mother is still unknown to the dangerous demons."

"And the Fae," I added.

"The baby is currently safe, which means you are fulfilling your role in the Great Plan. Now, let your Fae take you home, get some rest, and continue on your path."

My eyebrows pulled together with confusion, which didn't help the headache. "What?"

Movement of my hair, a hand gently pushing back the strands. A blink and the forest disappeared. Another blink and Orion was holding me in his arms. We were next to water, the cool evening air biting at my skin, and beyond Orion was the castle. "Cassie, are you okay?"

"Yes." No. My mouth was dry, the pain in my head worse than in the forest, which I didn't know was possible. "The baby's safe." It was hard to keep my eyes open, and I probably should have requested that CT, but then if I went to the hospital the mobs would find me in their new witch database. At the moment, I wasn't in the mood to be burned at the stake.

"How do you know?" he asked calmly, but I could tell he desperately wanted the answer.

"I do. She fled and is safe." I went to sigh and instead groaned with the headache. What did I hit my head on? A tractor trailing going ninety miles per hour? "What happened to Moloch?"

"He's gone," Orion said with finality.

"What he said," each word was a struggle against the pain, "about belonging with them. What did he mean?"

"Some witches choose to work with the Fae. Some with the demons. He was wrong. You belong with me."

"What did he mean that I freed him?"

"I don't know." Orion brushed my hair from my face again. "I don't know."

Before I could ask anything else, the warm bubble appeared around us again. He was silent, his hold on me tight, and I was just as tired and confused as the first time I shifted with Orion. I'd worry about everything tomorrow. Tonight, with the mother safe, I was going to rest.

CHAPTER 19

"*H*ow have you never had a corn dog?" I asked with a great seriousness Orion found deeply amusing.

He was wearing his wicked grin while he gingerly poked at the corn dog. "The question you should be asking is why would anyone want one?"

"Because they're delicious." We were on the main strip, standing at a high table, and two corn dogs lay in a paper bowl between us. I had the day shift at the restaurant, and after I'd gotten off work, Orion was waiting for me, leaning on his motorcycle, looking exactly like a royal prince of a motorcycle club—if such a title existed. He had been gone for a week for work for his family, and my heart galloped at the sight of him.

He had helped me onto his bike, I had cuddled close to him, and he had driven us to his penthouse. I had taken a shower, and before I could even have a chance to find my clothes in his closet, Orion had swept me into his arms and carried me to his bed. Needless to say, it took longer than I had expected to dress.

"Don't play with your food," I said. "And don't be a baby. Just try it."

He chuckled and the sound warmed me. "Did you call me a baby?"

"Yes. Try the corn dog."

I was on my toes, giddy with anticipation, willing him to enjoy it, for him to be the slightest bit like me. The divide between us was too great. Me: poor, him: rich. Me: uncultured, him: extremely sophisticated, even with his threatening motorcycle club vibes. Me: boring, him: mysterious and dangerous.

Behind us, gravity pulled the roller coaster over the tallest hill and the thrilled screams of the riders filled the air. People meandered along the boardwalk and couples held hands. Laughter and the bells and whistles of the carnival games provided the background music for the evening.

Orion followed my lead, dipped the corn dog in the ketchup, took a bite, chewed and his eyebrows raised like he was happily shocked. The smile on my face grew—Orion liked the corn dog. "It's good," he conceded as he took another bite.

"It's awesome," I corrected.

His eyes gleamed as though he agreed, but he wasn't going to grant me the gratification of acknowledging it. We finished the treat I had spent my hard-earned money on, a feat difficult to undertake when he was determined to pay for everything, and I was skipping on air. Orion wrapped an arm around my shoulder as we perused the busy seaside town. Within the shelter of his body, I felt wanted, loved and liked I belonged.

At the pavilion overlooking the ocean, a band played on stage and Orion steered me toward the middle of the dancing crowd. The song was slow, and as I laid my head on his shoulder, he gathered me near as if he could make me a part of his flesh. We swayed with the music, losing ourselves in the melody. He lowered his head and softly sang the lyrics in my ear.

I soaked up the lyrics as if they were a gentle rain and I were parched land, and I prayed each mention of love was meant for me. He hadn't said he loved me, but I had fallen for him. The song ended, and we stopped rocking, but he kept me close. "Walk the beach with me?" he asked.

"Yes." To absolutely anything he requested.

Out of the corner of my eye, there was a fluctuation, a hazy cloud that swirled like it didn't quite know how to fit in with the rest of the puzzle. Orion's arms squeezed snugly around me, as if he were attempting to gain my attention. I lifted my head from his shoulder. "This is a dream."

Orion rested his forehead to mine. "It is."

"This is the night you told me you were Fae."

"It is." When Orion shared his secret with me, I felt special. High that he trusted me with information that would cause him problems with other humans. He trusted me, and trust was a step toward love.

With his mouth near, my blood buzzed, and I licked my suddenly dry lips. "You're in my dream again?"

"It's time to wake, but I didn't want to scare you by walking into the room."

Because sometimes, doing so could make me scream in fright. After my grandmother disappeared and the police had found me living on my own, the state sent me to live with my mom and her boyfriend. He'd burst into the room I slept in, dragged me out of the bedroom and…I quaked with the following memories.

An ominous cloud in the corner of the pavilion began to grow. There were whispers from it, a coldness that nipped at my skin like frostbite. I squinted as the cloud took the shape of a face. I recognized that chin, that forehead, those eyes…a violent dry heave raced up my throat. My mother's boyfriend appeared, and he glared at me as he weaved through the outskirt of couples dancing. Hatred in his eyes, a sneer, and a promise of what was to come when we were alone. I faltered.

Orion placed his hands on either side of my face, forced my gaze from the monster, and reassuringly brushed his thumbs across my cheeks. "Don't allow the demons of your past to enter this dream, into this memory. Focus only on the joy that was us."

He kissed my forehead, and I woke with a start. My pulse drummed in my ears, and my body tingled from his touch. The pressure of his lips on my forehead was still fresh. I scanned the suite in Orion's wing of the house. The room was empty. The door to the terrace still opened, the breeze blowing in. I didn't like confined spaces and preferred for a window to be cracked, a door to be open, to know there was a way out if I were in danger. With the memories of my mother's boyfriend fresh, I shivered. The things he did to me at night, how he would lock me in confined spaces, leaving me in the dark….

"Orion?" I said aloud, and my voice trembled as I clutched the blanket. *Orion?* I sent telepathically. My mother's boyfriend wasn't here. I ran far from him. Multiple times. So many I lost count. The system kept finding me, and each time, they would place me with him and my mother instead of a foster home. Each time, I would run again. But at eighteen, I left for good. It had been years since the last time I'd seen him, but he still haunted me.

"You're safe here, Cass." Orion appeared at the terrace door. Was I? To be honest, I wasn't sure. "I'm sorry to wake you so early," he continued, "but the Council wants to meet with you to discuss the baby. My mother said she left a dress for you. When you're ready, meet me on the terrace."

~

How did one prepare to meet a Fae Council? Make-up? No make-up? Hair up? Hair down? I had absolutely no idea. I slipped on the white, lace sundress. It had spaghetti straps and fit me like a glove, and when I walked the dress gave the impression I was floating. With the stunning simplicity of the dress, I decided to leave my hair long, no style or hair-spray, and absolutely no make-up. Here was the thing about entering the lion's den: it was best not to do anything to draw the beast's attention.

I brushed my hair, smoothed wayward strands, slid the clasp of my necklace that held the small gold cross to the back of my neck, inhaled deeply, and left the bathroom. Orion was outside, staring out onto the ocean, and my nerves lessened as my breaths automatically matched his. He was wearing black pants and a black button-down shirt that was left open. The tails blew about with the breeze.

"What time is it?" I asked.

"Just before dawn." Orion's eyes widened as if in rever-ence. "You're beautiful."

"I'm a mess."

In that lazy, unhurried way of his, he moved toward me and offered his extended hand. "You're beautiful," he said gently, softly, slowly.

Missing his touch, yearning for it, I laid my hand in his and briefly closed my eyes, thrilled by the warm, tingling electricity that shot through me with the contact. Orion's thumb caressed the top of my hand, and my heart ached with the tender sight of our entwined fingers. His sculpted muscles were exposed, and I blushed with memories. I used to skim my nails along those muscles, trace the indentations, and kiss along his skin.

I wanted Orion, and from the way his dark eyes smoldered, he wanted me, as well. What was unexpected was how much I emotionally missed this. How just his hand holding mine mended broken pieces. Stripped away of the animosity of his lying to me about his death, at my rawest, what I desired most was this moment—this touch.

"Come." Orion led me to the edge of the terrace. With my hand still in his, we followed an aging wooden path up and over the dunes. The beach was cool beneath my feet, and I hadn't realized how much I had missed the sand between my toes. We walked to the water's edge, to the spot where the waves were on the verge of lapping over my feet.

"Fairy is of this world, but not." Orion said as he regarded the ocean. "As is hell and the spiritual realm where we wage war with our enemies."

Great—more chaos thrown into the unknown. "What does that mean?"

"Think of it as dimensions. Other worlds existing among us, but unseen." He paused, as if waiting for my inquiries, but I was questioned out.

"I got it. The world is weird. Up is down. Down is up. The sky beneath my feet, the ground above my head. The clouds are green, the grass blue. Life is never going to be the same. I'm as caught up as I'm going to be."

His eyes twinkled as if he found me amusing, but he kept the sober expression. "Since the dawn of time, humans told stories of Fae because they caught sight of us in the liminal."

That I definitely didn't understand. "The liminal?"

"Liminal means threshold—an entrance and an exit. The sill of a window, the door of a house, the place of entering or beginning. A place that neither is nor isn't."

Like my relationship with Orion. We neither were nor weren't. As if he'd read my thoughts, his thumb stroked the top of my hand.

"We use glamour to create our earthly image. In the

liminal, humans can see us as we really are. It is in the liminal the walls between our realm and your world are the thinnest, and it is through the liminal I will take you into our world to meet the Fae Council. Humans can only enter our world as long as they are accompanied by a willing Fae."

Interesting. "The tabloid stories of people disappearing to Fairy and returning years later are true?"

"They are called fairytales."

I overly rolled my eyes. "Leave the bad jokes to Mercutio."

He chuckled, and I allowed myself to smile. "Where is this liminal?"

"Everywhere," Orion said. "It is the in-between. The stronger the liminal force, the easier it is to see Fae and to enter our world. The edge between the forest and the grasslands, the opening between the ground and a cave, the hills between the mountains and plain, where a great river meets the sea, the mysterious place between low and high tides, and more importantly, daybreak and dusk. The dawn and twilight of life is the closest our world is to yours."

The clouds on the horizon glowed pink with the dawn. We were on the verge of the liminal. Orion released my hand. "Are you ready to see me for what I am?"

It was a slicing inquiry. I had believed when we were together that I did know him, all of him, and I forced myself to nod. Orion slipped the shirt from his arms, allowed it to fall to the sand, and stepped into the water that was neither high tide nor low. The great in-between.

With the backdrop of the exquisite reds and pinks of morning, Orion turned to face me, and I yelped. As the sun rose, Orion stretched great beautiful wings from his shoulder blades. Thousands of splendid, glittering gold feathers fluttered with the breeze. Already tall, Orion became taller, his muscles thicker, his beauty so blinding it was hard not to sob. He was glorious and terrifying, and in his presence, I was unable to breathe.

Like he did on the terrace, Orion extended his hand to me. "Come, Cassie."

I was frozen, as a fight ensued between my instinct to survive telling me to run and my soul begging me to follow.

"It's the same action as when you joined me on the terrace. A few steps forward and placing your hand in mine."

Was it the same? Because this felt ferociously different, severely more dangerous. At the same time, there was a call in my blood pulling me toward the sunrise and Orion. A siren song as beautiful as the mist settling into the valleys in the mornings at my home in the mountains. Orion's offered hand created within me a swirl of adventure, the longing of passionate risk, the same wild freedom as being on the back of his motorcycle at nineteen.

My entire body trembled in fear and awe as I lifted one foot, then another. Through the sand shifting beneath my feet with the tide, I reached out, and when my fingers touched Orion's there was a flash of light, the warmth of the sun hugging me close, and the tickling of feathers on my skin as his wings folded around me. As the brightness faded and Orion withdrew his wings, I gasped at the world around me. This wasn't the beach, not South Carolina, no longer the earth. This had to be heaven.

CHAPTER 20

a great waterfall spilled over a mountain, higher than skyscrapers, wider than Victoria Falls. A curtain of sparkling blue water with white foam cascading from rock ledge to rock ledge. The magnificent garden surrounding me stole the air from my chest. Green-leaved, towering trees mixed in with smaller ones producing every fruit imaginable —apples, peaches, pineapples, and pears. There were vines, vegetable plants, bushes full of berries, and multiple types of blooming flowers that created a sweet fragrance. A breeze blew through the garden and the leaves made the tinkling sound of wind chimes.

Above me, there were countless stars and comets streaking across the cosmos with their long icy tails. The sun was in the east, the full moon in the west, the light upon the surface just bright enough, but not blinding, and that light touched my skin like a warm hug. Everything was in sync, was beautiful, and was how the world should have been from the beginning until the end.

"This is heaven?" I whispered, terrified the sound of my

voice in such a perfect place would be too harsh and would shatter this resplendent reality.

"No," Orion answered in a normal tone. "This is my home. Heaven, from what I understand, is far more beautiful."

"Impossible." Maybe it wasn't. While this aesthetic beauty nearly cracked my mind, it didn't have the same overpowering sense of peace the portal held. "Why would you leave?"

"It's our punishment for participating in the fall. We aren't allowed to linger here long. Eventually, we can choose to return to Earth on our own or the realm will thrust us out. God allows us peace and rest, but we're constantly reminded why we exist—to protect humans."

As the beauty overwhelmed me, I became aware of how small, plain, and insignificant I was—not only in this place, but by Orion's side. Maybe mascara would have been a good idea.

The forest in front of me swirled and a dirt path appeared. I glanced over at Orion, and he watched me with that emotionless expression that gave nothing away. Giggles from a child and I whipped my head toward the sound. And then there was a laughter, a familiar belly laugh that was full of joy. My heart clenched. My grandmother. My grandmother was here.

"Cassie," Orion called, but I was already bolting toward the echoing sound through the dense forest, and as my legs hit against the brush, I heard the tinkling of bells.

The laughter grew louder, and I ground to a halt at the sound of my grandmother's voice, "Cassie."

My grief dripped like blood from a deep wound. I frantically scanned the woods for my grandmother, but there was nothing but green leaves, thick trunks of trees, and colorful flowers. "Gran! Where are you?"

A giggling squeal of a child and my grandmother laughed

again. "Cassiel, I do believe you love those puppies as much as they love you."

I blinked rapidly. The voices were coming from within the massive glittering oak tree. "Impossible."

From the top of the towering tree, a green vine with velvet leaves began to grow down toward me. Twining around and around the tree. When it reached eye height, a flower similar to a poinsettia with golden, glittering petals bloomed. One breath in and my body relaxed. The heady and sweet scent was intoxicating—the same feeling as drinking a potent wine.

I closed my eyes and when I opened them, I saw her—my grandmother. She was smiling and laughing as my five-year-old self—pigtails in my hair and knees scraped from climbing trees—sat in the middle of the Labrador litter. Little yellow puppies were crawling over me, licking me with love, and were wagging their tails as I picked up and hugged each and every one.

"Gran," I whispered, but she didn't look my way. Instead, she cradled the smallest puppy.

"Which one do you want to keep?"

The excitement I felt at five overwhelmed my soul. I smiled and said at the same time with five-year-old me, "We can keep one?"

My grandmother's smile could have lit up the blackest hole in the universe. "Yes."

"Gran?" a child's voice called out, and my stomach sunk as I understood the fear in that voice. A lump formed in my throat as my hands started to shake. I turned to the right, toward my younger self staring out the window of the cabin. Both of my small fingers wrapped tight to the window ledge. The waning evening light was about to disappear, and my lower lip trembled as I didn't know what to do. Should I turn on the light or keep the room dark? Should I do what Gran said and stay inside or should I go look for her? What if she were hurt? Sick? What if she was dying and I didn't go help? What if she were already dead?

Pain ripped through my chest, and unable to handle the memory, I squeezed my eyes tight and only reopened them when the sound of my childish whimpers faded and was replaced with the sound of the ocean crashing onto the beach. I dared to open my eyes again.

I was casually walking the boardwalk, Orion was beside me, both of his hands shoved in his pockets, and he was giving me the most charming smile. His white T-shirt was stretched tight against his broad muscles, and he was utterly adorable with a baseball cap hung backwards on his head. "Go on a date with me."

Butterflies took flight in my stomach and I snuck a peek at him, as he was too beautiful to stare at for too long. How was it possible that this angel on earth was walking next to me? He had come into the restaurant several times over the last two weeks and sat in my section every time. His intense dark eyes always lingered on me, and when I waited on his table, he greeted me with a pirate smile and had just the right words to make me laugh. And when I laughed, he would shine as bright as the sun. Just to see him with that expression, warmed me from the inside out.

"Hello, Orion," a beautiful, tall woman with come-hither-mascara eyes tried to catch his attention, but he didn't once acknowledge her or look her way. Instead, he kept his eyes on me.

My ankle twisted when I stepped into a crack in the boardwalk, and as I pitched forward, Orion caught me. His arms tight around me, his dark eyes boring into mine with concern, and when I was steady, I could barely catch my breath with the light touch of his fingertips caressing my back. "Are you okay?" he asked.

Besides the fact that my heart was skipping several beats due to his feathering touch? "Yes." I waited for him to let me go, but he hadn't.

He breathed in, I breathed out, and my mouth went dry with how Orion's smoldering eyes watched my lips. "The date," Orion said in that deep voice. "Will you grant me the honor?"

"Yes."

"Cassie," Orion whispered into my ear, his hands caressing my cheek. "Cassie, wake up. You're lost in a memory."

Lost, hypnotized, captured, vanished...

"Cassie," Orion said again with more force, and I opened my eyes. I blinked repeatedly, and the garden came back into view. Shock bolted through me, and I pushed away from Orion. The poinsettia with golden leaves shriveled up and fell to the ground.

"What was that?" I asked.

"That is the garden." Orion surveyed the towering trees with reverence. "This forest contains memories."

My forehead wrinkled with confusion. "My memories?"

"All memories."

I wasn't sure if that made me feel better or worse. I spun in respect of the dazzling giants surrounding us. "Is all of Fairy like this?"

"No," Orion said. "Elsewhere, there are pools of water that are a mirror of yourself. You will see yourself for what you really are instead of how you think yourself to be. There are mountains where you can visit the dead, and rainforest-flower jungles made for couples."

"Couples?" I repeated.

"Couples." The look he gave me sent shivers of pleasures through me, and I found myself blushing like a schoolgirl at the idea of visiting places like that with him.

Thankfully, Orion continued, "Then there are caves meant for you to explore your deepest fears."

"Just what anyone needs, another area of the Fae with monsters lurking."

"The monsters there aren't the work of the Fae—it would be monsters of your own creation. Fairy is a glimpse of heaven and hell. It is a wicked and beautiful garden."

Unease crawled along my insides, and I didn't want to hear about the garden anymore. "You have wings." Massive wings that, even folded as they were now, spanned above his head and ended near his calves.

"What do you think of them?" He studied me, his gaze containing the same scrutiny as when I attempted to read someone's mind through their emotions, and they were fuzzy.

"They're magnificent." I worked to hide my hesitancy. "Do all Fae have wings?"

"Some don't. Some do. Only Sidhe have these types of wings."

"Do the wings disappear when you enter earth?"

"No. I use glamour to appear like a human."

His answer made my stomach drop. Unable to look him in the eye anymore, I pretended to take interest in the over-grown forest. When I was dying in the dream with him, he asked me what was real. Evidently the answer was nothing, at least when it came to my history with him. Our physical intimacy was a huge part of our relationship, and each memory I had was now tainted. I never felt wings, just the scarred back of my lover—a human lover. The Orion I had experienced was a fraud, an illusion. He had, over and over again, lied to me.

"Cassie?" My name from his lips was an arduous recognition of my pain.

"Yes?"

"Tell me what's going on in your head."

"Why?"

"Because it's eating me alive to not know what you're thinking."

"It ate me alive when I thought you were dead, so I guess we're even."

"You're angry," he stated, and if I wasn't before, I was now.

"What do you want me to be? Happy? The man I loved kept…" I pointed to his wings then stretched out my arms at my sides and spun in a circle as a show of our surroundings, "*this* from me." My mouth hung open as I searched for words, but failed. Fallen angels, demons, a warrior and another realm…I shook my head. "You kept nearly everything about you from me."

"You didn't share everything either." The pained look in his eyes caused me to feel sick. "I saw the memory of you as a child calling for your grandmother. You never told me about that. In fact, you hardly spoke of her."

My head whipped around so fast I was surprised it didn't snap off. "We are not even on the same level. So, I didn't tell you after my grandmother disappeared it took a few weeks for the town to figure out she was gone. Nor did I tell you my mom's sick boyfriend was so disgusting that I constantly ran away from home. That was nothing compared to what you kept from me."

"You never told me the depths of your heartache."

"I told you they hurt me."

"You never told me how much. You only gave me high-lights of a bigger picture."

"I told you more than I told anyone else!" I shouted. "And you act like that was easy for me, and it wasn't. Telling you was one of the hardest things I ever did."

"I didn't know—"

"Of course, you didn't," I cut him off. "What happened to

181

me when I met you was in the past. You," I gestured at the beautiful cousin-land of heaven and hell, "were living this when we were together. You're still living it. This is not only the past for you, but your present and future."

"I told you what I could."

"So did I! I poured myself out to you like a cup full of my blood at your feet, and you gave me crumbs." I ran a frustrated hand through my hair. "It doesn't matter."

"It matters," he said softly.

It didn't. "You're missing the point. I loved a man I didn't know."

"You knew the parts that mattered."

I swept away the hot tears threatening to spill. Mad for the emotions. Madder that I felt at all. I needed to become cold and cool like marble. Maybe I knew the parts that mattered. Maybe not. "As soon as we find the baby, we'll go our separate ways. According to you and your mother, we're cursed, and because of our blood link, your enemies find you through me. That doesn't sound like the secure foundation for a relationship."

Orion said nothing. Stood there stoically still like the stone I wished to become, and it drove me absolutely insane. "All those years ago, why did you choose me? You could have had any woman, yet you told the hostess to seat you at my table. You flirted with me. You escorted me home every night. You asked me out. Why?" I slammed my hands to my chest. "Why me?" Why put me through all this pain?

His eyes searched my face. "Do you regret it?"

Honest answer? "Yes." A sharp ache in my chest. "No." The absolute honest answer. "Both."

I winced with a contraction of his pain and placed a hand against my stomach to fight the sensation of being punched in the gut over and over again. A wave of dark blue light emanated from Orion's soul and I followed it. A swirl as I tumbled down the rabbit hole in his mind. Orion alone in his penthouse. My shirt was bunched in his hands, and his knees buckled as he yelled out as if wounded. Mercutio and Shaw appeared and tried to hold him up, tried to convince him to leave, but Orion crumbled again. His mind whirled, and he was at the beach, again on his knees, facing the sunrise. He stayed there, in that spot, as time fast forwarded around him. Day into night. Night into day. Mumbling to himself, head bowed. "Save her, save her, save her, save her…. please."

I became one with his despair, his emptiness, loneliness, the dark pit he festered in. His pain was my pain, twisting my gut. My forehead furrowed. "You grieved for me."

"Letting you go is the hardest thing I've done. I don't know how to describe to you how you're a part of me. How you will always be a part of me. That without you, I'm lost."

I blinked, stunned at the strong red threads of honesty, of how open he was, of how, if I chose, I could have easily waltzed through his mind, set up camp, lived there, and plundered his emotions and secrets. As much as I wanted answers, I shoved my way out of his head. "You let your walls down," I said in confusion.

"So you can see me, Cass. I have never lied about how I feel for you."

Needing space, I wandered to a gurgling stream. Gold and silver glittering fish glided through the crystal-clear water. I sensed Orion move more than I heard him. With each step, the magnetic force between us strengthened, our breaths and heartbeats synchronizing, the fever of passion burning along my skin like tiny, pleasurable flames.

His desire for me was so intense, I was nearly consumed. The strands of his lust were fire red and drew me into his head. The images were intense, crisp, and clear. Seeing myself through his eyes, not as I was. Not as plain, but as a goddess to worship. Long, rich chestnut hair, eyes that were dark pools of water that he could drown himself in, skin so soft he'd happily die for one touch. I was in his arms, sighing his name, moving underneath him in our own creative rhythm. My hands were on his skin, in his hair, my fingernails digging into his muscles.

While we used to sleep, I'd feel protected with his massive arm possessively tucked around me. Every part of him touching every part of me. Many times, Orion woke me at dawn with his insatiable need. Kissing me awake, whispering sweet words into my ears, bringing me from the dream of sleep to a waking dream as his kisses carried me to a beautiful high.

"I want to touch you, Cass, but I won't. Not without your permission." His voice was a velvet caress along my bare back where the dress didn't cover. "I want to. The need is nearly driving me insane."

I craved his touch and basked in the intimacy with how he called me Cass. Just like he had on the nights we had made love under the stars. "Where do we go from here?" I asked. "I loved you. You loved me. Our attraction is very real, but as you've said...we're cursed." It didn't take a rocket scientist to use our wake of destruction in each other's lives as proof the curse was real.

"Where do you want to go?" he asked.

Home. Back to the simple times of the front porch of the cabin with my grandmother. Back before my mother's boyfriend, back before my mother even thought of returning home. Back before death and pain entered my life. Back to my own personal Eden—the world before original sin.

"Do we need to have it figured out?" Orion asked when I didn't answer.

"I let myself lead with emotion last time. It sounds like you did, as well. That didn't turn out well for either of us."

"Tell me what you need, and I'll give it to you. Anything.

Everything. Even if you tell me to leave you. All I want is your absolute happiness."

Truth was, I longed to forget the hurt and pined to be with him. To have him touch me, kiss me, love me in such ways I would forget all that destroyed me. But what did that say about me if I allowed it? "Nine years ago, I was a girl in love with a Fae I didn't understand. While I miss parts of that girl, I like who I am now. How can you offer me such words when you don't know me, and I never truly knew you?"

"Give me a chance to learn who you've become and for you to understand me." Orion was slow as he reached out, giving me an opportunity to retreat, but instead I edged nearer.

His fingers skimmed my cheek. My heart beat hard twice, and I didn't know if the reaction of nerves was from him, me or both. "What about the curse? According to you and your mother, if we stay together, we die."

"I will move heaven, earth, and hell to undo the curse. Just give me this chance."

"Orion," Mercutio called from a few feet away. "It's time."

CHAPTER 21

*O*rion claimed my hand. With nerves wreaking havoc in my stomach, I not only allowed it, but grasped his hand back. He met my worried gaze with confidence. "I promise you will be fine. You're my amans, and therefore under my protection."

"Of course you'll be fine," Mercutio said. "Orion had the title of Honored Warrior bestowed upon him, which means he's as badass as they come, and ninety-nine percent of the universe is terrified of him." Mercutio wore the same silk loose black pants as Orion. He was taller and thicker than on earth, and his wings were full of luminescent, glorious silver feathers. "If that doesn't make you feel secure, I'll be beside you." He gave me a wink. "We both know I'm stronger than him."

"What does amans mean?" I asked.

Orion gently traced the crescent scar on my neck, and a liquid warmth traveled through my veins. "It means you gave me the honor of your blood and that we are forever connected. It's a bond respected by Fae."

"Let's get moving and this meeting over with," Mercutio said.

As we exited the forest for a field, Shaw pushed off a tree he had been leaning against and joined us as we walked through the tall grass. My mouth dropped at the sight of him, and I faltered. Gorgeous wasn't the proper word, and neither was perfection. Shaw, on earth, was a fine male specimen, but here he was breathtaking.

"Like what you see, kid?" Shaw gave me a blinding smile.

"You don't need to be staring so hard at him." Orion nudged me forward. "He already has a complex."

"Stare away. I'm a growing boy and my complex needs to be fed."

Ahead of us was a large opening on a sheer rock on the edge of the falls. Oddly enough, there wasn't a roaring of the crashing water, but instead the soft tinkling of wind chimes and the subtle quiet voice of a woman singing. The chimes and the song were beautiful, alluring, yet at the same time, with each step we took toward it, my gut twisted, and nausea raced up my throat. I froze in my tracks. My skin became cold and clammy, and Orion released my hand as I bent over in an attempt to keep myself from dry-heaving. "What's happening?"

"Great," Shaw mumbled. "She falls in love with a Sidhe but has the natural rejection to a siren. What are the odds?"

A siren? Like a mermaid? But I couldn't ask as I was fighting the urge to vomit. Orion rubbed my back as he gathered my hair from my neck. I welcomed the cooler air against my hot skin.

"Shaw," Orion said, "go ahead of us and tell Calypso to stop singing."

"She's doing it on purpose. She's testing you and Cassie."

The singing evolved into a chorus, and I wrapped my

arms around my stomach as pain flashed through my intestines. Dizziness ensued and I dropped to the ground.

"Telling her to stop is going to make Cassie look weak," Shaw continued, "and show your weakness for her. I bet her intent was to lure Cassie to her and to make a show of Cassie at her feet, worshipping her. Humans typically don't reject sirens."

"Cassie's in pain," Orion seethed. "If anyone is concerned with weakness, then the Council can watch as I pull Calypso's vocal cords out of her throat."

"This is Nessa's doing," Shaw argued. "You know how close she and Calypso are. Nessa wants Cassie to appear unstable."

Nessa. Her name alone caused my blood to boil. How dare Nessa put me through this. How dare they stand in the way of my finding this baby. Wind gusted through the field.

"Aw, hell," Mercutio muttered. "Cassie, there're no storms here, and it's going to cause a problem if you create a hurricane. We don't have tornado sirens because we don't need them."

The song sliced me as a dagger, and my anger grew as I thought of the baby, of how she needed me, my protection. Of how helpless she was, and adults were blocking me from her.

"Breathe in and out," Orion whispered close. "I need you to stay in control. Don't do it for me or for anyone else, but for the baby." Control. The baby needed me to stay in control.

"Hey, Cassie," Mercutio crouched beside me. "What did the sea say to the water nymph?" As I fought the song and the sensation of being lost at sea in rolling waves, I glanced at him like he was insane. "Nothing. It just waved."

It was funny. One of his jokes actually was funny. I didn't

laugh. Didn't smile. The humor did still the chaos within me, but the song was still pummeling fists.

"Okay, okay, I see how this is going. The weather calmed for a second. You got this so let's try again. Where do Water Nymphs go to see movies? The dive-in." Mercutio cracked a smile at his own joke. Amusement flared in his eyes. "Where did the fisherman and the sea fairy meet? On line. Get it? On line…like a fishing line, on the internet online? Last one, last one. Where does a water nymph sleep? On a waterbed."

I grabbed onto the humor budding within me, the sense of belonging—Orion tucking my hair behind my ear, Shaw's concern, and Mercutio's attempt at making me laugh, at distracting me from danger.

The song persisted, the voice of an angel grating against my skin, but by focusing on the sense of laughter, the nausea waned. The air returned to its normal state of perfection, and slowly, with Orion's help, I stood. He cradled my face in his hands and studied me as if I had been injured. "You okay?"

"Feeling a bit sick, but I'll be okay. Anything else I need to be aware of? Are Pixies going to eat me alive? Is a Leprechaun going to beat me over the head with a pot of gold?"

"Naw, we told the Pixies to eat before they came." Mercutio waggled his eyebrows. Problem was, I had no idea if he was joking or not.

Orion's thumbs gently brushed across my cheeks, but pure rage flowed from his eyes. "It's against our laws to hurt another's amans. I can end her, and I would be within my rights."

"Because that wouldn't be a public relations nightmare," said Mercutio.

"Not a fan of what just transpired," Shaw said. "And I'll admit Calypso does like to play on the lines, but I have a hard time believing she meant you pain."

Orion shot a glare at Shaw that frightened me, but Shaw remained unruffled. I placed a hand over one of Orion's. "No harm, no death. I'm here to save a life, not end one."

"I promised to protect you."

"And I walked away from heaven so I could find your queen. Our focus is on her."

"My healer." He pressed his forehead to mine, and the siren song faded into the background as my and Orion's synchronized heartbeats grew louder. He gathered me into a hug, and I allowed myself the brief respite that came with the embrace. "You ready for battle?"

Nope. "Sure."

Orion didn't reclaim my hand, but instead positioned himself in front of me and stalked to the clearing. Mercutio and Shaw flanked Orion, forming a protective V with me at the center.

The clearing was filled with Fae who had formed a loose circle. They scrutinized our approach as if I were taking my last steps. A striking Latina woman broke from the group. She had long, wavy raven hair, brown skin, purple wings and light brown eyes that contained specks of gold, knowledge and danger. She wore an off-the-shoulder black lace one-piece jumper that fitted her figure. Her lips curled in a devilish smile as she passed Orion and Mercutio.

"She is one of us," Shaw said to me, and he watched her as if he were in a trance. "Part of my, Orion and Mercutio's team."

"How many teams are there?"

"Not enough. As the rest of us have, she has sworn to protect you and the babe."

"Sworn to who?" I asked. Nessa?

"To each other. The morning you refused the portal, we swore an oath to you. You sacrificed much for us, and we honor that."

Like a moth to a flame, Shaw pivoted toward the woman. As his attention was solely for her, her gaze was only for him until she slid beside us. Then she studied me. "You must be the healer." Her voice was as beautiful as church bells.

I raised an eyebrow. Coincidence that this was what Orion had just called me? "I'm Cassie."

"Tierney." Realization dawned—the woman who had a room at Orion's home. Suddenly, green jealousy coursed through me. She was poised, beautiful, Fae….

"It's an honor to meet you." She crossed her arm over her chest and placed her hand on her heart, as if making a pledge. "I've learned much about you in a short time. As a Sidhe warrior, I possess much respect for those who breathe life into souls, especially when many of us are called to kill in order to protect."

A quick glance at Shaw for his reaction as I was unsure what to do with her seriously stated compliment. But I wasn't sure he'd heard it, as he was still lost, admiring her. My eyes flickered from him to her—there was something between them.

"Run along, boys." Tierney inclined her head toward the groups. "She's in more capable hands with me than the three of you combined."

The way Shaw's eyes traveled around her body told me he was making promises to her, and the way her mouth turned up was her telling him he'd better fulfill his oaths. With Orion and the boys no longer by my side, the power within me danced along my skin. I rubbed my hands together to try to keep it under control.

"Not only are you the first outsider to meet with the Council, but you're the first witch in our realm," Tierney said. "Some see the great power within you that is starting to awake. All of us see the strengthening link between you and Orion. You make us all curious."

"Is that good or bad?" I asked.

"Both."

Whisperings of the siren song I heard earlier tickled the inside of my brain, and I looked toward the origin. Perched on a large rock was a woman glaring at me as if she were Medusa and I was her enemy. Except there was nothing revolting about her. She was power. She was beauty. She was the merciless sea during a hurricane. Long, unruly golden hair that rippled in the wind as if the strands were caught in a water current. Bold cheekbones, skin the color of ripe peaches. She possessed an ample bosom that nearly flowed out of the green see-through strip of lace that wrapped her chest, her pink nipples sticking out. Her short skirt, of the same material, revealed her long legs stretched out beside her. If sex were a flesh-and-blood being, she would be it.

The longer I looked at her, she morphed…changed. From human to not. From mermaid, to selkie, to something else aquatic and back to human, but it happened so quickly it seemed like my imagination. "I'm assuming she is Calypso," I said to Tierney.

"Yes. She is the leader of the Undines, or Water Nymphs. The smaller groupings to the other side are the Sprites and Sylphs."

I gave Calypso a snide lift of my lips to let her know her song didn't work. She glowered, and fury swept through her and punched into me. I raised my head to keep her emotions from penetrating my control.

Are you ready for this, witch? a voice whispered in my head, and startled, I jumped. Tierney studied me. She said nothing of my behavior, but she did follow my line of vision. To where I believed I had heard the voice.

"It would be best to avoid Ignis," Tierney whispered to me.

"Who is he?"

"A Salamander. They are a rare breed of Fae, and they are extremely powerful. Not only are they able to control fire, but they can create it at will. In fact, they are the parents of the flame. Without them, there would be no fire anywhere, ever."

Ignis sat on a black throne made of charcoal, and his stare felt like a red-hot brand upon my skin. His spiky hair was fire red, the scruff along his face the same color, and his eyes were the color of emeralds. He was slouched in his charcoal throne as though he was bored, but his serious expression told me he was anything but. He had one leg swung over the arm of the chair, the other sprawled out to in front of him. His bare chest exposed chiseled muscle, and he looked like a god straight from a Greco-Roman statue.

The power within me could appreciate the power within him, and it was an inferno. The longer I stared at him and the longer he stared at me, my hands felt heavy with electricity, and I moved them to contain the sparks of lightning begging to be released from my fingertips.

"He, out of everyone here, will be able to see the depths of your power as a witch," Tierney whispered to me.

I severed the connection and balled my fingers. The baby. I was here to save the baby.

"Holding court are the Sidhe." There were three great marble chairs higher than the rest of the group. "The man on the left is Finvarra. He is the leader of the Sidhe of the Eastern Hemisphere."

"Eastern Hemisphere?" I asked.

"Before the Americas were colonized, we had one governing body for the Sidhe. We have populated and worked in the Americas since the dawn of time, but when the Europeans found the Americas, the Sidhe decided it was best to have two centers of rule instead of one."

"Why?"

"Because two different families laid claim to the Sidhe throne, and there was anger that was threatening to spill over into violence. To keep us from civil war, the Council split the Sidhe and created another ruling body with equal voting rights." She eyed me in a conspiratorial way. "Be careful in our world, Healer. Fae can mirror humans in their lust for power."

Like the other Sidhe, Finvarra wore silk black pants, and he had great golden wings. He sat stoically in his seat like a king should over his court. Upon his chest were many wounds, countless scars. Part of his flesh looked as if it had once been peeled off and was now chunks of mutilated skin. His face contained two long mirroring scars from his temple to his chin. The midwife in me who brought babies into the world wanted to weep. The nurse practitioner was wondering why there weren't better ways to heal. The empath lived his pain. Physical retching agony. Suffering that was similar to nails being driven into my body. My legs wobbled with the acute, razor-sharp spasms, and Orion, who had been standing off to the side, whipped his head in my direction. Tierney gripped my elbow in support, and I focused on centering myself.

Knowing I couldn't look at him again without collapsing to my knees in anguish, I glanced at the throne on the left and sighed heavily. "Nessa."

"She is the leader of the Sidhe of the Western Hemisphere."

Of course, she was. Why wouldn't she be? This entire realm was a contradiction—as Orion said, it was a beautiful and wicked garden. "Who sits on the middle throne?"

"No one…as of now. That throne is for our queen."

"When was the last time you had a queen?"

"Centuries. Morgan le Fay was our last queen."

I did a double take. "Morgan le Fay as in Morgana? Like King Arthur's court, Morgana?"

"The very one."

"I thought she was a witch."

"Morgan le Fay is a direct translation: Morgan the Fairy."

My grandmother told me stories of her—she was a great witch who healed King Arthur after he had been mortally wounded in a battle. "With no queen, who rules over the court?" I asked, even though I had a feeling I wasn't going to like the answer.

"Each of the Fae groupings—Sylph, Sprite, Salamander, Undine, the Eastern Hemisphere Sidhe, and the Western Hemisphere Sidhe—have one voice and one vote."

Didn't take long to do the math. "What happens when the vote is three to three?"

"That rarely happens, and it is one reason why we want so desperately to find our queen. But when things end in ties, the council will bow to the Sidhe for final decisions."

Fan-freaking-tastic. Nessa, the woman who hated me, was one of the most powerful Fae in the universe. My life kept getting better. In sync, Nessa and Finvarra flicked their wrists and gold staffs appeared in their hands. In unison, they lifted the staffs and banged them to the ground. A resounding gong rang through the realm. Everything went silent, everything stilled, even the great waterfall behind them.

A cluster of women who had the giant wings of the Sidhe stepped from the forest. They wore yellow dresses and pantsuits, and each woman bowed before the Council then took a seat at what looked like a golden juror's box. One peaked from behind her hood and I caught the glowing smile of Relle. "Those are our honored prophetesses," Tierney whispered.

More Sidhe came forward, men and woman dressed in

black, and they bowed before the council before creating a circle around the entire area. Their group included Shaw and Mercutio.

"Our warriors are setting a perimeter of safety," Tierney explained.

That caught my attention. "Are we unsafe here?"

"Our enemies cannot enter this realm. It is a symbol of our pledge to defend our Council."

Finally, Orion presented himself before the three thrones and knelt. He stayed there, head bowed, on one knee, and I caught the pride rolling off Nessa and Finvarra.

"Why is Orion separate?" I whispered.

Tierney met my gaze and studied me before answering. "Because he is their son. Orion is the offspring of our purest bloodlines. Once he finishes his final rites, he will take over for Nessa and Finvarra, finally merging the Sidhe."

CHAPTER 22

*N*essa and Finvarra rose from their seats. Orion also arose. He turned toward the circle of Fae, and every knee in the area bent in honor of the three of them. I didn't kneel, and neither did Ignis. He stayed bored in his chair, studying me, but Orion held my attention. I stood there, slack jawed. Orion would someday be the leader of not only the Sidhe, but all the Fae.

"You are a guest here, Cassie Strega," Nessa called out. "I'm assuming that is why you don't understand you are to kneel."

I cocked an eyebrow. Kneel to her? Never. And I wasn't about to give Orion the impression I was beneath him. He and I were on unsteady ground as it was, and I was not in the mood to create an even greater imbalanced power dynamic.

"Cassie is my guest," Orion said as he met my eyes. There was a wild spark there—not that of a regal heir to a throne, but of the man who broke the rules while riding his motorcycle. "And she doesn't kneel to me."

He could say that again.

"Cassie chose to forgo the portal to save our queen."

Orion addressed the entire circle. "She's also a healer who has saved many lives, and she deserves our gratitude and respect."

I tossed a glance at Mommy and didn't bother to keep the snide smirk off my face. She seethed with wrath. Someday, I would more than likely regret it, but I'd worry about that later.

"As you were," said Nessa, and the Fae returned to however they had been before court had been called into session.

"Come with me," Tierney said. When we reached Orion, he moved to box me in between the two of them. Tierney flicked her wrist and a huge sword appeared in her grasp. She knelt to Nessa and Finvarra, placing her sword on the ground. "May I present Cassie Strega. Human, healer, and, according to the visions of our prophetesses, the bridge to our queen."

"You left out witch," Nessa said, drawing a rush of anger and fear from the crowd that a "witch" was in their presence.

"An unfortunate turn of events," Finvarra said, and I rolled my shoulders back. First time I was meeting dear old dad, and he obviously liked me as much as mommy did. Orion subtly shook his head for me to remain silent.

"Everything between them has been an unfortunate turn of events," Nessa continued. "Do I need to remind the Council this is the woman who will bring Orion's doom?"

"A prophecy that has been fulfilled," Orion said. "Cassie and I parted in tragedy. Neither of us whole, and both of us have suffered."

"I saw your death," Nessa continued. "And she will be the cause of it."

"She is my amans," Orion said carefully, slowly. "I have been without her for nine years. That is death."

A variety of emotions from everyone tiptoed along my

skull. Orion felt protective of me, Nessa was furious, Calypso had a fine ring of jealousy, and Finvarra was still radiating physical pain. When I forced my focus away to prevent myself from falling into his pit of agony, I caught the amusement of Ignis.

"But the prophesy could still come true," Calypso said. "It more than likely will. We need to find our queen, but we cannot do so at the risk of losing the last of our royal bloodline. If something happens to our queen, we will need you, Orion. You are the future of the Fae."

Murmurs from the crowd, and my skin itched as the differing emotions clawed at me, trying to find a vulnerable place to tear off a scab and burrow inside.

"Orion and the other Sidhe warriors can find the queen without the help of the witch," Nessa said. "She is not one of us, and as we all know, a witch's loyalty blows where the wind blows. They cannot be trusted. It is appalling she's even in our realm."

A muscle jerked in Orion's jaw and he squared his shoulders. "Through me, she is entitled to be here."

"She is a witch," Nessa hissed with hate.

"She is my amans," Orion countered. "My home. If she is not welcomed here, then neither am I."

Multiple gasps, a tense stare off between mother and son, and one of the prophetesses stood from her jury box. "We have seen the healer holding the babe."

Yeah, Nessa, explain that one.

Nessa waved her off. "Your vision happened after Orion found the witch on his hunt to save the child. What you saw wasn't prophecy, but Orion's clouded judgement at seeing this witch whom he gave up nine years ago. He saw her, wanted her in his bed again, and it briefly changed the trajectory of the future. Once we vote to no longer use the witch and she moves on with her life, the prophecy will change again—to a future that does not involve her."

"Our queen has reached out to Cassie," Orion started, but Nessa cut him off.

"So she says. That witch has been scheming to be part of your life since the start, and you have fallen for it. She is your annihilation, and your destruction is the collapse of the Fae, which leads to the ruin of the human world." A distinct word came hurtling out of Nessa's head and it was a blow straight to my chest: *whore*.

My spine straightened, Orion and Nessa continued to argue, and as if sensing my vehemence, Tierney placed a hand on my arm in warning, but I had been silent for too long. As my hair moved with the wind building in me, a deep voice entered my mind and shocked me. *Listening to them drag their family issues into such a public place amuses me.*

I glanced wildly around.

Don't look surprised, the deep voice spoke again. *I'm not so different from you. You play with lightning, I play with fire. Between the two of us, we could burn down this entire realm.*

I knew I shouldn't, especially after Tierney's warning, but unable to fight the temptation, I met Ignis's eyes. There was a simper on his face as he casually stroked his chin. *I see you, healer. I see your power. Power you haven't even begun to understand. Orion has lied to the Council about the depths of what you can do. A dangerous play to make with your inability to control yourself, and my ability to see through you. Talk to me, healer. Talk to me as I am talking to you. I see you can as easily as I can see you are able to push yourself into my mind and read not only my emotions, but my thoughts. Nessa will destroy you if she discovers that neat little trick. She'll leave you bleeding out on the spot on which you stand, but I have a feeling you are already aware.*

Nessa was talking, trying to convince the Council that my involvement would lead to Orion's death. Orion was arguing with her, and I realized this wasn't a meeting about how to find the baby. It was my witch trial.

You are correct. If the Council rules against you, you will die. Orion will fight for you. His mind is resolute, but there are enough Fae here to incapacitate him. The fight will be bloody, bringing him to the brink of death, but Nessa will not allow him to die. But your death will surely come at her hands.

More Fae were speaking: Calypso agreeing with Nessa, the Water Nymphs joining her like a Greek chorus saying Orion's life was not worth my involvement. The prophetesses rising to their feet, demanding their visions be taken into consideration. Orion invoking the fact that I was his amans, that his mother had no right to demand anything when it came to me. With the subtle way Tierney and Orion edged closer, this meeting wasn't leaning in my direction. Death—I wasn't scared of it, but there was an edge of panic that I wouldn't be able to find and protect the baby.

No, as a witch, you wouldn't be scared of death. Witches have a kinship with the underworld. In order for a witch to find their power, they have to die, whether it be emotionally or physically, and you have experienced many deaths. You are friends with the underworld, bound to it as much as you are to Orion. The link between you and death is strong. Strong enough, even, that you have piqued my curiosity. You amuse me, healer, and Nessa annoys me. I will save you, for now. That is, if you can save yourself.

If I could save myself, I wouldn't need your help, I shot back at him, and his dark grin widened.

You are more than Orion's obedient bed servant after all. That is good to know.

"Look." Calypso pointed at me. "Her energy grows. She's stronger than Orion let on."

Orion's head snapped in my direction. He pushed me behind him, his wings spreading just enough to become a barrier between me and his mother. "If you kill her, you kill me."

Anger from the crowd, and I was swamped by the same vile emotions as when the mob had dragged me from my home. My head throbbed, my temples pounded, and a storm swirled inside my soul.

"We need to protect ourselves," Nessa preached from her throne. "The Fae are obligated to fulfill our purpose given to us by the Creator. This witch is a danger to the Council, the Fae, and our job on earth. She's a menace, an infant witch who can't control her powers. She has no business anywhere near our queen, and our queen is who you are bound to, Orion. Not this whore. Any other bonds you have made, blood-created or not, cannot supersede the one with our queen. Remember that before you go too far."

She's right, Ignis said. *Oaths for Fae are not mere words spoken allowed. It is a magical pact we are obliged to keep. No matter the blood bond between you and Orion, he will be compelled by his original oath to choose his queen. Makes you wish you had been able to read the fine print of the agreement before you allowed Orion to drink your blood during a Fae rite.*

Wind blew about as I met Ignis's gaze, wondering why he was torturing me. *I feel great emotion in you,* Ignis said in his bored, calm tone. *Use it.*

I rolled my neck as I fought the storm within me that was begging to lash out. *I will not harm these beings, even if they try to harm me.*

While that would bring me joy to watch, that isn't what I was referring to. Are you not a healer? If so, heal. Maybe I have overestimated you. Maybe you are nothing to be curious over.

Heal. He said it simply, like I had any idea what that meant. There wasn't someone bleeding, there wasn't a mother in labor—but I stopped breathing as I realized there was pain. Finvarra's head dropped in agony. *Why is Finvarra suffering?*

A demon blade nicked his soul during battle before Orion's birth. Thirty years to be tormented is long enough, wouldn't you agree?

My forehead furrowed. *I don't understand his injury, and even if I did, I have no equipment, no medicine.*

You are not human anymore, witch. The faster you figure that out, the better your odds of surviving. Either heal him or I will allow Nessa to do what she pleases with you. I have no room for someone with little faith in themselves. You are either audacious or not. Live or die. What happens to you is your choice, not mine.

What about your queen?

The queen will be found with or without you. I'm bored of you, Cassie Strega. I wish you well in death. With a disinterested twist of his wrist, he broke off the connection.

Past the battering of emotions, past the electricity at my fingertips, I tilted my head and did exactly what Orion told me not to do—I pushed into Finvarra's mind. The orange thread of pain was a massive rope around his throat and lungs. As I followed the thick, durable chain to the source, Finvarra clutched his chest as if he could sense me within him.

"She's doing something to Finvarra!" Calypso shouted. "The witch is pouring energy into him! She's hurting him!"

Orion rounded on me, his face paling. "Cassie, what are you doing?"

Finvarra's pain was becoming my own and nausea swam within me. He needed the inexhaustible agony to end, and as I dove deeper, I became one with his suffering. I was drowning in the feeling of my skin being boiled off, my muscles cut by a thousand knives. I raced along the rope, whiplashed in spot when I came to the end and found a complicated and bloody knot on the essence of his heart.

"Restrain her!" Nessa roared, and bright lights flashed around me. Shaw and Mercutio appeared by my side and boxed me in along with Orion and Tierney.

"Stay back!" Orion commanded. "I will kill for her. Don't doubt me on this."

I needed to undo the knot, but how? Sparks sprouted off my fingertips, and as I wiggled them, awe flooded me as the knot moved. The emotion surrounding me, the emotion within me, it powered the electricity in my fingers. Since the accident, I had repelled emotion, terrified of what would happen if I called it into me. Taking a deep breath, embracing the emotions, I latched onto the knot and tugged. Finvarra's chest spasmed, and while the knot moved position, the tangle was still in place.

"The witch is killing Finvarra!" Calypso yelled. "Orion, she harms those you love!"

Roars from the crowd, Orion and his friends taking battle stances, a shadow of a Fae racing toward us and the sound of metal clanking against metal as someone released a battle cry.

I reached out with both hands, sucked in a breath, and gathered more emotion into me: Finvarra's pain, my pain, Orion's fury, the anger, the fear, the hatred from the Fae. I drained them of it all, my entire body shaking, everyone shouting, Orion capturing my face, staring into my eyes, booming my name. I stared past him and forcibly pushed into Finvarra's soul. I grabbed the knot and screamed as I drew every last bit of emotion into me and then threw it out from my hands to yank and pull the knot apart. An explosion in my fingers, pain ripping through my blood, a bright light, and as I collapsed to the ground, I couldn't hear anything. Silence, pure silence, even though Orion was on the ground with me. He crouched at my level, his hands on my face, his mouth moving, and then, with an ear-piercing screech, there was sound again.

Chaos. Shouting and yelling and Nessa calling for my death.

"We have to get her out of here." Mercutio held his sword firm as if ready for battle. "We need to move! Now!"

A reverberating ring of a mallet on heavy metal—the striking of a huge ceremonial gong— drowned out all other sound. Heat flooded the ground beneath me, and flames licked the sky above. When the bang rang through the area again, I trembled with the vibration. Everyone quieted. Orion hauled me to my feet, keeping me secure to his side. A sword in his other hand pointed out toward anyone attempting to come near. Standing at his throne was Ignis, staff in his hand, and he was looking at me. *Well done, witch.*

Witch? I thought you were calling me healer.

With the slightest movement of his fingers, the staff disappeared and he slumped into his seat. *You cannot be a healer without being a witch. The meaning, for you, is synonymous. Be careful with me, Cassie Strega. Gaining my attention isn't good. It saved your life for now, but I will easily take the breath from your body myself if you pose a problem for me. Anger me, and I'll hand you to Nessa to be tortured before your death.*

Exhausted by healing Finvarra, I wavered. Orion's hold on me tightened.

"How did you do it, witch?" Finvarra's voice was full of wonder and empty of the earlier strain. He was slow standing, as if he were afraid his legs would give, but he found them to be strong. A weathered face that had been gray was filling with color. "How did you break the curse of the demon blade?"

Every eye, once again, was on me, and Orion's grip on me loosened. With a short glance at Ignis, I left the safety of

Orion and stood on my own. "I saw you were in pain, and I wanted to ease your suffering."

"Seasoned witches rarely possess this power," said Finvarra, "and we have not seen a witch with this ability in fifty years. You are an infant performing the magic of the old."

It was then I noticed the world around me was clearer. It was easier for me to breathe, easier for me to think. The emotions of those surrounding me were mine to read at will, were mine to possibly control. "I have seen your queen. She has reached out to me through dreams, and she has come to me in a vision." If that's what it was. "She is healthy and vibrant." I paused as I remembered the pure happiness she shared with me. "Her soul is utterly beautiful, and she has yet to be born, but her mother is scared and in danger. I denied peace to help your queen, and you bring me here to decide if I should live? I don't understand any of you. Your queen has asked for my help, and I'm starting to understand why. I wouldn't trust any of you to get me a drink of water, much less save my life."

"Blasphemy," Nessa said.

Orion came to my side, sword still in hand, and rage was pouring from the glare he gave his mother. "My allegiance is to my queen and my queen has chosen Cassie. Nine years ago, I performed the Amans Rite with Cassie. Through our laws, she is protected."

"The ceremony you performed with Cassie was not complete." Nessa waved her hand as if suggesting I was trash to be dragged to the curb. "You had no consent from this council and the rite was not properly performed. Cassie Strega is nothing more than my son's witch whore. She has no rights here, and I will not hear that argument from you anymore, Orion."

So quickly it caused me to jump, the sword switched to a

dagger and Orion slashed open his palm. Bright red blood poured out.

"No." I frantically searched the area for something to bind his wounds. My dress. I raised the hem to tear off pieces for a bandage, but Orion laid the sharp edge of his dagger on the ground at my toes, and he snatched both of my hands in one of his, preventing me from tending to him. He fisted his bleeding palm, squeezed, knelt in front of me, and bowed his head as his blood dripped onto my toes and his dagger.

I thought of my words to him earlier... *I poured myself out to you like a cup full of my blood at your feet, and you gave me crumbs.* A strange floating sensation in my head. This moment had happened before between me and Orion.

"I, Orion MacAleese, honored warrior, leader of the Sidhe Bellators, son of Nessa MacAleese, son of Finvarra Ri, heir to the consul of the Fae throne, swear an oath to you, Cassie Strega, human, witch, healer and my amans, that I will protect you from any threat, great or small, from human, Fae or from any threat from the gates of hell itself. My blood runs through you, your blood runs through me, we are one, and anyone who harms you will face my wrath. My blood, my soul, my body is yours, as is my life."

Shaw, Mercutio, and Tierney joined Orion in kneeling and placed their swords at my feet. Around the outer circle, I lost my breath as the other warriors fell like dominos onto their knee toward me.

"This does not complete the ceremony," Nessa seethed.

"But he will complete it," Finvarra said. "Unless there are objections, Orion's oath to the healer will stand and Orion will finish the rite by Beltane. If the rite is not concluded by then, Cassie Strega will no longer be protected by the laws of amans."

"She will be his doom," Nessa said. "This witch will cost

us Orion. He is the last blood heir to the Sidhe. You are choosing a path that will ruin the Fae."

"I'm choosing Cassie Strega," Orion said. My heart somersaulted at the light radiating from him, from the peace on his face. His emotions were like a wave rolling out to sea, pulling me along with it, and his love and admiration for me left me buoyant in his ocean. I brushed my fingers along his cheek, and he briefly closed his eyes with the caress. He turned his head, kissed my open palm, allowed one more drop of his blood to land on my foot, then stood. His wound closed, and his palm healing before my eyes left me stunned.

The rest of the Sidhe warriors stood and Orion stepped closer to his parents. "The path I'm choosing will save our queen, and there is no need for an heir if she is found. I swore an allegiance when I was sixteen to protect the Fae, the rulers of our kingdom, and the human race. I understood then I was agreeing to my possible death. Cassie is the bridge to our queen, and if joining forces with her brings my death, then I welcome the portal that will open to me upon my last breath. My life for my queen."

"My life for my queen," echoed the warriors around us.

Orion looked over his shoulder at me and whispered again, "My life for my queen." But he didn't mean the baby, and there was a melting inside me.

"Let's vote," Finvarra said. "All those in favor of asking the healer to help the Sidhe find our queen and accepting her as Orion's amans with the rite to be completed by Beltane, say, aye."

CHAPTER 23

*T*wo thoughts circled my brain:

1. Nessa and Calypso voted against me.
2. Back on earth Orion no longer had wings and
   appeared human again.

After the vote and the subsequent discussion of how we
would find the baby, Orion returned us to my realm—to the
beach on earth. He led me to the garage, opened the door to
his car, and I hopped in without an argument. My mind was
a hamster wheel with all that had occurred in Fairy.

It was evening and I was famished, overwhelmed, and not
prepared for Orion to pull into the garage to his condo. He
parked in a spot near the elevator, and I could tell by his
pensive expression as he exited and rounded the car that he
was in no mood for small talk. Typically, that look meant he
needed silence, he needed me close, and—in the past— that
our lovemaking in bed would be intense.

He opened my door, offered me his hand, and I accepted,

as it was an excuse to taste his emotions. The intensity of his concentration rattled me from head to toe. He was thinking of a million scenarios at once. Playing games of chess as he tried to work out how to protect me as he searched for his queen.

The elevator opened on command, and he inserted his key for the penthouse. When we reached his floor he didn't rush in, but just held the door open, allowing me the time to process. The sight of the spacious room, the marble floors, the state-of-the-art kitchen where he had made me countless meals, and each piece of furniture we had christened by making love upon it caused my heart to quicken. There was excitement in my blood and a healthy dose of fear. What was I agreeing to by entering? Nothing. I was agreeing to absolutely nothing.

With a deep breath, I stepped in and slowly walked into a place that had haunted my dreams for nine years. It looked exactly the same as it did when I was nineteen. The leather sofa still faced the fireplace and the television was still mounted over the mantel. The high seats were still situated along the granite bar that separated the kitchen from the living area. The large balcony overlooked the sea. To the left was the master bedroom, and I caught a brief peek of the endlessly large four-poster bed where Orion and I had worshipped each other for days.

The memories of how he would touch me, kiss me, bring me to a fantastic high caused a tingle in my blood. I paused by the bar, and Orion's fingers lightly caressed my back as he passed me on his way to the fireplace. The brief and simple touch caused a quake of pleasure to vibrate along my skin. He lit a fire, checked the thermostat, then shrugged off his leather jacket and laid it on one of the chairs. Next, he washed his hands at the kitchen sink, put a tea kettle on a burner, and pulled items out of the fridge and pantry.

Orion methodically moved about as he chopped vegetables and seasoned meat. The kettle whistled, and he poured the hot water into a blue mug, then placed a teabag in the cup. He walked around me, placed the mug on the coffee table in front of the couch, and picked up a blanket from a chair. "You're in shock, Cass. You have been since you healed my father. Don't deny it, as you don't even realize it, but I can feel it. Take the tea, take a seat, and let me take care of you."

Shock. "I'm not in shock." Clinically, I checked off the symptoms. Cold, clammy skin, dizziness, rapid and shallow breathing, changes in mental status. I glanced at my hands and saw they were shaking. My entire body trembled with a chill, and there was a moment of clarity before my thoughts looped again. Maybe I was in shock.

I slipped off Orion's jacket, placed it next to his, and shuffled to the couch. I sat, drawing my knees underneath me, as Orion laid the blanket over my lap and gave me the tea. The heat seeping through the ceramic brought on a wave of peace, as did the scent of chamomile that drifted up with the steam. I took a sip, and the warmth flowing along my throat was heaven. Orion brushed his fingers along my cheek and looked at me as if he wanted to hold me close and then hide me away.

He returned to the kitchen, and I curled into the corner of the couch, enjoyed my tea and the heat of the fire, and watched as Orion relaxed with the rhythm of the kitchen. Soon my mouth watered and my stomach grumbled with the scents he was creating, and I thought of the countless nights I sat at the bar and watched him lose himself in cooking a meal.

"Fae like food," I haphazardly said as I chased after a random thought from a book my grandmother had read to me a long time ago. It was a book about magical creatures. I had loved the beautiful drawings of the Pixies and was entranced by the darker creatures hiding in the trees and caves. She had hugged me and told me there was truth in fiction.

"Yes, we do enjoy a good meal," Orion answered. "Every gathering we have is an excuse for a feast."

"Is it all true then? The fairytales? That Fae love music, dancing…?"

"Sex," he said with a sly smile, and I blushed. Sex was a given, at least it was between us nine years ago. "We also love a good fight." He gave me a conspiratorial wink. "You never asked about Fae when we were together. I waited for your questions, but they never came."

"I was scared to say anything or do anything that would cause you to want to leave me." I regarded the hot mug, thinking I was insane for answering honestly. It was more than likely the shock, but why not have an authentic conversation with Orion? He took me to Fairy, offered several times to die for me, and swore an oath to me in front of his mother that involved his blood. I could at least discuss this. "I also had this absolute blind faith and trust in you. I wanted to believe you knew me better than I knew myself. It made life easier—at least I thought I did. If you made my decisions for me, if I followed wherever you lead, then maybe I would be happy. Maybe the bad would disappear, I could pretend the world was perfect and I could hide." All sad, but true. "Weren't you relieved I didn't ask?"

"Yes," he answered as he prepared lettuce for a salad. "But I didn't like it. It didn't make us…real."

"Because we weren't real. I followed you around like I was your pet instead of your equal. Don't tell me you didn't enjoy it." The flash at how my words made him hurt created an ache in me.

"I did like it, but at the same time I didn't. There was a control I had over you that gave me the false assumption you were safe. That kept the worry at bay. But I stifled you. I saw it then but was too damn selfish to care. As odd as it sounds, Cass, I'm glad you broke away. I like that you became your own person. You're happier this way. It hurts to admit, but when you were with me you were full of fear. Now, you're strong."

I circled the rim of the mug with my thumb. "I'm still scared."

"Not of being on your own. That's good, and I'm glad you found happiness."

At the sad note in his voice, I met his eyes, and the devastating candor was there in his soul—choosing me was a death sentence and he was genuinely full of joy knowing I would find happiness after he passed. "Orion," I whispered. "What is this curse?"

"I've told you—my mother had a vision that if we are together, we die." He gathered the tray of food and two glasses of water and carried them over. There were two salads that contained cut veggies, cranberries, and his special vinaigrette dressing. The tray also had filet mignon, steamed asparagus, and mashed potatoes. "Wine would be better, but that wouldn't help the shock."

"It wouldn't."

Orion sat on the couch, pulled out a napkin, and as he went to place it on my lap, I grabbed his hand to force him to focus. "There have to be more curse details than that. What are they?"

"You need to eat and so do I. The curse will still be there when we're finished."

It was hard for me to listen, to not insist I get my way first, but I was starving, and as his knee brushed against mine, I sensed his hunger and his need for peace. I could give him peace, for at least the length of the meal. He handed me my salad and a fork, took his, and settled beside me.

The salad was pure ecstasy. Orion had an uncanny knack for inventing unique flavor combinations. The salad made me think of the lettuce I had planned on planting in the community garden this summer, and that made me think of my apartment and all that I had left behind. "I had a box of personal items. Pictures, cards, and such. I'd love to have any of it."

"Where can I find these things?"

Dread washed through me. This was going to make him aware how much he affected me, as there was no doubt he'd see the pictures of us. "I was going through the box on the couch the morning of the mob. I'm assuming everything is still there."

"I'll retrieve it for you. Anything else?"

I gave him a weak smile. "My plants?"

Orion chuckled. "You and your damn plants. Your apartment was one grow light away from being a garden nursery."

"You were jealous because I loved some of them more than you."

He laughed deeply and the sound soothed my own soul. "I should have seen then you were a witch. In hindsight, I feel like an idiot."

"You should have seen I was a witch because I liked plants?"

"Yes," he said as he cut into his steak. "Witches have a connection to the natural world. Where Fae guard over it and create it, witches can use it. You find healing for yourselves and others in nature. Witches can also sense shifting moods. Even before becoming an empath, you had a way of being aware of people's emotions and would twist yourself into knots to help them. That was some of what drew me to you—how you cared for other people, even strangers. I'm wondering if, when I gave you my blood, it awakened the part of you that's a witch and gave you the empathic abilities."

"Then the rest of me woke when whatever supernatural power was responsible roused the rest of us." It was definitely a sound theory. "Why do fairies hate witches?"

"Hate's a strong word."

"I felt some strong hate today, and some of it was merely because I was a witch."

"There is…distrust," Orion said as if he was searching for words. "Even knowing lives are in the balance, witches have been reluctant to involve themselves in the war with the demons. Some healers have helped, but only on their terms, and they demand great compensation. Some witches have chosen to help the demons. Overall, most have stayed neutral. We don't understand how they can stand back, see the losses we are taking, how the world is suffering, and not want to help. Many in my world see witches as selfish."

"Why did Moloch say I belonged with him? Did it have anything to do with me being a witch? Because the morning of the mob, there were demons there and they said something about them searching for me and about someone being freed. I'm assuming all that is Moloch."

Orion's jaw clenched. "Why didn't you tell me this?"

"I don't know. Maybe I was too focused on the fact I was dying, there was a baby who decides the fate of the world in danger, and my dead ex-boyfriend was back in my life. Tell me more about this Moloch. And to be honest, I have a hard time believing you don't have a theory as to why he's saying I belong with him. This is your world and I've been thrust into it. I need some answers. Solid, detailed answers."

Orion stayed silent, and rage burst through me. "I'm not doing this." Not anymore. I was no longer the nineteen-year-old girl who was happy to stay in my place. I sprang to my feet. Screw this. I was out of here. To where, I didn't know, but I'd figure it out.

"Cassie," Orion stood along with me. "Wait."

"I'm not doing this, Orion. I'm in this. With you. Either treat me like an equal or I'm leaving."

He rubbed his eyes then rolled his neck if he was annoyed. "I want to treat you like an equal."

"Then do it!" I shouted.

"My instinct is to protect you. To keep you safe and out of danger. It causes me physical pain to not keep you safe."

"You can't keep me out of this. I'm as deep as anyone can get. Deeper than even you. So staying quiet, not telling me things, that's not keeping me safe. That's a slap in face."

A war played over Orion's face, and my chest ached as his physical pain reached out and strangled my lungs. He wasn't lying about feeling this agony regarding me physically, and that caused some of my anger to dissipate.

With a heavy sigh, Orion finally answered, "Moloch is a demon prince, and he's damned proud to be named in the Bible. During our last battle, I stabbed him with a blade that caused him to be chained to the lake of fire in hell for what was supposed to be an eternity. That blade was old magic, hard as hell for me to find, and could only be used once. As for what freed him, I can't say if it had anything to do with you or with whatever mystical force that woke the witches, or if his newly found freedom had anything to do with either event."

I narrowed my eyes, pushed out to search his mind, and winced when I came in contact with the fuzzy radio waves. "Let down your wall."

He mashed his lips together and gave a curt nod of his head. Within seconds the fuzziness faded enough that I could search his emotions and his honesty was clear. He meant what he said. A second later, a swirling of lust crept out and weaved around me. His energy was like the brushing of his fingertips along my breasts, and my heart picked up speed as the delicious touch dipped further down toward my thighs.

I winced when Orion shut his walls. Drawing in a breath to control the runaway pheromones now sprinting through me, I turned away from Orion and toward the windows overlooking the ocean. I leaned my head against the cool windowpane and tried not to think about Orion's hands on my body. "How do you do it? How do you function feeling like that all the time?"

"You act like wanting you is a punishment."

No, the punishment was not giving in. I glanced at him from over my shoulder. He raised an eyebrow, and his adorable grin made me feel like he could read my mind.

"I was as shocked to hear what Moloch said as you were," Orion said as if knowing I needed the conversation to move away from kissing him. "I don't know why Moloch said what he said, but I don't like it. If he found you once, he'll find you again."

"He found us through our bond?"

"Maybe, but unlikely. It's not bright enough for a demon to see. He didn't even give it a second glance in New York, and I know because I was watching him."

Not knowing how to respond, I leaned back against the wall of glass. "How do I move about, searching for the baby, if I have a demon prince wanting to have side chats with me?"

"Wren can give you wards to wear. Speaking of Wren, she blew up my phone while we were in Fairy. She wants to meet with you tomorrow." That drew a dark, grim look upon his face.

"Why does that bother you?"

"She wants to take you someplace without me."

"You don't like that?" I asked carefully.

"I don't like a lot of things, but I need to learn to live with it. With much unknown, I don't like your being out of my sight, but Wren promises she'll protect you."

"Do you think it's safe for me to go with her?"

"No." That was blunt. "Wren's hiding something from me, but she cares for you. She always has, and she'll do her best to protect you. She's proven that in the past and recently. I'd prefer you stay with me, but if you want to go with her, I won't stop you."

There were moments when the conversation needed to shift, and this was one of them. "Are those your famous garlic mashed potatoes?"

"Why don't you find out?"

I sat back on the couch and happily picked up my plate full of steak and potatoes. "What is Beltane?" As that was our deadline to complete this Fae rite of amans.

Orion joined me and then sliced his steak into smaller pieces. "Beltane is a major celebration for us. All Fae will come home on May first. We are called home and expelled out, but there are certain times we are compelled in. If we don't show of our free will, then our realm will literally suck us out of the earth and back home. Beltane is an obligation."

"Wow." A combination of how weirdly his world worked and how awesome the mashed potatoes were. Orion gave me a crooked grin, as if he understood some of that was in appreciation of his cooking. "What type of dress is required?"

"Depends on which ceremony we attend. Some are formal and some," he gave me a pirate's wink, "are downright devious."

I nibbled on my bottom lip with the heat that spread in my belly with that wink. The conversation needed to change again. "I should try to connect with the baby. Do you think it was the combination of ocean and sleep that worked?"

"I think it's possible the baby connects with you when

she's ready, not the other way around." Orion took our empty dishes to the kitchen and started the process of cleaning. I went to help, but Orion froze me with a glare. "Sit. This is me taking care of you. Let me do it."

"I'm feeling better and can help," I offered.

"I feel your exhaustion," he said as he placed the plates in the dishwasher. "You wear it like a second skin. Even before things spiraled after you awoke to being a witch, I saw the dark circles under your eyes when you were taking care of Brittney, and then felt your weariness when we reconnected. It's going to be a fast-paced few days. Take the time to rest."

"We should try the water again."

"You also connected with her when you slept. You should try more of that."

"You're like a dog with a bone," I said.

"You know what they say about those who live in glass houses."

I snickered as I snuggled into the couch and pulled the fluffy blanket to my chin. "The meal was great, Orion. Thank you."

"Anytime," he said with a flicker of a glance in my direction to show his sincerity. "And thank you, for healing my father. What you did today….It took courage. You put your life on the line for him. I will not forget it, and neither will he."

"You're welcome."

He began to sing, his voice beautiful and deep. Not loud, more to himself than anything. I missed this. This shared intimacy where he was comfortable enough to move about his place without feeling like he had to entertain me. Like I was part of his home.

Contentment and peace caused warm colors to weave around Orion. He loved cooking, but he also enjoyed the rhythm to cleaning—to making his world, his home, belong to him. Soon, muscles that were tight from the day relaxed, and my drowsy eyes found the fireplace. I listened to Orion sing, to the fire crackling, and watched as the embers jumped into the air. Relishing the precious feeling of safety, I closed my eyes and drifted to sleep.

CHAPTER 24

*O*rion and I were in his penthouse that overlooked the ocean. The rays of the summer sun created a hazy glow, and the breeze was drifting in. We were sharing a bowl of chicken Lo Mein he had made. He was wearing his favorite about-the-apartment outfit: a worn pair of jeans that hung low on his hips, so low the line of reddish-blond hair that trailed south was visible.

He never bothered with a shirt when we were together in his penthouse. One, if it found its way off, we'd have to search for it when it was time to leave. Two, I loved the fluid way his muscles moved when he stalked about, and he liked the way I watched.

We sat at the bar chairs, laughing over the way he had slurped a noodle, and my heart was so full of joy, it felt as if it were going to burst.

"…and Shaw was so drunk he didn't realize how close he was to the surf and a wave hit him from behind. He smelled like fish guts the entire way home. You should have seen the look on his face when he woke in the morning and realized we had placed him in his bed…on purpose."

Orion chuckled and I giggled along. I twirled the noodles around my fork and glanced at him. His eyes were twinkling with mischief, but then there was a brief second of the sadness that had been consuming him when I first arrived. Something had gone wrong with his work. Beyond his haunted expression, there were the telltale wounds on his body: bruises, cuts, even a gash that appeared to be newly healing. I learned quickly that if I asked about his work or his injuries, he wouldn't tell me, but I could help him forget his misery—if even for a little while.

"Want to watch a movie here?" I asked. "You pick, and I'll make us popcorn later."

Orion put down his fork and threaded our fingers together. "The movie—yes. The popcorn—I don't know. It would be a shame if you set the fire alarms off again."

"I burned the popcorn one time!"

He picked up his fork again to continue to eat. "The building had to evacuate. Smoke filled the entire top floor."

I kicked his shin. Yes, the fire alarm went off, but after a few waves of a dish towel near the fire alarm, it quit beeping. "You are such a liar."

Orion gave me a wide grin. "I don't know, Cass. Should I trust you with the microwave?"

The corner of the room swirled as if trying to readjust, and the realization was a pins-and-needle sensation in my brain. "I'm asleep."

"Yes. This is one of my favorite memories. It's not fair of me to invade your dream like I have, but I needed to know if you still remembered this night."

"I remember it," I said absently, confused. "I would have thought your favorite memory of me would have included the bed."

"Oh, I have plenty of those." The raw intensity of his gaze sent a thrill through my chest.

"Then you chose it because Shaw fell into the ocean?"

He chuckled, and it was a beautiful sound. "That was funny, but it isn't why I chose this one." He circled his fork to indicate the shared bowl, me and then him. "Since we've been apart, this is the evening I've thought about the most."

My forehead furrowed. "What happened?"

"Nothing," he said simply. "I made us an early dinner, and we watched a movie. You fell asleep in my arms a quarter of the way in. You looked calm, peaceful. I carried you to the bed and watched you sleep until the sun rose."

"Why did you choose it for a dream walk?" I asked, half prepared for him to expose some life-altering truth he was scared to tell me in reality.

It was adorable how he focused on the bowl of noodles as if he were intimidated to meet my eyes. "I've missed what we had together. I miss our conversations, your laughter, and how I laughed when I was with you. I miss…." When he lifted his gaze, his dark brown eyes hypnotized me and butterflies took flight in my stomach. "You."

His words pierced my soul, and the stunning truth in them caused my eyes to flash open. The room was dark, the bed beneath me as soft as a cloud, my skin sensitive to the cool ocean breeze. I was in his massive four-poster bed. Feeling his heart beat with mine, my breaths in sync with his, I rolled onto my side toward that pull, toward the ocean, and Orion was standing at the open door. "I'll leave you to dream in peace." He moved to leave.

"Stay," I whispered. "Tell me why you think of that night."

Orion slowly walked toward the bed as if each step were heavy. "We had a mission go bad and I was in a living hell." He paused. "I lost a friend to a demon. A close friend. That's why Shaw was drunk. He couldn't take it. None of us could. The pain of losing Demetrius nearly killed us all. I had asked you to come over because I thought I could lose myself in you."

Could lose himself with me in his bed. "Is that what I was to you? Your human lover?"

"Yes," he answered, and pain rippled through me. "I thought that's all we were—an intense attraction neither of us could deny. But that night changed everything. From the way you breezed into my apartment, from your gentle touch to your laughter—you healed my wounds. When you fell asleep in my arms, I saw your trust in me, and I realized I loved you. I never thought a human could own me, but you did. You do."

It was a lot for my groggy mind to process, but I caught the strong conviction in his words, along with a whisper in his brain involving the curse. "Tell me about the curse."

"I can explain it in the morning."

"You left me over it. Your mother tried to convince the Fae Council to end my life over it. I deserve to know the details." More than deserve. I snagged his hand and forced him to sit beside me on the bed. "Tell me."

"Since my birth, my mother saw a woman standing over my dead body. My dagger in her hand, dripping with my blood. Nessa then slays the woman. A sword through her heart." Orion flinched. "Her body falls over mine, looking as if we are two lovers locked in a bloody embrace. When you entered my life, my mother realized the woman she sees in her vision is you."

Even at my angriest with Orion…."I would never hurt you."

"I know, Cass," he said softly, but his eyes were full of pain. "I know."

I searched his face in the dim moonlight, feeling like someone had opened a trap door and I was falling through it. "You believe the vision is real. You believe I'll hurt you."

"My mother shared the vision with me—several times throughout the years. She believes you will kill me. I believe the path you and I will take together will lead to my death. When I was younger, I believed I could keep you safe from any harm—that my love for you would change the course of the future. After the demon attack, I realized I couldn't, so I let you go. My mother's visions stopped, but now that you're back, she's having them again. We're on the same course as before. I never previously understood the vision, but now I do."

"What do you understand?"

Orion glanced toward the sea. "You should sleep, Cass."

"Stop stalling and tell me."

"I'll die in the quest to find the Fae queen. My only regret will be that my mother will blame you for my death, and I won't be here to protect you from the aftermath."

My gut twisted at his resignation. "You believe the curse is real?"

"Fae visions are very real. You have no idea how powerful they are."

"You said the purpose of the Fae was to stop the destruction of humans. To do that, you set out to change the visions. Does it work? Does what you do change the future?"

"It can."

"Then we will change this one. You said in Fairy if I were willing to give us a chance, you would move heaven and hell to break the curse. Did you mean it?"

Orion cupped my face with his hands and his expression turned deadly serious. "To have you by my side again, to be given the honor of being yours, I would fight Satan himself."

My mouth dried out. I was standing on the cusp of a life-altering decision. Trust Orion or not trust him. Love him or keep him at bay.

"To be with you, I will do anything," Orion continued. "To

protect you, I will give my life. If you give us another try, I will break every rule necessary to keep you by my side." His fingers continued their slow slide from my cheek to along my neck, and I shivered with pleasure. Orion pressed his forehead to mine. "I want you. I want to lie with you, feel your body beneath mine, on top of mine, to become one. I want to be consumed by you."

Me, too. "I'm not giving us another try if you're intent on dying. I grieved you once. I can't grieve you again. We must break this curse."

"Heaven, hell and earth, Cassie. I will move each and every single one for you."

My heart stuttered. This was me entering his world again. I almost didn't survive last time, and there was a good chance neither of us would survive round two—emotionally or physically. "You're wrong about me," I whispered as I cast my glance to the floor.

Orion tipped my chin to force me to look into his eyes. "How's that?"

"I'm very afraid."

He held my gaze for so long I was terrified he had found a way inside my brain, and he was burrowing into the places I was frightened to visit. "Of what, my amans? Tell me and I'll slay the demon for you."

"Of you," I answered honestly. "Of me. I feel so much for you, still caught in the emotions of nineteen. I'm not that girl anymore. A week ago, I was my own person and now I'm a witch without a home. It's too easy to lean upon you again and fall into the patterns we lived before. I need to understand who you really are. I can't fall back into your bed. I cannot go straight back into your heart, but I'm willing to give us a try."

The right side of Orion's mouth briefly lifted. "That's a hell of a demon for me to slay."

"I'm not asking you to slay it. I'm asking you to try to understand me."

"Sciens," Orion whispered. "The Rite of Knowing."

"What?"

"Not important. Tell me what you need, and I'll give it to you. Help me understand."

"I need…for us…to move slowly. At least slower than before. You entered my life, and I was fine as you completely took it over. I want you in my life, but I need room to figure out who I am without you. Especially when I don't know who I am now."

"Are you asking me to court you, Cassie Strega?" There was laughter in his eyes.

Feeling stupid, I pushed his hands away and slid off the bed. "Fine, make fun of me."

Orion moved with amazing speed and cut me off from stalking away. His fingers snagged the belt loops of my jeans and dragged me close, so close we were thigh to thigh. The friction caused a wave of pleasure my body begged to ride. "Don't be in a rush to run from me. Not when you're finally in my life again." He lovingly tucked a lock of my hair behind my ear. "Courting you would be an honor. We will be slow. I promise you will relearn every inch and part of me, and I will enjoy slowly re-memorizing every inch and part of you."

The way he said it made my knees weak, and with the heat building between us, I longed for him to pick me up and stretch himself beside me on that bed.

"What are the rules? Tell me and I'll follow every one of them." His thumb lazily stroked along the hem of my jeans and under my shirt. I sucked in a breath when the pad of his thumb came in contact with my skin. "But you have to tell me this is real—that you're working toward being mine again, along with all of the privileges that permits."

I briefly closed my eyes at the mere idea of "privileges,"

and how those "privileges" would make my body sing. "You don't follow rules."

"I don't." Orion leaned in. His hot breath danced along the sensitive spot behind my ear. "Tell me the rules so I know where to start breaking them."

He nipped my earlobe, and I bit back a moan of desire. "You're bad."

"Always have been, Cass," he whispered to me. "But together we were so good. Tell me the rules. Tell me how to love you." Orion pressed his lips to the scar on my neck, and I nearly lost my mind with the surge of energy that rushed through me. It was the rhythm we'd find in that bed, the passion of the nights he took me in the ocean, on the beach, it was him guiding me to straddle his lap when he parked his bike and the way he'd make me forget the world around me.

My pulse pounded, there was a curling within me, a tightening that was begging for release. As I dared to turn my head toward Orion, to concede to this driving need, Orion drew back. "I will follow the rules—for you. If we're working on us, I'll do my best to move at the pace you need, but you have to admit the fire between us will eventually rage out of control. What will happen when we finally do burn together in bed? Will all be lost?"

"No, it will not be lost." Because there was no use in denying the fervor between us was intense. To continue to fight it would be a war we would lose. "But I deserve this—I deserve to figure myself out and to truly know you. I deserve the right to be my own person as I choose to be with you. I deserve to fully know and understand the man I am with. If that can't happen, then yes, I will leave."

Orion captured my hands and held them tight. "If that's what you need, then you'll have it. I promise you, Cass, I'll give you the world."

CHAPTER 25

I woke to the sound of the waves crashing along the beach and seagulls singing to each other. When I cracked my eyelids open, sunlight was streaming into the room. I stretched, and it was a weird sensation; my muscles were heavy with a long sleep. My pillow was a hard chest, my legs were tangled with another set, and the blanket that had been keeping me warm was a muscled arm holding me close.

I raised my head and rested my chin on Orion's chest. He and I had ended up in this bed last night, talking and laughing. Sharing moments of our lives from the time we spent apart. I even told him how much I missed my grandmother. The exhaustion eventually caught up, and as I listened to Orion's heartbeat, as I enjoyed his fingers massaging my scalp and the pleasant sensations of his hands combing through my hair, I drifted off.

Orion was asleep—a state he didn't require much of, but when he did sleep it was deep. The scruff along his jaw was the same color as his golden-brown hair, except the red was more noticeable. His square jaw was relaxed and his breathing even. When he had joined me in the bed, he took off his shirt to be comfortable. I teased that he was attempting to seduce me. His eyes darkened with lust, and he answered, "Maybe." That maybe was a yes, but I stayed strong. Though in this second, I didn't know what I was waiting for.

I delicately leaned up on my elbow so as to not wake him and examined his chest. The circular wound he had received nine years ago, the one he denied was a gunshot wound, but was, scarred the area below his right shoulder. There were many discolored scars. A few that were so deep they were white and raised.

As I moved my fingers along his skin, I saw flashes, images that shook me to my core. Human faces with red eyes lunging, Orion shouting as Shaw was struck by a sword, and Orion appearing by his side, taking the blade that was meant to end Shaw. The tip ripping flesh from Orion's chest. He yelled as he lifted his own sword and cut off the head of a demon. My stomach churned as I felt the burning pain in Orion's body from the injury, of how it created a terrible metallic taste in his mouth, of how his life force started to drain from him, yet Orion found the strength to swing around and stab the demon who was rushing up behind him. There was quiet in the mist, and Orion fell to his knees. Tierney emerged beside Shaw, her hands pressing against his bleeding wounds. Mercutio appeared beside Orion, trying to hold him up.

"The blades were poisoned," Orion gasped, out of breath. "Get Shaw to a healer."

"You need a healer," Mercutio said.

"You and Tierney take care of Shaw first. There's still one demon out there."

Sorrow overwhelmed me for Orion, Shaw, Mercutio,

Tierney and the countless other Sidhe who battled beside them, and for how much pain his body had endured over the years. While he had many scars, the large, jagged one bothered me the most, and I wanted to erase it. A spark of warmth ignited in my heart and raced to my hands. Driven by instinct, I traced the scar and heat radiated from my fingertips. My soul poured into his, and my awareness of Orion moved further along than just our breaths and heartbeats. His cells perked up and my own cells reacted the same. It was as if we were merging, becoming one, and the same raw urge and hunger from when I drank Orion's blood tiptoed into my veins.

"Not that I want you to stop, but you can't heal a scar." Orion's drowsy voice was rough with need and caused a stirring in my chest. "Doing so is like trying to raise the dead. Healers can only help open wounds."

"I'm not healing," I said, yet still ran my finger along the scar. "Just touching."

"I've been to a healer more than once, and that's how it feels—a warm sensation exiting your body and pouring into mine."

I curled my fingers in and frowned. Was that what I was doing? "I didn't know."

"It's okay. You're new to this. Wren will help you learn."

So would the Grimoire. My frown deepened. When would she summon me again and how? Then another thought hit me. "Someone else healed you?"

He cocked an eyebrow. "How do you think I met Wren?"

"Wren's a healer?"

"For the type of wounds Fae encounter, yes. I'm unaware if she has other healing abilities. Witches differ in how their power in healing manifests. Some heal the body, some the mind."

Interesting. "I thought Fae healed quickly."

"We do, but there're some injuries that would take days to recover from, and we're unable to heal on our own from poison blades. Only witches can heal us of those wounds. As you saw with my father, there are some poison blades, even with witches' help, we can't fully recover from." He paused as if waiting for me to explain what I did with Finvarra, but I remained silent, as I had no idea. "With our enemies always on our backs and with new visions pouring in daily, we don't have time to recoup properly, so we see witches."

There was a rock in my stomach. "Do healers have to touch you like I just did?" My touch was intimate. It was me pushing a piece of my soul into him and him willingly accepting.

"Except for what you did for my father, I was under the impression healers needed physical contact."

My fingers brushed along his gunshot wound, and a pit of ugliness opened in my soul. "So, after your battles and before you came to see me, someone used to touch you like I just did?"

There was a hint of a devious grin that edged me toward ticked off. "Are you jealous?"

Yes, and as I went to push off the bed, Orion moved so quickly I squealed with surprise. He flipped us so I was no longer on top, but he was lying on me. My breath came out in a rush. I'd missed this. I missed how perfectly we fit together. I missed how parts of him sweetly pressed into parts of me as if we had been made for one another. Orion's face hovered over mine, a breath's distance apart. I licked my suddenly dry lips, and Orion tracked the motion.

"How deep the energy needs to go depends on the severity of the wound. When we were together, only once did a healing start to mirror the touch you just performed on me, but I thought of you the entire time. Then I came home to you, hungry for you, needing you."

My fingers touched the long, jagged wound. "This one."

He nodded his affirmation then took my hand, linked his fingers with mine, and raised them over my head. "Your magic must not like the remnants of hers."

"I hurt for you when I saw the scar and wanted it gone."

"Then heal me, Cassie," Orion whispered then nipped my ear. My entire body came alive and, desiring more, I moved underneath him. "Take away all the pain."

There was an energy in the wound I didn't like clinging to him, and as a storm in my chest began to build, I pressed my lips to his. An explosion. Brightness around me as our mouths opened and our tongues danced. Our hands were hungry, greedy to feel everywhere at once. I shoved Orion and rolled us, ending with me on top.

His hands were in my hair, gliding along my back, grabbing at my shirt, tugging it up, and I was lost as I kissed his neck, enjoying and drinking in his touch. My body pulsed, begged for more, needing more, desiring—

"Bad timing?" Wren asked, and the shock of her voice caused me to flinch away from Orion. I would have leapt off him and onto the floor if he hadn't settled his hands on my hips to lock me in place.

"Go away, Wren," he said with obvious disdain.

Wren folded her arms and cocked a hip against the door-frame. "Nope. You've had her to yourself for long enough. She needs to spend time with witches—which is long over-due, since besides me she has had no interaction with a witch since she…oh…became one."

"Thoughts, Cassie?" he asked lazily, and he looked damn good with his hair a tousled mess. His thumb made small circles on my inner thighs, and with how fast our hearts were beating, how hard it was to gain a breath, I wanted to tell Wren to go to hell. But that was what I would have done nine years ago—stay lost with him.

I leaned down, kissed his lips, and moaned when his hand slipped higher up my thigh. I didn't want to resist, but I did. He let me go as I slid off him and the bed. "We have a baby to save, and we might do a better job finding her if I understand my abilities."

CHAPTER 26

From Orion's dark mood when I left with Wren, it was clear he wasn't happy, but he also kept his mouth shut, which was an indication he was determined to uphold our agreement. Before I walked out the door, Orion pulled me against him, gave me a kiss that made me question why I ever left his bed, and then stalked away like a pissed-off grizzly.

Wren's response was a sugary smile. "Didn't take long for you two to end up in bed."

Weird. Nine years felt like forever.

After drawing strange symbols on my arms and legs, and then having me wear a necklace and bracelets on both arms and ankles that contained protection stones, we left.

"Just to let you know, you can't depend on wards to protect you forever," Wren said as we walked to her car in the parking garage. "One, wards fade. Two, if you continue to draw wards on a person, they will gradually go insane."

That caused me to freeze in place. "Then what am I doing wearing them?"

"Calm down. You're a long ways away from that fun side

effect, but don't go thinking you can go the rest of your life wearing them, okay? Using them for now is okay. But we can't keep putting them on you for too long."

After that exciting piece of news, Wren was unusually quiet behind the wheel of a sporty little black car with the top down. She drove with the precision and speed of a race car driver over the bridge that connected the island to the mainland and then she chose the freeway. We headed into swamp territory that was beautiful, eerie, and atmospheric. On a dirt road that looked like it would easily wash away with the flooding of a tropical depression, we passed cypress knees protruding from the dark murky water like spikes, curtains of Spanish mosses, and southern live oaks that were like islands in the dark water where snakes slithered and swam across the stillness.

Wren kept the radio tuned to a news station addressing the evil of witches, including information about how to find one, what to do when one was discovered, and finally, how many witches had been brought to justice by the mobs since, as the news stations had labeled it, the Great Unveiling.

The dirt road ended, and Wren parked to the side. We sat in silence, listening to the end of the news report, and she finally turned the car off. "The mobs are killing women who aren't even witches now. The first few hours of The Awakening," because Wren refused to use human terminology, "they caught many who were new—people like you, Cassie. People who didn't even properly have the time to understand they were witches before they were slaughtered. People who didn't have Orion to save them. Now, people are acting crazy, doing what they've done for centuries— hating women for being powerful and knowledgeable, and trying to shove us into a box. You don't like your neighbor —call them a witch. You don't like your kids' teacher— witch. Don't get that promotion at work—witch. Kill all you fear, use a scapegoat in order to cover your own insecurities."

"What about the male witches?"

"Overall, they're safer than women, but a few have been murdered. Let's go."

"Where to?"

"To meet my coven."

I followed Wren out of the car and to a small, rickety boat I wasn't sure could hold one of us, much less two. "I thought you said you weren't highly organized."

"We're organized, but not like the Fae. Truth is, you're an unknown. Your blood flows in the leader of the Fae army and his blood flows in yours. You'll have to excuse me if I decide to be overprotective of the people I consider family. We've lost more than we should have, and I don't plan on losing more. Help me push this boat."

Wren bent down, but I crossed my arms. "If you're over-protective of them and see me as a threat, why are you taking me to them?"

"Because they asked to see you. We're wary of you, but you're one of us. Every witch has the right to find her true home. Besides," she surveyed me, "we were once friends."

"Orion says that there are witches helping the Fae and witches helping the demons, but most are staying neutral."

Wren just stared at me as if I hadn't spoken.

"Which is this coven?"

"A coven acts and decides as one."

That wasn't exactly an answer, but I decided to take it as one. "Did you know I was a witch?"

"I saw the dormancy within you," she answered. "But rarely does a woman out of her teen years break through that wall to her power. The older we become, the more we close ourselves off to the possibilities of who we could be. Adults are good at accepting a boring and predictable life."

"Being a witch isn't boring and predictable?" I asked.

Wren gave me a crafty smile that belonged to a teenager caught skipping school. "Has it been boring or predictable yet?"

I sighed heavily and dropped my arms. "Not at all. So, this is how it's going to be? Running from the one situation to the next wondering how I'm going to die this time?"

Wren laughed, a soulful one I had missed. "This time. Classic. How many times have you died now? Twice? The coven read tarot cards for you last night and death will definitely be riding your back for the foreseeable future."

"Fantastic," I mumbled.

"Are you scared of death?" Wren tilted her head as if she were honestly curious.

I thought of the terrible fear I'd felt while being dragged through the street by the mob and shuddered. "I'm not a fan of fear, pain, and the unknown, but I'm more scared of not being able to help those who need me." Because I hadn't told Wren about the baby. That was a Fae issue, and they seemed to have a great deal of distrust, if not hatred, toward witches.

"That," Wren pointed at me, "is the answer of a true witch. Rest assured, the cards do say, eventually, after turmoil, upheaval, and much unneeded death, there is a slight chance the overall world of witches will return to normal."

"Which is?"

"Healing. Fae create the seasons and protect the earth, but we're the caretakers. We help life thrive, we help ease pain, and we help those who are ready to move on from this life do so without the burdens of this world following them. In the past, there was a reason why many midwives were witches."

A breeze gusted through the trees, and a delicate, white flower drifted toward Wren. She caught it and her eyes moved about it as if she were reading a page from a book.

"I've been told you need to mask your connection with Orion before I can take you further."

Stunned, I wavered on my feet. "How do you know about that?"

"Did Hecate not tell you she belongs to all of us and none of us?"

"Hecate?" Who was that? My mouth dropped open and it was hard to form a sentence. "But when I asked you about the grimoire, you said—"

"I said a grimoire could be handed down or you could create your own. I didn't lie. I'll say it again—I already lost too many people this past week. I will not lose anymore, not even for you, so I was careful with what I told you. Now, cast the spell or I'll drive you back."

"I've never casted a spell before."

"Sure, you have. I caught you casting one in the bathroom. Each time you created a storm and called for lightning? Spell. You've been an empath for years, and while I don't mean to dismiss how hard you worked in school, I'm betting you were using some mad healing skills with your patients."

I rubbed my hands together with the growing unease and frustration. "But that came—"

"Naturally," she finished for me. "Maybe you didn't catch on earlier, but that is the essence of being a witch—nature. Hecate said you have a spell that will mask your connection with Orion, now do it."

"I don't have anything. She showed me a spell in a book, but she didn't show me how to cast it."

"You're overthinking. Just cast the spell."

"What if I can't—"

"Cassie!" Wren threw her arms out in agitation. "Do it!"

A spark of anger, and though I wanted to glare at her, I closed my eyes and focused on the words the Grimoire had shown me: *to keep me and thine alive, hide the ties that bind.* She said I had to imagine what I wanted. To see the cord that tethered me to Orion still attached, and then to see me stepping outside myself, beyond that hold, just for a brief period of time. Gone short enough I wouldn't be missed, gone long enough I could learn what I needed while keeping my teacher safe. The more I focused, the lighter I became, but I also felt this weird, hollow emptiness. Then my body spasmed as if I'd been shot. The pain nearly caused me to faint.

"It worked," muttered Wren. "I told the coven you were a badass. They were like, but she's a new witch, and I said it doesn't matter—you've always been as badass as they come."

The severe pain lessened, and after making sure I was steady on my feet, I opened my eyes and stared in wonder at the golden ball of light. "What is that?"

"That," Wren pointed at the ball, "would be your connection to Orion."

As I walked around it, I placed a hand on my chest, to where a cold void was growing. It was a dark sensation, similar to what I experienced after I realized my grandmother wasn't going to return, or when I woke in the hospital and heard Orion had died. "I don't like this."

"It's not permanent," Wren said with surprising sympathy. "You don't even have to return to this spot to recall it. When you're ready, reel it back in, but please don't until we are far from my coven."

I touched the shimmering ball, and it was what I imagined running my fingers through a stream of liquid sunshine would be like. "Why do I have to do this?"

"Because we're being hunted," Wren said. "I don't trust the Fae, but more importantly, Orion's enemies are the enemies of the witches. The demons have found you before by following that link. If you're not careful, they'll find you again. While the wards on you are powerful, I can't promise how long they will hold or how fast they'll fade when they do break. We can't risk your leading them to us."

I nodded as I understood, but having my connection with Orion outside my body was like having my nails being ripped from my fingers, my teeth being pulled from my head, my brains being sucked out of my nose. "He won't feel it?"

"No," Wren said as she readied the boat. "The only way he'd feel anything is if you snap the connection." She made a scissor motion with her fingers. "Otherwise, he'll think you're happy here on the bank of the swamp."

"What happens if he shows looking for me?" I asked.

"Then you'll have a lot of explaining to do, but I'm betting dollars to doughnuts, Mommy is in his face trying to win him over. Either that or he's fighting demons. Here, help me push off the boat. And I hope you're good at paddling, because I suck at it."

I frowned, not liking either of those ideas regarding Orion, and it was too late to trace the connection to him to confirm if he was okay. With one last look at the floating golden orb, I helped launch the boat into the water, hopped on, and then paddled away from my soul.

CHAPTER 27

For an hour, Wren and I paddled aimlessly through the swamp, her multiple bracelets tinkling together as she rowed. We went north, then west, south, then north again, a bit east, until I gave up being a human compass. There were flies, mosquitos, and other bugs I didn't want to contemplate, along with alligators who stalked me with their beady eyes from across the placid water. Finally, far off in the distance was a wooden shack that leaned to the left on a small island that was surrounded by four towering cypress trees marking the four corners.

"Stereotypical, don't you think?" I continued to help Wren paddle. "Witches hanging out in a swamp in a scary shack in the middle of nowhere. Did you at least clean up where you left cookies and candies for children to follow so you could eat them for dinner?"

Wren snorted. "We use the forest for that nonsense. Out here, the damn alligators kept eating the kids before we had a chance to kidnap them. Speaking of stereotypes, I went to the store last night and there were some drunk morons near the front door screening women for being a witch. I was able to walk on by because they were searching for old, white women with warts, but the idiots did have the social grace to tell me to go back to my own country." Anger pushed out of Wren so quickly that it created flames from her fingertips. "I spent eighteen years in the foster care system. That makes me more American than his sorry ass. I wanted to shove my foot up his butt, then light his pickup truck on fire."

"You should have."

"I came close. Very, very close. I agree on the stereotypical, but how many people do you know who are going to come out here?"

"None."

"Exactly. If they do and they get up in our business, the idiot's friends, if they have any, will presume they became alligator fodder. This isn't our typical hangout. Two weeks ago, we met at a coffee shop and then hung out at the local park to perform a ceremony around midnight. Deep in the trees, but still, we weren't holing up in someone's basement, terrified of the light of day. But now that the world is changing on us, we're not taking chances."

Completely understandable.

We rowed beside other boats tied to the dock. Wren grabbed a rope connected to a post and worked on tying a knot to keep us steady. *I haven't told my coven you're an empath. I trust them, but I won't put you at risk. I suggest you keep that information to yourself. If Hecate joins us, there is no point in lying to her. She annoyingly knows all. It's beyond reading minds. She knows things about me even I don't know.*

Who is Hecate?

You've met with her. Wren finished off the knot. *She was who you summoned when I caught you casting in the bathroom. I could feel your energy swarming, felt the call in my bones, and I knew she answered your call when you disappeared as you touched the knob of the door. I felt her there in the room with you. Lying to you at the time was easier.*

Dumbfounded, I had to force my brain to turn. *I didn't summon anyone.*

You did. Most witches only have a small amount of power and then spend the rest of their lives training to make it stronger. Power comes naturally for you, but you're untrained. A word of warning —there are some witches who aren't fond of those of us who have natural tendencies. Wren raised her eyes to meet mine—a showing of solidarity.

Why didn't you tell me about Hecate?

Because I didn't know what to say. With my unsteady relationship with the Fae, I already walk a thin line, and it became even thinner when you reappeared. I thought my days of playing double agent were over. How wrong I was.

Double agent. There was so much I didn't understand.

Hecate is our link to God, Wren continued. *The Fae have Gabriel as their go between and we have Hecate. Hecate is and she isn't. It's hard to explain. Truth is, even I don't understand. Some say she is the Key of Solomon.*

I don't know what that is.

"Wren, we're glad you made it safely," said a woman from the cabin door. "We were worried." The woman had kind, dark eyes and shoulder-length, mouse-brown hair. She appeared as if she were nearing fifty, had laugh lines around her eyes and mouth, and had the smile I imagined a proud aunt would have at seeing a favored niece. Her outfit was simple, jeans and a navy-blue T-shirt. She held out her arms to Wren in the invitation for a bear hug.

Wren wasn't a hugger, so it shocked me when she accepted the embrace, holding on for several seconds longer than I could stomach touching most anyone. Wren then gestured toward me. "This is Cassie Strega. Cassie, this is Beatrix. The leader of our coven."

Beatrix tilted her head as she surveyed me, and her eyes softened with pity. "No wonder you and Wren became sisters so quickly. Hardships have a way of creating deep bonds."

"Beatrix can read auras," Wren said as an explanation.

"Easier than I can read books," Beatrix said. "I'm severely dyslexic." The leader of the coven stepped closer to me, and it took everything I had to not recoil. She intensely examined the air around me with the same focus I had when studying for a nursing exam.

Hands have not been kind to you, child. Beatrix's voice was like being wrapped in one of my grandmother's hugs. *Neither has love. Deep love has brought you intense suffering. Like Wren, you're too young to have felt pain so severely. We welcome witches into our circle with open arms and love, but I see that a stranger's touch creates unease. We will respect the wounds you have that still bleed, but please know even though we are not taking you into our arms, there is great joy in our hearts that you are joining us.*

I tried for a smile, but failed.

"Auras are snitches." Annoyance radiated from Wren as she leaned against the wall of the shack, thumbs hitched in the pockets of her jeans. Then to me Wren said, *Beatrix heals souls.*

"Auras give nothing more than what the universe needs us to see so we can help with the healing of someone in pain," Beatrix said in a patient school-teacher voice. "Come, meet more of your family." She physically turned from me for the door, but in my mind's eye, Beatrix's spirit was still there, and she offered me her hand. There was so much compassion in the gesture, graciousness, and unconditional love. My soul leapt at the welcoming, and a ghost of myself linked fingers with her spirit and started forward. My physical self moved a few beats later.

Welcome to Oz. Wren inclined her head to the shack and then followed me in.

I expected darkness, dirt, and spiders, but instead I was in the middle of a great forest. Rays of the bright sun crept through the thick blanket of new green leaves. I breathed in and immediately was at ease with the scents of home: the freshness of green grass, the rich scent of soil, lilacs growing wild amongst the trees. I tasted the summer tomato off the vine, the sweetness of the spring strawberry, the tartness of the ripened blueberry. The trees swayed with the gentle breeze, applauding my arrival, and butterflies danced in a delicate tornado before me.

Wren winked as she walked past me and hiked toward a group of women who had made a circle in an open field.

"When you have accomplished the first part of the task the universe has asked of you, you may join us if you'd like," Beatrix said beside me. "Though you are connected to the Fae, you're still our sister and we will be here for you when you are in need. Wren is a good teacher. She will do well by you, but if you need additional help, call on me."

This seemed like a goodbye, and I didn't understand why. Why drag me halfway across the state, into whatever this place was, to leave me here alone? "How would I reach you?"

"The same way you called Hecate. Though I should be easier to summon." Beatrix lightly laughed as if we were sharing a private joke. She stayed still, yet a shadow of herself —a ghost—a spirit—reached forward and lovingly clutched my hand. "You have great power within you for healing, but I'm concerned for you. There are many broken and muti-lated pieces within you. While the upmost part of being a witch is helping others, with a coven you will find peace in a world that is unforgiving and dark. I implore you, once there is a calm moment, make time to join in unity with us, to take time for yourself. If you constantly heal and help others without a break, where will you find the strength to heal and help yourself?"

I nodded, as I had no idea how to answer or whether an answer was needed.

"By the way, this is truly a beautiful place. I can see why your soul calls for it. Our coven will bring honor to your home, as well as prayers for its peace, and for your peace as well."

My soul calls for it? A blink, and my heart acknowledged where I was before my mind. My chest squeezed hard at the sight of the carvings I made in the great towering oak tree, at my grandmother's encouragement, as a child. Two simple letters: C.S.

My grandmother took me into the forest, and we had a feast. Fresh vegetables, fruits, cheese and breads. She gave thanks for our food, for our lives, for the gifts bestowed to us, and then she took my hands and we danced in a circle. My grandmother sang and I joined in, singing along with the parts I could understand, as some of it was in a different language. We were lost in the dance, lost in the joy, and when we finished, my grandmother told me to remain still, to close my eyes and become one with the earth. So, I did. I shut my eyes, delighted in the warm, soft dirt beneath my bare toes, breathed in the heady forest scents, and raised my arms to welcome the playful breeze of the trees. A light appeared in my mind's eyes.

"Do you see it?" my grandmother asked.

"The light?"

"Yes, the light. Is it moving?"

As if waiting for her cue, the light began to skip away. "Yes."

"Follow it."

And I did. Past the familiar woods, over steep rocks, past the cold waters of the creek, and it led me to this tree.

"This is where you are grounded," my grandmother had said behind me. "To where your roots run deep. When you're lost, this is where you must return to burrow yourself into the dirt. Remember, from dust you were made, and to dust you will return."

That memory felt like lifetimes ago, and my fingers trembled as I traced the letters I had carved into the wood.

"Hello, Cassie Strega." The Grimoire stood under the shade of a neighboring grand maple and regarded me with interest. Her long black hair was pulled back with a pink ribbon and she wore a blue sundress, the hem of which kissed the tops of her bare feet. "I see you have left the confines of the Fae and their realms and that you mastered the spell to mask your connection."

"You're not a book?" I hedged.

"I am. Whether it be a book or a person or a voice in the wind—I am."

"Wren and Beatrix called you Hecate."

"They did."

"Wren said some call you the Key of Solomon."

"Some do."

"What should I call you?"

"I respond to many names. I know who and what I am, so I'm not as concerned with what my children call me. I'm more interested that my children find the right name for them to call me by. Who am I to you? Answer that question and that is how I will answer."

"I don't understand."

"Cassie Strega is not your given name, yet you respond to it, and you have responded to other names people have had for you."

My mother's boyfriend called me pathetic. My mother called me a mistake. Nessa said I was a whore. The cruel world called me forgotten. "Some names hurt."

"Those are not names, they are chains, and I am not speaking of chains. You, too, have been given many names, and like me, you respond with love to the names spoken with a true heart. Many have called you nurse, and by doing so gave thanks to the Creator for you, and in return the Creator named you as 'healer.' Many have called you 'friend' and 'confidant.' There is a Fae lover who calls you Cass." She paused as if giving me time for her words to sink in. "Tell me, when you originally summoned me, what were your thoughts?"

"I was in the bathroom, focusing on the book on my coffee table that appeared when Wren woke me from the dream. I needed help to find the baby, to protect the baby."

"Yes, but that was not the first time you summoned me. Our initial meeting, what did I appear as? What was the name you gave me?"

I blew out a frustrated breath. "After I woke, I saw the book and thought of you as a grimoire."

"What were you thinking then?"

"I wasn't thinking. I was confused. I felt fear. I needed…." My forehead furrowed at the connection. "Help."

"Yes." Her eyes brightened. "I am your help."

"But I flipped through a book to find the spell."

"You flipped through the knowledge within you. The book was a reflection of you sifting through power within that you have yet to understand. You've asked for help, Cassiel, and that is what I will give to you. Now, tell me, what is it you need help with?"

I was curious how she knew my given name. The one my grandmother gave me when, after my birth, my mother refused to name me herself. But that wasn't the point of my being here. Besides, Wren said the Grimoire knew all. Guess she was right. "Everything."

The pressure of the past few days crashed down around me, and the burdens weighing upon me made me too heavy to stand. So, I conceded, allowed myself to drop to the ground, and used the tree that contained my initials to prop me up. The Grimoire had an easy, graceful way as she closed the distance between us and sat on the forest floor across from me.

With a wave of her hand, clover flowers sprang from the ground, and I recalled how I would sit for hours with my grandmother, weaving the small flowers into garlands so I could crown her and myself royalty of our enchanted land.

"You don't tell people about her." The Grimoire weaved the flowers, just as my grandmother had taught me. "Not to Wren when you were as close as sisters. Not even in the dark nights full of whispered secrets when you were a cherished lover in the Fae's bed. Why?"

There was no point in asking how she knew any of this or how she knew I was thinking of my grandmother. I had plummeted down the rabbit hole days ago. I ran my fingers over the flowers, inhaling their sweet, spicy scent. "The pain of losing her hurts too much. It's an infected wound that won't stop oozing. Remembering her rips it open further. Talking about her—" A flash of pain stole the breath from my lungs. I couldn't finish the sentence so instead I shook my head.

"She is a part of you, correct?"

I nodded.

"Then how can they know you without knowing her?"

My eyes snapped to the Grimoire's, but she didn't notice as she tied one clover into another. I changed the subject. "The Fae Council has approved my helping to find the baby."

"I have heard."

"Will I do it? Will I be able to find her?"

"The baby is intent on finding you, but I will warn you, there will be peril. Her mother runs, but the darkness is closing in on her. I'm afraid once you and the baby are connected, it will expose you to grave danger. You must work with Wren and refine your abilities to protect yourself and the child."

"Once she's found, the Fae have sworn to protect her."

"The Fae will have their own battles to fight and you will have yours."

I nibbled on my lip as that hollow place created when I masked my connection with Orion became wider and deeper. "Do Fae visions come true?"

The Grimoire studied me with a hint of sadness. "If you are concerned for your Fae, then focus on understanding your magic. That will be your best weapon and defense."

"Can I change the outcome of the vision concerning me and Orion?"

"Free will changes everything. I say again, learn to understand your magic."

"How? I don't control it as much as it just keeps…happening."

"At first, you saw me as a book because that's how you see your abilities. Something outside of you to study then shelve. Your magic is already inside you. You've not become a witch; you're realizing you've been one all along. Magic is not complicated. To wield it, you need to have a clear mind, become one with the world around you, and have a pure heart."

Annoyed, I made a slip knot in a stem and then threaded a flower in. I repeated the action two more times. Was she not listening? "I don't know how to control it. I don't know how I summoned you. I don't know how I created lightning or a storm or how I masked my connection with Orion."

The Grimoire flickered and there was a sly smile stretching upon her lips. "You're trying to make me into a book again, and I'd prefer you wouldn't. Being confined is uncomfortable."

"Sorry," I said sheepishly. "I don't understand."

"That is because you are making magic complicated."

"If I closed my eyes and asked for a million dollars then would a million dollars appear?"

The Grimoire stopped her flower weaving. "You are a witch, not a genie in a lamp."

I didn't want to ask if genies were real. Just the thought of more magical beings divided my brain and the split hurt.

"If I told you that you have the ability to summon a million dollars, would you do it? Could you close your eyes, root yourself into the earth like you did when you were with your grandmother, breathe in the air of this forest, taste the honeysuckle you helped your grandmother plant, feel the wind that carried you when you were too tired to continue, and with a pure heart summon a million dollars?"

With a pure heart. Why would I want a million dollars? I could donate the money to those in need, to the hungry, to the poor, but when I searched my heart further, went into the dark and dirty crevices I purposely overlooked...while there was a good possibility I would give much of it away, I would find excuses to use the money for myself.

Could I summon a million dollars with a pure heart? "No."

"Witches are healers. We take on many forms. Some can heal the mind, some the soul, and some the body. There are some who are like Wren and can heal two out of the three and then there are some like you who can heal all three. The elements are drawn to us and allow us to call upon them in our time of need. We were given our gifts to help. Never for selfish reasons and never to harm."

I thought of the night of the mob. "I've summoned storms and lightning to use against others."

"You're allowed to protect yourself and the ones you love, but it's important for you to stay focused on a witch's oath to heal."

Orion said that some Fae believed witches worked with the demons. "Are there witches who use their abilities for selfish reasons or to harm?"

"Free will is a gift and it's a burden," she said. "Our power used in harmful ways has terrible repercussions for the one who cast the spell. Consider what we have discussed, Cassiel, but do not over think it. There's a reason why humans say the devil is in the details, as he loves when we get lost in our overanalyzing." After giving me a pointed glance for me to listen to her wise words, the Grimoire beamed at me and placed a garland of clover on my head. "There, my gift to you. A crown for the queen."

My heart ached, yet I smiled. "That's what my grandmother used to say."

"I know." She stood, I joined her, and I took courage in how I felt much lighter.

"Work with Wren on the meditation of magic and be careful in your plans with the Fae. They are our allies, but, like you, they have free will to choose their path. Free will is one of the Creator's greatest gifts, but it can also be a curse, as we can choose the wrong path as easily as the right. Now, I leave you in peace and love, healer." She inclined her head toward me in a sign of leaving, of respect, and it was natural to bow to her in return. As she turned to leave, a part of me called out for her to stay. It was my soul, and it wasn't ready for her to leave.

"Grimoire," I exclaimed, and she glanced at me over her shoulder. "I don't like that name for you, especially if it makes you feel confined."

"What would you like to call me?"

I shrugged. "Anabeth?"

She belly laughed, hands holding her stomach, as if she knew that was what I had named every one of my fish when I was younger. "To properly know someone, you must look into their heart. Look into mine and tell me who you see."

As I had done as a child, I closed my eyes, dug my feet into ground beneath me, breathed in the surrounding mountains, and focused on the air moving across my skin. I cleared my mind of anything else but the bright light dancing in my mind. I peered into the light, curiously looking about as a child seeing a rainbow for the first time. Who was she? She was kindness, understanding, love, compassion, my helper, my... I opened my eyes. "Teacher."

The approval that shined from her filled me with pride. "That is a wonderful name."

There was a blinding light. I closed my eyes against it and when I reopened them, I was standing outside on the dock, near the entrance of the dark, dirty shack and the only light was coming from the fading evening sun. I spun on my toes and found Wren at the end of the dock, readying the boat. I spun again and found Beatrix watching me with sympathetic eyes.

I blinked repeatedly, trying to grasp what had happened. "Was it real?" Orion's question echoed in my head...*What is real, Cass?* "Was I there? Did I talk to..." Teacher?

"The coven you saw in the distance was real," Beatrix responded. "But instead of joining you in the forest of your mountains, they surrounded you in this shack in a circle of protection and love as you walked with Hecate."

I glanced around again. "Where is everyone?"

"I sent them home. We want you to eventually join us once you complete your task, but you're on a path of great peril. I hope you understand, especially with our being hunted, I must protect my family."

"Great peril because I'm associating with a Fae?"

"My coven has scattered for safety. Today, we arrived separately and will return to our safe places separately. This is to protect you, as well, as to protect the others. But make no mistake, you're on a strenuous quest. One that means death. Hecate has told me that the task you've been given is important to saving our world. If you should need me and this coven, we will aid you however we can. You are our sister, and we help our family."

"Was it a dream?"

"You weren't asleep. Deep meditation, but not a dream. Whatever you and Hecate shared was real." She paused, and I was so bewildered I couldn't form a coherent thought. "When we closed our eyes, we saw where you're rooted. It's a beautiful place, and we were honored to have been allowed to visit such a sacred place to you."

The blood drained from my face. How was any of this real? "Are you rooted?"

Her smile was a hug, and I felt the ghost of a hand taking mine. "All witches are. How can we draw power from the earth if we aren't connected to it?"

"But I only recently became a witch," I whispered.

"But your grandmother was, and she made sure you were on the path to become one."

My mouth dried out. "How do you know?"

"Because she was my friend."

Through the shock, I stepped toward her, a million questions tripping up my tongue. "How did you—"

Beatrix held up her hand. "This isn't the time or place. I understand your questions and someday I will answer them. For now, you need to stay focused. Your life and the lives of many others depend upon it."

CHAPTER 28

he moment the boat landed where Wren had parked the car, I jumped out and eagerly reconnected with the ball of light that was my link to Orion. Rejoining with it was like the warmest and tightest hug. Unable to stop myself, I gave the thread between Orion and me a tug. In a split second, in my mind's eye, I flew through space and watched as Orion lifted his head in recognition. I felt his heartbeat, his even breaths, and his relief that I had wanted to reach out to him. *I'm coming home to you*, I whispered to him, but wasn't sure if the message could be delivered from so far.

I helped Wren hide the boat under branches, and then returned to the passenger side for the ride to the island. As we drove into the waning evening and toward the dark of night, we listened to a rock station with music that had loud guitars and even louder people shouting lyrics that hit too close to home. Throughout the drive, I closed my eyes and tried to focus on the baby. *Are you there? Are you still safe? Where are you?*

"If you've forgiven Orion, will you find a way to forgive

me, too?" Wren broke the silence between us. "We were once friends."

"Then why did you leave?" I asked.

"Because I didn't approve of Orion making you his amans. You didn't understand his world or the real implications of being his lover, and you sure as hell didn't understand the fallout of going through the rite with him. I couldn't stop you, I couldn't stop him, and I would be damned if I sat back and watched the train wreck happen, so I left."

We drove past two more exits until I found the courage to continue the conversation. "Orion claims me as his amans, but the council says the ritual wasn't executed properly and that we have until Beltane to complete the rite."

Wren tapped her fingers against the wheel. "Are you going to complete the ritual?"

"Orion acts like doing so will give me protection. What *is* an amans?"

"That's a question for Orion, not for me. I thought for sure you'd be asking a million questions about your grandmother."

Logic suggested I would, but I couldn't bring myself to do it.

"When we were friends," Wren continued, "except to tell a few stories about what life was like on the streets when you were running from your mom, you never discussed your past."

I felt a flare of anger, as this was the second time today someone pushed me on my grandmother. If Wren desired to speedrun memory lane, we'd sprint. "Did you know my grandmother was a witch?"

"Yes."

"Did you know when we met?"

"Yep."

"Why didn't you say anything?"

Wren switched the hand she was driving with. "Besides the fact you were a dormant witch and witches weren't real to humans at the time? Beatrix told me not to."

I chewed on that. Beatrix told her not to, and Wren had also previously admitted she became my friend at Nessa's directive. "Who sent you to spy on me first? Nessa or Beatrix?"

"Spy is such a strong word, at least in Beatrix's case. Watch would be better. We were curious. What were the chances the granddaughter of a lost coven member would choose to live near us?"

"When did Nessa get involved?"

"When isn't Nessa involved? I'm one of the few who heals Fae warriors when they're seriously wounded in battle, but the only one the same age as you. When Orion set his sights on you, Nessa was all over me."

There was a dangerous tensing of the muscles. "Did you heal Orion?"

"Put the claws away, tiger." Wren rolled her eyes. "Yes, I've healed Orion, but stopped when you two became involved. I'm a double agent, not a bitch. Unless I was the last witch available, I would have never healed someone you were involved with. After you two hooked up, he saw someone else for his healings. And if you remember correctly, while I'm not against dating the occasional guy, my preferences typically swing in the opposite direction."

Unhappy with my jealous kneejerk reaction, I sighed heavily. "Do you care to explain the double agent thing?"

"Nope." She glanced at me. "You think you're the only one the universe has asked to save the world? You can get that lone-savior complex out of your head. You're a piece of a bigger picture, and all of us have to play our parts precisely or we'll lose."

"What happens if we lose?"

Wren was silent for a few beats too long. "If we fail, then hell will overtake earth."

We were driving along the two-lane beach road, still twenty minutes from Orion's condo, and a tingle entered my blood along with a tickling touch that teased along the curve of my waist. Images flashed through my mind. Candlelight, the silk sheets of Orion's bed, him standing in the doorway of his bedroom at the penthouse. Shirt off, the soft light of the candles flickering on his sculpted chest and ripped abdomen. His arms were flexed as he rested them above his head onto the top rim of the door frame. His feral gaze was pinned solely on me as I seductively and slowly unbuttoned my shirt. Orion had the build of a fighter, the aura of a hunter, the presence of an untamed warrior, and he was my lover.

Orion stalked across the bedroom, his muscles rippling with the movement. He scooped me up so our naked chests were pressed tight, and his lips devoured mine. A wave of pleasure swam through me and caused my cells to spark to life. Liquid heat warmed my belly, fanning the flames of this delicious desire.

A blink and I was back in the passenger seat of Wren's car. "Orion's near." And he had let his walls down to welcome me home. A glimpse in the passenger side mirror and I caught how my cheeks were tinged red. My breaths were coming out in a rush, and my pulse pounded in my ears. All I wanted was to feel the heavy weight of Orion's body on top of mine.

Why was I waiting?

"There's something in the road." An edge of panic in Wren's voice and she moved her hands on the wheel to do a U-turn.

"It's Orion," I said. Even though I couldn't make out the figure, I knew it was him.

"How do you know?"

"It's him," I said, and she merely cocked an eyebrow as a response.

Wren slowed the car to a stop, I placed my hand on the door handle, and as I was about to hop out, I was startled by a knock on my window. Mercutio grinned from ear to ear. How did he get here so fast? "Knock, knock!" he called.

With the push of a button, the window rolled down with a whine. I was going to regret this. "Who's there?"

"Alex."

"Alex who?"

"Alex-plain when you let me in."

Before I could tilt my lips up in appreciation, he was in the backseat, causing me to jump again. Good God he had speed. "Shaw and Tierney are grabbing tables at Riptides. Pizza, beer, karaoke. You two in or what?"

"Aren't witches being herded into extinction?" I asked.

"Yeah, but one, things are chill on the island. Two, Riptides is mainly a Fae hangout. Three, you're heading out with four badass Fae warriors. No one is going near the two of you. Humans may not know we're Fae, but their instincts tell them we're trouble. Mad attractive trouble, but trouble all the same. Four, thanks to Wren's wards, no one who is looking for you can find you."

"I'll need to reapply Cassie's wards, but I'm in," Wren said. "As long as you're paying."

Mercutio gave her a nod. "I have you covered, but I wouldn't mind a ride."

Something in how Wren gave a small frown gave me the impression they were talking in code, as if he were telling her something private and it worried her. She scanned him, and I couldn't help but wonder what she was searching for. "Sure."

"Don't know how your day has been, Cassie," Mercutio said, "but Orion's been a bear all damn day. Mind heading out and giving me a break from his bad mood?"

Wren's headlights spotlighted Orion. He was lazily leaning against his motorcycle, wearing a pair of loose-fitting jeans and a white T-shirt that hugged his muscles perfectly. His arms were folded over his chest. The moonlight highlighted the curve of the muscles in his biceps, and he was staring straight at me.

"Are you lost?" I called out to Orion as I slipped out of the passenger side.

"I was concerned of the same for you." He pushed off the bike, and my heart quickened when he placed his hands on my hips and dragged me into him.

"Miss me?" I asked with a knowing smile.

His dark eyes were full of all sorts of suggestions for our plans for the evening as he drank me in. "Immensely." It was nice to be missed and even nicer to be welcomed home. "How was your day with Wren?"

"Educational."

Orion's jaw hardened, but he kept whatever he was thinking to himself as he pulled me in for a hug. I melted into him and closed my eyes the moment my head rested on his chest. This was what I so profoundly missed. Having someone's arms around me, being caught up in an embrace, to know I was needed, that I was loved.

"What do you say?" he asked as he snagged his fingers into the belt loops of my jeans. "Pizza? Beer? Maybe a dance or two?"

"Is this you courting me?"

The right side of his mouth quirked up. "How am I doing?"

"I'm impressed, but I'm giving it a seven."

"A seven?"

"I have to see how the evening progresses."

Orion chuckled. "You're going to make me work for this, aren't you?"

"Is that a problem?"

His fingers started a slow climb beneath my shirt, and I sucked in a breath at his devious touch. "Not at all." Orion leaned his head toward my neck, placed a kiss on the scar there, and I shivered, my blood instantly running hot. "I'm enjoying this slower pace." This forever tease between us may burn me alive. He skimmed his lips up my neck then whispered into my ear, "You didn't answer about the date."

Because I had lost the ability to speak. "Yes." I drew in any air that would snap me from the spell I was under. He handed me his leather jacket, and as I slipped it on, I paused at the sight of a cut going up his arm. The power inside me sparked to life like steel against flint, and my fingers went to the wound. "What happened?"

"Typical day at the office." He caught my hand before I could make contact with the cut. "I'm all about your healing me, Cass, but doing so has sexual undertones. Combine that with our blood lust and we will be an unstoppable inferno. Because of that, think hard before you agree to heal me. That may not line up with moving slow."

Lust rolled through him and into me, and suddenly it was hard to breathe. I craved to lay my hands on him, pour this energy out of me into him, and then let him loose to ravage me in exactly the way he was detailing in his mind. But we were taking things slow…we were…courting. I stepped back, accepted the helmet he offered, straddled his bike, and wrapped my arms around him. After Orion started his motorcycle and took off, he placed one of his hands over mine, keeping us connected as we drove next to the ocean.

CHAPTER 29

*R*iptide's—my home away from home. Worn wooden floors with matching wall paneling. Neon beer signs and mounted, large opened-mouthed stuffed fish. Plastic menus that listed the numerous fried foods and seafood available, and all the beer anyone could ask for in a bottle in addition to the cheap beer on tap. This wasn't the place where anyone went when they wanted a salad, but they did have hushpuppies that were so good that you thought were you having an orgasm when you took your first bite.

Years ago, I noticed the help-wanted ad on the door. The manager gave me the job on sight, I started waitressing that afternoon, and I met Orion at this very table that evening. He returned every night and asked the hostess to seat him in my section. Then one night, he asked for my number and walked me to my apartment. From that moment on, the axis of my entire world tilted.

Now, Orion strutted into the restaurant, went for the bar, pulled out his wallet, and dropped his seductive grin, green bills and then his credit card. The waitresses went to the corner and fought over who would earn Orion's tips at the end of the night and the opportunity to shamelessly flirt with him. But to his credit, he kept his focus on me.

After an initial round of sliders for everyone, the hush puppies and seasoned French fries flowed freely, as did the beer. Self-preservation kept me to finishing off one beer when we first arrived, then nursing a second as the evening progressed. Though I was all in for the hush puppies and French fries. Wren and Mercutio dominated the karaoke machine, and Orion and Shaw were at home at the billiards table, but it was Tierney who was a pool shark with the uncanny ability to hit the most precarious shots with ease. Watching her was like witnessing an artist at a canvas.

There was storytelling and laughter. Orion split his time between playing pool, watching his friends make fools of themselves on stage, and slipping behind me. He'd put his arms around me, feather kisses along my skin, and then lead me to the dance floor.

"Tell me something about you," Orion whispered into my ear as we swayed lazily to a slow song. My head had been on his shoulder, and, keeping my arms around his neck, I pulled back to look at him. His hands were on my hips, keeping me close. Orion was absolutely adorable with that glint in his eyes and amused slight slant of the corner of his lips.

"Like what?"

"You said you want us to get to know each other, so tell me something I don't know."

"I'm allergic to shellfish."

"That's new."

"Five years ago new. I had shrimp at a wedding buffet and I blew up like a balloon." I puffed out my cheeks for effect. "Your turn."

"My parents are married and they hate each other. They

haven't been on the same continent since they conceived me. They only see each other at Council meetings."

If that's how things were between them, I was slightly impressed Nessa didn't go praying mantis and tear off Finvarra's head after they had sex. "How does that make you feel?"

"Besides Council meetings, I never see my father. My only memories are of him being in pain. I'm curious what he'll be like now. Did you know you could heal like that?"

"Nope, and I'm not sure I can do it again."

"Tell me something about your childhood," he said.

I didn't like this game anymore. "There's not much to tell."

The glimmer in Orion's eyes faded, and I caught the fuzziness of his disappointment. We were standing there, dead in the water, and I was the one who had messed up the rhythm. How could I explain there were portions of my life I didn't want anyone in?

"Orion, Cassie!" Mercutio called. "More food!"

As we gathered around the table, Orion encouraged me to sit on his lap. I happily complied and tried to forget the awkwardness on the dance floor. I settled comfortably into him, enjoying the fast comebacks and long stories. There was tranquility in being this close to him, to feeling so relaxed.

As Mercutio came to the climax of his story, that moment when everyone had a smile and was waiting for the belly laugh, I had a weird sensation of déjà vu. I had sat at this table before with this group—everyone but Tierney. I had experienced this edge of acceptance, this preface of belonging, and when I had fully embraced it as mine, it had been ripped from me. Blood drained from my face, and I didn't want to be here anymore. Orion's head turned toward me, away from the conversation, as if he sensed the shift. His arms around me tightened. "Cassie?"

I edged off of his lap. "I need air."

Orion stood with me and placed a hand on my lower back as I weaved through the crowd toward the nearest exit —the one toward the beach. We stepped into the cool spring night, and I walked to where no one else was near. My heart was racing, my lungs tight, and I realized I was having a mini panic attack. Maybe a huge one. Maybe it wasn't one at all. Maybe my mind was finally cracking. Resting my arms on the railing that separated the walk from the dunes, I searched the stars above. *God, help me.*

"What's wrong, Cass? What happened?"

"How does this end differently? You say the connection between us makes you vulnerable to demons' finding you. If that's the case, I'd always be putting you in danger. We're always at risk of whatever terrible attack happened nine years ago happening again."

"We'll be okay," Orion said gently. "We won't make the same mistakes."

I listened to the waves crashing along the beach and breathed in the salty air. God, I missed this place. I missed the ocean, the sea, the stars, the friendships, the sense of belonging, of feeling loved, and I missed Orion. I missed the way he could make me laugh, the sound of his laughter when I amused him, the simplicity of his hand holding mine, the comfortable silences as he held me in his arms, the absolute sense of peace of being in his presence.

"I don't understand," I said. "Why did you want to make me your amans? Why did I agree and allow you to take my blood? Why, when doing so created this bond that left us both vulnerable to your enemies?"

Orion leaned forward, both of his arms on the railing, his hands clasped together as he stared at the dark horizon. "You're not going to like the answer."

So far, I hadn't liked many answers since my life exploded. "I deserve to know."

"You do." He dropped his head as if defeated. "You were different nine years ago. So was I. We were younger, strong willed, and didn't think a damn thing through."

I couldn't argue with any of that.

"But I loved you." His eyes met mine, and I was swept up in the overwhelming affection that emanated from him. "I still do."

Nine years ago, I was desperately in love with him, and in truth, I still was, but pain and love were synonymous, and I wasn't sure I wanted to play the game anymore. Not just with him, but with anyone. I had lived life without love for the past nine years and it was a half-life. A safe life, but a half one. Like watching an inferno from a distance. Too far to enjoy any of the warmth and every night was spent shivering in the unbearable cold.

"Why did we do it?" I pleaded with him. "What does being your amans mean besides I allowed you to drink my blood and it created a connection between us?"

"I wanted to be with you, Cassie. Forever. God willing, we can still have forever. If that is what you choose."

Hope surged through me, but I fisted my hands at my sides to try to stop the unwanted emotion. Hope was dangerous. Hope was ruthless. Hope had caused me pain again and again and again. I couldn't afford hope. Not anymore.

"My mother saw how close we were becoming," Orion continued. "And how attached I had become to you. Her visions of my death at your hands became stronger, clearer, so she started to move against you in the Council. My first step to making us forever was to tell you I was Fae, and my mother made sure I was punished greatly for that offense. She knew the path I was choosing, and I feared she would end up harming you. I hadn't planned on making you my amans so soon, but I couldn't risk allowing you to be unprotected any longer.

"By taking you on as my amans, my mother couldn't harm you. No fey could harm you. You would be regarded as my mate, with all the privileges bestowed on you thereof. When we were attacked, we were on the way to your apartment because there were things you refused to leave behind. Because it was the initial connection, it was very bright. I wasn't prepared for that. I begged you to let me take you immediately to Fairy. One, to complete the ceremony with the Council. Two, to keep you safe. I offered to go to your apartment for you, but you wouldn't tell me what it was you wanted." Orion ran a frustrated hand through his hair. "You were so damn stubborn."

I didn't remember any of that, but there was a sinking inside me at knowing what it was I was after and why I wouldn't tell him—the items from my grandmother. Yes, I was absolutely stubborn in my grief. Was I still?

I went numb as part of his declaration sank in. Mate. I was his mate with privileges thereof. "Your mate?" The words sounded distant, even though they came from my own mouth. "Mate as in…married?"

"Not in your traditions," he said and avoided my gaze.

That wasn't a no. "Are…we…married?"

"We have marriage ceremonies, but those are only allowed between Fae."

Still not a no. "Does the amans ceremony mean we're married?"

Orion briefly closed his eyes as if in pain, and then there was a surge of his sadness, guilt, love and pride—such a strange combination. "We're not married in human traditions or in the traditions of a witch, but in what marriage is between a Fae and a human—in what marriage means to me —yes."

Air rushed out of my body, and I was so dizzy I tipped to one side. Orion reached out to steady me, and as if sensing this was not the moment for contact, he withdrew.

"Fae don't view it as a marriage, but as a bond between a Fae and a human that cannot be broken. But in our traditions, taking on an amans is a sign of great love and respect. Oftentimes, the love for an amans is even greater than that of a Fae wife. To take your blood into my body means from now until the end of time, I belong to you. That without you, without our connection, I'm lost. When we're not linked, I experience pain. Agony that never goes away. Suffering that never lessens. Torture that finds new and awful ways to turn me inside out."

I shook my head, not wanting any of this to be real. "I didn't feel this pain when we were apart." Was that true? Without him, even after nine years, I felt empty and hollow….

"Because you're human, you wouldn't feel the tortures I do. By taking you as my amans, I am laying myself at your feet. You control the link. You control my happiness and my pain. I have handed you my heart."

A hazy memory of standing at the beach at night, wearing the same white lace dress I had when we had visited the Fae Council. The moon was full, the light bright, and Orion was on his knees as he cut himself with his blade and then squeezed his fist to drop his blood at and on my feet. He'd then stood and gazed deeply into my eyes. "Are you sure, Cass?"

Joy had blossomed through me. "Yes. Absolutely."

"Just a prick," he said as he stood. "Then I promise there'll be no pain." My heart had fluttered in anticipation as he took the sharp blade and created a nick in my neck. I flinched as if I were currently feeling the pain of the cut and then closed my eyes at the memory of the erotic rush of his lips at my throat. I forced my eyes open and held myself tight.

"I made you my amans to protect you from my mother and the Council and because I want to be with you forever."

He wanted to be with me forever…. "But that traded one problem for another." I pulled at the ends of my hair causing pain at the roots. "Making me your amans left us vulnerable so why did we do it?"

Orion's jaw twitched and my insides froze. He had yet to get to the part I wouldn't like.

"Tell me," I pushed.

"Once the ritual is completed with the Council, amans don't stay on earth. The completed bond is too bright and is a danger to all of us. Because of that, amans stay in Fairy."

My head whiplashed as if I had been punched in the face. "What did you say?"

"Amans live in Fairy. We…" he struggled to find the words, "provide for you there."

"And I would have done what?" My voice rose higher in anguish. "My sole purpose in life would have been for me to wait for you?"

His throat moved as he swallowed hard. "Yes," he said gruffly.

My hand went to my mouth and then drifted to my stomach as it twisted. The thoughts in my brain slowed as it tried to reject his words. "Is there…." Repulsed. I was repulsed at myself, at him, at both of us. "Is there some bustling community in Fairy I didn't notice before? Maybe when you took me there, we were on the outskirts of civilization? I'm assuming in Fairy there was a…productive life I had planned on living?"

Orion stayed stoic, emotionless, and then eventually shook his head.

Knots formed in my stomach and I turned from him.

Cassie Strega is nothing more than my son's witch whore. Nessa had been seething when she spat those words, and I was sick because it wasn't a euphemism. "Did I understand what I was giving up?"

"How can I answer that? Nine years ago, if you asked me if you understood what you were giving up, I would have said yes, but now…." He threw out his arms out in frustration. "*I* didn't understand what you were giving up, but I do now. I see who you've become. For the first few years after I left you, I watched you from a distance. I watched you fail, fall and succeed. I watched you struggle to relearn to walk and talk. I watched you work endless days and nights to earn your degree. I watched you walk across the graduation stage. I saw the look on your face the night you delivered your first baby on your own. I saw you happy…without me. When I saw that joy on your face, I never checked on you again. I wanted happiness for you, and you found it. Did you understand what you were giving up nine years ago? No. At nineteen you had no idea what life had to offer, and I'm a selfish bastard to have put you in the position I did."

I wanted to yell at him, to push him away for wanting to make me nothing more than his whore, but I instead turned from him and started to walk. I walked quickly, I walked brokenly. I walked with my arms wrapped around myself, as if that could salvage my broken pieces.

There was anger within me and I wanted to lash out at him, but that wouldn't be fair. There was no doubt he had told me the truth. He did ask me to deny myself for him, but *I* had agreed, and that was the important part. I could only lose myself if I allowed myself to go down that path. And the proof was there in that brief squeeze of forgotten memory—I was all in. I'd wanted to be his amans. I had wanted it more than I wanted air to breathe.

My shoulders tensed as Orion's emotions became so

strong that they battered me. His overwhelming grief, his sadness, his guilt, his love for me, and there was this pain. This wrenching pain that stole my breath. I spun on my toes and shouted at him, "What now? You expect me to complete this ceremony to officially become your whore so I'll be safe from your Fae Council?"

Orion shoved his hands into the pockets of his jeans. "Yes, to the ceremony, no, to living in Fairy. I'm not that ignorant bastard anymore, and I would never ask you to give up your life. If you're willing, we'll complete the ceremony on Beltane. We'll find the baby, and then I'll help you settle into a new normal life—one where you can continue as a nurse practitioner, a midwife and healer without the fear of being hunted as a witch."

None of it made sense. "But you said amans have to stay in Fairy. That the bond between us after the completed ceremony would be too bright and I'd be forced to stay there."

"If we don't find the baby before Beltane, we'll stay in Fairy during downtimes and then you'll cut the link whenever we're on earth."

There was a weird movement inside me, the hollowness growing, whispers of rejection in my brain. This was why I hated hope. Hope only led to pain. The realization of his words shredded my lungs. "You're going to leave me again?"

"No. If you'll allow me by your side, I'll never leave you again. We'll have Wren teach you how to use wards for when I'm with you on earth. Each time we're apart, you'll cut the link. Again, during down time together—I'll ask you to come to Fairy."

My brow furrowed. Hecate had said cutting the link would cause him agony. He'd just admitted that doing so caused him inconceivable pain. I didn't like that idea. In fact, I hated it. "But doing so will hurt you. You said a cut link causes you constant torment."

"I told you before I will move heaven and hell for you. I mean every word. From the moment I shed my blood for you in an oath and your blood entered my veins, it has never been about me, and it never will. I understood what I was taking on when I made you my amans. I understood the pain I would suffer if the connection were broken, I understood I was officially putting another life, your life, above my own. I don't regret it, and no matter what you choose—whether to be with me or without—as long as you're happy, when it comes to your being my amans—I will never regret the decision."

We stared at each other, a distance between us.

"I don't want you to be in pain," I said and meant it.

"I made that choice, you didn't. I never told you the consequence of a severed link. I love you, and I want to be with you, but more than that, I want you happy, Cassie. I can take whatever torture there is as long as I know you are safe and happy."

"What about this cursed vision from your mother?" I asked.

"I didn't take the vision seriously before. I do now. We will prevent that vision from happening."

We stared at each other for what felt like an eternity. How would this end well for either of us? I go with him to Fairy and give up a life that I loved….

Or

I stayed here, sever the link, and leave Orion in physical agony. Plus, there was this vision of our curse….

"If you need time to process, I understand," he said. "I'll ask Wren to let you stay with her. Just know that I love you, Cassie. I never stopped. You're a part of my soul, and all I want is your happiness."

Happiness. Did I even know what that was anymore?

Orion turned to leave, and my heart dropped at the sight.

The hole that existed inside me grew larger. I didn't want him in pain. I didn't want the pain inside me. I wanted to be who I was now, and I wanted to be with him. Orion was asking me to try with him, he was asking me to have hope, but what if I trusted in hope and it failed?

What if I did nothing and I never saw Orion again?

But what if I tried having faith? Tried trust? What if…I gave him a piece of myself I had never given to anyone else? What if I did and I finally found happiness? Orion was almost far enough away that he was becoming lost in the darkness, and I felt sick with the idea of losing him again.

"When I was younger, I ran away," I called out, and Orion stopped with his back still toward me. "After my grandmother died and the state found me living by myself, they sent me to live with my mom and her boyfriend. He was a…." My tongue twisted as nausea shot through me. "Awful. I never had a plan when I left. At least not one that worked. I was always found, but I couldn't stay with them. I had a home in the mountains with my grandmother. There, I was loved and I was safe, and it was taken from me. Then I lived in hell. When I ran for the coast, I found a home with you and that was taken from me, too." My heart beat hard in my chest and my throat thickened as sickening heat flashed through me. I didn't talk about this—my misery, my hurt—and doing so was making my body revolt.

"There's this screaming inside me that tells me love never lasts. That if I allow myself to feel happy, real happiness, then that happiness will be ripped away, so I don't know what to do with this—with you and me." Struggling to breathe, I pulled at the neckline of my shirt. "I…I don't know how to accept what you're offering. If I truly find happiness, does that mean I'll hurt worse when it goes wrong?"

One second, Orion was farther down, and then he was in

front of me. "Heaven and hell, Cass. For your happiness, I will move both."

My eyes frantically searched his resolved face. "But this bond between us causes you pain. Each time I break the connection—"

Orion framed my face with his hands. "I understood what I was taking on. Search me, Cass. Use your ability and explore every inch of my brain. My walls are lowered. You won't find regret, you won't find pain. You'll find a man who wants nothing more than to love you."

Orion's mind was crystal clear, and within it was a sunrise after the darkest night. Out of the cold, dark abyss there was an explosion of color of passion, devotion and love. Rays of the sun swaddling me in their embrace, keeping me safe and secure. And all of that love was for me.

I rose on my toes, Orion leaned down, and when our mouths met it was fireworks. Our lips moving in time, opening fully to each other. Orion's hand glided along my back, drawing me tight to him as the other messed through my hair. I couldn't get enough. Not of his touch, his kiss, of this fire spreading along my insides and licking upon my skin. As I broke free for air, Orion began the delicious assault of kisses along my neck, and my knees went weak.

"Orion," I whispered. "I want you." I was consumed with this powerful need to lie with him, for us to shed our clothes, worship each other's bodies, and find union in becoming one. To finally fulfill this driving, aching need.

Orion lifted his head from my neck to stare into my eyes. "I've missed those words coming from you. I have missed every inch of your body and soul."

I grabbed hold of his shirt to drag him to me again. "Take me to your condo."

That mischievous gleam I loved touched Orion's eyes, and he had that pirate smile that held naughty promises.

Orion and I were going to end up in a bed, but this would be a wickedly sleepless night. He linked his fingers with mine and we started for the parking lot.

"Do we need to tell the others we're leaving?" I asked.

"It's you and me, Cass. They'll figure it out. Do you want to try some protective wards? Because I need you to make sure Wren can't interrupt us again. Not when I plan on making love to you for the next several days."

I laughed. The type that originated deep in my belly and rocked through my entire body. Orion gave me a glorious smile, ear to ear, and when we reached his motorcycle, he swung around to draw me into his arms. "I love your laugh."

"I love your smile."

Orion's eyes darkened with lust as his hands wandered to my hips. "I love your body. Especially when it's close to mine."

"I love you," I said and melted all over again with how his entire expression softened. Orion reverently caressed my face, his fingers whispering against my skin, and I felt his love for me down to my toes. But then my forehead furrowed at the niggling in the back of my brain, and I stiffened with the strange intrusion. "Orion, there's something wrong."

CHAPTER 30

*O*rion wore a mask of death as he flicked his wrist and his dagger appeared. He hovered near me, reaching out to stop me as I began to wander toward where the strange energy was originating. "Mercutio, we're in the parking lot and there's problems."

I shrugged off his grip as I realized it wasn't one niggling in my brain, but two. One that was dark and angry, the other…familiar. The familiar pull contained a beautiful and melodic song, and I was completely enraptured. "It's the baby."

"What?" Orion slipped in front of me, blocking me from the direction I wanted to go.

Yes, the baby. I felt her, from the core of my soul to the tip of my toes. "She's near and she's calling to me." Flashes of light and Mercutio, Shaw and Tierney appeared. The menacing pull grew stronger, coming from the south. "There's something else besides the baby. It's a lot like before Moloch arrived in Alex Bay, but it's not as strong."

"Demons," Shaw spit out and produced a sword with a

wave of his hand. "Get her out of here, Orion, to the beach. That's the closet liminal link. Take her to Fairy."

Orion tangled his fingers with mine. "Let's go."

I yanked out of his grip. "The baby is near. She's the priority. Not me."

Orion searched my face. "Are you sure she's close by?"

"Yes."

A war of emotions overtook Orion's face. "Take us to her. We'll get you, her and the mother to safety."

To Fairy. I understood and agreed. Following her was easy. Her pull was a lullaby that became louder with each step, became more enchanting. As if in a haze, I could no longer sense the demons, could no longer sense others around me, could no longer taste the salt in the air or hear the waves crashing on the beach. Nor was I aware of touch, not even when Orion snagged my wrist. But I didn't care; I was consumed with the need to find the one who was singing.

I moved through the parking lot and down the street, speeding my walk close to a run as I cut through an ally and emerged onto an empty street full of trinket shops closed for the night. My head whipped to the left, and my mouth hung open—Brittney. A very pregnant Brittney, cradling her overdue stomach, looking absolutely scared, pale and exhausted. Impossible.

Orion froze beside me and I swung my gaze to him. "You said she had the baby."

Sensing danger, he edged himself in front of me. "I held her baby."

"Cassie," Brittney called, and her entire face clenched as she cradled her belly. "Cassie, I'm scared. I don't understand what's happening and I'm scared."

"Did you see her deliver?" I demanded of Orion. "Did you see her deliver the baby?"

He absently shook his head as if he couldn't believe what he was seeing. "I drove her to the hospital, but when it came time to deliver, the doctor asked me to leave the room. I did. I later held the baby in the nursery and discovered she wasn't our queen. Then I left."

"Orion, the demons are coming," Shaw said. "Does she carry our queen?"

"No," I struggled out as I tried to expand my mind to understand the siren call coming from Brittney's womb, and to weave through the tangle of Brittney's fear to figure out what was happening. The baby was calling to me, but with an instinct I couldn't explain, I *knew* this baby wasn't their queen. The Fae shot a look toward me. Unable to stop myself, I took a step closer to Brittney. "She doesn't carry your queen, but she is about to give birth."

"This is the woman we originally thought was carrying our queen," Orion said as he matched my steps. "The one who I drove to New York. Cassie, don't get closer to her. She's been marked by demons."

"I have to see to her." I was compelled to.

"Orion, take Cassie to Fairy," Shaw said as he, Mercutio and Tierney created a wide circle around us. "The demons could be using this woman to track and harm the two of you."

Brittney let out a blood curdling scream and fell to her knees on the pavement. I shot forward. Orion grabbed me, but a gust of wind from the sky pushed him back. I sank to the pavement next to her. "Tell me what's happening."

"There's pain." Brittney rocked as if doing so could bring her relief. "There's been pain. For days. But the baby won't come. She won't. I don't like my brain anymore. I don't. First, I was obsessed with coming home to New York. The thoughts wouldn't stop. Every damn second of every day, my brain screamed to go home, and when I did, I met you. The screaming stopped, but then it started again, but louder. Telling me to find you again. I'm scared, Cassie. I'm scared." She wept freely, her body trembling, and I was terrified to touch her due to her intense emotions. Brittney screamed again, and I quaked as I felt her pain in the marrow of my bones.

"The demons are nearing!" Shaw shouted, and I winced with the screaming sound of metal nails against a chalkboard that was growing from the south.

Orion appeared by my side. "We need to go."

"Brittney's having this baby and she needs a hospital. I can't leave her until she's safe." My heart beat hard in my ears as I sensed the rising fear and tension in Orion, saw the images in his head of me bloody and broken nine years before. "Can we take her to Fairy?"

"No. She reeks of demon. Even if I wanted to take her to Fairy, the realm wouldn't allow her to enter. My oath is to protect our queen and to protect you. You have to leave—"

"And my oath as a nurse and midwife is to protect this child and her mother. If you don't understand that then you don't understand me. It's a baby, Orion. Not a monster. And this is the baby's mother. A woman who needs me. Neither of them will live if I leave them."

Orion let out a string of curses as he picked up Brittney and carried her across the street. He kicked open the door of a gift shop, stalked to the back of the store where items were stored, and laid Brittney on the floor. She shrieked again, and I rested a hand on her forehead to soothe her. The psychic impact of that touch caused me to convulse, but I fought through the energy whiplash. "Lie down, Brittney. Let me examine you so I can see how much you've progressed."

More tears fell from her eyes. "It hurts."

"I know," I cooed softly to help her relax. "Let me take a

look." I helped Brittney take off her shorts and suppressed a frustrated sigh. Ten centimeters.

"Is the baby okay?" Brittney asked with a shaky voice.

I mentally prepared myself then placed a hand on her stomach for a quick read. The baby was aware, and fear pulsed from her. "How long have you had the urge to push?"

"Too long."

"Why didn't you go to a hospital?"

Brittney struggled to get up. "I had to find you. You have to be the one to deliver her."

I gently edged her to the floor. "Okay, Brittney. Just lie back. She's doing okay. But if you have another contraction, don't push. Do you understand? Don't push."

"Don't push," Brittney repeated. "I won't push."

Orion hovered over us and Mercutio stood in the doorway. "Wren's on her way with my SUV to get this woman to the hospital, but the demons are closing in fast. Having both you and Cassie here is a hell of a risk for us." A pause. "Orion, whatever you two did when you left the bar made your bond brighter. Demons will see it now."

"I know," Orion said, "but the baby is on its way."

"I need blankets, scissors and water," I said. "Hand sanitizer and or rubbing alcohol if you can find it. I also need a string for the umbilical cord." I hoped against hope I wouldn't need it. *A scalpel—something sharp to make a cut,* I sent to Orion.

He spoke to Mercutio in a low voice, hopefully repeating my requests. "Cassie, I need to talk to you," Orion called from the door after Mercutio disappeared.

I squeezed Brittney's hand. "I'll be back." Then went to join Orion.

His expression grew pensive. "I need you to cut our link."

"What?"

"I don't want to run the risk that they might be able to follow our link to find you."

The idea of cutting the link shook me to the core. "How do I cut it?"

"Close to the same way you masked the link," Wren said as she entered and moved between me and Orion as she continued forward. "Except see yourself cutting it in half. You need to go, Orion. I'll ward the place and keep her safe."

"Thank you," he said with deep sincerity.

"Yeah, yeah, whatever. Get out of here."

Mercutio appeared, dumped the items I asked for at my feet, and then disappeared again. There was also a huge medical bag EMS workers carried. Wren scored a thick black marker from a desk and drew circles onto the wall with symbols within them.

"Orion," Wren said under her breath, as if scared of being heard, "I healed Mercutio earlier this evening. He's not one hundred percent. Watch his back."

"We're indebted to you, Wren," Orion said.

"You have been for a while." Wren moved to another wall and drew circles on there. "Cut the link, Cassie, and save this baby. These are crude, Orion, and won't hold for long. If I have to fight, this entire building will burn around us. You need to win this battle fast."

Orion cupped my face, leaned down, and took my lips. The pure determination of his love poured into me. He ended the kiss and rested his forehead to mine. "I love you." He released me then braced his arms against the doorframe. "Break the link."

Brittney shrieked as another contraction rolled through her. I raced towards her, grabbed her hand, and let her transfer her pain into me. "Don't push," I reminded her.

Drawing in Brittney's pain, Wren's concern, Orion's

protective fear, a ball of energy in me grew and I cleared my mind by whispering the same words over again: *to keep me and thine alive, break the ties that bind.* The cord that tethered me to Orion was bright, was beautiful, and the thought of harming it made me want to weep. But this was to keep him alive, me alive, Brittney and this baby alive. In my mind's eyes, I walked along the connection and marveled at it. I didn't want to do this. Didn't want to hurt me or Orion, but this had to be done. I raised my arms, felt a wet streak cascade from my eyes, and like scissors, snapped my arms shut. The breath rushed out of my body as the broken link reverberated and slapped me hard.

The muscles in Orion's arms strained as he fought to keep himself upright. His knees buckled, and as I jumped to move toward him, Wren grabbed my arm. "You touch him, and he'll have to go through it again. Leave him be."

As Orion continued to grimace and struggled to find his land legs, I had to fight the urge to hug him and make him better. He clutched his chest as if he were having a heart attack. Knowing I could do nothing, I forced myself to turn my back on him, though doing so was like ripping off my skin. It was hard to take in air when my lungs weren't working, hard to see as my eyes kept filling, hard to stay upright when I was shaking so hard my teeth chattered.

I fell to my knees next to Brittney, who was still suffering through the contraction. On the inside, I was hollow… empty…and there was a flash of a bright light that told me Orion was gone. The baby. I needed to save the baby. I laid my hands on Brittney's stomach and concentrated on the baby within. *I'm here.*

The baby stilled and turned her head in recognition. Happiness radiated through her, and her tiny arm moved as if trying to reach me. I pushed along Brittney's stomach, tried to see the womb through the eyes of the baby, and there was a sinking foreboding with the confinement, the panicked feeling of something blocking her progression. I pressed just above the pelvic bone and gave the baby a mental nudge. *Move your shoulder.*

The baby twisted, but there was no room to move and her anxiety heightened. "Brittney, your baby's shoulder's stuck, preventing her from moving down the birth canal. In order to save her I'm going to need to—"

"Do it!" Brittney yelled. Sweat poured off her brow, and she shook on the floor, her teeth chattering. "Do what you need to do to save my baby." She was going into shock.

"You need a hospital."

"The baby doesn't want a hospital. Each time I go to one, the contractions stop and then her father finds me and takes me out of the hospital. His brother then helps me run, but then her father finds me again. She wants you to deliver her, and she doesn't want *him*."

I moved the hair stuck to her sweaty face. "You don't know that."

"I do. I don't know what it'll mean to be a mom, but I know she needs you."

Wren crouched to Brittney's side and took her hand. "How can I help?"

"Do you know anything about childbirth?" I asked.

"No, but I can ease her pain. If there are injuries, I'll be able to help."

I moved to between Brittney's legs. "Help her any way you can. Brittney, this will be painful. Do not push unless I say. Your baby is in trouble and I'm going to try to help her."

Another contraction rolled through and Brittney screamed. I went to work, zoning in on what needed to be done. I sanitized my hands and the items I would need to deliver the baby. I took the scalpel in hand and spoke to Wren. *From here on out, she will be in excruciating agony.*

Wren nodded and held Brittney's hand tighter. She closed her eyes, dropped her head and began a whispered chant. I said my own prayers as I made the necessary cut to widen the opening as part of the problem was the baby was huge for a newborn. Brittney moaned with pain, not screeching, which meant Wren was helping.

"I need you to pull your legs to your stomach." As Wren and I helped move her legs into the position, I gave her the bad news. "I'm going to have to use my hand to free her."

Brittney squeezed her eyes shut as tears fell down her cheek. "Get her out. Please," she begged. "Just get her out."

Wren stroked Brittney's tears away and soothed her hair back as she continued her whispered words that not only relaxed Brittney and the baby, but also me. I took a deep cleansing breath and then let it out slowly. I had done this before, especially when working in the rural areas and the mother wasn't going to reach the hospital in time.

The building around us shook, and when I glanced at Wren, she was focused on Brittney. *The demons have arrived and the Fae are in battle. If you walked out onto the street you wouldn't see them as they fight in another realm that is parallel to ours. When the fighting is intense though, it can reverberate into our world.*

Yes, I had done this before, but not while Fae and demons were battling. Not when I knew the man I loved was in danger. I mentally readied myself and then reached into the birth canal, relying on my training, using the baby's sight to guide me. Brittney tensed, Wren held her down, and Brittney emitted a low moan of torment. I located the baby's shoulder, moved it, and the baby slipped along the birth canal. As I withdrew my hand, the contraction rolled through her. "Push, Brittney! Push now!"

As the walls around us shook again, Brittney pushed and the head crowned. "Good job, Brittney." Wren continued her vigil of words, and my gut clenched with anxiety. This baby needed out so she could take a breath. "Next push, I need you to give it everything you have, do you understand? I want her out, and I know you do, too."

The contraction began and I maneuvered to catch. "Push, Brittney! Push!" She did, and I held my hands out as Brittney's hard work released this precious new life into the world. There was a strange stillness as the baby emerged. Ten toes, ten fingers and all sound became muted, as if the entire universe were holding its breath. Going into that calm place in my soul when the situation was going grim fast, I focused on the task at hand. *Come on, baby. Don't do this. I know it's scary, but this life you're just starting is worth living.*

The building shook again, and this time, pieces of dust and drywall fell around us, forcing me to shield Brittney and the baby with my own body.

Something's wrong, Wren sent telepathically. *The demons are pushing against my wards.*

"Why isn't she crying?" Brittney's voice was thick with tears she leaned up on her elbows. "Isn't she supposed to be crying?"

How long do we have? I laid the baby on the towels, quickly cleaned her, and suctioned her nose and mouth. Most babies didn't come out automatically crying, but they would react to these movements. Parents were oblivious that it took a few seconds for their baby to take their initial breath. While I knew this happened, it still caused a deep pit in my soul as I, too, waited. *Come on, come on, come on.* I placed her on another clean, dry towel, swaddled her, and picked her up. Through the blanket, I flicked the bottom of her feet. *Come on, little one, breathe.*

286

My wards won't hold long, Wren answered. *They were crude at best. We're going to have to figure out how to leave.*

Then I heard the most beautiful sound in the world. The gasp for air followed by the cry. Tears pricked my eyes as I held her close.

"Is she okay?" Brittney asked.

"She's beautiful."

CHAPTER 31

The baby opened her eyes, and I was startled as she looked straight at me, causing our gazes to lock. Newborns didn't have that type of awareness. Not the sense of recognition she exhibited as she reached her hand out toward me. She had gorgeous blue eyes, a head full of blond hair, and a strong heartbeat. My head tilted as the low pulse I had detected from her when she was in the womb grew stronger.

She's demon, Wren pushed into my mind, her voice dripping with menace. *The baby is a Nephilim. A child of a fallen archangel. I once caught scent of a Nephilim off of an old relic and this baby has had the same smell since the moment you delivered her.*

You can smell demons? I asked.

It's a trait of mine, and she's not just a demon. That's demon royalty. The world hasn't seen a demon baby since the dawn of time. I'm going to be honest with you, Cassie. I'm officially freaking out.

It's a baby!

Wren looked me square in the eye. *That is the child of the devil.*

The baby stirred in my arms. She reached up again and I took her small fingers. The skin-to-skin contact was a rush as her emotion poured into me. Joy and curiosity at this new world around her. *She's part human.*

Which makes her even more dangerous. Humans were the ones trying to burn you at the stake for being a witch.

"She's a baby," I snapped at Wren, and Brittney's eyes widened as I handed her child to her. "Keep her swaddled and warm, and protect her head. If you can't support her, let me know." Then to Wren, *Brittney needs healing from the episiotomy. Are you capable of that or does Brittney not deserve your help?*

Wren glowered as I clamped the umbilical cord. I then laid the baby on the ground long enough to help Brittney through the afterbirth. The baby didn't cry when placed by herself, and that unnerved me. Not all babies wailed at birth, but this baby had a contentment I had never encountered with a newborn before. And the pull was still there, a lullaby being sung to my soul.

Pissed off at the world, Wren started to heal Brittney, but then swiveled her head toward the wards on the wall, acting as if she could see things I could not. The hair on my arms stood on end as did the fine hair on the baby's arms. The building shuddered again, and my blood pressure dropped at the sight of the wards fading.

"We have to go, Cassie." Wren's face was strained with concern. "Now."

Is the car close? Brittney is bleeding badly and moving her is a risk. Which one do you want to carry, Brittney or the baby?

Neither! The demons are coming for Brittney and the baby! This is their child! Let the demons have them!

"And the baby called for me!" I shouted. "She still is."

The building shook again, and Brittney swiped up her baby and held her tight. "He's coming for me, isn't he?"

Both Wren and I turned to face her. "Do you know who *he* is?" I ask slowly.

"He's something wrong." Brittney tucked in the corner of the blanket swaddling her baby. "I don't know what he is… but I know it's not good. I swear I didn't know there was something wrong with him. Not until after I became pregnant. He was so angry I left. He didn't understand I had to find you. He said he'd protect our baby, and when he got angry his face became weird. So did his eyes." She shuddered. "I don't want him near my baby."

"He's the father," Wren pressed. "Are you sure he isn't who you want?"

"I thought he was who I wanted, but I realized too late he wasn't. She wants you, Cassie. From the moment I first saw you, I just knew my baby needs you in order to survive."

I shot a glare at Wren. *Go if you want. I won't leave her behind. She's asked for my help and I'm giving it. You can leave. This isn't your battle.*

Wren angrily clapped her hands together as if doing so would keep her from throttling me. *That baby is five minutes old and has no idea who is or isn't on her side. If the Fae are searching for their queen, why wouldn't the demons be looking for theirs? And witches know the Fae are seeking their queen. Our job is to protect humans from the fallout of this bloody war. God and the devil are setting up the final chess game between them and they have placed their queens on the board. Hell…* She rubbed her hands over her face. *Maybe we're the pawns and the game has already begun.* Wren shook her head as if exhausted and annoyed. *That's the demons' queen and they won't stop until they find her. If you don't hand that baby to them, then the demons will hunt us, and we risk our lives for what? For her to grow into her demon genetics? Can you imagine her as a preteen? One bad hair*

*day and the entire world burns to the ground? And even if we keep
her, the Fae will not allow her to live.*

I couldn't imagine Orion harming a child, but Nessa
wouldn't bat an eye. *She's also human, so that means free will.
She can choose her own path. This infant called to me for weeks. I
don't know why she chose me, but she did. Maybe she's using her
free will to choose her human side.*

Wren placed her hands on her hips. *You were a dormant
witch and a Sidhe's amans still in the human world. Maybe that
made you a weird demon-baby beacon. Not everything is fate.*

*This baby chose me, and Hecate said when I refused the portal,
I chose her, as well. She may have demon blood in her, but she is
free to choose differently.*

Wren let out a frustrated sigh. *She has to live long enough to
be given a choice, Cassie. How are you going to protect an infant
when you're an infant as a witch? And what about the Fae baby?
Did you have no connection to her, or was it always this baby?*

Looking down at the baby, seeing how she watched me
with absolute trust, I had no doubt that this was the baby I
had connected with. But Relle said she had seen me with the
Fae queen so what did it all mean? *I'll deal with that later.*

Another shove against the building, as if there was a giant
outside attempting to tackle it to the ground. The wards
faded into the paint. The electricity shut off, and in an
instant, there were two flames. One each being held in
Wren's palms. "The storms and the lightning—it happens
when you're emotional, right?"

"Yes."

"If I'm staying to defend a Nephilim, you better light them
up when they come at me and then make it rain so you aren't
burned alive by what I'm about to do."

"You don't have to stay," I said.

"I do. I promised myself I would never leave a friend in
need again."

A hissing sound caught our attention, and a gray, choking mist seeped into the room from the floor and windows. My eyes burned, and my hands went to my throat as it felt like strong fingers were closing in on my windpipe. Wren, Brittney and I began to cough. I grabbed Brittney, forced her to look at me, and shouted in her mind. *We have to get out of the building. Can you hold the baby and keep her safe?*

Brittney's eyes widened with the use of telepathy from me, but then nodded. As she tried to stand, she collapsed. I took the baby from her as Wren snaked an arm around Brittney and hauled her toward the exit. But each way out we tried, we were met with rapidly rising smoke. The smoke solidified yet shifted, reminding me of Calypso. Instead of half-fish though, their faces twisted into a gray cloud, then to a human. Their eyes were red as flames, and they had forked tongues that slipped out as if smelling the air like a serpent. One formed next to me, and when it reached for the baby, Wren released a battle cry.

Fire protruded from the palms of her hands like a flame thrower and hit the demon as I used my body to cover both Brittney and the baby. I shoved them into a corner, thrusted the baby into her arms, and pushed her toward the floor. *Keep her safe. If you see a way out, if you are strong enough, run. I will find you.*

"She wants you." Tears streamed down Brittney's face. "She needs you."

Other demons raced forward, and Wren shot fire at them. The desk and chair caught on fire and the flames quickly spread. Anger flared within me and the wind picked up. Thunder clapped outside the building, and my ears popped as the air pressure dropped. The building shuddered with the wind, the roaring of a train filled our ears, and the roof flew off the building. A hurricane gale burst through the room and hurled the demons into the wall. They dissipated into smoke, but quickly restructured.

The demons formed a line then shot out in unison. Pain burst against my cheek as a fist pounded my jaw. I fell to the ground and there was blackness then stars. I opened my eyes to see Brittney crawling toward the back door with her baby close to her chest. Wren yelped as a dagger caught her in the shoulder. We were losing. The baby was in danger. She came to me and I was failing.

I pushed myself up to my hands and knees, and there was an explosion of agony as I was kicked in the stomach. I rolled away and the boot caught me in the spine. Not willing to quit, I tried to get up again as a smoke monster stalked toward Brittney. No. Not the baby. I pushed off the ground and screamed, "Leave her alone!"

"Watch out!" Wren yelled, and she shot fire at the demon, and he disappeared before it hit him. More smoke poured into the room, more pillars of the mist turning into demons. The newly formed demons merged together, becoming one big ball of heads, eyes, forked tongues, arms, and legs. Each pair of hands started to move in a circle, and they created a huge ball of black smoke.

"Don't let them finish!" Wren yelled as she shot flames at the sickening formation.

Lightning danced in my veins, and as I reached my arms to aim the strike, the baby began crying. The herd of demons shot black smoke in my direction right as lightning sparked from the clouds above, and I was shoved to the floor by Brittney. Her terrified eyes met mine. "She needs you!"

The smoke struck her, and I screamed as the light in Brittney's eyes died. She went from rosy cheeks to pale, her body dropped from life to death, and by the time she hit the floor, she exploded into dust.

"Enough," shouted a familiar voice, and the entire room

froze. Even the small particles of dust that were Brittney became suspended in the air. I desperately tried to catch my breath as I glanced over at Wren who was as still as a statue then scrambled up at the sight of the cemented black ball of demon parts. The many eyes caused a shudder to go down my spine.

"Wren?" I shoved her arm, and she didn't move. *Wren?* But my telepathic call was bounced back by an invisible wall.

Nausea flipped my stomach—what happened to Mercutio, Shaw and Tierney? What happened to Orion? What was happening at all?

The baby continued to sob, and I stumbled over broken pieces of the ceiling as I raced to her. The moment I gathered her in my arms, her big blue eyes met mine, and she immediately fell silent. I moved the blanket and did a quick check. No bleeding, no bruises. No signs of distress. I shivered with the sound of a lullaby being sung with no words. The voice sweet was enchanting, and the song came from the baby. "Impossible."

"What's impossible?"

I spun, cradled the baby to my chest, and then staggered backwards at the sight of Moloch. He leaned casually against a burning wall with his thumbs hitched into the pockets of his jeans.

The building convulsed as if it were about to cave in, and I was swamped with a sick relief. Orion was alive, still fighting. Around us, fire crackled and burned. In the corner near the front, a dangling, burning roof beam fell to the floor, and the flames rose along the wall.

"I asked what was impossible," Moloch said.

"The lullaby coming from the baby. It's…" Beautiful, alluring… "Impossible."

"Yeah, I heard Nephilim can be like that. I also heard you

have the ability to make it rain." Moloch jerked his head toward the flames. "Do you mind?"

"Afraid of fire?" I asked.

"Not at all. In fact, it reminds me of home, but while your friend there won't burn, she can die of smoke inhalation, plus how good is the smoke, fire, and heat for our baby?"

Moloch had me and he knew it. *Orion*, I sent out. *Moloch is here.* But there was a sickening sensation of my words being bounced back at me as if undeliverable. I tucked the blanket close around the baby and then took a deep breath to focus on the energy. My body buzzed with the moisture forming overhead. With a roll of my neck, the skies above opened and a cold rain dripped onto my skin.

"She likes you." Moloch nodded toward the bundle in my arms. "I can tell. Just so you know, that baby is ours."

"The baby is Brittney's."

Both of his eyebrows raised as he did a quick glance at Brittney's ashes. Swamped with grief, I twitched, thunder rolled through the sky, and the rain came down harder. "What did you do to Wren?"

"The other witch? She's suspended in time. If you cooperate, I'll make sure she lives for now. No promises with future run-ins. I'm surprised to see you still alive," Moloch said. "Word on the street is that there are powerful figures on the Fae Council who want you dead."

"Sorry to disappoint you."

"Oh, I'm not disappointed. Fae failures make me damn happy." He scanned me as if trying to see past my skin. "I watched the birth, and I saw what you did. You saved the baby." He crossed his arms over his chest as if uncomfortable. "Thank you...for that."

"Are you the father?"

He gave a dark chuckle. "No." And he sounded thankful. "I'm more of a...uncle. Be thankful I found her first. Her *daddy*," Moloch used finger quotes, "created a game for me and my three other brothers. Whoever our queen chooses is the one will who shares in the glory when we finally conquer earth so we're all scrambling for her to be in our possession. Only way for her to know how to choose wisely is to be the one who raises her. My brother Belial is out there fighting with the Fae, and trust me, you don't want him to get his hands on her. He's a real son-of-a-bitch."

Reading Moloch was difficult. He remitted the same low pulse as the baby, but it was loud, like the pounding of a bass drum. I caught a single word in his head, and it was like a kick in the gut. *Queen*. She was their queen.

"Demon blood flows in the baby's veins," Moloch said. "To save her, you must hand her to me. The Fae will kill the baby. Nothing you do or say will change that. And if you think you can influence Orion to save her, you won't be able to. His allegiance to the Fae will force his hand. I am the baby's only hope."

"Why you? Why not her father?" As if I were handing her over to either of them.

"Her father is…shortsighted."

"What does that mean?"

Moloch crossed his arms over his chest and annoyance flickered over his face. As I waited for his answer, rain continued to pelt us. My soaked hair stuck to my face, but the rain never touched Moloch. He stayed as dry as noon in the desert. The clouds above us swirled and cloud-to-cloud lightning danced in the dark night.

"She's an infant," I said when it was clear he wasn't going to answer. "Human blood also runs in her veins. She asked for my protection, calling to me in dreams, and I promised her I would."

"I'm aware," Moloch said. "Imagine our initial surprise when the witch who freed me is the same witch our queen chose. Then, after a few minutes of thought, it wasn't surprising. It makes perfect sense. I don't know how much more proof you need that you belong with us."

"Small problem," I said. "You want to destroy humanity."

"No, we want to destroy the cages the Fae and their god have built for humanity."

"I don't believe you."

"A question to think about—why believe the Fae, especially when they want to kill you?" Moloch looked up toward the sky then back at me. "Come with me. The baby has chosen you as her protector, and I, in turn, will protect you."

There was a tingling in my fingers as I felt the electricity building in the air surrounding me. "No."

He gave me a ghost of a smile. "Is that static electricity I feel brewing?" He didn't wait for an answer. "You can't kill me, witch. I'm not some worker-drone demon you can strike down with wind and lightning. Bring on a whole damn hurricane, and I'll still be standing because I am the furious winds surrounding the eye of the storm."

He pushed off the wall, crossed the room, and the buzzing of the electricity in the clouds above grew in me to the point I was able to snap my head to the side and cause lightning to crash into Moloch. I shielded the baby and when my ears quit ringing, the breath was stolen from my body when Moloch loomed over my smaller frame. His diamond cutter blue eyes slashed through me. "I am death, witch. You cannot kill me."

I believed him.

"And you, witch." His cold gaze roamed to the baby. "Are life. She chose you and she chose me. There is no coincidence in that."

My stomach dropped as the baby turned her head in his direction. Anger shot through me as she reached out to him. It felt like a betrayal, and as I went to take a step back,

Moloch said, "Do not move or I will make you stay still. She likes you holding her, so for now, I will not take her from you."

Screw him. I didn't want him anywhere near this baby. But then I couldn't move my foot, my calf, my leg…my muscles froze up, keeping me in place. The coldness overtaking me swept up my body, and I started to shiver.

"She definitely likes you." Moloch reached out to the baby, and with my teeth chattering so hard, I was unable to protest when the baby took his finger. It was if my blood was solidifying into ice. The baby, though, was warm in my artic cold arms. Moloch's frigid blue eyes melted as he admired the baby's grasp on his finger. "It turns out she likes me, too. You're not the only one she's been communicating with through dreams. For weeks in my imprisonment, she visited me. Kept me company, promising she would help free me when the proper witch was born as long as I promised to protect her. She kept her promise, and I will keep mine."

"I don't believe you," I sputtered out through my frozen lips.

"Believe it. Why else do you think she brought you to Alex Bay? Who do you think had taken Brittney out to dinner that night? How else did Brittney arrive just in time to the exact place you were in order for you to deliver the baby? The baby has been leading me to you."

His eyes met mine again, and I could barely see him through the icicles forming over my eyelashes. "Are you cold enough yet?" Moloch removed his finger from the baby, turned his back to me, and walked toward the statue of circling demons. I, on the other hand, broke from the glacial hold and gasped for air.

Moloch surveyed the petrified demon ball and Wren. "The baby wants us both to protect her, and I would like to fulfill her wishes. But we're running out of time. Last time I'm asking, come with me, witch."

The baby stirred in my arms and fear pulsed out of her. My forehead wrinkled, and then I felt hate, absolute hate soaring in from above. Wren stirred, and the fire that I had put out flared up. The screaming of an incoming bomb pierced my ears. Moloch rammed into me and tried yanking the baby from my arms. I kicked at him and desperately attempted to pull away. The building shuddered so hard that pieces of the already collapsed ceiling sprinkled around me, and our struggled stopped as we both used our bodies to shield the baby.

"Cassie!" Wren shouted as she reanimated and staggered toward me.

"You're coming with me, witch." Moloch placed a hand on my face, began to speak foreign words and his hand became hot on my skin.

The baby started to wail. The incoming scream grew louder, making me feel as if the bones in my skull were going to shatter. The light of a nuclear bomb blast blinded me. The heat made me feel as if my skin was going to melt off, and I felt the yank of someone trying to rip the baby from my grip.

I screamed and the baby cried. I mentally fought, physically pulled, spiritually willed the baby to be safe. *This baby— be safe, be safe, be safe, be safe, be safe....*

I attempted to open my eyes against the horrible sound of steel fingers on a chalkboard, against the feel of the burning heat, but the motion was heavy, as if I were wading through quicksand and I kept the mantra up in my head *be safe, be safe, be safe, be safe....*

A splitting pain at the top of my skull, this feeling that I was about to be torn into two, and I willed safety for this child. This baby deserved the love I had with my grandmother. She deserved warm fires on cool evenings, long walks through the meadows on warm days. She deserved evenings of catching fireflies, mornings of sitting on the steps of the porch, being in awe of the morning fog settling in the valley, and the feel of the cold dew upon bare feet.

Arms around me from behind, were pulling at me as if I were the middle knot of a tug-of-war. The baby in my arms began to vibrate, the low thrum growing louder. It was a powerful beat against the metallic scream, and my lips moved with my mantra, *The baby safe, safe, safe, safe....*

A rush of hot wind, the force of a hurricane gale. My hair blew wildly about my face, the pull of someone trying to take the baby lessened and I was able to cuddle her close. The feeling of flying, falling, my stomach tumbling like the drop from the highest roller coaster with no restraints. And then I slammed onto the ground hard, on my butt, my spine jarred with the impact.

Silence.

Terrible silence.

Welcomed silence.

My heavy breaths filled the void. The baby moved in my arms, and when I opened my eyes there was darkness and everything was blurry. But I almost sobbed with relief with the feel of tiny fingers against my skin. I sucked in a breath and stiffened with the familiar scent of earth, honeysuckle, and the fragrant scent of a forest.

I blink repeatedly, desperate to clear my vision, and when the shadows finally merged together to create a clear image, I lost the ability to move. Above me was a clear, full moon night. Surrounding me was a thick forest of old trees, and I sat in the shadow of the cabin.

My home.

And there also were Moloch and Wren. Both passed out on the ground beside me.

What in the hell was going on?

CHAPTER 32

The medical bag Mercutio had found for me had also made the journey with us. It was beyond odd, but so was this entire scenario.

We were far, far away from South Carolina, and we were at the quiet cabin I had shared with my grandmother. I hadn't been to this place since I was a teenager. I had often wondered if it was still standing, if it would still be empty, and if it would still be haunted by the memories of the happiness I had shared with my grandmother. With the baby who was very calm and content in my arms, I checked on Wren and Moloch. They were breathing and had no signs of physical distress, but they were unconscious.

Asleep.

The word pushed easily into my brain, and it wasn't my voice. Wasn't my thought. I glanced down at the wide blue eyes looking at me. "Was that you?"

The baby blinked, and I didn't want to think too hard about whether that was an answer. I sighed heavily, not sure what to do, but the only thing I had control over was getting the baby into a safe shelter while I decided what to do with Wren and the demon prince.

The key to the door was still under the small rock next to the boulder. The furniture was still covered with sheets I had stolen from the store when I was sixteen and knew I couldn't return anymore—that was, if I didn't want to be caught by my mother. The cabin was still tidy, as I had left it, but now there were many years' worth of spider webs and dust.

What was also still there were the ghosts. The good memories, the bad, including the time I had dragged myself here after my mother's boyfriend had beaten me when I was fifteen and left me for dead at the bottom of the stairs of their condo. My mother had stood back and watched him as a storm raged on around us. I breathed out slowly. A storm. I guess I'd always been a witch.

I laid the baby on the wooden floor, opened the attic, and immediately found what I was searching for—the cradle my grandmother had used for me. It was still in good shape, and after a good wipe down, I placed the baby in it and stared at her as she fought sleep. Her little eyelids blinked repeatedly as she tried to force them open, but eventually the human side of her won out and her breathing turned light with slumber.

She would need to eat soon. Thankfully, there were diapers, blankets, a bottle, and formula in the bag. Not a lot, but enough to give me time to think of how I could find more. She also needed safety from all of the beings in the world who wanted her dead or wanted her for their own power. What was I going to do now? How could I keep her safe?

"Hey," Wren said in a groggy voice. She was leaning against the frame of the door that led to the front porch, holding her stomach as if she were considering vomiting.

I sprang up, and as I went to help her come in, she stum-

loved God more. Lucifer caused a revolt in heaven that led to a bloody war, but the Creator won. Everyone held their breath, waiting to see how the Great Designer would punish Lucifer and his followers. Even though Lucifer had caused much pain, God couldn't destroy what he loved, so instead he cast Lucifer and his followers to hell."

"Why didn't God force Lucifer to love and obey?" Cassie asked. Seemed like that would be easier than fighting and war.

"Because the Creator wants his children to choose to love him. That's why he gave us free will. Love is a choice. If God forces love and obedience, then it isn't love, but puppetry."

Cassie frowned. Her mother had chosen to abandon her, but at least her grandmother loved her. Each and every smile from her made Cassie feel as if she were as free as the birds of the air, and that she, at any moment, could literally grow wings and fly.

"Lucifer," her grandmother continued, "realized free will meant he could convince more of creation to love him, so he proposed a game to God: allow humans to flourish on the earth for a set period of time while God and Lucifer would fight over the humans' souls. Lucifer wanted to prove he could win more souls than God."

"Is the game like chess?" Cassie asked.

Her grandmother's eyes brightened with approval. "It's exactly like chess. God and Lucifer have played many chess games, but they're preparing for what might be the final match. We're nearing an end. It's either the end of the beginning or the beginning of the end. Either way, Cassiel, the world is changing. God and Lucifer have slowly been placing the pieces on the chess board that is Earth."

Her grandmother picked up a pawn. "These are the humans. They may not look like much, but without them, we cannot win. Then," she lifted the rook, "close to eighty years ago the world figured out Fae are real. Fifty years later, on the exact same day," her grandmother raised the knight, "millions of people across the world claimed they saw an angel appear to them. Some of the angels were bright lights of hope and love, but some were terrifyingly demonic. Red eyes, tongues of serpents, a great in-between of human, ash, and smoke."

Uncomfortable, Cassie unfolded her legs and sat on her bottom. "My teacher said the angels aren't real. She said a sun flare affected people's sight."

"Humans rationalize what they don't understand. But make no mistake," her grandmother waved the knight in the air, "angels and demons are real."

Cassie kicked out her legs faster in an attempt to comfort herself. Angels she could live with. Demons, she didn't want to think about because what if her mother's boyfriend was a demon masquerading as a human? The idea alone caused her to shiver.

Her grandmother raised the bishop. "You'll be twenty-eight on the one hundredth anniversary of the world's learning of the Fae and the fiftieth anniversary of the day the world saw angels. I believe that's when the final pieces of the concluding game will be revealed."

"What about the queen?" Cassie pointed toward the crowned one without the cross.

"Great question. One you need to contemplate as you become older. See how the pieces surround the king and the queen? The queen is powerful, but in order for her to succeed, the other pieces create a safe place for her at the beginning of the game. Do you understand how much courage that must take to put yourself in harm's way in order to protect someone else?"

Probably the same amount of courage it took for her

bled back down the stairs of the porch and stood next to the still sleeping Moloch. Wren nudged his shoulder with her foot and his breathing didn't even hitch. "That's a demon prince."

"It is."

"Damn," she said. "They're impossible to kill."

"Orion called him Moloch. Moloch himself told me he was death."

"He's not death. But Moloch is still pretty damn dangerous."

"Moloch's immortal?"

Wren shrugged. "Orion's tried to kill him and hasn't succeeded yet. To be fair, Moloch's also tried more than there are stars in the sky to kill Orion. Orion isn't easy to kill, but he's not immortal."

She lifted her hands into the air, began spinning them in a counterclockwise motion, whispered to herself, and a rolling fire erupted from her fingertips. As she thrusted her arms forward, the fire smacked into an invisible shield and dispersed into the air as tiny embers. Her eyes widened in shock. "What was that? I should at least be able to maim the bastard."

I sighed heavily. One more unexplainable item on the checklist. Wren stared at him like he was a puzzle then flicked her fingers into the air as she muttered more words and the sparks that came out of her fingers also slammed against the invisible shield. I put my hand through to make sure some magical wall hadn't been created, and my fingers went right through. Weird.

Wren turned her back on him and performed the same spell away from Moloch, and I was seriously frightened by the amount of flames that came from her. She immediately closed her fists to keep the woods from catching on fire. She pursed her lips, snapped her fingers over him, and little warming lights floated over his sleeping body. Annoyed, she frowned and then clapped her hands together to make the lights disappear. "It's some sort of protection spell. If we don't mean him harm, I can use magic. If I mean him harm, I can't get in."

Not encouraging. "We can't use magic to protect ourselves against him?"

Wren nudged him with her toe again. "This type of magic is intent. I can only touch him if I intend to do good. That's a fine piece of magic. I hate it, but it's a fine piece of magic all the same." She ran a hand over her face then cracked her neck to the side. "Let's ward him. Create a box he can't get out of. Once he wakes, it won't hold him for long, but we might be able to keep reinforcing it so he can't get out and kill us. That'll give us time to figure out what to do." Wren glanced around. "Even better train of thought, where did you and demon baby snap us to?"

I blinked with the shock of her words. "What?"

"Back on the island, I felt your magic swirling in an attempt to cast a protection spell. Demon Prince was using his magic to force you and the baby to shift with him, so I pushed my magic into yours. Then demon baby magically joined in and...." She threw her hands out to her sides. "Ta da."

"We're at my grandmother's cabin."

Something like awe crossed over Wren's face. "No kidding? I've heard she was an amazing witch."

A spark of bitterness, as I had no idea she was one until Beatrix told me.

"I bet if we walked out into the woods, we'd find old wards protecting the place. I've heard she was powerful and powerful wards can hold centuries. Except for the fact one of the most dangerous demons is snoozing in the front yard, I can't think of a safer place for us to be." She paused. "If you and demon baby were casting a protection spell, why is the prince of all things awful here?"

Because Moloch was right. The baby also wanted him, and there was no part of me that liked it. "It's a long story."

"You can tell me as we ward the place. Do you have something for me to write with? Paint would be best."

I shoved my hands into my back pockets and stared at the long grass surrounding us. "You can go if you want. I wouldn't blame you." I tilted my head to the dirt road that was close to being swallowed up by the encroaching wilderness. "It's a long hike, but you can make it to civilization by morning."

"I already told you, I won't abandon a friend in need again. I'm in this, Cassie. Don't know where the hell *this* is headed, but I'm in this no matter how it ends."

WE FOUND paint in the storage shed, and I practically had to push Wren out when she noticed the containers that contained my grandmother's "recipe" journals. I realized now they were her grimoires. Wren knew she wouldn't be able to read them, but she wanted to know if I would be able to, and I wasn't mentally ready to deal with whether I could or couldn't.

After telling Wren the story of Moloch and the baby, we dragged his sleeping body into the cabin, placed him in a corner and Wren warded the hell out of the area. We then set to cleaning the cabin. I started a fire in the stone fireplace to help fight off the cool spring air, and Wren painted wards on the walls of the cabin, but she took her time, making them look like works of art as she muttered the words that would hopefully make us safe.

"Will you teach me how to do that?" I asked.

"Yes. You'll need to learn. Wards are going to be our lifeline."

I made formula, changed the baby's diaper, fed the baby as I rocked her in the same chair my grandmother rocked me in, and held her close as she fell asleep. It was hard to believe she was a demon when she looked and felt like such an angel. "It wasn't enough."

"What wasn't?" Wren asked as she painted a particularly intricate design.

"Brittney held her child for only a blink of an eye. The baby won't even have the memory."

"Maybe Brittney was lucky. Some of us don't get a chance to hold the people we love."

My instinct was to pry, to ask what she meant, but the way she went back to work told me it wasn't the time. I returned to rocking the baby and watching the fire, and I thought of the night Orion took care of me after the Council meeting. Was this it? Was this how Orion and I were supposed to be? Two falling stars who occasionally crossed paths? Was this our curse, or were we looking at it wrong? Were we lucky to have had any time together?

If so, I wished I would have done it differently. I wished I could have loved him without thought. Wished I would have given myself to him a thousand different ways, because here was the truth—my grief was deep. I had no idea how much I cherished memories until I realized, at least this time around, I didn't even bother to make them with the man I loved.

I tucked the baby into the cradle and stared a little longer than needed to make sure she was safe. Wren hadn't touched the baby, and I had no idea if she would. She was here, by my side, and I couldn't ask for more than that. "I'm going to get some air."

Wren thoughtfully glanced over at me. "Have you tried to contact Hecate?"

I gave a defeated nod. Obviously, Hecate wasn't in the office at the moment. I even tried leaving a message after the non-existent beep.

"Yeah, me, too. Maybe, after we get some sleep, we should try together." Wren painted another line then risked another look at me. "Are you going to contact Orion?"

That was the million-dollar question. My forehead furrowed with the pain at not knowing if he were alive or injured. Worse was the emptiness, this hollow place where my heart should be. I rubbed my chest as if that could help, but it didn't. If I felt this lost, what type of pain was he suffering? "Each minute that I don't reach out to him feels like…." I couldn't find the right words. "It gets harder to breathe…It…." I trailed off and rubbed my chest again. "I didn't feel like this before—after the accident. I didn't feel this…loss."

"Because that was part of the deal Orion made with his mother. She saved you, took away the memory of the Amans Ritual, and lessened the emotional fallout for you of a broken link. In exchange, he cut you out of his life. Orion is a mated Fae, and now that the deal with his mother is off, he won't stop until he finds you."

"What type of pain is he in?"

Wren dropped her hand from her painting as if the idea caused an ache in her. "It's awful. He suffers without you. He's stoic. Never lets the pain stop him from doing his job, but he's a shell of a man." Wren let out a long, sad sigh. "I don't tell you this to make you feel bad. I'm telling you this because it's only a matter of time before he finds you or you reach out to him. You need to decide what you're going to tell him about this baby. It appears your job is to protect the infant. His job is to…" she trailed off.

Destroy her. I didn't want to hear her say it aloud any more than she wanted to say it. "Do you think we can alter her course? Do you think we can appeal to her human side to not destroy humanity?"

"I don't know, but how can we live with ourselves if we don't try?"

I stepped out into the night and sat on the cracked wooden porch steps that lead to the overgrown yard. The sky to the west glowed with the pink and golden sliver of the coming dawn. Once upon a time as a child, witches and demons were fiction. Life was just the world around me—the forest, the trees, the birds of the air, the rabbits of the bush, my grandmother's hand in mine.

"Could you do that?" my grandmother had once asked me on this porch. *"Can you protect a queen so she can, in turn, protect her king?"*

"I brought the queen home," I whispered to my grandmother. "Is that what I was supposed to do?" Beyond the sound of an owl in the forest, there was no answer.

I closed my eyes, and my thoughts circled back to Orion. The grief and pain in his eyes during our argument, the twisting agony in his heart, the wound on his arm I had promised to heal….

I breathed in deeply and was shocked to inhale the salt of the ocean breeze. My eyes flashed open, and I was standing on the edge of the ocean wearing the white sundress I had worn when I visited Fairy. My bare feet were sinking in the cool sand and tendrils of my hair blew about with the light breeze. Facing the growing sunrise and the ocean, Orion was on his knees. His head was bowed, and he was whispering in a foreign, ancient language, and his tone was full of anguish.

He made no move to acknowledge I was there, even when I slowly circled him, just an arm's length apart. Mediation. Orion was deep in mediation, and I was somehow lingering here within that spiritual rumination.

When Orion came to me in dreams, he had control. Since

I was visiting him, was the control mine? What were the rules of meeting with each other in this spiritual realm of existence? The link of our bond had been broken, and a simple touch would reconnect us. Did that mean only physical contact in the real world, or if I touched him now, would the reconnection still happen?

Better question, did I want to reestablish the connection?

Yes. Definitely yes.

No, because then he could find me and the baby.

Before I could make the decision, Orion's head snapped up and his eyes opened. In mere seconds, he flashed to in front of me, and the moment he took me into his arms, there was an explosion of light. Electricity zapped through him into me, an electrical current that originated in my chest raced into him. The two sparks connected and there were fireworks of warmth, joy, and passion. His lips were on mine, hungry, greedy, and I immediately opened to him. We kissed like an out-of-control wildfire. Each of his touches along my skin were like little licks of flames.

I gasped as Orion swung me into his arms. Within the blink of an eye, we were in his room, and he carried me to his bed. He laid me down and his body covered mine. He kissed his way along my skin, toward my breasts, and a niggling in my brain told me that this wasn't why I was here, but the pleasurable goosebumps forming on my skin as he swept his hand along my bare shoulders told the rational part to keep quiet. Especially when Orion pressed his lips in the space between my cleavage and liquid heat raced through my body. I wanted him to make love to me, I wanted to love and cherish him in return, but the niggling returned.

In a blink, I was on top and he was on the bottom. My legs straddled his hips, and a slow, lazy smile crossed his lips. "You're becoming bold in my dreams."

My suspicions were confirmed. He thought he had fallen

asleep during mediation and I was his dream.

"I'm becoming bold in real life." I caressed the stubble along his chin. "You can't come after me, Orion. Not yet."

He frowned, and I felt a stirring of recognition in him that I was in his mind.

"Don't become fully aware. Stay in the deep meditation, otherwise we'll lose this moment. I need you to hear what I'm saying. I'm okay, Wren is okay, but don't come after us."

Orion pushed up and wrapped his arms around me to keep me locked to him. His serious dark eyes flickered around my face. "Moloch doesn't scare me if that's what you're concerned about. I will destroy him, not the other way around. Describe to me where you're at."

My forehead furrowed. "How do you know about Moloch?"

"I came in as another demon prince was trying to get to you. As I protected you from him, I saw you, Wren, and Moloch disappear."

My heartbeat hard in my ears as I cupped his face in my hands. "Are you okay? How about Shaw, Mercutio, and Tierney?"

He pressed a strong hand over mine. "I'm fine. We're all fine. The battle was hard, but we won." He tilted his head and sadness washed through his expression. "I'm sorry about Brittney and the baby. We saw...the ashes."

A lump formed in my throat and I had to blink away the hot tears forming there. Brittney. God, poor Brittney. At least he thought the baby was dead, but the grief of losing Brittney was eating me alive. Orion swept his fingers along the rim of my eye, catching a tear I hadn't realized had fallen. He leaned forward and brushed a kiss where another teardrop had slid down my cheek. He cuddled me closer, lovingly rubbed my back, gently kissed to my ear, and said, "Describe to me where you are, Cass."

My eyes narrowed. "I thought we just reestablished the link."

"Spiritually, yes. Physically, no."

"Are you still in pain?"

"That's not the concern now. Tell me whatever you can about your whereabouts. We will come for you."

"You can't."

"Whatever Moloch has told you is a lie," Orion said. "He will not harm me or my team. Now tell me where you are."

My heart broke—he thought I was protecting him. I knew what I needed, and being in control of this, his dagger appeared on his bedside table. I grabbed it. Before Orion could react, I cut the blade along my palm and dripped my blood onto the wound on his chest he said I could not heal.

"Orion MacAleese, warrior and leader of the Fae army, I make an oath to you. I, Cassie Strega—your amans, healer and witch—promise to return to you. Maybe you aren't the one who needs to move heaven and hell so we can be together. Maybe that quest belongs to me."

I leaned forward, kissed his lips, then yanked myself out of his head and back to the porch. My heart beat hard in my chest, my lips were swollen from his kisses, and as I opened my palm, there was a stinging sensation and blood still dripped from the cut.

Yes, I was becoming bolder. If God and the devil wanted a chess match, and Orion and I were pieces on the board, then game on.

∗∗

Read on for a preview for A Stormy and Sultry Sea:
Book Two of the Witches of the Island Series

∗∗

Orion

My dearest Cass,

You've disappeared, and I can't find you. Through our muted connection, I can tell you're alive, but I have no idea if you are hurt or in pain. Not knowing is a living hell. This situation requires patience, and my patience...it's wearing thin.

The last time we were together, you told me to not look for you. Your voice like a warm breeze caressing my skin. It was hard to concentrate on your words as your fingers skimmed my chest. You told me we'd find each other again. I want to believe you. I need for you to be right.

Having become a witch only recently, you still have so much to learn and not enough time. Fae and witches exist to play a specific role in the fight to protect humans against the powers of evil. And your assignment of finding the Fae queen is perilous. It puts you in the path of the most dangerous depravity in the universe—demon princes like Moloch.

I'm going to be honest with you, I'm tired. Tired of the fighting, tired of the bloodshed, tired of losing people I love, tired of the war. Since I've been on this earth, darkness has won too many battles and we've lost too much...too many souls, too many stars...too many friends. And we've lost each other. But I've been watching, abiding by the rules, being...patient.

Have I been known for my courage, for my wrath against my enemies? Yes, but never have I been known for my patience. But you...you've always made the impossible possible. You're facing the impossible, and, Cassie, you're losing. Relle had a vision, and it's bloody. I'm tormented by the vision day and night. The demons are intent on causing you pain, giving you the worst in life, and turning you away from the light and into the darkness. The demons are intent on destroying your soul. I can't lose you. I refuse to lose you. Not in life and not in death.

During our limited precious time together, you told me you didn't know me. I told you that you knew the parts of me that mattered. You know my heart. But you were also right. There is much you don't know about me as a Fae, just as there is much you don't know yet about being a witch.

Still, our draw to each other is intense—and more. Exceptional. Extraordinary. All-consuming. But why? It wasn't until you disappeared that I found the courage to discover the truth. You and I are connected, Cassie. Beyond space, beyond time. You are my soul. You are the heart that beats in my chest. I understand that my role in the universe's plan is to save you. Our relationship is not a curse. We're fate.

If you're reading this, it means I died while saving you. I need you to know I don't regret my decision. Your life is worth more than mine, and you have always been worth the battle. This war... the loss, the things I've seen and done...I fight, always, for you.

I love you,

Orion

I folded the letter, placed it in an envelope, and sealed it by breathing across it. Doing so ensured the letter could be opened only by the intended person—my Cass.

Sitting across from me at the table on one of the two wooden chairs in the dark, dingy, one-room apartment we used for emergencies was Mercutio. There was no grin from my typically jovial friend. Not even a joke. A rarity, but not unexpected. There was nothing amusing in this moment.

Even though Mercutio was in a relaxed pair of jeans and a red T-shirt, his pissed off demeanor reminded me of a guard I had the unfortunate opportunity to encounter when once imprisoned in the outskirts of hell. If Satan had an in-the-flesh, bitter son with daddy issues, that guard would have been the man. He had been a sadistic, deranged lunatic. I still carried a few scars and a grudge. In theory, I wasn't supposed to advocate personal revenge, since Fae were once angels, but that experience came close to making me believe in an eye for an eye.

Mercutio had arrived minutes after I had entered the safe room and had sat silent and stoic as I wrote the letter—because that's how my friend was. He could simmer for days, weeks, months, years, before he pondered the thought of boiling over. Odds were he'd never lose his temper. Unlike me, he had patience.

Mercutio was over six feet tall, had dark umber skin, and dark eyes that saw everything—even the things I didn't want him to see. He crossed his huge arms over his chest and eased back in his seat. "Why are you here?"

I shrugged one shoulder. "I figured it had been a while since anyone had cleaned the place, so I thought, why not?"

Mercutio snorted, but kept his eyes locked on me. "Orion, the Leader of the Fae Army, is on cleaning duty?" I was betting Mercutio the Negotiator had been sent by the Fae Council.

"Someone's got to do it."

"Yeah, but that someone isn't you, and last I checked, cleaning doesn't require you to write a Letter of Testament to Cassie."

True on all accounts. In the apartment below, a couple began to fight, and a child whimpered. Reminders of the broken world.

The latest report I had heard was that we were making progress in the war against the demons, but I didn't believe it. Not many did. We were on the losing end, and it was getting worse.

The man's drunken voice, rising in volume below, scraped my raw nerves, dislodging an old memory from the year I spent working the streets of the human world hunting a demon who fed off domestic violence and hate. What I saw during that tour of duty, what I'd experienced….

"You can't get involved," Mercutio reminded me, reading my body language. Just flat out knowing me better than most. "With the family below *or* with Cassie. You've got orders to follow. We both do and we made a solemn pact to obey the Council. They're demanding you return to Fairy, immediately."

"Maybe that's why we're losing the war. Maybe the Council is wrong." On a lot of issues. Not only on how they handled the war with the demons, but with their diplomacy with the witches, and their lack of concern about the growing number of witches who had gone missing over the last several months.

Due to that lack of concern, more and more witches were starting to believe that the Fae were to blame for the disappearances. What didn't help was the growing Fae hatred of witches. That hatred stemmed from what the Fae viewed as the witches' scarcity of help during the demon war. It was a cyclical problem, and I believed that the Fae were the ones who needed to act first to heal the divide, but the Council disagreed.

Disagreed. That was a popular word between me and the Council. It would have been easier to list things that we agreed upon, as that was at about zero.

I pushed away from the table, opened the only drawer in kitchen, dropped the letter inside, closed it, then waved my hand over the wood. If I failed, if I died while trying to save her, Cassie would feel the loss, morn me, and then she'd be compelled to come here, open the drawer, read the letter, and only she would be able to undo what I had sealed.

I glanced around the one-bedroom apartment. The place looked the same since the last time I had been here. The once white walls were brown, encrusted by years of dust and dirt, and in the adjoining room was a worn bed covered by even older blankets. The same table, chairs and ripped blue couch inhabited the cramped living space, and the same annoying slow drip fell every five seconds from the facet into the ceramic sink.

This apartment had never been on the warm, fuzzy side. In fact, it was raw, just like any Fae would be if they had to crash here. Like now, I felt exactly like one of those torn out electrical sockets that revealed exposed wires, and I was as closed off as the boarded-up windows and as shut-down as the nailed-to-the-frame door.

This place was a firetrap, an earthly version of hell, and it was one of the few remaining places on the planet where Fae were completely safe from our enemies. A place we could go to when we were mortally wounded and needed to be healed by a witch—without the threat of a demon finding a way in and finishing us off. Warded by Wren the witch, using magic that nearly cost Wren her life, no human or demon could enter this place without a Fae—unless they literally possessed the power of the gates of hell.

No doubt my unauthorized visit to this place had sent up warning alarms to my mother, Nessa. Mercurio, being loyal, must have volunteered to be the welcoming committee. Question was, in this moment, who owned Mercutio's allegiance? Did it remain where it should? With the Fae Council? Or was he here as my friend? My best friend. The closest I had to a brother.

With his arms still crossed, Mercutio drummed his fingers. "You don't have permission to be on earth. With the disappearance of Cassie and Wren after the battle on the island, I was under the impression you were ordered to stay in Fairy. We all know it was Moloch who kidnapped them, and we all know that Belial left as soon as he did because he was chasing Moloch. Two of the biggest bad-ass devils in the universe are pissed with each other, and Cassie and Wren are caught in the middle of the fight. You and I both know that if two of the four demon princes are going at it, the other two aren't far behind. Retrieving Cassie and Wren isn't going to be easy."

No, it wasn't, and because I was the last of the bloodline to the throne, the Fae Council had voted for me to stay in Fairy. My mother was convinced that if I died, the Fae, and therefore the human race, would be doomed. A grim lift of my lips. Permission. What did that word mean? Nothing. "I don't have permission? What happened to free will?"

"You got it." Mercutio rested his arms on the table and leaned forward. "Look, I know the last few years have been hard on you," he said in that annoying, calm tone. That understanding one he thought made him relatable. The tone that ninety-nine percent of anyone else did relate with. "And I know that being without Cassie has made it worse—"

Hearing her name from my friend's mouth pinched a bruised nerve and poked the enraged beast living inside me. I grimaced from the bitter taste of anger. "When it comes to Cassie you understand nothing. She is my amans. She is flesh of my flesh. Bone of my bone."

Two beats of silence passed. Five more. Each beat, Mercutio kept his placid gaze locked on me. Eventually, he tried again. "There are many who are concerned about you. Many who wonder if the Council has asked too much of you. If you were given missions no one would have been asked to endure to further our cause."

All of this was beyond correct.

"You're a hero, Orion. The most revered in our world. Your name will be forever engraved alongside the saints. Many of us believe you've done enough, and there are those who wonder if you've been lying about your pull to return home to Fairy."

"Are you one of those?" Orion asked.

"Yes," came a quick and un-hesitated answer.

Home. Fairy. The words struck me hard, struck me deep, and I recoiled. Why? Because every cell in my being screamed to flee from the earth and let my soul finally find the peace of home—of the realm of Fairy. I needed rest. I was weary. Exhausted. And each minute of staying in the fight was tearing me apart. My power came from resting in Fairy, but…. "I can't go home. Not without Cassie. If I return to Fairy and she finds a way to contact me through our link, there's a chance I won't be able to feel it. I can't take that risk."

A shadow of sad compassion crossed Mercutio's face. "She wouldn't want you to be in pain. She'd want you to go home if you're being called. Shaw, Tierney and I are working on finding Cassie and Wren. With their disappearance at the hands of a demon prince and our prophetesses no longer having visions, the Council is scared. They ordered you to Fairy to keep our royal bloodline safe and to comfort their own fears."

Rage rumbled deep within my bones, and my voice came out as a low, warning growl, "You think I could leave Cassie behind?"

"No, but I do think you're in trouble, and I think you know you're in trouble. Why else would you write a Letter of Testament to Cassie and seal it in this room—the one place we would bring you if you had a fatal wound? You're my friend, and because of that I will stand in your way. Talk to me Orion. Tell me what's going on with you."

Stand in my way? Mercutio thought *he* could stand in *my* way? A shockwave of anger bounced through the room. The walls undulated, wavering as if in a breeze. The man downstairs stopped yelling, and his fear beat at my skin. Guilt pulled me under as if caught in a strong undertow. I sucked in air, reined in my anger, and knew everything Mercutio was saying was right. Being on earth was dangerous, but there would be no peace without Cassie.

"Feel better?" Mercutio asked in a bored voice.

No. Not at all. I leaned back against the counter and scrubbed my face. "The reason I exist is to protect Cassie."

"I know you love her and the bond you share is strong—" Mercutio started, but I cut him off.

"It's more than that. Relle's still having visions, but she's not sharing them with the Council because she fears their reaction or their history of inaction. Relle shared it with me, and then I visited the Mirror. My sole purpose in the universe is to protect Cassie. The Council wants me to be their leader, but that's not my fate. The fate of the world rests on our queen, and our queen has chosen Cassie for protection. The demons know this, and Cassie's soul is their target. I need to find her. Now."

"What has Relle seen?"

I shook my head. "The vision was for me."

Mercutio twitched as if he understood the unsaid—that Relle had seen my death. We stared at each other then—two warriors who had been fighting a battle against evil for too long. "Is there another way?"

Truth? "We both know there is always another way. I'm just telling you what has been seen."

Mercutio sat up taller. "Then we look for Cassie and Wren. We won't lose them, our queen, or you." Mercutio held his hand out to me, and, after a second, I accepted it. With our hands combined, Mercutio's promise, a covenant that was too powerful for words, seeped into my veins. An agreement that he was going to fight for Cassie, for our queen, and for me. Then with a flash of light, Mercutio disappeared, and I had the answer to my question—Mercutio's allegiance was exactly where it needed to be—with me and with Cassie.

Hold on, Cassie, we're coming for you.

Printed in Great Britain
by Amazon

13652110R00183